OMEGA CLOISTER

By John Wilson

Turmfalke
The Disappearance of Lyndsey Barratt
(originally published as *Flatmate*)
Omega Cloister

OMEGA
CLOISTER

John Wilson

HarperCollins*Publishers*

HarperCollins*Publishers*
77–85 Fulham Palace Road,
Hammersmith, London W6 8JB

Published by HarperCollins*Publishers* 1999
1 3 5 7 9 8 6 4 2

ISBN 0 00 225800 5

Typeset in Postscript Lynotype Sabon by
Palimpsest Book Production Limited,
Polmont, Stirlingshire

Printed and bound in Great Britain by
Caledonian International Book Manufacturing Ltd, Glasgow

Thanks . . .

To Herta, for everything.

To Sue, for her poetry.

To Layne, who went through a bad time
and came out okay in the end.

To Peter Abraham, Professor of Military Psychiatry,
with whose information on battle-shock
I have taken a few liberties.

To the management at Rampton, Broadmoor,
Ashworth and Carstairs high-security hospitals.

AUTHOR'S NOTE

None of the characters in this book is meant to
portray or resemble any real person, and any similarity
with real people is unintentional.

If a company called CareCorp plc exists, I apologise.
As far as I know, Lindisholm Hospital does not exist in the
United Kingdom, and neither does Omega Cloister.

Readers can contact the author by e-mail:

argoed.hall@btinternet.com

All hope abandon, ye who enter here . . .

Dante Alighieri, Italian poet,
commenting on hell

The fact is, you got it wrong, didn't you? Tough shit!

Geoffrey Abbott, mental patient,
commenting on Lindisholm Hospital

THE UNIT

The Unit was Colonel Henry Clarke's baby. A covert group of soldiers with a specific mission: to spread alarm and despondency among the enemy.

Battle-shock.

Colonel Clarke's presentation to his superior officers had been based on military expediency and the rising cost of artillery shells.

'We lay down a barrage of mixed ordnance,' he said. 'If the enemy is well dug in, we achieve a few minutes' disorientation and a few hours' partial deafness. If we get lucky, maybe five per cent of the enemy are killed, wounded or rendered dysfunctional. All that means in real terms is they get shot for cowardice or pulled back for medical treatment while their chums carry on. Meanwhile, depending on the scale of the exercise, we waste over 100,000 pounds' worth of artillery shells. Air strikes are even less effective. A unit such as I suggest – the Unit – could operate at a fraction of the cost and achieve five times the dysfunctionality.'

Someone suggested that this kind of thing was best left to mercenaries. Colonel Clarke was ready for that one.

'If we could guarantee control, fine, but the last thing we need in a theatre of war is a bunch of mavericks screwing things up. Besides, they cost too much.'

It was a good argument. It was also the reason why Colonel Clarke was flying along the Adriatic coast below radar cover. Two of the Unit's most effective members were out of control and behaving like mavericks. Major Christopher Leamington and Sergeant Geoffrey Abbott. Word had it they were turning battle-shock into some kind of religious crusade.

Clarke had requested permission to X the two men, but someone else got into the act. Someone with another axe to grind. Leamington and Abbott represented an investment, and you don't throw an investment away because it malfunctions. You examine it. You find out what's gone wrong. People were worrying about the mental condition of soldiers. Too many disciplinary incidents. Too many suicides. Isolate these two men and find out what went wrong.

Sergeant Geoffrey Abbott was very confused, but that wasn't surprising. All that gunfire, all that killing. And the smarmy voice, talking to him. He couldn't tell if it was coming to him over the Unit radio or what, but then someone had stuck him so full of morphine and chlorpromazine that he couldn't figure anything properly. Maybe he was having a bad dream. He recognised the speaker, though. Staff Sergeant Melton, laying down the law, as usual. Or was it ex-Staff Sergeant Melton? Yes. He'd left the Unit and set himself up in civilian life. Clever sod, Melton.

'Come on, Geoffrey. Tell me about Major Leamington.'

The trouble with a morphine cocktail is, it does your head in. Scrambles your grey matter. Was he in Bosnia, Zaire or back in the UK? He remembered that hard-nosed colonel offering him and Chris a deal. Colonel Clarke. That was definitely in Bosnia. Not much of a deal, actually. Comrades from the Unit trapped them when they were taking a crap together. Buddy crapping. One looking one way, the other the other! Only no one would have thought to look down into all that shit, would they? Tranquilliser darts in the arse – how degrading. A man couldn't even crap in peace! As he felt the dart he remembered wondering who had volunteered to lie all morning in the latrine. Jamie Batson, of course. Jamie liked that sort of thing, the dirty helmet. He almost fell on the little bastard as he passed out. Next thing, this Colonel Clarke and his helicopter landed almost on top of them, lying there, all trussed up, with that fucking sniper having a field day with its rotor blades! He could still feel the gravel as he lay next to Chris. What the fuck was going on? Why had they been taken out like this? It wasn't right. They were the best. Better than the best. The ultimate.

He strained to hear what the colonel was yelling at Chris above the roar of the turbines.

'We can't have you two running amok in a theatre of war, Major. Bad for public relations.'

'Yeah, but we get things done, you arsehole,' Chris yelled back.

2

'You wanted data on battle-shock, and we gave it to you on a fucking plate.'

'That's not the point, Major. You and Sergeant Abbott have been giving the Unit a very bad name. You can't go round X-ing friendlies just because they set fire to villages and crops and leave dead bodies floating down rivers, for Christ's sake. If it was up to me, we'd hand you over to Mladic for him to sort out. Unfortunately, I am instructed to offer you an alternative.'

There are times when you have to let the rhythm of nature take charge, and this was one of them. Batson and the others carried them into the Mess tent, still trussed up like turkeys. Maybe they could have bust the Kevlar straps, but not with various high tensile nine millimetre steel tubes pointing at their heads. Anyway, according to this colonel, their old friend ex-Staff Sergeant Keith Melton needed help with something he was running for the Ministry of Defence. Experimental rehabilitation, no less. Seems they were worried about suicide rates among ex-paras, so they wanted a couple of men from the Unit to spend time in some new-fangled hospital he was running. Bearing in mind that Leamington and Abbott had taught Mladic's Tigers some of their less pleasant tricks to play on helpless prisoners, it was not a difficult choice to make.

He couldn't hear the chopper any more, so he reckoned he was definitely back in the UK. Keith Melton's voice seemed to be coming from that TV monitor above the bed. And there he was, in the digital flesh. Pug-nosed little shit! But what could he tell Melton that would do any good?

Chris and I got religion, Keith. Not the usual crap. More into Mother Earth and the life cycle, like the Druids. We have sworn to serve the gods so we can get salvation. The people we slew were polluters of the land, and the Lord Beltane is well pleased with his children's work. He converted Chris to his Way and took him into his bosom. That's where he is now, and where Chris goes I follow.

Christ, he'd never get out of here if he went into all that, would he? He was a very specialised case, not mad like the other poor sods. People like Melton marked you down as mad if you even mentioned the word 'God'.

'Tell me about Chris,' Melton said again.

An aimless giggle was called for. People talking to patients in mental hospitals can handle aimless giggles. It gives them a sense

3

of superiority, of control. Makes them feel comfortable with their own sanity.

The huge bulk lying strapped into the hospital bed giggled aimlessly.

'Okay, Geoffrey.' Melton made his voice sound soothing. 'I know it's tough, but it really would help me to know what happened. Chris couldn't possibly get out of Lindisholm. That means he's still inside, and *that* means I have to presume he's dead. So where's the body? If you don't tell me, we'll have to pull the bloody place apart.'

Pull away, old mate. Won't do you any good. I'll tell you one day, though. I'll tell you the day we take a journey to the Great Upstairs to see who was right and who was wrong about all this peace and war stuff. Meanwhile, I've got a lot of work to do. And I mean a lot of work. The Lord's work!

Another aimless giggle.

Keith Melton switched off his video link viciously and turned to the two security men, both ex-members of the Unit.

'That mother-fucker is taking the piss. My bet is he snuffed Leamington and chopped him into pieces small enough to stuff down lavatories and U-bends. For all we know he could have buried bits in those bloody gardens everyone was so keen to cultivate between the cloisters. There's bound to be traces. Batson, I want you to check Delta Cloister. Tell Alex Searle we've had a fault warning from one of the equipment suppliers. That'll keep him happy.'

'What do we do if we don't find anything, sir?'

'We lean on Abbott, that's what we do. Hard.'

They were capable men, very loyal. And very well paid. They'd find Leamington, and then Melton could report the situation to Colonel Clarke and dump everything on that lunatic Geoffrey Abbott. As things stood, he could hardly tell the Army that one of its trained killers had vanished from the country's most secure facility for the criminally insane.

WESLEY

Elm Park Senior School, on the outskirts of Wolverhampton, prided itself on its conversion from a run-down dump for social and educational no-hopers to an establishment of which pupils, parents and staff had good reason to be proud. After several decades of zero attainment, public exam results improved to the point that five children had gained entrance to universities; morale was high, and the school had just been awarded a prestigious commendation from the discerning Singleton Education Foundation. But all this was far from the thoughts of games coach Anne Squires as she waited in the games pavilion. It was six o'clock in the evening. Lessons were over, and training sessions had long finished, except for one of the pupils. Wesley Freeman: long-distance runner, and a contender for the national championships.

Despite all her training and common sense, Anne had found herself drawn to Wesley as he progressed through the school. At first she had merely noticed his physical beauty, the way his musculature flowed as he walked, ran and performed his exercises – the way you might, from a distance, notice the grace of a Derby winner or a champion ice dancer. But as Wesley moved from third year to fourth and then fifth, she found herself performing silly deceptions to meet him in corridors or at the school entrance, and even in the town, once she had discovered where he and his friends liked to hang out. Needless to say, she fought this compulsion. She began avoiding the places Wesley might be, only to find that somehow or other – there he was!

Anne decided that the reason for this was because Wesley was feeling the same way about her. Time and again, when she brought herself to look into his eyes she discovered that he was looking into hers. She was feeling almost ill because of it, and in the end she knew she had to face up to the situation. She had to meet him, to talk with him, somewhere private. Tell him. Find out what he felt. After that, who knows? All these stories about teachers seducing pupils! It was usually a male teacher with a female student, but there were exceptions. Notable exceptions. Sensational newspaper story exceptions. And God help the female teacher concerned. Sacking was the least she could expect. All Anne knew was, she could not carry on this way. She had to deal with it. That was why she was here, in the changing rooms, hoping that Wesley would turn up and hoping at the same time that he wouldn't.

Anne had a sudden urge to vomit. As she fought back the nausea she staggered to the door, only to find Wesley barging through in his running shorts, sweat running down his wonderful features, breath hanging like a silver cloud in the cold evening air.

'Are you all right, miss?'

'Yes . . . yes thanks, Wesley. Must have caught a tummy bug. I'll be fine in a minute.'

'I'll get some water.'

She watched as he went to the dispenser and manipulated a conical cup from the holder, brought it back, passed it to her. The way his hand caressed the cup almost made her heart stop. One of his fingers touched her wrist, and she dropped the water.

'Oh dear!' she said.

Wesley went back to the dispenser. This time she managed to drink some.

'Thanks, Wesley. That's better.'

'No problem, miss.' He paused, then turned away.

Why did he pause?

'Wesley,' she managed to say. 'I need to talk to you.'

'Yes, miss?'

Now what? There he stood, three feet away. Her legs took over, and she found herself moving towards him. Two feet, one foot. He smelled so sweet, and he looked so vulnerable, swaying away from her. But his feet stayed where they were. And his eyes were fixed into her eyes, his breath mixed with her breath. All she wanted to do was touch his lips. What was wrong with that? It wasn't sex. It was beyond sex. It was totally pure. Her hands cupped his face and she pulled his head down. If he resisted she didn't notice, but in any case his lips were close enough for her

6

to stand on tiptoe and press into him so she could touch them with her lips.

And Wesley did what any red-blooded youth of seventeen would do. He got an erection, and as she felt it rising between her legs thoughts of purity evaporated. All she wanted was to get him inside her, to feel his skin on her skin, to quench the fire that was threatening to burn her soul. When he began responding to her movements, she tore at her blouse, feeling the buttons popping into the air and hearing them hit the floor and roll into corners. She dragged one of his hands into her bra and then pushed her own hands into his running shorts.

Almighty God, the size of it!

Ordinarily, the force of him ripping the bra away would have been unbearably painful as the straps cut into her and then snapped apart, and so would the force of his fist connecting with the side of her jaw. But there was no pain, only a series of thuds as his knuckles smacked into her cheeks and her arms and her breasts, and a voice shouting: 'Stop that, you young thug!' It sounded like the groundsman, Joe Carver.

After that, everything was a jumble, for her and for Wesley.

And it stays a jumble, right, even when the police come and call him names and slap him around, then take him to the police station to slap him around some more and take his fingerprints and sit in front of him for hours yelling and shrieking for a statement. Only he wasn't going to give them no statement, was he? No way, man! Plus, he wasn't going to talk to no lawyer, or no doctor. He wasn't going to talk to nobody, never mind all that psychiatric report shit. He wasn't going to say nothing. How could he, for Christ's sake? No matter what they done to him. No matter where they sent him.

Ruby Freeman looked through the hatch in the reinforced front door and sighed. It wasn't the first time the police had called round over the past couple of years. Usually it was because of something stupid Wesley had done. A young boy growing up. Joy riding, graffiti. They even arrested him once for loitering because he and some friends were dancing on the pavement. No charge, of course. Just a caution. But it went on his record all the same. Never drugs or muggings, though. Wesley was different from the other kids like that, but still

7

they came knocking on her door. This time it was a young, white police constable with a hard face and an Asian policewoman looking determined, angry.

'Mrs Freeman?'

'Yes.'

'Can we come inside?'

She opened the door.

'What is it? Has something happened to Wesley?'

'Perhaps if we could come inside.'

She didn't want them in the flat, but neither did she want them standing where her neighbours could see. She stood to one side and let them in.

'Which is Wesley's room, Mrs Freeman?' the policewoman asked.

'What's happened? What's my boy done?'

Something more serious than spraying paint on a wall. She could tell by the stiffness, the outrage.

They pushed past her and went upstairs, opened her bedroom door first, then Wesley's. In America, this would not be tolerated, not according to the TV programmes. American police had to get a search warrant from a judge, or anything they found would be inadmissible in court. That's how it worked in America. Here, in Britain, it seemed to Ruby that the police could do anything they liked and get away with it. Searching homes, planting evidence, beatings, even killings, so she heard. She couldn't understand how this could be. British justice was supposed to be the best in the world.

'Got a clean plastic bag, Mrs Freeman?' the policeman called down.

Ruby tried a quick prayer, but it didn't work. Her heart was thumping too much. What had Wesley done, that they needed to put something in a plastic bag? What could he hide away that she didn't know about? Not drugs. Never drugs.

'You can't take anything from here unless you have a warrant,' she called.

It was worth a try.

'There's a carrier bag in the bathroom, Paul,' the Asian police-woman said.

They came downstairs. She stood in front of them. Determined.

'Where's my son? What has he done?'

8

'We'll be informing you in due course,' the Asian policewoman said.

'My boy is seventeen. He has to have his mother with him.'

'We haven't charged him with anything yet, Mrs Freeman,' the constable said. 'When we do, we'll let you know.'

She soon discovered what they had taken. The girlie magazines that her son hid under his mattress and the packet of condoms that he kept at the back of a drawer. She'd known about them for months, of course, but she didn't know what to do about it. This was the sort of thing best left to a father to deal with, but her husband, Steve – Wesley's stepfather – had left home again. There would not have been any point mentioning it to him anyway. Either he would have ignored her or flown into one of his rages. Better that he'd gone when he did. More peace that way. Until now. What in God's name had Wesley done?

Ruby put on her Sunday clothes, went to the police station and found out. Assault and attempted rape. His school teacher. The one who helped with his training. Miss Squires. And they said he had assaulted the man who put the white lines on the sports field. The shame was overwhelming. They let Ruby see Wesley, and all she could say was: 'How could you, how could you?' He just stared at her and said nothing. It was not until she was back home that she remembered: he was innocent until someone proved he was guilty, and that's when she started to cry.

The lawyer appointed by the court set his briefcase on the table and scanned through the documents relating to Wesley's arrest and charge. A victim with cuts, bruises and damaged clothing. Buttons all over the changing room floor. The accused caught, trousers down, attempting the act of rape. Forensic evidence: her blood on his fists. Additional corroborative evidence: the collection of soft porn magazines and condoms from his bedroom. She was saying she did not want to prefer charges. That might make things easier when it came to sentencing, but there was the second victim, the groundsman, and he was outraged. Cut and dried. Signed, sealed, and delivered. A quick five thousand for his firm and more for the barrister. Play it by the book, the one that says, 'The less hassle, the better'.

'We'll enter a plea of guilty and try to find some mitigating circumstances,' the lawyer said. 'You've got no previous form, so with a bit of luck and a sympathetic judge you might get away with three years in a young offenders' institution.'

He paused, leaving space for a comment.

Wesley stared at him.

'I need more information about your family. When did your stepfather leave home, for example? Why? Did he beat your mother? Did he beat you? That kind of thing.'

The lawyer was accustomed to silence from young offenders. They fidget and stare at the attending constable or out of the window. Seldom look him in the eye like Wesley was doing, because they're trying to figure out how many lies they could tell him. This lad was different, but he'd open up with a bit of coaxing.

'I know how you feel, but if we can convince the judge that this was an uncharacteristic act for which you feel great remorse, we might be able to shave a year off.'

Wesley carried on looking at him. It was slightly disconcerting. Not exactly a stare. Certainly not a glare, like some of his clients gave him. A quiet, almost serene gaze, as if Wesley had figured something out.

'Look,' the lawyer said, flapping his hand between them. 'We have to start communicating, right? Otherwise I'm wasting your time, and you're wasting mine.' He scanned through the documents again, read the photocopies of handwritten police notes. *The accused made no statement. The accused remained silent.* 'You'll need to give a statement at some stage of the game, so the sooner the better. You'll forget things, otherwise. I mean, did this Miss Squires provoke or encourage you in any way? Did she do or say anything that you or any other reasonable person might have interpreted as an overture?'

Silence.

'Okay, Wesley.' The lawyer stood up and packed the documents into his case. 'Sleep on it. I'll be here tomorrow, and I'll expect a little more co-operation.'

The social worker got the family history from Ruby. Wesley's mother was only too eager to talk to someone who might help her son. She certainly could not discuss this shame with her family. So by the time the social worker sat in front of Wesley, she knew all about the divorce, the stepfather, the violence and the infidelities. She knew how Wesley had tried to help, ever since he was old enough to understand why his mother cried every day; how the stepfather eventually turned his brutality onto Wesley. It was only during the last year that he stopped turning up occasionally to demand his conjugal rights from his unwilling but terrified wife. That was when Wesley grew big enough to turn the tables. It was not what you'd call a fight. The stepfather unbuckled his belt and swung it across Wesley's shoulders, and Wesley hit him once, in the stomach. It was more of a surprise than a beating. When he got his breath back, he tied the belt round his trousers and walked out.

'How are they treating you, Wesley?'

The police had probably pushed him around a little. The odd slap. But few of these young people made a complaint, even if the odd slap turned into a frenzy of blows. It wasn't worth the risk of further, more subtle trouble.

The expected 'okay' was not delivered.

'I'm here to help you, to make sure that all the relevant factors are taken into consideration. I'm not supposed to take sides, but the more we know about your circumstances, the more it might be possible to understand what happened.'

Wesley's gaze made her feel uncomfortable, and she quelled a rising irritation. Her caseload was tough enough without this young sod making it worse. After ten minutes of totally one-sided conversation, she made her mind up and closed her notebook with a snap. Her report would recommend a psychiatric examination. That would sort him out.

Wesley was brought in front of the magistrates the following day and remained silent throughout the proceedings. His lawyer entered a formal plea of not guilty, and the police objected to bail. He was sent to the young offenders remand centre at Brinsford, pending a psychiatric examination and report. At his next court appearance the psychiatrists, frustrated by his continuing silence, informed the magistrates that Wesley was suffering from an obsessive-compulsive sexual disorder with schizoid tendencies and was therefore unfit to stand trial. In view of the seriousness of the alleged offences and possible further danger to the public, the judge ordered that he should be sent to a high-security hospital for treatment, under Section 1 of the Mental Health Act 1983 and Section 4 of the National Health Service Act 1977.

Throughout the entire procedure, Wesley refused to utter a word.

I

The Kirbys had been trying to relocate from London for over a year. Not because they were tired of the place; it was more like a tacit understanding that the pressures of city life were beginning to affect their relationship. Too much pollution, too much crime, too much niggling at each other. Time for a change. They wanted somewhere Ben could concentrate on his writing, somewhere Janice had more space to set up her clay bins and her ceramics kiln. They wanted peace and quiet, but nothing too remote. Reasonable access to shopping and other facilities. Somewhere not too expensive.

Brianne Mill was the last property they had lined up to see on a two-day visit to mid-Wales, and they were beginning to like the place. It was big enough for them both to work there without bumping into each other all the time. The property was far enough from the village of Penford to give them privacy, but not so far that you couldn't walk there if the car broke down. A hospital was marked nearby on their Ordnance Survey map, which could prove useful, if they had an emergency to deal with. The grounds were very attractive, particularly the ancient, moss-covered ruin on a hillock overlooking the river that flowed through the front field. Nice to have fishing rights, too. Not that Ben Kirby had ever fished, but some of his friends knew a silver butcher from a hairy mary. The twenty acres of pasture created a problem, though. What were two urbanites going to do with twenty acres?

Mr Fletcher, the young estate agent with inflamed pimples on his cheeks, showed Janice the kitchen, the room in which most house deals are made or broken. Ben stuck his head round the door.

'Lots of work surfaces,' he observed brightly.

Janice ignored him.

'How much oil does that Rayburn use?'

The pimply estate agent shuffled through his papers nervously. 'The vendor gave us some information on running costs, but I think I've left it in the office.'

Janice muttered impatiently under her breath. After a year of dealing with the breed, she was in no mood to make concessions.

'We can sort all that out later, if we decide we like the place,' Ben said agreeably. 'What I'd like to know is, what's the catch?'

'Catch?' The young estate agent managed to look astounded and perplexed at the same time.

'The place is on the market at £135,000. This size of house, plus all those fields, is generally going for more than that, even round here. There has to be a catch.'

'Oh, I see. No, no, there's no catch. The vendor wants a quick sale, that's all.'

'Sorry to push, Mr Fletcher, but why does he want a quick sale? Motorway coming through, is there? Or has the council granted planning permission for an incinerator or wind farm?'

'Gosh, no. It's just that he landed a job in Birmingham. He needs a quick decision, because he's found a house near his new company.'

'Would you mind very much if I had a quiet chat with my husband?' Janice asked him.

The estate agent backed out of the kitchen, and Janice walked round turning the taps on and off, opening the oven, opening cupboards.

'You like it, don't you?' she said.

Ben nodded. 'The study is ideal, and you could use the barn for your pottery, always assuming the local power supply could stand the loading from the kiln. It's those fields I'm worried about. The last thing we want to do is take up farming.'

'The kitchen's filthy. So is the bathroom. The whole place needs redecorating.'

'So we clean up and find a paint shop.' He was dog tired of looking at bloody houses. Houses in Cornwall, Devon, Hereford, Shropshire. It was so disruptive. He hadn't been able to get down to serious writing in months. 'But only if you really like the place.'

'You're right about the price. Why is it so cheap?'

'It's not exactly cheap, but you'd certainly expect it to be around £150,000. Maybe more. On the other hand, if the bloke wants a quick sale £135,000 would be about right.'

'Can we afford that?'

'The Façade is selling well, so if Andrew negotiates a decent advance for my new book, we could – especially once you're set up.'

Janice opened more cupboards and wrinkled her nose. 'Christ, what a pigsty.'

'We could get a new kitchen fitted before we move in.'

'And a new bathroom?'

'If we beat the guy down to, say, £125,000.'

Janice took a mobile phone from her bag and clicked an auto-memory button. 'Shit! There's no signal.'

'Who are you calling?' He already knew. Big sister.

'Eileen. I'd love her to see the place before we make our minds up.'

He kept his voice calm, but couldn't hide the edge. 'Don't you think we should make our own decision? It's us who've got to live here.'

'But she'll be so excited. I wonder if that estate agent has a phone that'll work.'

The pimply young man scurried back through the door.

'None of the mobiles work round the mountains, Mrs Kirby. They keep promising.'

'We're worried about those fields,' Ben said. 'Far more land than we were looking for.'

'Lots of people moving from the city find that, but there's usually no problem renting it out. In fact, the previous owner signed a tenancy agreement with a local farmer that had six months to run. The rent more or less pays for the council tax, and the farmer has to look after the fencing and the fields. Of course, the agreement ends when the house is sold, but I'm sure . . .'

'We're prepared to offer £125,000,' Ben interrupted, in a voice that he hoped sounded final.

They agreed on £130,000 and settled for a new kitchen. The bathroom would have to wait for Ben's next royalty cheque to come in from his book *The Façade: An Exposé of Business Ethics*. He had written it after years of investigating the activities of leading multinational companies as a business journalist. Each of the carefully scripted libels was backed up by documentary evidence and tape recordings of telephone conversations and meetings with dozens of directors, managers and press officers who had lied and cheated their way up the promotion ladder, plus evidence from many disaffected employees and ex-employees. No one sued; the rights sold to more than twenty countries, and the paperback version had just got into

America's top ten business books list. Now his agent was chasing him for the next book. He had no idea what it was to be, and he was beginning to worry about it. Writer's block was something he had ridiculed all his working life, because the ideas had always flowed faster than he could deal with them. Ben thought the move might jolt him into the old creative frame of mind, the old frenetic output.

The purchase of Brianne Mill took twelve weeks to complete, and the Kirbys moved in a month later, after the new kitchen had been installed. Eileen had offered to help with the move, but Ben insisted that they should get on with it themselves and invite her to stay only when everything had been finished. Including the bathroom. With luck, that would give them at least six months on their own, sorting things out. Maybe longer.

Four days after the move, the front doorbell rang. Ben was in the cellar trying to figure out which of the power cables went to which of the ring mains, so Janice opened the door. Their visitor was a tall, rather gaunt man. Diffident, but determined to do his good-neighbourly thing.

'The name's Tom Attwood. Live just over the hill. You must be Mrs Kirby. Thought I'd call to see how you're settling in. See if I could help.'

'Janice. Hello. Still knee-deep in packing cases, as you see. Do come in though.'

'No, no, mustn't disturb you . . .'

'Ben's just about to make a pot of tea, aren't you, Ben?' she called.

'What's that?' Ben came up the cellar steps, banging his head on the lintel. 'Shit! Oh, hello.'

'This is Tom Attwood. He called to see if we needed anything.'

'You mean apart from ten more arms, infinite energy, more shelf space and a foot more head room in this cellar?'

'I said you were just about to make us a cup of tea.'

'Absolutely. One lump or two?'

'Well, as you insist, black, weak, no sugar.'

They moved into the kitchen, Ben pushing crates to one side to clear the way, Attwood nodding at the walls and tapping his knuckles on the plaster here and there, as if he knew his way around.

'A good, solid building, but not without its little idiosyncrasies,' Attwood observed. 'I see you've changed things around in here.'

'Those ceramic hobs had to go. Bloody awful things,' Janice said. 'And once we started, one thing led to a completely new kitchen.'

'I know what you mean. Bob Cryer was going to switch to gas, but that would have meant storing the containers right outside the kitchen window, so he decided not to.'

'We got the contractors to put one of those big cylinder thingys on the other side of that wall,' Janice said.

'Cryer left a list of Dos and Don'ts,' Ben said. 'Very useful.'

'Bob was like that. Helpful chap, on the whole. Sorry to see him go . . . not that . . . oh, you know what I mean.'

'What's your line of business, Tom?' Janice asked.

Ben held his hands out in mock despair. 'My wife is very direct, you'll find.'

'Accountant. Retired. How about yourselves?'

'Writer, potter,' they said simultaneously.

'I'm a writer.'

'And I'm a potter.'

'Fascinating. Will I have stored fruit in one of your bowls or read one of your husband's books?'

'I'm more into abstract work than utensils,' Janice said, 'but you might have come across Ben's opus, *The Façade*?'

Attwood pulled an apologetic face. 'Afraid not. What's it about?'

'Taking the lid off industry slime machines, he says. Personally, I think he was just venting his spleen after a decade of rubbing shoulders with Mammon.'

Attwood's eyes were taking on the glassy look that people got when faced with this kind of response to a polite question.

'Exactly how weak?' Ben asked as the kettle began to boil.

'Wave a tea bag over it, and that'll be about right.'

'Biscuits?'

'Very kind, but I'll be having lunch shortly. Thought it would be a good time to pop up, though, in case you needed something. Did Cryer leave you any phone numbers, like where to get help if something crops up?'

'Just a list of which switch turns what on. Where the electricity meter is hidden. Where the thermostats are. That kind of thing.'

Attwood pulled an envelope from his pocket. 'This could come in handy then. Doctor, dentist, vet, builders ... my number's on it, too, with a few other neighbours you'll no doubt run into soon. Everyone's very curious about you, but I suppose you expected that. Small communities being what they are.'

'Not half as curious as we are,' Janice assured him.

'In that case, maybe you'd have time to meet some of us in the Blue Lion on Saturday around lunchtime. Informal. Couple of pints and a pie. The guvnor's a good chap. Harry Price. Knows everybody worth knowing, and his wife Sian runs an excellent kitchen. Best restaurant for miles.'

'Seems nice enough,' Ben said as Attwood strolled down the drive towards the road.

'Mmm.'

'Does that mean he *doesn't* seem nice enough?'

'I thought he was creepy.'

'Where did you get creepy from? The guy turned up to see if we needed anything.'

'He was looking at everything, like he was taking inventory.'

'He probably was. For Christ's sake, you were always complaining that no one took any notice of anyone in London, and here you are bellyaching when someone does.'

'It's one thing to take notice,' she said. 'This looked as if he was sizing us up, for some reason.'

The Blue Lion was one of those pubs that city dwellers dream about being their local. Ancient. Forming part of a small square. Low oaken beams that didn't have an embossed plastic sign saying 'Duck or Grouse'. No juke box. No piped music. No red and green fairy lights nailed over the doorway. Just a gaggle of warm, comfortable rooms with huge mantelpieces and open stone fireplaces. A free house with a wide range of real ales and an equally formidable array of exotic drinks, plus a bar menu that promised a cut above the average in terms of choice and quality of meals. Ben and Janice stuck their heads into the various rooms, but there was no sign of Tom Attwood.

'It's only twelve thirty,' Ben said.

'Let's see what kind of rubbish they serve as dry white wine.'

As she was peering over the counter, a burly man with a beaming smile appeared.

18

'Frascati, Muscadet, Chablis . . . your choice. I'm Harry Price, and you must be Mr and Mrs Kirby.'

'Oh shit,' Janice said sheepishly.

Price gave a deep chuckle. 'Don't worry, Mrs Kirby. Most pubs round here serve paraffin and diesel oil. I try to cater for the more discerning palate.'

'I'm really terribly sorry.'

'It's not a problem. So what'll you both have? This one's on me, by the way. New customers and all that.'

'That's very kind,' Ben said. 'I see you serve Donnington's.'

'I have to bribe them to bring it over here.' Price began pulling a pint. 'And you, Mrs Kirby?'

'A Frascati would be lovely, thank you.'

'Tom gets here about one o'clock. Normally sits over there with his cronies. That tall chap is Alan Walters. He's the fishing bailiff, among other things. You introduce yourselves, and I'll bring these over.'

Walters stood up as they approached and held out his hand. 'Welcome to the Blue Lion. Tom said he'd called on you. How are you settling in?'

'Still stumbling over packing cases,' Ben said.

'It's a lovely old house. Solid as a rock, but they do say the east wind rattles the sash windows. Let me introduce Gwyn Evans who farms down river from Brianne Mill. Gwyn is trying to keep the local hunt alive, against all odds.'

They all smiled and shook hands.

'Do you support hunting, Mr Kirby?'

'I know so little about it that I decided long ago not to take sides.'

'That's reasonable,' Evans said. 'You'll always be welcome to any of the meets. We'll see if we can't swing you over to our side of the business.'

Janice sipped her wine. Light, dry and surprisingly good. 'What is a fishing bailiff, Mr Walters?'

'I'll only tell you if you call me Alan.'

'What's a fishing bailiff, Alan?'

'Not as exciting as it sounds, and it doesn't sound very exciting to start with. I keep an eye on the anglers to make sure they conform to the seasons and the regulations. Permits. That kind of thing. Do either of you enjoy the sport?'

'Never held a rod in my life,' Ben said.

'You've got a good stretch below the Mill. Bit of trouble with otters over the last year or two. Used to be pike. Either way, we lose a lot of fish. Damn nuisance. Fred can confirm that, can't you Fred?'

The stout man who had just ordered a pint at the bar turned and raised it. 'Afternoon, Alan. Confirm what?'

'The otters. I was just telling our new neighbours that we've been losing some fine trout.'

'Ah, the new neighbours. How do you do? Fred Newson.'

'Pleased to meet you, Fred. Ben Kirby, and this is my wife Janice.'

'Janice Kirby, and this is my husband Ben.'

'Janice took a course in political correctness before we moved here.'

Newson looked blank, then laughed. 'Got it. Political correctness! Very good. Must tell my colleagues that one.'

'Ben is a writer,' Attwood told him.

'Is that right?' Newson paused. 'I thought your name rang a bell. Let's see. Something about corporate corruption, wasn't it . . . *The Façade*?'

'That's me.'

'Well, well, well,' Newson said. 'So you're my new landlords.'

'Landlords?'

'That's right. I signed a grazing agreement with your vendor. Legally, it's all off since he sold the land, but I'd like to discuss a renewal.'

'We haven't got our heads round that kind of thing yet,' Janice said.

'That's right, but I don't see why there should be a problem,' Ben continued.

'We pay a fair price per acre, wouldn't you say, Tom?'

'More than fair.'

'Good business,' Newson said. 'Keeps things stable. So, what's all this about trout? You people fish, do you?'

'No, but Alan was explaining that we've got munching machines in the river that gobble them up.'

'Otters. Not to mention zanders. Nasty bastards. But there's far worse up in the mountains. We've got the Beast of Bont to contend with up there. Course, it's not fish we're worried about with the Beast. It's lambs mainly, and sometimes a full-grown ewe.'

'I've heard of that,' Ben said. 'People think it's a puma, don't they?'

Newson laughed. 'Wild cat, puma, panther. Maybe a maverick dog. Who knows?'

As they were trying to get their heads round the notion of a wild puma in the heart of the Welsh mountains, Tom Attwood came in with an elegant blonde woman whom he introduced as his lady friend, Mary Drover. 'Who knows what?' he asked.

'We were telling Ben and Janice about the Beast of Bont,' Newson told him.

'Mary's seen it, haven't you, Mary?'

'I saw something in the garden a few nights ago. Great yellow eyes glaring at me in the dark. Very frightening, I can tell you.'

More drinks arrived, bar meals were ordered, and yet more drinks, as everyone got to know about everyone else's business. By the time Ben and Janice made their farewells, everyone was mellow and firm friends with everyone else.

'Be sure to visit us at Lindisholm Farm,' Newson insisted. 'Just turn left out of your gates, left again at the next fork, and right when you come to the bridge. We're about three miles further into the hills, just before the hospital. White building, on the right. You can't miss it. And any help you need, just ask.'

'He means it,' Attwood nodded. 'His tenancy works very well for my fields. I don't know what we'd do without Fred and his youngsters when there's work to be done around the place.'

'Funny old lot,' Ben said as he and Janice began the two-mile walk back to Brianne Mill. 'Friendly enough, though.'

'Was that Mary Drover serious about the Women's Institute?' Janice asked. 'She certainly doesn't look the type. I mean, they're all into knitting and making jam, aren't they? I can't imagine her elbow deep in a tub of damsons, can you?'

'It's difficult for women in a place like this. What else have they got to do, with the menfolk out farming and fishing all day?'

'It's not like you to miss an alliterative opportunity. Whatever happened to fucking?'

'It's only randy writers who are interested in fucking, this time of day. How about it?'

'Chance would be a fine thing. By the way, did someone mention a hospital?'

'Yes. Our tenant farmer. We saw one marked on the map when we were finding this place, remember?'

'Could come in handy if one of us chops off a finger.'

'I doubt if it's that kind of hospital, not stuck out here. Probably a sanatorium. You know, all this clean, healthy air.'

'Not to mention clean, healthy people. Our neighbours don't seem short of a bob or two.'

'They probably think the same about us. People always think writers and conceptual potters are loaded.'

'We're not doing too badly.' They came to the stone bridge where the road crossed the river, and she stopped. 'Pooh sticks!'

'Hey, I thought we were on our way home for a quick one.'

'You're so bloody common sometimes, Ben. It's enough to put a girl off sex for life. Tell you what. If your Pooh stick wins, I'll give you a blow job.'

'And you call me common, you slut!'

'They seem a nice young couple,' Harry Price said as he relieved the table of empty glasses.

'Very friendly,' Tom Attwood agreed. 'Have to get hold of that book of his. "Know thine enemy."'

'He's not an enemy, darling,' Mary Drover said. 'He's a new neighbour. Nice eyes. Pity about the nose.'

'Figure of speech, my dear. Just so long as he doesn't upset our little arrangement with Fred, like that idiot Cryer, with his bloody drugs. The last thing we need is the police swarming all over the place again. They charge you with anything these days. Safety belts, tyres . . .'

'Well, he's safely off the scene, enjoying the delights of Birmingham,' Alan Walters said. 'And good riddance, I say.'

'I wonder how that nice Mr Kirby broke his nose,' Mary Drover mused. 'Actually, it makes him look quite handsome.'

'He probably got punched by a husband whose wife fancied him,' Walters grinned. 'I'll ask him next time we meet, shall I?'

'Don't you dare.'

Next Saturday morning the Kirbys took a phone call from Fred Newson inviting them round for tea at Lindisholm Farm so they could see his farming operation and talk about his tenancy of their twenty acres of pasture. They accepted the invitation, and Janice began hunting through the sale documents to find the copy of the agreement between Newson and the farm's previous owner, Bob Cryer. It was a single page of small print, crammed with sections on grazing rights, access, fertiliser application, fencing responsibilities and milk quotas. Some entries had been crossed out and initialled.

'I think one of the things is to make sure a tenant doesn't establish permanent rights to anything,' Ben said. 'That's why it runs from the first of February to the end of December, for instance. Not a full calendar year.'

'It doesn't say anything about what Newson wants to graze, I mean sheep or cows or what?'

'Don't suppose it matters.'

'And what's all this stuff about poles that's been crossed out?' She peered at the document. 'Ping Poles, it says. What are Ping Poles?'

'God knows. Probably something to do with electricity supply or phones.'

'It seems our predecessor didn't want them on his land, anyway.'

'Maybe it was the other way round. Maybe they were his Ping Poles, and Newson didn't want them stampeding his buffaloes.'

'Don't think so. Cryer didn't draw up the agreement.' She pointed at the bottom of the page where a tiny line of print stated that this was Lindisholm EE/5432: CareCorp plc. 'All very official-looking.'

'I suppose the best thing is to see what the bugger wants before making a decision.'

'Is £150 an acre a fair price for grazing rights round here?'

'Absolutely no idea. I'll phone Toby. He's got a farm somewhere. If he doesn't know, I'll call the local National Farmers Union on Monday.'

Toby Jennings was a friend and also their solicitor, and he told Ben that the price was about fifty per cent more than he would have expected, especially as Newson made it clear he would maintain the land and all the gates and fences.

'Curiouser and curiouser,' Janice said.

The route to Lindisholm Farm took them to the head of a valley nestling in a range of wooded mountains. The farmhouse was surrounded by trees, so it was difficult to see how much land there was attached to it, but Ben decided it must be a relatively small estate, otherwise Newson wouldn't need tenancies. As they turned into the farm, two large, sleek Dobermanns ran up and escorted the car to the front entrance where they sat quietly with their tongues lolling out, looking at the visitors with fathomless brown eyes. Ben sensed Janice stiffening in her seat.

'For Christ's sake, darling. They look harmless enough.'

'I'm not setting one toe outside this car until those brutes are locked away,' Janice said emphatically.

She meant it. Ben knew there was no way she would move until the dogs were under lock and key. He sighed and tooted the horn, and two youths and a girl, all wearing green overalls, appeared from behind an outbuilding. The tallest, a teenager with a small gold ring in his right ear, came up to the driver's side of the car.

'We're here to see Fred Newson. Ben and Janice Kirby. He is expecting us.'

'Good afternoon, Mr Kirby,' the boy said stiffly. 'Mr Newson says he's sorry he's not here to meet you. One of the calves has been hurt. He says I can let you into the house, unless you'd like to go to the fields.'

'Thing is, my wife has a problem with the dogs.'

'We aren't going anywhere until you lock them away,' Janice said tightly.

The youth leaned down so he could see into the car. He glanced at her and looked away, quickly. 'We'll put them in the kennels.'

They watched as he fondled the dogs' powerful muzzles and patted their rumps. The stumpy tails wagged, and the animals turned and loped towards the gates. The girl and the other boy followed. After a few moments, the youth said, 'They won't be no bother now.'

Ben helped Janice from the car.

'Very kind of you,' Ben said. 'Er, you didn't tell us your name.'

Again, that quick look at Janice. Not sneaky, Ben decided. More embarrassed. Shy, perhaps. Or maybe something else.

'Wesley.' Almost a whisper.

'Okay, Wesley. Lead the way.'

Wesley strode towards a metal gate and along a footpath through a wooded area. When they emerged from the far side of the trees, Ben stopped dead.

'Jesus Christ! What's that?'

Wesley turned and saw where he was staring. 'That's Lindisholm Hospital, Mr Kirby.'

Newson's farm was on a hillside overlooking a large valley several hundred feet below. Unlike other valleys in the area, this one seemed, even from that distance, to be heavily cultivated. But it wasn't the pattern of fields that had caught Ben's eye. In the middle of the valley was a glistening white structure, laid out in concentric circles connected by spokes. The spaces between the circles and spokes were occupied by people in coloured garments. Even from this distance he could pick out the colours: green, blue, red and yellow. Kaleidoscopic dots of humanity in the afternoon sunshine. Hundreds of them. Lindisholm Hospital. Ben shook his head. Of course! How could he have failed to recognise the name? It was even on the bottom of the tenancy form with the name of the company that owned it. CareCorp plc. Very sloppy!

'Hello, there!' Fred Newson's call came from a hedgerow over to their right. 'Bring our guests down, Wesley, so they can see a horny-handed son of toil at work.'

Newson was kneeling by a calf whose legs were being held by yet another youngster in green overalls. He was sewing up a jag-ged gash in its throat. As they approached, the calf managed to kick the youngster away and jerk its neck free. Blood spurted as Newson struggled to stop the animal getting to its feet, and Ben threw himself on the calf's shoulders. Wesley followed, and between them they kept the calf immobile as Newson opened a pack of sutures.

'Right,' Newson gasped. 'Keep the blighter still for just two more minutes . . .'

It took a little longer than two minutes, and by the time Newson had tied off the last stitch and plunged a hypodermic needle into the calf's backside, Ben's wax jacket and Wesley's overalls were covered in blood.

'Off you go, you little bugger, and stay away from those fences, if you please.'

The calf kneeled itself upright, shook its head tentatively, and went dancing off to find its mother.

'Sorry about this, but animals come before visitors. No offence meant. Let's get to the farm so I can get one of the kids to hose your jacket down. You better clean up, too, Wesley.'

'Absolutely. No problem,' Ben said. He stared after the calf. 'That's a pretty deep gash for barbed wire.'

'The little fellow must have struggled to get free, I suppose.'

'I put the dogs away. I don't know if I should let them out yet,' Wesley interjected.

'They are guard dogs, Wesley. They should be guarding.'

'Oh dear,' Janice said. 'I'm afraid I'm responsible. I go all weak at the knees if there are dogs around, don't I, Ben?'

'Utter collapse.'

'Not to worry, then, Wesley. You can keep them locked up until our guests have left us. Meanwhile, I reckon we could do with a nice cup of tea after all that, and thanks a lot for your help, Mr Kirby. Plucky thing to do, for a city chap, wouldn't you say, Mrs Kirby?'

'My husband tends to get stuck into things. Bleeding calves, truculent taxi drivers. It's all the same to him, isn't it, darling?'

Tea, hot buttered toast, jam and small cakes. Not just good. Outstanding. Everything except the tea and sugar was made on the premises, Newson told them with considerable pride. Farm-grown organic wheat, stone-ground at the mill next to the river, bread baked in a wood-fired oven, home-made gooseberry and redcurrant jam, hand-churned butter from organically reared cows' milk . . . Janice was finding this fascinating, but Ben's contribution to the conversation grew increasingly monosyllabic, so the farmer directed his attentions to Janice, explaining how grazing tenancies could benefit both sides, especially as the Kirbys did not plan on using the land themselves.

'You'll hardly know when we're there,' Newson was saying. 'If we move the animals, it's either first thing in the morning or last thing at night. Every now and again we'll turn up with a tractor and spend maybe a few days tending to the grass or repairing the fencing. Your fields have gates opening to the lanes, so there's no need for my people to come near the house, unless you want them to help out with maintenance or cleaning, things like that.'

Janice was nodding appreciatively, when Ben asked, 'Those young people you have working for you – do those green uniforms mean they come from Lindisholm Hospital? Is your farm part of the hospital?'

Newson's affable manner changed subtly, and Ben got the impression that the question was not unexpected.

Janice stared at him. 'Is that something that concerns us, darling?'

'Not if you don't mind dealing with the largest institution for the criminally insane in Europe.'

'No one uses the expression "criminally insane" these days, Mr Kirby. Lindisholm is a high-security hospital for people who have been diagnosed as having a treatable mental illness.'

'So you use these people to help you run your farm, and from what you tell us you'd use them on our land, too.'

'Yes, but all the patients concerned have been assessed by the consultants as being fit for work release schemes. It's part of their treatment.'

'And you offer rents for your tenancies that are well above the prevailing market rates. Is that because you are getting cheap labour from the hospital, or what?'

'From your tone, I suspect that my explanation may not satisfy you.'

'Why don't we give it a try?'

'If you like, but I can only outline the local significance of the farm with regard to the hospital. If you want to go deeper, you'll have to contact a colleague of mine, Roy Ormley. He's the director of public affairs for CareCorp. That's the company in London that owns the hospital.'

'I know.'

'Then you'll understand that we have to run a very tightly controlled operation, and my main responsibility is to help the hospital achieve self-sufficiency. The farm produces over seventy per cent of all foods for patients and duty staff, including meats, vegetables, bread and some processed foods. We use hides, wool, and vegetable fibres to manufacture clothing and other products, some of which we sell at a profit. We also supplement our labour requirements by using hospital patients, which is considered to be an excellent therapy and a great mutual benefit. I can only hope you agree that kind of thing is in the best interests of the public and the patients.'

'I think it's a great idea,' Janice said.

'You make it sound very impressive,' Ben said, 'but our predecessor wasn't altogether happy with the situation, looking at the deletions in the contract you had with him. Was there something wrong?'

Newson sighed. 'Bloody stupidity on our part, I'm sorry to say. Our security people fed him some bullshit about the Ping Poles being part of an anti-rustling drive, you know, where you inject a transponder into the neck of an animal and a sensor at the top of the poles monitors its movements. One morning Cryer went into the fields and prodded a couple of cow necks. No transponder. He was understandably annoyed. Said he'd been misled. We had to take the Ping Pole down in your field and amend the grazing agreement. It left a security gap in the outer perimeter until Tom Attwood agreed to let us install one on his land. There's still a flat spot at the southern boundary of your fields that we'd like to cover, though.'

'What are the poles for?' Janice asked.

'Electronic tagging of offenders,' Ben said quietly. 'The kids in green are wearing alkathene bracelets, or didn't you notice?'

'No, I didn't. It sounds awful. Like animals.'

'It's in everyone's interests,' Newson said quickly. 'Society gets more protection, and the patients get more freedom. And I must correct you. The residents of the hospital are not offenders, Mr Kirby. They are patients. They are here because a court or an independent medical authority decided they suffer from a treatable illness, regardless of what they might have done.'

'That young man, Wesley, who was looking after your dogs and the calf. He seemed very nice, didn't he, Ben? What on earth did he do to get himself assigned to Lindisholm?' Janice asked.

'I'm sorry, Mrs Kirby. I'm not allowed to discuss the patients. In any case, I don't know. When they come to the farm, I get a profile outlining their general needs and problems, and that's it.'

Ben stood up. 'I think we're going to have to sleep on all this, Fred.'

The Kirbys drove back to Brianne Mill, mulling over what Newson had told them, suspecting that they had differing views about it all. When they arrived home Janice opened a bottle of wine and poured them both a glass.

'There's a problem, isn't there?' she said.

'Damn right, there's a problem. I don't want anything to do with that plausible bastard.'

'He seemed like a nice man to me.'

'Nice? What exactly is nice?'

'I don't want us to have a row.'

'Why should we have a row?'

28

'We're having one already.'

'I'm sorry,' he said. 'Come here.'

They had a long, close hug.

'You were very brave with that calf.'

'Brave? I was bloody heroic. Bit of a mystery, though. Newson said it was hurt by the fences, but there's no way barbed wire could have caused that gash. Did you see how deep it was?'

'Maybe there was some glass or something.'

'Maybe.'

'It was very brave of you, anyway,' she mumbled into his chest. 'So. Are we going to sign his bloody agreement, or what?'

'Like I said, I think we should sleep on it. I'll check a few of the legal aspects with Toby on Monday, then we can make up our minds.'

'Good thinking, Boy Wonder.' She tightened her grip.

'What made you ask about Wesley?' he asked after a few moments.

'I liked him.'

'Oh yes?'

'Not like that, silly. He just seemed, you know, nice.'

'I thought he was a bit odd, myself.'

'What do you mean, odd?'

'I don't really know. I think you made him uneasy.'

'Don't be ridiculous. He seemed perfectly normal to me. That's why I asked about him.'

'Maybe he suffers from "Janophobia", like you suffer from "Canophobia".'

'Janophobia? Ha, ha, very funny,' Janice responded.

When his visitors' car had bumped its way down the farm track to the road back to the village, Fred Newson stared out of the window towards the woods that led to the fields and the valley beyond. He did not think he would have any problem dealing with the Kirbys. They would soon learn that their fields needed the animals as much as the animals needed the fields. Without grazing and care, the grassland would be overcome by dock and thistle. But Newson wanted to tie things up as quickly as possible. The idea of waiting for that snotty writer to make his mind up was not appealing. Then again, the arrival of the Kirbys might be put to all kinds of advantages in his close-knit community. Advantages to Newson.

The young girl who had been with Wesley when the Kirbys arrived was carrying a can of mixed corn to the chicken sheds. He tapped on the glass and beckoned to her. She put the can down and came into his room, standing straight and quiet. Thin shoulders. High cheek bones. Pert little breasts. Narrow, provocative hips. A compulsive thief and liar, according to the unofficial reports that circulated within the hospital.

'You were in the courtyard when our guests arrived, Janie, weren't you?'

'Yes, Mr Newson.'

'What's all this about the dogs?'

'The lady didn't want to get out of the car because the dogs was there. She was scared.'

'And . . . ?'

'Wesley got the dogs away from the car, and John and me took them to the kennel and locked them up.'

'And that's all?'

'I don't know, Mr Newson.'

'What I mean is, did anyone say anything to the lady?'

The girl's face remained blank. 'No one said nothing, sir.'

'We can't be too careful with our visitors, can we Janie?'

'No, sir.'

'You know why?'

'A visitor can make or break a patient's future.' A catechism.

'Exactly. "A good word from a visitor is manna from heaven. A bad word can bring the wrath of hell." You will remember that, won't you?'

'Yes, Mr Newson.' She paused. 'Wesley fancied the lady. I saw him watching her. He wanted to stick his willy into her. She fancied him, and all.'

'Really? How do you know that?'

'A woman can tell these things.'

Newson stifled a sigh. 'Thank you, Janie. Carry on with the chickens and ask John to come here.'

Newson had no time for religion, but found its homilies and clichés very useful when dealing with simple and disturbed people. He also shared one abiding principle with many religious people: he believed everything was for a purpose. In Newson's case, the purpose was the continued well-being of Fred Newson, and he left absolutely nothing to chance in his efforts to establish this. The arrival of the Kirbys at

Brianne Mill had to be assessed and measured and integrated where possible into Newson's life-improvement plan. And apart from the tenancy, Newson was curious about Janice Kirby's question about Wesley Freeman. Was little Janie the Liar correct? Was the sexy Mrs Kirby attracted to Wesley? Was it mutual? These things happen.

'Come in, John,' he said when he heard the tap on his door. 'I want you to tell me what happened when our visitors arrived.'

The same story. The dogs. The frightened lady. Wesley calming them down. John and Janie taking them to the kennels. No, he had not spoken to the lady. Did he think Wesley liked the lady?

'Don't know, sir.'

'Come, now, John. You can tell if a person likes someone, can't you?'

'No, sir.'

God, it was like pushing water uphill with a pin. How the hell did the counsellors cope with this kind of thing?

'Did you like her, John?'

This boy was a persistent bed-wetter who had kept trying to smother his six-month-old baby sister. He was eighteen years old.

'I don't know, sir.'

Newson believed him. 'Thank you, John. Ask Wesley to come here, will you?'

Wesley Freeman. According to the hospital grapevine, young Wesley had assaulted two members of his school staff, and he was silent as a trappist about his transgression. A challenging case for the social workers and consultants. An arousal of interest for the foxy Mrs Janice Kirby. Maybe Wesley could provide some leverage for Newson in his constant battle for self-aggrandisement.

LION

I look around majestically as the sun appears over the eastern horizon to send long dawn shadows across the darkened veldt, with its brown grass and teeming herds, feeling the shiver of anticipation as the final stage of the hunt begins. The Offering is still trying to satisfy the demands of Lamb and Spiderlady out there in the corridor. What a way to go! Perhaps, next time, the Beaters will bring a young female, so that I can sow my seed into her womb as she lies on the altar. It has been weeks since that happened, a long time, and my head is full of the howling, rushing wind that drowns the unclean world in pain. But this young male Offering will help. Better than nothing. First me, then the Jackals, then the others. I wonder what pleasure White Eagle gets out of all this, sitting there in Omega Cloister, cut off from the world; but that gaunt, blank face gives nothing away. No emotion. No reaction. Only intellect. That is why White Eagle is who he is and where he is. That is why we are who we are and where we are. That is why we do what we do. Without White Eagle we would not be born again. Without White Eagle we would be names and numbers, without hope. White Eagle brings us purpose, gives our lives meaning, lets our imaginations soar to anywhere in the world we want to be: out of this sterile place with its featureless impact-proof surfaces and camera-scanned walkways, out to sun-lit beaches and high mountain peaks, out to the killing fields of the great plains . . .

'Any time, any place,' White Eagle promises us from his eyrie in Omega Cloister.

'Any time, any place,' the priests chant back in their heads.

'A new beginning is a new beginning,' he intones.

'And a new ending is a new ending,' we respond.

White Eagle is brilliant. He discovers meaning in non-meaning and gives it to his people.

32

The entrance to the UK headquarters of CareCorp plc was squashed between two ancient Elizabethan buildings in a narrow alley opposite St Paul's Cathedral and protected by an ancient wooden door lined with steel sheeting that had been installed when the IRA bomb campaigns started. City of London planning permission had been flouted by the mounting of a high-resolution security camera slanting down from the wall of the next-door building. But then, the company chairman Lord Balacombe was a formidable part of the City establishment, and planning officials trod lightly on issues involving him.

In general, CareCorp was not a company that advertised its presence, preferring to impress those it sought to woo with an image of discretion and financial success. In the entrance lobby, visitors were greeted by a girl whose main responsibility was to look cool and beautiful, no matter what. She was supplied with perfume by the company, a tactic introduced after a survey carried out by a firm of image consultants showed that fragrancing and body language were vital components in the constant battle to establish group and social domination. You not only had to look good if you worked for CareCorp plc, you had to smell good. You also had to be absolutely meticulous. Lord Balacombe was very fond of corporate mission statements, and one of his favourites was: 'It's just as easy to get it right as get it wrong'. Another was: 'If you can't do it yourself, think twice before passing it upstairs'.

This was why Roy Ormley, the company's director of public affairs, was rereading his computer screen. Something had been passed upstairs.

E-MAIL
FROM: F Newson, Lindisholm Farm
TO: HQ: Public Affairs.
COPIES: Hospital Departments: Finance, Security,
            Clinics, Counselling.
SUBJECT: Monthly report.

I attach my monthly report and submit the following summary:

1. Arable and animal production targets achieved within average variation of 5%. Three animals injured on barbed wire. Suggest review of fencing materials.
2. Low rainfall during summer months has affected flour mill efficiency. Need to adjust next month's buy-in quota by 50 sacks.
3. Grazing rights for Brianne Mill discussed with Mr and Mrs Ben Kirby, the new owners. May not go as desired. Suggest we offer rent increase per acre-year from £150 to £175 in first instance. If this fails, suggest involvement of RO, public affairs.
4. Reference Para 4: IT confirms Ping Pole flat-spot at south-western boundary of outer perimeter at Brianne Mill. Suggest hospital security adds the Penford-Buryton road to patrol schedules until further notice.
5. Mrs Kirby made personal enquiry re Wesley Freeman (Alpha 99-52-7301). A patient commented on a possible mutual interest between them. Suggest query during counselling.

Fred Newson's e-mail irritated Ormley. Newson was a reliable man, especially when it came to the practical matters of farm management and its interplay with hospital affairs. But there was a certain lack in his grasp of strategic matters. Ormley stared at the e-mail circulation list and then at Point 3. Local matters affecting the Lindisholm complex should not be reported to HQ unless something drastic happened. A negative reaction on the part of a new landowner was not a matter that Ormley considered drastic. Either Newson had made an error of judgement or he had failed to explain why he had directed his comments to HQ. Ormley picked up the phone and started with an open-ended question. That always caught people off-balance.

'Fred? Good morning. Roy Ormley here. What's all this about Brianne Mill?'

'Morning, Roy. I take it you've read my e-mail.'

Of course he had read it. Why did people like Newson always ask such stupid questions? Ormley created a silence, and Newson smiled

35

to himself at the obvious tactic. The man was a control freak, and not a very subtle one.

'It's all tickety-boo, Roy, but under the circumstances I felt it advisable that you should be fully appraised of the situation.'

It was Ormley's turn to double-think. Under *what* circumstances? He stared at the computer screen for several seconds before it hit him. Ben Kirby! The bastard who wrote *The Façade*. Bloody hell! The fucking paperback was sprouting up in bookshops all over the place.

'Quite right too, Fred. But you're the man on the spot. What do you think?'

Newson acknowledged the slick way Ormley changed mental gear. The man was an arsehole, but a very professional arsehole.

'The way I read it, there's nothing particular in his reactions. He's just an awkward sod who doesn't like large companies. I plugged the social responsibility and benefit to society stuff. If that and the extra rent for the fields doesn't make an impression, we'll need another approach. His wife might be less negative. More sympathetic to patient requirements, for instance. Incidentally, she's what we country bumpkins call "a bit of a cracker".'

'Really? Well, keep on it, and let me know if you want my personal support. Bye.'

Newson grinned at his telephone. Ormley had missed the significance of the name Kirby, first time round. He thought that would happen, and the good thing was that Ormley knew that's what he thought, but there was nothing the smooth prick could do about it. Plus that bit about Janice Kirby was a good move. Fancied himself as a ladies' man, did the public affairs director, and Janice was one tasty lady. Maybe Ormley would make it his business to turn up at Lindisholm, and who knows what would happen from there. The whole thing was one in the eye for the patronising Lord Balacombe and Mission Statement No. 38: 'Remember: your colleagues are your brothers and sisters, so treat each other with respect'. What a load of crap. A bit of cut-and-thrust between colleagues was what made the business world go round. Newson had plans for his work at Lindisholm Farm, and his key ambition was to take early retirement much sooner than CareCorp was likely to offer it to him. If that meant putting spokes like Ben Kirby into various company wheels, so be it. It couldn't do Newson any harm, and it might do him some good.

*   *   *

36

Ormley put down his phone, added a note on the e-mail and forwarded it to Admin. He restarted his computer, went into the set-up program and altered the date. His memo informing the company that an antagonistic author had settled right on the perimeter of the company's flagship operation would go straight into the archives, pre-dated by a month, and everyone would wonder why only Roy Ormley had noticed. He then reset the date and replied to Newson's e-mail congratulating the farm manager on how he had dealt with the Kirbys. Meticulous back protection is the first level of fire-proofing. He wondered if Fred Newson's observation about Mrs Kirby was accurate.

Professor Petra Jonser, Lindisholm's Head of Psychiatric Medicine, read Newson's e-mail and cross-checked Wesley Freeman with her patient files. Alpha 99-52-7301 aged eighteen, from Wolverhampton. A social worker had noted a disturbed home background but a good school record. At the age of seventeen he had been discovered in the sports pavilion by the school caretaker attempting the violent rape of a female teacher, Anne Squires. He had also physically assaulted a male member of staff. Strangely, the female teacher had chosen not to make a statement. Even stranger, Wesley had presented no defence and refused to plead. In fact, the records showed that he had said nothing at all to anyone involved in the case. He had been in Lindisholm Hospital for almost a year, showing no sign of remorse. However, neither did he show any sign of violent tendencies, so after the statutory six-week period of induction he had been assigned to Alpha Cloister under a regime of routine medication and regular counselling. His case was being handled by a new member of the psychiatric team, Dr Nikki Congleton. Professor Jonser sent her a copy of Newson's report, with the message, 'Please check this, and report to me.'

With the reputation of Lindisholm Hospital always on the line, the methodical Professor Jonser was not about to let would-be rapists like Wesley Freeman endanger the system.

Tim Johnson, Head of Physical Security, read Newson's report, groaned and called his deputy, Mervyn Jessell.

'Fred Newson wants a patrol on the Buryton road. How are you fixed?'

'You have to be kidding. We haven't got enough staff to patrol an ice cream van. He knows that, so what's his problem?'

'We've got a blank spot at Brianne Mill.'

'Really!' An ooze of sarcasm. 'Have you checked any of the other perimeter sites recently?'

'Something wrong I should know about, is there?'

'I've been reporting it for the last year, for Christ's sake.'

'Ah, your bird-shit-rain theory.'

'What theory? The birds shit on the solar panels, the Ping sensitivity goes down. The rain washes it off, the sensitivity goes back up again. The bloody things are totally unreliable.'

'You want me to make your complaint official?'

'Don't drop this on me, Johnson. It's not my responsibility to make technical reports. I'm just telling you what the situation is.'

'Okay, okay, but that's the system we're stuck with, and the company's not going to spend another penny on perimeter security for at least five years. Why don't you make a couple of sweeps and send me a report every now and again. That'll keep Newson off our backs until we can find some way of keeping the bird shit off the panels.'

'So you believe me about the bird shit?'

'No, but maybe it'll keep you off my back.'

'I can see Wesley. It's Wesley's turn for thirty minutes in the garden. I see him sitting on a seat by the flower beds with some of us other patients. They are playing "I Spy". Educational and stimulating. To spy it, you have to be observant. To clue it, you have to be able to spell the first letter. To get it, you have to be smart. And quick, if Pedro Sharez is playing with you. Pedro is a walking dictionary, plus he has one of those memories that can't forget anything he looks at. He can recite the complete works of William Shakespeare, Pedro can. An autistic savant, is what the counsellors call him. Just like me, but I remember other things. Pedro is in Lindisholm because they get him on one of those TV programmes, don't they, and this lady puts a big tray of this and that in front of him, and they show it to him for ten seconds then throw a cover over it, only one of the TV people sticks something else on the tray, so when they ask Pedro what was on the tray he tells them all these things except the thing they stick on the tray, because he never saw it, did he? And they say, sorry pal, you missed out the thing, and Pedro tells them it wasn't on the tray when he looked, and they go Oh yes, a likely story, and this and that. So Pedro goes apeshit and does the studio and does the idiot who stuck the thing on the tray, and that's why he's here in Lindisholm. I'm here because I'm too clever by far and I hit people who don't like me . . .'

'That's very good, Harold,' Dr Nikki Congleton said, interrupting the flow. 'You can stop looking out of the window now.'

The wizened little face turned towards her. 'I can see your face and your boobs, and I know what boobs are for, don't I?'

'Of course you do. Was Wesley the first person you saw when you looked out of the window?'

'Yes. Wesley is my friend. Mr Dagby is my friend, too. He lets me play with the system.'

'We're glad you've got friends, Harold. Can you go to Wesley and tell him to come here as soon as his break is finished? Can you do that for me?'

'Yes, I can do that.'

Dagby? That would be Robert Dagby, Manager of Information Technology. Now why would this patient claim his friendship? Dr Congleton made a note on Harold Jenkins's file to query that when she had a moment and watched through the window as the stunted figure appeared outside and made its way along the footpath to Wesley Freeman. He looked towards her window briefly, nodded to Jenkins, and continued his game. She checked that security was monitoring her interview area and got Wesley's file on the screen. Some of his companions were very disturbed young people, but Wesley never seemed to antagonise them. He just kept himself to himself and got on with things. Many psychiatric patients were like that, hoping that by keeping a low profile they would be released back into society.

In the few weeks she'd been seeing him, Dr Congleton had decided that Wesley was a very dangerous young man. The teacher he attacked had withdrawn her statement for some reason, but Wesley had also assaulted the caretaker of the school, who had not, and the case of assault against him was still pending in the courts. If a patient committed one spontaneous assault, he could commit another. As far as she or any of her colleagues could see, Wesley was making no progress whatsoever. Maybe this information from the farm manager would provide some insight, maybe not. One had to keep an open mind.

Wesley came to the doorway and stood waiting. Not many doors within Lindisholm's cloisters, just security sensing stations, barriers and partitions to give an illusion of personal privacy in designated areas. The only exceptions were the lavatories and the operating theatres in the well-equipped medical centre, but so many cameras and microphones were in those places that they might just as well have no walls.

'Come in, Wesley.'

As he moved past the sensing loop, his tag was registered with that distinctive electronic 'ping'. The loops were also attached to the Ping Poles that were situated in the area surrounding the hospital. The physical location of every patient was logged into the central computer every minute of every day. No need for time-consuming and costly personal checks by staff. The system kept track of all patient movements. It knew that Wesley Freeman was now alone in a counselling area with Dr Nikki Congleton. The CCTV camera auto-focused on his chair, and his image came up on the Alpha Cloister security room monitors. If Wesley tried to attack Dr Congleton, a riot-proof barrier would be dropped between them and guards would appear with tranquillisers. When Lindisholm began operations, quite a few adjustments had to be made before they got the timing right. It was a balance between protecting the staff and guillotining a patient, and the staff knew where their priorities lay. Eventually the word got round and the attacks stopped. Another positive statistic to pass to the board of directors – and CareCorp shareholders.

'Do you know why we want to see you, Wesley?'

'No, miss.'

'It's not a problem. We're just checking how you feel about your work on the farm.'

'I like it, miss.'

'Well, Mr Newson's recent monthly report puts your work there in a good light. You were with Janie Dolstead and John McWeeney last Saturday, weren't you?'

'Yes, miss.'

'And Mr Newson gave you the responsibility to greet his visitors. He says you handled that very efficiently. Well done.'

'Thank you, miss.'

'How did your game of "I Spy" go just now?'

'Sammy Entfield kept forgetting what he was doing, and Peter Upton kept giving us stuff that was in his head.'

'Did you win?'

'No, miss. Nobody won. We was just enjoying ourselves.'

A classic interview structure. Greeting, praise, query irrelevant topic to remove important issues from front-of-mind, ask key question. Now was the time.

'Apparently you showed an interest in Mr Newson's guests, especially the lady. Would that be correct, Wesley?'

'I don't know, miss.'

'You helped the lady out of the car, and you kept looking at her. Is that true?'

Wesley stared straight ahead.

'Is that true, Wesley?'

'No, miss.'

'It's not that there's anything necessarily wrong here, Wesley, but why would anyone say that if it didn't happen?'

'I don't know. She wouldn't get out of the car. That's all it was.'

'She wouldn't get out of the car? Why was that?' She noted that his eyes were shining.

'The lady was scared of the dogs, so I calmed them down, and Janie and John took them to the kennels.'

'What I'm trying to get at, Wesley, is: did you look at her? Did you touch her? Did you want to touch her?'

'I didn't touch nobody. I just sorted the dogs and then we went to the fields to see Mr Newson.'

His eyes were not so much shining as swimming. Something here worth pushing. 'Did you find Mrs Kirby attractive?'

He sat very still, and his tears flowed down his cheeks. He mumbled something.

'You must speak up, Wesley.'

'She was in the car, and then I went to the gate, and they followed me to the fields. I didn't look at her.'

'Okay, I can live with that, but did you want to look at her?' He was trembling now, and his tears were dampening his collar. 'I should imagine you did want to look at her. Most boys would at least look at a lady to see if she was attractive, wouldn't they?'

'No, no, no,' he muttered. Then louder. 'No, no, no!' It turned into a wail, and he curled up in the chair, sobbing uncontrollably.

Dr Congleton looked at the CCTV camera and nodded, then waited while two orderlies arrived, injected Wesley and helped him out of the room. She wrote her report and e-mailed it to Professor Jonser with an attachment of the interview video: 'My conclusion is that Alpha 99-52-7301 is developing schizoid reactions under stress, and he still shows no remorse for attacking his teacher. I recommend that we increase his medication and upgrade his security to Beta Cloister.'

Professor Jonser had a reputation for reacting quickly to clinical situations. She replied half an hour later.

'I agree with your conclusion and have sympathy with your recommendations. However, the hospital board will question the cost of such a move. They might also comment that you pushed a little hard during the interview. I suggest you give Wesley more time to develop possible abreactions so that we have a stronger case for recloistering, if that is necessary.'

Congleton glared at the screen. Pushed a little hard! This young thug assaults his teacher, gets sent to this luxury hotel, sits in the sunshine playing with his friends, and she pushes him a little hard! To hell with that! If the good professor wanted Wesley's problems to develop so a decision could be made she, Nikki Congleton, could play that game, no problem.

She started typing another e-mail, then paused. A phone call would be wiser.

'Mr Newson, it's Dr Congleton from psychiatric counselling.'

'Hello, Dr Congleton. What can I do for you?'

'Professor Jonser passed me your note on Wesley Freeman. I've looked into it, and you might just have stumbled on the very thing that could help Wesley. You say that your visitor, Mrs Kirby, showed some interest in the boy.'

'Well, she asked why he was in Lindisholm, if you call that interest.'

'What did you tell her?'

'Nothing, because I don't know anything. How can this help Wesley?'

'It may not. But more outside contact might be therapeutic for him. It was common practice in my old hospital to let low-risk patients get a little more involved in the community.'

'And which hospital would that be, Dr Congleton?' He already knew, of course. The staff grapevine at Lindisholm was faster than e-mail.

'Rampton.'

'I see. Well, as you know, I have no authority to take part in any medical activity or patient treatment. Anyway, the patients have plenty of outside contact with farm visitors and the agency labourers we take on.'

'Naturally. But if the Kirbys have shown an interest of any kind, it could be just what we need to help Wesley make that all-important move back to normal behaviour.'

No harm in that, Newson thought; in fact it could prove to be very useful. If that toffee-nosed writer and his sexy wife were interested in one of the patients, he could send the kid along there to do a bit of general handiwork or rubbish clearing. It might help them to swing in the right direction. If not, no one had lost anything. All-in-all, his innocuous little e-mail was creating some very satisfying reactions. According to Tim Johnson, it had even resulted in those lazy sods in security driving up and down the mountain road to check things out and report that everything was satisfactory. They'd soon get pissed off with that, of course, and that meant they were less likely to stick their interfering noses into any of his work parties. Now this new kid on the medical block was asking a favour for one of her patients which involved the newcomers. Newson neither knew nor cared why. It was none of his business. But it couldn't do any harm and it might build a few bridges. Things were stacking up very nicely.

'I'll see what I can do,' he promised Congleton.

ROSEHIP

There's Lion, there's Lion. Good Lion. Lion is strong and clever, that's what Brother Lion is. And poor Rosehip is not strong and clever. But she listens and hears and she wants to tell everybody the wonderful things she has in her head, only she's better at listening and hearing than she is at speaking. And she can read and write, too, read and write, can Rosehip. Only no one knows that because when she tries to tell them, the words won't come out like they should, and she is very unhappy. But Rosehip has a lot of friends, a lot of friends, and she wants to help them, so she does, and here is Lion lying on his bed with another tube sticking out of his arm. Poor, poor Lion. But Rosehip knows exactly what to do because her friend Monkey Boy explained it all very, very carefully, didn't he? She has to talk to Lion until the camera moves away, and then she has to empty some of Lion's medication into the bag that Spiderlady gave her. And then she has to go to all the others in the restraining ward and do the same thing to them, a little bit here, a little bit there, and she can spell all the names of the medications she is taking from their drips. There was chlorpromazine, haloperidol, lorazepam, imipramine, phenelzine, lithium, plus things from the farm stores.

Good to sleep, good to dream, good to sleep, good to dream. Here I am, there I go, here I am, there I go. Look at sleepy-head, dreaming dreams, so peaceful. And me, and me, why not here, why not there? Only one match needed for all this, only one match, and the air rushes in and carries dreams to the sky.

When my plasma bag is full, the Jackals will be ready for Antelope. Poor Antelope.

TUTOR NOTES
Interesting. This student refers to a fellow student's nom de plume and seems to be extending his storyline. Perhaps this is not too

44

surprising. They have probably talked about the writing project among themselves. Her contribution mixes hospital procedures with fantasy, partly coherent and partly rambling, but showing a potential of sorts.

3

The Kirbys' morning post included a carton of eggs brought direct by the postman from the fishing bailiff, Alan Walters, with a note saying: 'Surplus to requirements. We've also got three spare hens. Good egg-layers. All you do is chuck a handful of mixed corn at them every day and collect the eggs each morning. Just say the word.'

There was also a package and letter from Ben's literary agent, Andrew Connolly, an aristocratic Irishman who had lived, breathed and consumed publishing since he had graduated in Classics from Trinity College, Dublin.

> My dear Ben and Janice
> I trust you are both settled in. Enclosed is a belated house-warming gift. It should be champagne, of course, but bubbly stuff does not travel at all well, as you know. So accept this with my compliments and a word of warning. Stand well clear of naked flames. By the way, horrendously short notice and all that, but I've booked a table at next week's Journalist of the Year Awards at the Savoy, and a couple of my guests have let me down. Mary quite rightly says I should have invited you in the first place. Mea culpa. Invitation cards enclosed. Will not – repeat, not – take no for an answer.
> Ever yours
> Andrew
> PS: Mary sends her love. She'll be there, of course.
> PPS: Black tie, by the way. Don't let that put you off.
> PPPS: Don't want to press you, old boy, but I really need a synopsis of your next book ASAP if we are to capitalise on your current success.

'Christ, that's next Thursday,' Ben said. 'He's got a hope.'

Inside the package was a very large glass medicine bottle with a gift label tied to its neck saying in Connolly's handwriting: 'The only thing guaranteed is the age. At least fifty years, matured in oak in a secret location. Seventy-five to twenty-five dilution recommended. Enjoy!'

Ben opened it and gave a cautious sniff. 'Bloody hell! Where are those chintzy glasses Eileen gave us?'

Janice opened a cupboard. 'You really must learn where we put things in this house. Two Waterford crystal tumblers coming up, with one water jug.'

An hour later, when the medicine bottle still contained four fifths of its contents and they were both warmly content, she exacted an irrevocable commitment from her reluctant husband that they would graciously accept Connolly's invitation.

'If we don't go, I will never, ever, let you touch my body again.'

'Rubbish!'

'I mean it, Ben. I need to do some shopping. And it will give me a chance to see Eileen and . . .'

'But what about these hens that Alan Walters says we can have? They'll need looking after. We can't go to London.'

Janice poured him another slug of potheen. 'Yes we can. I'll tell that bloke Newson that we'll go ahead with the grazing agreement. You get the hens, and Newson will send someone to look after them while we're carousing with your chums at the Savoy. What could be easier than that?'

'Are you serious about your body?'

'Deadly serious.'

'This is fucking outrageous.'

'You have such a way with words, lover. You go round to Alan in the morning and get his hens, and I'll phone Newson to sort the other things out.'

When Ben set off for the hens after breakfast the next morning, Janice picked up the phone.

'Hello, Mr Newson,' she said. 'It's Janice Kirby.'

'Mrs Kirby, how nice to hear from you.'

'We have this problem. We have to go to London next Thursday and stay overnight, only the thing is Ben has gone to pick up some hens from Alan Walters, and we wondered if we could arrange to have one of your people look after them while we are away. Oh, and we think we should go ahead with your grazing agreement.'

Newson couldn't believe his luck. He needed the grazing agreement, and Tim Johnson wanted to plug the gap in perimeter security. New kid Congleton wanted Wesley Freeman to get some more contact with people like the Kirbys, and here was the ravishing Mrs

47

Kirby, putting everything into place. Just like that! And everyone would owe him a favour. Lovely!

'You know the boy who sorted the dogs out for you when you came up to the farm? His counsellor would like him to get a little more experience outside the hospital. Could be just what you're looking for.'

'I think we'd be happier with one of your regular farm workers rather than a patient.'

'I can understand that. You can certainly have someone from the agency, but there would be no problem with Wesley. He is absolutely reliable, and we wouldn't have to charge him out to you like we would one of the agency lads. What do you think?'

'I need to talk this over with Ben. I'll get him to call you when he's home.'

Ben drove back from Alan Walters with three hens in a large cardboard box on the back seat of the Shogun, a bale of straw in the boot and a plastic bag filled with mixed corn to be going on with. One look at his face told Janice that he was having second thoughts about the whole thing.

'There's serious hen shit all over his yard, and his lawn. They peck all the bloody flowers, they scratch holes in the soil, and they give you the evil eye. I've a bloody good mind to take them back.'

'Think of all those lovely free-range eggs.'

'Fuck the lovely free-range eggs.'

'And they eat all kinds of garden pests, like those horrid red centipedes and slugs and earwigs.'

'They do?'

'I promise! And Mr Newson says we can borrow one of his workers to feed the hens while we're away. Actually, he suggested that nice boy Wesley who sorted the dogs out.'

Ben sighed. 'That "nice boy" is a patient in a high-security mental hospital, for heaven's sake. We can't have him traipsing around here, especially when we're away.'

'That was what I thought to start with, but we wouldn't have to pay for him like we would the agency people. Mr Newson doesn't think there'll be a problem.'

'Oh, doesn't he!' Ben picked up the phone, dialled, stood jiggling from one foot to the other irritatedly until Newson answered. 'Mr

Newson, it's Ben Kirby. I understand my wife spoke to you about arranging for one of your workers to come over here while we're away.'

'That's correct, Mr Kirby. I'd be glad to oblige.'

'She said you suggested that young fellow, what's-his-name. The patient.'

'Wesley. Only if you feel comfortable about it. His counsellor, Dr Congleton, is keen to help him get some experience in the community. She would never suggest such a thing if there was likely to be a problem.'

'Well, fine, but is there anything we need to know about Wesley, in case anything should go wrong? That is a heavy-duty place you have there.'

'Now, Mr Kirby, you know I can't be drawn into discussing that. All I can tell you is that Wesley was assigned to the farm by the psychiatric committee for Alpha Cloister, which is the cloister for patients with minimum security problems. We have Beta patients in our work placement scheme, and we even get occasional patients from Gamma Cloister who are showing significant improvement in their behaviour. Dr Congleton is suggesting that Wesley could benefit by having some contact with people like yourselves. She thinks there's a mutual benefit to be enjoyed.'

'But we won't be here, so what about security?'

'The tagging system takes care of that.'

'You mean your Ping Poles?'

'Right. It's all automatic. Security knows where every patient is, every minute of the day. If someone did try to leave their authorised area, we have a global positioning system that can track them to within a few feet within seconds. Wesley really is a reliable lad, and we'll indemnify you with the usual insurances, of course.'

'At the very least, I'd like to know how long he's been at Lindisholm. I mean, has he become institutionalised?'

'Not at all. He was admitted to Lindisholm last January and assigned to Alpha Cloister because he represents no threat to anyone. I'm able to use him on the farm, because his clinical prognosis has thus far been encouraging. He, in turn, has contact with Beta Cloister patients, which does them good, and so on, right through the hospital cloister system: Beta helping Gamma, Gamma helping Delta. The cloister system is designed so that the more able patients can positively affect the less able.'

'I imagine the reverse is also true,' Ben commented dryly.

'Good point, but the medical staff are able to encourage the positive effects and minimise the negative ones. There is a net gain for everyone involved. That's the beauty of the system. What do you say?'

'Hang on a minute.' Ben turned to Janice and held his hand over the phone. 'He says Wesley doesn't present a threat to anyone, and they'll indemnify us against anything that might go wrong. What do you think?'

'Well, he did seem nice, and if it's going to help him . . .'

'My wife says why not.'

'Splendid,' Newson said. 'What say I bring him round at ten o'clock next Tuesday, so you can show him the ropes? He can look after the hens on Thursday and Friday for you, and if all goes well he can come over once or twice a week for a while to give you a hand on a more regular basis.'

The Lindisholm Farm pick-up truck turned into the drive on the stroke of ten, with Fred Newson at the wheel, a mountain bike in the back and a solemn-looking Wesley Freeman in the passenger seat. The Kirbys met them at the door and offered a cup of tea.

'Not for me, thanks,' Newson said. 'Got to get back.' He produced a clipboard with some forms attached. 'All we need is your signature on this stuff.'

'What is it?' Ben asked.

'Agreements for the indemnity. Confirmation that the hospital remains responsible for Wesley in every respect, providing you meet a couple of rather obvious stipulations, such as no alcohol, cigarettes or money. There's an emergency telephone number for you, if anything should go amiss. The patients understand their part in this, so everything is above board. Isn't that right, Wesley?'

'Yes, Mr Newson,' Wesley said.

'He has to be at the farm by six to get the coach back to the hospital, so he should leave here by five at the latest for safe-ty's sake.'

'I shouldn't think that'll be a problem,' Janice said. 'There's not that much to do.'

'Gracious, don't tell him that, or he'll spend the day lying in the sun, won't you, old son?'

'No, sir. I'll find things.'

'That's the spirit,' Newson smiled. 'I'll leave you to get to know each other, then.'

When Newson's pick-up truck started back to the road, Janice turned to Wesley. 'I'd like a cup of tea, anyway. I'll make one for all of us, shall I, while Ben shows you around?'

Wesley stared at the ground and didn't say anything.

'Good idea,' Ben said. 'Come on, Wesley. We can look at the main buildings and check the hens on the way.'

Janice could see them both from the kitchen window for parts of Wesley's tour, Ben pointing out this and that, vanishing into the barn, emerging from the stables to walk up the hill and into the spinney, tapping this tree and that, waving his hands in the air as if he knew what he was talking about. She felt a sudden rush of affection. He hadn't been looking forward to this, but there he was, pitching in whole-heartedly, as he usually did. By the time they came back she had put out a selection of Mr Kipling's cakes and chocolate biscuits and was pouring boiling water into the teapot.

'Milk and sugar, Wesley?' she asked.

There was a silence, and she saw that Wesley was staring at Ben with a strange expression. A kind of pleading, she thought. All of a sudden she felt utterly out of her depth. The boy had been polite and communicative when they visited the hospital farm, and now he seemed incapable of speaking or even looking at her.

'Not to worry!' she said, a little too brightly. 'I'll let the two of you get on with things.'

She left the kitchen, and Ben said bluntly, 'It looks like you've upset my wife, Wesley.'

At that, the lad went to pieces, trying to tell Ben something, fighting back sobs, wringing his hands, shaking . . .

'Janice!' Ben called. 'You better come back here.' He poured Wesley a mug of tea and put three heaped spoons of sugar in, on the basis that sweet tea never did anyone any harm in a stressful situation. 'Let's all sit down and see if we can sort this out. First of all, Wesley, should I call Mr Newson?'

It was an effort, but the boy managed to get the words out. 'No, no.'

'All right. But I want some straight talking. It looks to me like you're frightened about something, and the first point I'm going to make is that there's no need to be frightened of us. We're just two ordinary people who moved here a few weeks ago, and we want to fit into things. On the other hand, maybe you can see that we should be a little concerned about you. Lindisholm is a secure hospital for the criminally insane, and, while we can understand that there are ranges of insanity and all kinds of security checks, how do you think we feel now, after we got on so well with you at the farm?'

'I don't know.'

'Frankly, we feel pretty nervous. We've no idea why you're at Lindisholm, and we certainly don't want to pry into your business. We simply want you to know that there is no need for you to feel frightened while you are with us. Not on our account, anyway.'

'If there is something bothering you, can you tell us what it is?' Janice asked.

'I'll be all right,' he said, still looking at Ben. 'Please don't call Mr Newson.'

'I tell you what,' Ben said. 'We have things to get on with. You grab that mug of tea and have a wander outside. If you see anything that wants tidying up or fixing, have a go, and if you need any help, come right back inside and knock on my study door. Around four thirty, we'll look over things, and then you can pedal your way back to the farm in good time.'

He was rewarded with a slight nod.

'Okay. We'll leave you to it.'

At the end of the afternoon, they were relieved and pleased to see that Wesley had done exactly what Ben had suggested. Logs that had been lying at random were now arranged in piles in the barn, and the farming implements that Bob Cryer had left behind were stacked neatly against a wall. He had replaced the straw in the henhouse and put out fresh water for the hens to drink.

'Looks like you've done us proud,' Ben said.

Janice found herself looking at the implements: spades, garden forks, rakes, buckets, brushes. Fine. But she found her eyes drawn to a group which Wesley had set to one side by the barn door. A pitch fork, various axes, a thing that looked like a cross between a machete and a sickle, and a selection of saws.

'Yes,' she said. 'Very tidy.'

Ben noticed where she was looking. Guessed what she might be thinking.

'Any reason you've put those things over there?'

'Yes, sir.' Very soft. Almost a whisper. 'They need fixing or sharpening. I can straighten the prongs on the pitch fork and put an edge on the axes and the brushing hook, but you need to send the saws to a hardware shop.'

'Right. Very helpful, Wesley. Thanks. By the way, Alan Walters told me the hens probably won't lay for a few days while they settle down. If they pop any eggs into an unsuspecting world while we're in London, you take them back for your supper. I'll leave a note, so Mr Newson won't think you're nicking them.'

When Wesley left, Janice suggested she and Ben go for a walk by the river.

'We haven't been to those old ruins yet. I'm dying to see what's inside.'

'More old ruins, plus impenetrable brambles and lethal stinging nettles.'

'Don't be a spoilsport.'

'Me, a spoilsport? Rubbish. I'm as interested in old ruins as the next man. Married you, didn't I?'

'Charming! Come on. What d'you say?'

'Okay. Let me get my boots. It looks pretty muddy over there.'

When they climbed the hillock ten minutes later, they saw that the ruins appeared to be a random jumble of stones rather than the remains of a building.

'Gracious,' Janice said. 'Our very own pagan circle. Look at that altar.'

'The farmers probably carted off the smaller stones over the years.'

'No, it's definitely a stone circle. Can't you feel the elemental forces?'

'All I can feel are the pangs of hunger.'

She stood close to him and slid her hands round his thighs.

'Where's your imagination? That rock is just asking to be christened.'

'Pagans didn't christen things.'

'Don't be so pragmatic. Come on, for God's sake.'

53

She started undoing his trousers, and her urgency became infectious. They almost fell onto the flat stone.

'Christ, where did that come from?' Ben gasped, several minutes later.

'Who cares?' Janice murmured.

They set off for London at dawn on Thursday and arrived as the morning rush hour traffic was subsiding. Andrew Connolly had booked them into the Langdon Hotel in Knightsbridge, hugely expensive but an ideal location for a lady with expensive shopping tastes and only a short time in which to indulge them. He explained that the client who couldn't make it to the Journalist of the Year awards ceremony was a Japanese publisher and his wife for whom only the best was good enough, so the Kirbys had 'got lucky'. Janice was delighted, and as soon as they had unpacked she phoned her sister Eileen and Andrew's wife Mary before disappearing towards Harrods and the expensive boutiques of Brompton Cross. Meanwhile, Ben met with Connolly to talk about his second book. Their conversation was restricted by the fact that he had no idea what it would be.

'Problem is, you've given yourself a hard act to follow with *The Façade*,' Connolly said. 'When you've pulled the plug on some of the biggest industrial corporations in Europe, where else do you go?'

'France? America? Korea? China . . . ?'

'Not where literally, for God's sake. Where in terms of hot subject matter?'

'You're my agent. So tell me what's hot . . . armaments, politics, sport, sub-sea exploration, information technology, drugs . . . ?'

'It's not *just* what's hot, it's what you are hot *about*. You know that.'

Here we go, Ben thought. The infernal cycle: we don't know what we want, only what we don't want. 'I'm hot about lots of things. I'll tell you what they are, you pick the most likely one, and I'll write the book.'

'Aren't you the most exasperating fellow?' Connolly sighed. 'Maybe something will spark off this evening when you see your newspaper and TV friends collecting their gongs.'

Andrew Connolly sent a chauffeured limousine to take the Kirbys from the hotel to the Savoy, where they were led by a hostess to the agent's table, at which his other guests were already sitting. To

54

Ben's surprise, Janice's elder sister Eileen was also there, talking animatedly to Mary Connolly. She held her cheeks to him and kissed air. Mwah, mwah.

'Lovely to see you, Ben. Wasn't it thoughtful of Janice to ask me along? She's been telling me all about Brianne Mill. Can't wait until it's ready for a visit.'

'Few things to get on with, yet,' he said.

When he had first met Eileen, he wondered why she irritated him so much. Eventually he realised that she was quietly monitoring his relationship with Janice, who began saying things like: 'Eileen thinks it would be better if . . .' and, 'Eileen suggested that we ought to . . .' What made matters worse was that Eileen was often right. Which made him dig his heels in. Which led to arguments. For months he wondered whether Eileen was interfering because she was protecting her sister or simply because she did not like him. In the end he decided her reasons didn't matter. It was a threat to their relationship and one of the reasons Ben had been willing to move away from London.

He said hello to a couple of fellow clients from Andrew's agency, plus the editorial director from his publishers, Jimmy Webb, and his wife. There were two other couples whose names he didn't catch in the flurry of greetings and handshakes. After they had settled down, Connolly slyly showed Ben the neck of a medicine bottle tucked into an inside pocket in his dinner jacket.

'How are you getting on with Old Poky?' he grinned.

'Don't ask. It's the nearest thing to lawful euthanasia we've come across, isn't it, Jan?'

'What's that, love?'

'Andrew's house-warming present. Bloody lethal, I was telling him.'

'God, yes. Couldn't get to sleep, and when we did get to sleep, couldn't wake up, and when we did wake up, couldn't function.'

As they were chatting, a tall, assertive man in his fifties came over and nodded to Ben. Norman Shelling had been a front line reporter in overseas conflicts before becoming a tough TV interrogator. Ben had worked with him from time to time.

'Liked the book. What's next on the list, or should I say "who"?'

'It's an exposé of investigative TV reporters, mate.'

And Jimmy Webb said, quick as a flash, 'Write that for me, and it'll be one of next year's lead titles.'

They all had a good laugh, and Janice knew how pleased Ben would be. Her husband was not immune to a little flattery from people he respected, and there were few enough of those.

At that point the master of ceremonies banged his gavel on the lectern, and the formalities began. The final award of UK Journalist of the Year went to someone whose work was a major contribution to national issues in any field of reporting. There were four contenders including Shelling, and everyone knew the judges would have a hard job making a decision.

'And this year the award goes to . . .' the compere said, opening an envelope with a flourish.

Janice squeezed Ben's hand. 'Be wonderful if Norman got it.'

He nodded.

' . . . Norman Shelling of Global TV for his outstanding work in covering the Hong Kong conflict.'

People rose to their feet, clapping and cheering, as images of Shelling's work appeared on the monitor screens around the room. He shook the hands, accepted the award, posed for the cameras and leaned down towards the microphone.

'I can't say anything clever except to point out that none of us in this room could do our jobs without each other and without the hundreds of people who back us up twenty-four hours a day, every day of the year – and who generally risk far more than we do. Thank you.'

As he started to leave the podium, the compere stopped him.

'One more thing, Norman. As you all know, ladies and gentlemen, the judges have the discretion to add a further award at this stage in the proceedings, to any journalist whose work has made an outstanding contribution to the profession. This year they have decided that one of your number merits that special award, and I'd like to ask Norman to open this envelope and present his – or her – award.'

Shelling looked at the piece of paper and turned towards Connolly's table.

'I'm delighted to tell you that the winner is Ben Kirby, for his book *The Façade*.'

The clapping and cheering started again, and Ben realised that everyone at his table was standing and beaming at him. He then understood how hard they'd worked to get him there without giving the game away. Janice was failing to wipe away tears, and Connolly was pushing him forward with a wide grin on his face. When he reached the podium, Shelling handed Ben a cheque, a carved wall plaque and a crystal brandy bowl. The compere motioned him towards the microphone.

'This is a great honour and a great surprise,' he said. 'But apparently I'm the only one who *is* surprised. Thank you, Janice and Mary and Andrew. I now know the meaning of the word conspiracy. And thank you all for this award.'

The biggest kick for Ben was to see the happiness and pride on Janice's face when he returned to his table, a moment that rewarded all the research work in libraries, the furtive meetings with company informers, the hours at his keyboard.

Only a slight shadow remained when Connolly brought up the subject of his next book again. He still had no ideas.

SPIDERLADY

No tears. Just a deadness and fear.
What will happen to me?
I have no anchors.
Everything is slipping about;
There are no absolutes: what am I?
I try to understand, but I can't.
I try to explain, but I can't.
I am a negative force –
An angel of death;
Yet conceived and nourished by love.

Love is dangerous,
So I am dangerous
To those I love.

TUTOR NOTES

This is astonishing. Primitive, yes, but what power, what pulsing energy! Not for me to comment, of course, on anything but the creative writing aspect, but 'Spiderlady' seems to be able to encapsulate her innermost thoughts in the medium of poetry.

4

When the Kirbys returned to the Mill late on Friday night, they found that Wesley had tidied the outbuildings and various heaps of rubbish that had accumulated in odd corners since their arrival. The hens seemed happy, clucking contentedly in their coop.

'He seems to have done a very good job,' Ben said.

'Maybe we should have left him a little present.'

'Like what? Newson said we shouldn't give him money.'

'I don't know. At least we can say how pleased we are.'

'Absolutely. I'll let Newson know first thing Monday.'

On Sunday they decided to have a lazy morning in bed. They were sipping tea and foraging through the newspapers when Janice put the magazine section down and said, 'I think Wesley is frightened of me.'

'You what?'

'Really! How else can you explain what happened the other day?'

'Rubbish. Why should he be frightened of an inoffensive lady like you?'

She hit him with a pillow. 'I'm serious. Quite apart from that breakdown of his, he hasn't looked me in the eye since he came to work here, and I can hardly get a word out of him.'

Ben remembered the odd way Wesley had glanced at Janice when they had arrived at Lindisholm Farm. Maybe she had a point. Maybe he was shy. Surely not frightened, not of Janice.

'Maybe he's from a broken home, suffering from some kind of anti-social phobia. Whatever it is, it can't be too serious, or he wouldn't be an Alpha patient. You're being oversensitive.'

The pillow hit him again. Hard.

'That's not very nice.' There was no banter in her voice, so he knew he'd upset her. 'You tell me one thing: if you'd known about that bloody hospital, would you still have wanted to move here?'

'Don't be bloody silly.'

'I'm not being bloody silly.'

Definitely upset. Very upset. Where had it come from?

'Don't say you're having second thoughts about being here!'

She gave him that small-girl-lost-in-the-big-world look, the one that brought out his protective instincts. He pushed the newspapers off the bed and took hold of her. 'Hey, come on! This isn't like you.'

'You're being horrid.'

'No, I'm not. But how do you think I feel, you banging on like this?'

'I'm sorry.'

A hug and a kiss did some good.

'Tell you what,' he said. 'We'll keep ourselves to ourselves for a bit and give this thing with Newson and Wesley the elbow. How about it?'

She snuggled into his shoulder and sniffed. 'Wesley likes it here, though, doesn't he? The hens follow him around as if they're dogs. They adore him. It's just . . . it's just that you can't tell me that he's really happy, not with me around.'

It was true, Ben had to admit. The boy was on edge near Janice. Come to think of it, he was like that when Newson was around as well. Not surprising, considering the situation.

The front doorbell rang – an appalling clanging, like a fire bell.

'Jesus!' He jumped out of bed and peered down through the window. 'It's a woman, and she's got a blue Volvo. Any ideas?'

'Haven't a clue. I do wish people would phone before they call round.'

The bell rang again, and he dragged a T-shirt over his head and staggered into his jeans.

'You don't have to answer the bloody thing,' Janice said. 'She's probably a Jehovah's Witness or a Women's Institute person.'

'I'll get rid of her.'

He opened the front door to a short, thin woman wearing a tight business-style suit and clutching a document case. She had cropped brown hair, pale bluish eyes and a slightly hooked nose covered in freckles. His first impression was that she was mousy, but the voice that crackled from thin lips gave immediate lie to that.

'I take it you're Mr Kirby.'

'And who do I take it you are?'

'Dr Nikki Congleton. I'm Wesley Freeman's counsellor from Lindisholm Hospital. May I come in?'

It was one of those moments that Ben hated. He wanted to say something like, 'No, you can't come in, partly because it's Sunday morning and partly because I've taken an instant dislike to you, so fuck off, or I'll set the hens on you.' But other issues were involved, like his incurable curiosity.

'Well . . .'

'I'd like to see Mrs Kirby, if that's all right.'

'As a matter of fact she's still in –'

'Who is it, Ben?' Janice had come downstairs in her dressing gown and was peering over his shoulder.

'It's Wesley's counsellor, from the hospital.'

'Nikki Congleton.' And then, as if she had remembered that the occasional nicety is called for at such times, 'Pleased to meet you.'

'You better come in,' Janice said. 'I was about to make some coffee.'

They moved into the kitchen, Ben performing an indecisive ritual of backing in front of her then getting behind her as they went through the connecting doors.

'Not for me, thank you. I've no wish to impose.'

That's rich! The thought hit them both at the same time, and they shared a slight grimace.

'You don't mind if we do,' Ben said. 'Only we need a good stiff coffee when we wake up, don't we darling?'

'Absolutely.'

Dr Congleton glanced at her watch. It was eleven thirty. 'I hope I'm not intruding.'

Ben's curiosity almost suffered a terminal beating, but a concern for Wesley took its place. The woman was highly irritating, but maybe her visit would throw some light on the boy. Maybe it would help them to help him. So he kept his mouth shut and let Janice field that one.

'Not at all,' she said brightly, piling ground coffee into the percolator. 'I was only just saying to Ben, wouldn't it be nice if someone came along so we had a really good reason to get out of bed, wasn't I darling?'

'That's right, darling, so you were.'

Irony and sarcasm did not seem to be on Dr Congleton's list of understandable words and phrases. She opened her document case and took out a file with a large Greek alpha printed on it in green.

'I need to run through a few questions about your perceptions of Wesley, Mrs Kirby.'

'You don't want my perceptions, then?' Ben asked.

'No thank you, Mr Kirby.'

'Actually, Ben spends more time with Wesley than I do.'

The pale eyes flicked up briefly; the thin lips pursed. 'It's not so much a matter of who spends time with a patient. In Wesley's case we need to know how specific intra-relationship fusions relate to his clinical needs. If we can understand that, we might see a way forward.'

'Does that mean see a way forward with Freud, Jung, Adler, Eysenck or Watson?' Ben asked. 'I mean, exactly what brand of specific intra-relationship fusions are you into?'

The humourless face turned towards him. 'I'm into anything that can further our understanding of the criminally sick mind, Mr Kirby.'

'So Wesley has a criminally sick mind, then?'

'We want to help if we can, Dr Congleton,' Janice said quickly. 'Don't we, Ben?'

'Why don't I leave you girls to it?' Ben said, not bothering to hide his irritation.

When he was out of the kitchen, Congleton poised her pen over a clipboard.

'It's *Mrs* Janice Kirby?' She made the Mrs sound like an insult.

'That's right.'

'And how old are you, Mrs Kirby?'

'Thirty-five.'

'Any children?'

'No, and I'm afraid – '

'We need some details about you so we can put your observations in context.'

'Right. No children.'

'Any qualifications?'

'MA in Fine Arts from Reading. Teaching certificate.'

'Were you a teacher before you married?'

'Yes. I gave classes at a number of colleges until we moved here.'

The ballpoint waggled over the paper furiously. 'Why did you move here?'

That did it! Janice wanted to help Wesley, but all this questioning had as much relevance to that as a pig laying an egg.

'Dr Congleton, I better make it clear that giving personal information to you is not how I think I can help. Perhaps you'd be kind enough to ask questions that are relevant to Wesley.'

Congleton began to say something but stopped, nodding stiffly. 'Very well. My main concern is to ask how you would describe Wesley's behaviour towards you. How do you feel about that?'

'His behaviour towards me? He acts like a gentleman. He is very polite, and he always does what he says he's going to do. He's done a lot of good work around this place, but that's something you'll have to ask my husband about.'

Janice got the impression that Congleton was disappointed to hear this. Maybe it was a subtle change in her body language, a tightening of the already tight lips, a setting of the stiff shoulders that gave Wesley's counsellor away.

'You never feel . . . threatened?'

'Good God no! If anything, it's the other way round.'

The ballpoint paused, hovered over the notepad. 'Wesley feels threatened by you?'

'I don't know how he feels. You'll have to ask him.'

'I'm sure you realise that's exactly the kind of question that I can't ask him, Mrs Kirby.'

'Fair enough. I don't think I make him feel threatened, exactly. But I feel he's upset about something, and he's pretty withdrawn as far as I'm concerned.'

'Upset?'

'Yes, well, no, not upset, exactly. More frightened.'

The ballpoint deluged the paper. 'Frightened. And has he ever done or said anything that you felt was rather . . . personal?'

'Absolutely not. Like I said, he's extremely polite.'

'And how do you feel about Wesley? Are you attracted to him?'

Janice decided this exercise had gone far enough. She stood up and opened the kitchen door, waited while Dr Congleton stared at her and then slowly gathered her items together.

'I'm sorry if I have upset you, Mrs Kirby, but we seldom get a

63

chance to conduct this kind of interview. It's all for the patient's good.'

'If I ever figure out how that can be, I'll invite you back. Meanwhile, we have a lot to be getting on with.'

'She said *what*?' Ben was absolutely scandalised. 'I've a good mind to write to the boss of that bloody place. In fact, that's exactly what I'm going to do. Of all the bloody nerve!'

'Oh, come on. She's just another weird shrink. You know what they're like.'

'Dysfunctional, you mean? Lacking in social graces? Unaware or unaffected by social conventions? I'd say we were describing a pretty advanced case of personality disorder of some kind, wouldn't you?'

Janice laughed. 'Absolutely. Why else would she be working up at the hospital?'

'The mind boggles. Mind you, she's given us a clue about young Wesley, hasn't she?'

'She has?'

'Think about it. She didn't give a damn about my opinions or anything about his capability to work. Only your impressions. Like, did you feel threatened by him? Were you attracted by him? I bet he's in there for some sexual offence.'

'Wesley? You have to be joking.'

'Okay. You come up with something.'

Ben had a point. Congleton was certainly directing her interrogation down those lines, but it didn't gel with what they knew about Wesley.

'I keep thinking we're getting out of our depth,' she said.

And that's exactly how Ben felt, which did two things. It surprised him, because he found it hard to believe that two reasonably smart people could end up feeling out of their depth over a relatively trivial matter, like an uptight shrink descending on them to ask questions about a poor little sod who seemed, on the face of it, more sane than the shrink. And it was making him curious, because he was facing a situation that was throwing more questions at him than he had answers for.

'I wonder if Wesley knows she called round,' he mused.

* * *

Dr Nikki Congleton viewed her appointment to Lindisholm as merely another step up the professional ladder, and she placed little faith in this kind of procedure. As far as she was concerned, face-to-face treatment and detailed descriptions of meetings and other patient matters were far more effective. But effective was not the same as efficient, and the Holy Grail of Lindisholm was efficiency. So Congleton played the efficiency game as hard as she could, but looked for ways – or at least one way – to pursue her own researches. These were directed to prove her unshakeable belief that even the most mentally ill patients and criminals – especially criminals – were always capable of distinguishing right from wrong. If a psychotic rapist truly did not know this difference, why did he lurk behind bushes in the dark to attack a solitary woman? Why not wander through a well-lit shopping mall and have a go, with hundreds of people around? Same with murder. But no. Your average homicidal schizophrenic does his deed and rushes off to hide. And to cater for the few people who did commit such crimes out in the open, Congleton had her theory for that, too: they were control freaks who did not give a shit who saw them do what.

In Congleton's book, a control freak was not mad, merely an exaggerated example of men in general. Women did not do this kind of thing. It was a Man problem. It was not a mental illness.

Congleton used this line of reasoning with young Wesley Freeman. Here was a cunning young brute who had viciously attacked a teacher. The prosecution evidence included her clothing: bra torn right away and skirt ripped into shreds. His running shorts were halfway down his legs when the groundsman foiled his attempts. Congleton thought of the London expression, 'Caught bang to rights'. Well, Freeman had been caught bang to rights, and the cunning little shit had decided he could avoid punishment by keeping his mouth firmly shut. So firmly shut that the social workers and the local psychiatric board agreed he was suffering from a depressive illness that warranted Sectioning under the terms of the Mental Health Act.

So here was young Freeman, enjoying the best that the mental health service had to offer instead of spending his time in a penal institution. Outrageous.

As far as Congleton was concerned, Freeman's presence at Lindisholm, along with many others, was based on the so-called experts' agreement that he was ill and could be treated and perhaps cured. Their approach to all their patients was founded on this assumption, and Congleton intended to prove them wrong. All she had to do was wait for young Freeman to make a move on Mrs Janice Kirby so Professor Jonser would sanction his transfer to the more rigorous confines of Beta Cloister, then she'd see how curable or incurable he was.

JACKAL ONE

It is a pity about Antelope. Antelope looks all set to drop us in the brown stuff. Despite all the oaths about keeping the secret of Omega Cloister and White Eagle and all that, her pathetic relationship with her counsellor is tempting her to reveal secrets about secrets, and harm will duly follow. Now let me see . . . a short story about Antelope and myself entitled Rosehip and the cartons.

'*Rosehip was assembling cardboard cartons when Jackal One went into the assembly room to do his shift. He picked up an empty carton, and she slid her plasma bag into it. One more step on its way to Antelope in Beta Cloister. Antelope had taken the name of White Eagle in vain. She had even mentioned the things we did in Omega Cloister to her counsellor, and the counsellor had asked others about it. That's how the People had found out. Pretty little Antelope has to be taught a lesson that none of the others will ever forget.*'

TUTOR NOTES

There is clearly a collaboration among the students. Perhaps this is not a bad thing, although I was keen to have each one work independently. Maybe for our next exercise we can undertake a chain-paragraph creation so they can collaborate within a structured framework.

5

Hay-making. The time when farmers get the weather forecast and decide whether or not to cut the hay and, having cut it, whether or not to turn it so it can get good and dry and, having turned it a few times, whether or not to bale it and, having baled it, whether or not to leave it in the fields or store it in the barns. Get it right, and they can make hundreds of pounds profit per field. Get it wrong, and it's another visit to the bank manager.

The worst aspect of all this is that the machinery they use to do all the work is in short supply – and expensive to hire. So everything might be ready for the next step, but the baler is across the valley at another farm, and by the time it's available it's pissing down again, ruining the hay.

Which is where the landlords of Fred Newson scored, because they were not dependent on the availability of machines. They had teams of young farm labourers to do the work. The profit they made on this activity plus the high rentals Newson paid for using part of their land kept them very happy indeed, and none of them bothered to question the arrangement or work out what was in it for Newson.

What none of them knew was that Newson owned the agricultural employment agency that supplied labourers to work on Lindisholm Farm to augment the work put in by low-risk patients. He received the equivalent of one day's pay for each month or part-month they worked, and if quite a high proportion of them went on their way before a month was complete, well, that was all right by Fred Newson. He received his agency commission anyway. The hospital's finance department was happy too, because Alex Searle, the hospital's general manager, was Newson's fellow shareholder in another enterprise. Between them they submitted enough statistics to convince the money men that this direct labour system was not only viable but desirable – and enough to convince Janice Kirby that signing Newson's tenancy agreement was a smart thing to do, because after all the hay had been cut, dried and baled, Newson stored it on his farm, sold it to other farmers and local horse owners, and promptly gave half the money he received back to the Kirbys in cash.

Ben Kirby was not so sure about all this, and that made him irritated.

'There has to be a snag. Someone, somewhere, is on the fiddle.'

'He explained all that,' Janice reminded him. 'Because the patients provide free labour and because his farm is so productive, his profit margins are very high. By using the profits to subsidise work for his landlords, he is simply securing his lines of supply. He says that's good business, and I agree with him.'

'What would you know about good business?'

'Thank you very much.'

'That's all right. I mean, you swallow all this shit, knowing full well that every other farmer in the country is clinging desperately to every subsidy he can get, while smiling Fred Newson had found a way to beat the system. It does not make sense.'

'What would you know about sense,' she threw back at him.

'Ha-bloody-ha!'

'Laugh all you want, matey. Then ask yourself how your new book is getting along.'

'What new book?'

'Precisely. I can understand why you wrote *The Façade*. You were having a go at the creeps, but now all you do is sit here criticising someone for doing well. Write a book about that, why don't you?'

They broke a long-standing agreement by going to bed without a goodnight kiss, but in the morning Ben woke Janice with a breakfast tray decorated with giant daisies from the garden.

'You were absolutely right,' he said. 'I'm going to start work on it today.'

'Start work on what?' She was very sleepy.

'On Lindisholm. Not just the farm, the whole shebang.'

'You're joking.'

'I am not joking. I should have seen it weeks ago. It's the ideal subject.'

An earwig dropped out of the daisies and fell into her bowl of cornflakes. He fished it out and threw it through the window.

'I can't eat that now.'

'It's only an earwig from the garden. They're pretty clean, as far as pests go.'

'How can you possibly write a book about that horrible place?'

'Precisely because it is a horrible place. A successful horrible place, unlike its horrible counterparts.' He began striding around the bedroom, waving his arms, warming to the theme. 'It won't be just about Lindisholm. That's the whole point. It'll be about the other secure hospitals as well. There's a lot of question marks hanging over them at the moment. People are worried about safety and patients returning to society too soon. Traditional secure hospitals like Broadmoor are horrendous and expensive. Lindisholm is horrendous and cheap. And according to your friend Newson it's also highly effective. It's high tech. It's modern, and my bet is that it'll frighten the shit out of people. Why do you think they keep such a low profile, stuck away in the middle of the mountains? It's not human. It's space age technology taken to the extreme. It's Soylent bloody Green. Hell on earth.'

Janice was silent for a while. 'I don't think Andrew will go for it.'

'Yes, he will. Everyone is scared witless at the prospect of mental debilitation, so it's always shoved under the mat. I'm going to pull the mat from under their feet and shake the dust in their faces until they can't think for sneezing. Fucking Ping Poles! Did anyone check that out with the European Court of Human Rights?'

'It's boring. No one will publish it.'

'Boring? You have got to be joking. We're talking about some of the most depraved people in the world, stuck in that bloody place. Killers, torturers, rapists, arsonists, klepto-fucking-maniacs, plus the whole paraphernalia of modern medical science and appalling people like that awful Dr Congleton. Plus electroconvulsive therapy. Drugs that put your mind in reverse. Electronic tagging. Shit, it's a gothic horror story. Don't you tell me it's boring.'

'You really think you can do it?'

'Just watch me.'

'God, I love it when you get all fired up! Where are you going to start?'

'No idea. Some background research, probably. You know. Companies House. Newspaper archives. That sort of thing. Then again, I've got the ideal opportunity right here at the Mill, haven't I?'

'You have?'

'Certainly. I've got a living, breathing, fully functioning patient from the bloody place cleaning out our henhouse twice a week. I can suck all kinds of things out of young Wesley. What more could a man ask?'

As the Kirbys suspected but did not understand, Wesley Freeman was frightened, and the fear grew daily. His fear had taken seed when Miss Squires touched his face. It wriggled tap roots into his mind when she kissed him. It blossomed when she held his penis. Fear of disgracing his family. Fear of discovery. The moment he saw Mr Carver the groundsman his fear took a quantum leap, and instinct took over. Say nothing. Take the consequences, no matter what. Nothing he could say would make any difference. No one ever took any notice. Silence was the only way out. So he remained silent and failed to understand what was happening to him. None of his family or his friends came to see him while he was on remand; only a social worker and doctors and Mr Franklin, the pale-faced solicitor, who spent hours trying to get a word out of his client about the assault on Miss Squires. But Wesley kept his mouth clamped. He knew they'd twist anything he said to make matters even worse. So the social worker sat patiently in front of him despite the silence and explained that the judge would probably send him to a secure hospital where they would help to make him better. That didn't sound too bad, but what did he know about places like Lindisholm? He knew shit about them. If he'd known then what he knew now he might have tried to explain what happened with Miss Squires in the changing rooms, even if it meant telling lies and going to prison for years and years. But he hadn't known.

He also didn't know about the shit the doctors would pump into him that made the world hazy and hateful. He didn't know about the consultations with therapists and counsellors, or how they could poke into his brain. He didn't know about the cloisters or the patients milling about in their coloured uniforms with their blank faces and their secrets. He didn't know how they could suck you into their own madness, until you thought it was them that were sane and everyone else was off their trolley. And he certainly didn't know that they would start sharing their secrets with him, making him one of them. The only peace he got was working at Brianne Mill for the Kirbys, and even that peace was threatened. Everything was okay, as long as he was dealing with Mr Kirby. It was Mrs Kirby that was Wesley's problem.

*   *   *

71

When Ben phoned Andrew Connolly, his agent was even more dismissive of his idea for a book about Lindisholm than Janice had been.

'I understand all this stuff about antiseptic horror and human rights, but where's your peg?'

'I don't have a peg,' Ben admitted. 'I just have this feeling that everything is too squeaky clean to be true.'

'Jimmy Webb won't go for that.'

'So find another publisher.'

'Christ, you writers are arrogant. Have you any idea how hard it was to get Webb to give you a contract for *The Façade*?'

'You told me. Many, many times. You also told me I didn't have a peg for a book about corporate corruption, and I told you that the entire business world was involved, so the entire business world would buy the book. I was right.'

'This is different. You're telling me you want to write a book about a new-fangled secure mental hospital that on the face of it seems to be a screaming bloody success and that people will want to read about it. You're nuts, my boy. It would bore everyone to death.'

'That's what Janice said.'

'She was right.'

'She was wrong, and I'll bloody well prove it.'

'Ben, Ben, how can you expect me to handle something I don't believe in?'

'You don't have to. I'll get another agent.'

A long silence.

'You mean that?'

'Yes.'

It happened to all his writers, at some time or another. The crisis point. A clash of creative will against commercial common sense. Connolly sighed.

'Right, you've convinced me about your commitment. How do you intend to convince me about the book?'

'I'm going to write it.'

'I'd like a synopsis and a few sample chapters.'

'You haven't been listening, Andrew. How can I write a synopsis when I don't know what the fuck this hospital is all about?'

'It might be all about being what its publicity says it's all about.'

'Then again, it might not.'

'And you're willing to take that chance, are you?'

'Unless you can come up with a better idea.'

Another deep, long-suffering sigh. 'Jimmy wants to know what you're working on. What do I tell him?'

'Anything you like. Tell him it's a secret.'

'What does Andrew think?' Janice called after Ben had slammed the phone down.

'He thinks it's a wonderful idea.'

She came into his study. 'In that case, why are you sitting there looking so dejected?'

'Me, dejected? Whatever gave you that impression? I'm about to start work on the definitive critique of the country's high-security hospitals for the criminally insane. It'll make *The Façade* look like a corporate cover-up.'

'You hope. What if the hospital is the way Fred Newson says it is – you won't have a book, will you?'

'If the hospital is the way he says it is, they've discovered a whole new law of economics. Anyway, the man is simply the farm manager. What does he know?'

'He knows what he's talking about.'

'Oho! What do we have here – founder of the Fred Newson fan club?'

'Don't be ridiculous.'

'Ridiculous in the sense that my wife fancies him, or in the sense that he is the world's first perfect individual?'

'You're bloody impossible!'

'That's what Andrew thinks. I must be doing something right.'

Ben was always like this when he started work on a new project. Excitable, irascible, irritable, argumentative. Wandering around as if Janet didn't exist. Pounding his keyboard late into the night. When she first met him, it was exciting, stimulating. Now, the excitement had palled into habit. She wondered how she put up with it.

Over the next few days Ben hit the phone to press officers from a variety of organisations connected with the mental health service, and large brown envelopes containing information began arriving. The Mental Health Review Tribunal, Carstairs State Hospital in

Scotland, Ashworth, Broadmoor, Rampton ... but nothing from CareCorp about Lindisholm. So he phoned Fred Newson.

'I'm trying to remember the name of the PR director at CareCorp who you told me about,' he said.

'You mean Roy Ormley?'

'That's him. Do you have his number?'

'Only the general switchboard number and his e-mail address, but that's on LISA, the company intranet. Can I help?'

No you bloody well can't. The less you know about my new book the better.

'Not unless you have a list of CareCorp subsidiaries or an annual report. I'm thinking of offering my writing services to the group. Ormley would be a good starting point.'

'He does all that kind of thing through PR agencies, but it might be worth a try. You never know.'

'You're probably right. I'll give him a call. Thanks for the help.'

Ben rang off. Company intranet? Maybe he could hack into it. There was usually a way.

Ben's call gave Newson something to think about. The last thing a company like CareCorp wanted was to have someone like Kirby sticking his nose around the place. Newson had read *The Façade*, and the guy was poison. All this crap about writing services! Kirby was up to something. Newson's problem was, should he let Ormley find out for himself or should he warn the bumptious, over-sexed shit that Kirby might contact him? He decided that he could score an easy Brownie point without any downside risk by e-mailing Ormley about the phone call. He got an immediate reply: 'Thanks for your note about Ben Kirby. In fact he's already left a message with the press office that he would like some information. I'll check to see if they've sent it yet and take appropriate action.'

Ormley discovered several corporate information packs in the press office out-tray. The one addressed to Kirby had been there for four days because the press manager was on vacation and his assistant was off sick. A graphic example of Lord Balacombe's Dictum Number 84: 'If an army marches on its stomach, business management survives by backup'. This was lousy backup! Ormley got the Kirbys' ex-directory telephone number from an Internet site. Whatever else, an apology was in order. He presumed that the woman who answered was the sexy wife that Newson had mentioned.

'Penford 719.'

'Am I speaking to Mrs Kirby?'

'Yes. Who am *I* speaking to?'

'My name is Roy Ormley, Mrs Kirby. I work for CareCorp plc. I'm phoning to apologise to Mr Kirby.'

'That makes a change.'

'I beg your pardon?'

'It's usually the other way round. I mean, it's usually Ben who has to phone and apologise, or rather it's me doing it on Ben's behalf.'

Ormley was intrigued at all this. Mrs Kirby's voice sounded nice, but was she drunk?

'The thing is,' he explained, 'your husband recently phoned our press office and asked for some information. I've just discovered it's been lying in the out-tray for a few days. Very inefficient. Is your husband available?'

'I'm afraid not, Mr Ormley. Shall I ask him to call you when he's finished cleaning out the pigsty?'

'You have a pigsty?' She wasn't drunk. She was jousting; playing games with an unknown caller. Ormley liked that. It showed spirit.

'It might be stables. We won't be sure until Ben's scraped all this damp brown stuff off the cobble stones. He tried to get the boy who helps us to do it, but I put my foot down. The poor lad's got enough problems without leaving here covered in unspecified animal shit. What did you say your name was? I've just found a pencil.'

'Roy Ormley.'

'And what's your telephone number?'

He gave her his direct line. ' . . . but there's no need for him to call me. Just say that the material is in the post, with my profound apologies.'

'What exactly do you do in CareCorp, Roy Ormley, apart from apologising for mistakes that someone else has made?'

'I'm Director of Government and Public Affairs.'

'Does that mean you're in charge of parliamentary infidelities?'

He laughed. 'You could put it that way.'

'You have a lovely laugh, Mr Ormley.'

He has worked on his laugh for years, until it came out as a deep chuckle that warmed everyone within earshot. All his many women

75

had appreciated the Ormley laugh, but this was the first time he had felt really, truly complimented. By a person he had never seen, on the telephone. He found himself responding, with absolute sincerity: 'And you have a lovely voice, Mrs Kirby.'

There was a pause, and then Janice said, 'How very gallant you are,' before replacing the phone.

The *UK Press Gazette* had published a photograph of Ben Kirby at the Journalist of the Year awards, sitting at a table, smiling at the lens. On impulse Ormley called the company librarian and asked if she still had the issue on file. It arrived in the internal post that afternoon. The woman next to Kirby was also smiling into the lens. Although she was seated, he got the impression that she was quite tall and slender. Her blonde hair was cropped short in the way that only very beautiful woman can get away with. Janice Kirby was very beautiful indeed. And if he was any judge, if their phone conversation was any guide, she was also very bored. Or maybe she was lonely. Ormley had enjoyed many beautiful, lonely wives.

'Who was that?' Ben called from the upstairs landing. Naked from the bath. Washing off the pig shit.

'You're dripping all over my nice new rug.'

'Sorry.'

'Bloke called Roy Ormley. He's a bigwig who wants to apologise to you. Says the pack's in the post. Some idiot forgot to post it.'

'Bigwig, my arse! He's the director of PR for the company that runs the hospital.'

'That's not a bigwig?'

'Not in my book.'

'Which book – the one you've just written, or the one you're just about to write?'

'Ha ha. Where's my towel?'

'The one your freshly scratched mosquito bite bled into is in the wash. You will find a clean one in the place where we keep clean ones.'

HEN

Hens work hard and so do I, so I am Hen. Here is the carton of bright yellow scouring pads what Rosehip and me have been packing all morning. Rosehip would go on packing the damn things for ever, if the Bastards didn't come along and tell her to stop and go for lunch. Rosehip is great. Wind her up and let her go. You tell her to jump out of a window, and off she'd go. Actually there ain't no windows, as such, in the Place. Certainly there ain't in Delta Cloister. Just padded walls all round and them lights glaring at you all day. Even a fly couldn't get out of Delta Cloister, not without a ping tag it couldn't. What you get in Gamma Cloister is portholes with armoured glass, and even if some clever sod managed to figure a way to blow the armoured glass the portholes are too small to climb through. No point any way. You'd only end up in the gardens and they don't lead nowhere. Beta Cloister ain't much better but Alpha Cloister has windows what are more like windows. They are square anyway and they don't open but you can't have everything. At least the patients in Alpha Cloister can stand and look out of the bloody things and see the trees and the hills and that and the market gardens. Anyway, these scouring pads are due for delivery to the store room where all the tools and other things for looking after the vegetables are. I like the store room. Everything has to be spick and span or the Bastards get all uptight, don't they? The word is that the pads absolutely have to get to the store today or else. I dunno or else what. Just or else. Something to do with Antelope.

TUTOR NOTES
I think the students are ahead of me on the method of writing. They seem to have developed a chain-writing technique. Not surprisingly this student's work is disjointed, but interesting nevertheless. I am beginning to wonder what they have 'in store for Antelope'.

6

Toby Jennings was small, neat, well groomed and very laid back, with a smiling mouth full of uneven teeth through which emerged a well-modulated voice that reeked of irrefutable authority. He maintained a small and cluttered office just off London's Strand, close to the High Courts of Justice. His clients came mainly from the world of publishing and entertainment, and his specialities included contract law and libel. Ben Kirby had known him professionally and as a personal friend since Ben's early days as an investigative reporter on television and radio. Their friendship began the day a new producer for the TV programme sat halfway through the studio screening of an item about a City financier who had been fleecing thousands of small investors with the protection of the whole City establishment. No crime, therefore no investigation by the regulatory authorities, and certainly no police involvement.

'We can't broadcast this, for Christ's sake,' the producer had spluttered.

'Why not?' Ben asked him.

'It's . . . libellous.' He spat out the word as if someone had smeared his lips with vinegar.

Toby Jennings sorted it before anyone else could open their mouths. 'Of course it's libellous, Julian. Everything we do is libellous. Why would Ben have done the piece in the first place?'

The new producer rushed off to vent his panic to the head of current affairs programmes and was told to let the professionals do what they were paid to do or to piss off.

Ben was very impressed with Toby's understanding of the publishing process and had remained so throughout the years. The day he finished writing *The Façade*, he e-mailed the book to Toby. Two days later he received Toby's annotations, showing which passages would agitate the publisher's legal advisers and how to counter their arguments for amending or removing a word, phrase or section. Jimmy Webb had been duly impressed with Ben's work, and he accepted the book without any changes. Ben sent Toby a case of champagne, which he insisted on sharing with Ben and Janice in his converted warehouse apartment in London's Docklands. That's how it was. Toby did favours for Ben, and Ben bought the champagne, an amiable quid pro quo.

When Ben decided to write his critique of high-security mental hospitals in general, and of Lindisholm in particular, he arranged a meeting in London with Toby to check out his initial thinking.

'Let me understand you,' the solicitor said after flipping though Ben's notes. 'You need something to follow your first act, and this is it?'

'Don't you start. I've already had Janice and Andrew stamping on the idea.'

'You can hardly blame them. Everything here is surmise. When you started *The Façade*, you'd already spent years dealing with the bad guys and collecting evidence. The only reason they didn't screw you all the way to the libel courts was that it was true and you could prove it was true and they knew you could prove it. It was also in the public interest. This is completely different. You're starting from scratch, and even if you think someone in Lindisholm is elbow deep in a monumental fiddle, how the hell are you going to prove it?'

'If it's true, I'll prove it.'

'And if it's not true?'

'Then I've wasted a few months. So what!'

'You asked me, and I told you. Think of something else.'

'You think of something else. You all know what the fuck I shouldn't do, but not one of you can come up with what I should do. Everyone's full of shit.'

Toby sighed. 'Can I take a copy?'

'Be my guest. In fact, take the original and stuff it down your crapper.'

'That's another reason I like you, Ben. You have such a wonderful control of your emotions.'

Later that night, Ben called Janice from his hotel room to tell her about his meeting, but the phone kept ringing and the answering machine didn't kick in. He called a few old chums, crawled round a few jazz pubs, and got completely drunk.

Janice picked him up at Carmarthen station the following afternoon. He had a headache, and she was being quiet about something.

They were halfway back to Penford before he found out what it was.

'Why didn't you call?'

'I did. Last night. You didn't answer.'

'I don't mean last night. I mean this morning. You didn't call this morning.'

'Never mind this morning. What about last night?'

'I was in the bath.'

'And of course you forgot to put the answering machine on.'

'I hate that bloody thing.'

The next silence took them almost all the way home.

'The reason I didn't call this morning is, a, because you didn't pick up the bloody phone last night, b, because I was still pissed out of my mind and, c, because there wasn't much point, seeing as how you were collecting me from the station.'

'That's pathetic.'

At the mountain road that led to Brianne Mill they came across a group of men unloading shotguns and rifles from their cars and vans. Alan Walters was among them, and he gave them a wave. Janice slowed down.

'Afternoon,' Walters said. 'How are the hens?'

'Fine, thanks,' she said. 'Averaging two eggs a day.'

'Jolly good.' Walters ducked his head so he could look into the car. 'Not seen you for a while, Ben.'

'Been away for a couple of days. What are you chaps up to?'

'I forgot to tell you,' Janice told him. 'One of the farmers lost a sheep yesterday.'

'There's another sheep been reported dead up in the hills this morning, towards Fred Newson's place,' Walters said. 'Doesn't usually happen this far south, so we thought we'd get onto it right away. Come along, if you like.'

'Your mythical Beast of Bont, maybe?' Ben asked.

'More likely a pet leopard that someone let loose when it grew too big,' their neighbouring farmer Gwyn Evans said. 'Bloody idiots. Could be a couple of them, lurking in the forest.'

'You mean, like alligators in New York?' Ben asked. He received half a dozen blank looks. 'I thought everyone knew about that. These idiots bought all these exotic pets, and when they got too big they flushed them down the loo. Alligators, snakes, piranhas.

They're down in the sewers, breeding away and living off . . .'

'For Christ's sake, Ben,' Janice said. 'All Alan wants to know is if you want to go along.'

'No gun.'

'That's all right,' Evans, said. 'Borrow one of mine.'

'Shit,' Ben whispered. 'I've still got this fucking headache.'

'He'd love to go,' Janice told them. 'It's okay, darling. Your boots and Barbour are in the trunk. I'll go home and get dinner ready, like a good wife.'

They followed the track into the mountains for about a mile and turned north along an old drovers' trail towards the pass that led to Lindisholm Farm. At this point the group fanned out and headed over grassland where dozens of sheep were grazing, towards a pine forest above a granite escarpment. Gwyn Evans teamed up with Ben.

'Better keep a friendly eye on you,' he grinned, motioning at the shotgun. 'Used one before, have you?'

'Couple of times, at a clay shoot. Didn't manage to hit anything, though.'

'Let's have a look.' He took Ben's gun and removed the cartridges. 'Show me how you set her up.'

Ben swung the gun into the air and aimed at a couple of crows that were winging their way towards the cliffs.

'Ah! You're well behind. It may help if you line your forefinger along the stock and point at your target . . . Yes, that looks better already.'

'Makes that much difference, does it?'

'Not for everyone, but mankind has been pointing at targets for thousands of years. It's an instinct we've got. Have a go at those crows. There's plenty about, and Fred Newson will stand you a pint for every one you shoot on his land. Leave the buzzards and the red kites alone, though, or you'll end up looking the wrong way at a magistrate.'

'Don't forget I've spent a lifetime in the city,' Ben said. 'The nearest I ever got to killing birds is running over pigeons.'

'Fair enough,' Evans said amiably. 'The buggers are always going for the young lambs, though. As far as we're concerned, they're costly vermin.'

He brought his own gun effortlessly to his shoulder, and two large bangs downed two crows out of another flock. They carried on walking up the steep hillside, towards the granite cliffs, and then Evans's sheepdog, which had been dutifully keeping a few paces behind them, began whining and darting from side to side.

'She doesn't like bangs,' he laughed. 'Quiet, Jess!'

The dog stood still and then hunkered down, quivering, wagging its tail, eyes fixed on its master.

Ben walked a few paces forward, up an outcrop of rock. 'Jesus Christ!' he said. Then he retched, as a crowd of birds rocketed into the air with raucous protests.

Up to that point he had given little thought as to how he might react if he were to clap eyes on a sheep that had been killed by a predator. The animal was lying a few feet from his face, and it had not merely been killed; it had been ripped apart with great violence and left lying on its back with its legs spread-eagled, eviscerated, its intestines bundled between its hindquarters. In a corner of his mind he expected Evans to be amused at his display of weakness, but a firm hand took hold of his shoulder and another shoved a brandy flask at him.

'Never a pretty sight. Get some of this down you.'

'Sorry,' he gasped. 'I must have sounded utterly stupid. All that rubbish about alligators in New York sewers.'

'Don't you worry about that.' Evans gave a loud shout and waved his arms to the farmers on each side. The birds, still shrieking, flew above their heads and made tentative efforts to get back to the sheep. One or two landed on the far side and hopped this way and that in a state of agitation, darting towards the carcass, then leaping away. 'That's a damn funny thing. Still got its eyes.'

Gasping for breath, Ben forced himself to take a closer look.

'Been here at least overnight, but those birds don't seem to have touched it,' the farmer muttered.

Their nearest neighbour arrived and stared at the carcass.

'I'll be damned. We got any gypos in the area, Gwyn?'

'Not as far as I know.'

The newcomer went up close. 'Ribs are all busted and its heart's missing.'

As the other farmers arrived, they heard a high-revving engine, and Fred Newson on a quadricycle and trailer erupted out of the fir forest at the edge of the cliffs, heading straight towards them, bouncing over the rocks.

'Thanks for turning out, gentlemen.' He looked at the carcass. 'Messy business.'

'We've got to nail this bugger before he does any more damage, Fred,' one of the farmers said. 'He took one of mine, night before last. Clawed to bloody shreds, it was. Mind you, this one of yours seems more like it was torn apart by a bloody tractor. Look at those ribs.'

'If you'll give me a hand dumping it in the trailer, I'll check it out,' Newson said. 'We've got people in the hospital labs who should be able to pinpoint what did this.'

Ben listened as the farmers discussed their next move. Most of them wanted to spend a couple of hours checking the fields to see if they could discover tracks. No one had any illusions that they would actually find anything specific; it was more a case of adding to the collection of evidence as to what was killing the sheep and where the killer might be. None of them gave any credibility to the idea of a panther or a puma. More likely a family of wildcats.

'Why not dogs?' Ben wanted to know.

'It's the way they're disembowelled,' Alan Walters explained. 'A dog might break an animal's neck or back and savage its throat, but a wildcat claws at the stomach and takes its first meal from the intestines. Then the birds take over and make a messy job even more messy. Like this one. Only the birds have left it alone, for some reason. That's why we think whatever is doing this may still be hanging around.'

The Mill was in darkness by the time Walters dropped Ben at the entrance to the drive.

'You never have to apologise for being a beginner round here, Ben,' Walters said. 'The lads appreciated you coming along, and so do I. This Beast of Bont stuff might be a load of crap, but something's out there costing us hundreds of pounds a year, and we've all got a stake in sorting it out.' He handed Ben his jacket. 'Many thanks for joining us, and give the lovely Janice my regards.'

The lovely Janice was wide awake in bedroom darkness when Ben pushed the door open, white sheets pushed to the foot of the bed in the heat, brown body covered in a silk nightdress. He walked to her

83

side and carefully placed the mug of peppermint tea on the bedside table. A hand reached up and turned on the side-light.

'Mm, that smells nice.' She eased herself to a sitting position and sipped the tea.

'Sorry I'm so late.'

'That's all right. Did you find the Beast?'

'Only the remains of its supper.'

'Was it beastly?'

'About as beastly as a beast can get.'

'Did you throw up?'

He laughed. 'I think that's why I love you so much. You have no idea of subtle.'

She put the cup down and held him very hard. 'Do you love me?'

How many times had he told her? How many times did she need to be told?

'Of course I do, for Christ's sake. What's wrong?'

She was crying now, softly at first, but then in shudders. Her words came out staggered, punctuated by sobs. 'I just think we're growing apart.'

And the devil of it was, she was right, so there were no words he could find to persuade her otherwise. Maybe it was the move to the country, or maybe it went deeper than that. It frightened him more than he would have believed possible.

'Hey,' he said softly. 'Let's not go jumping to the wrong conclusions. I still love you.'

A snuffle. 'And I love you, too.'

LION TAKES CONSUMMATION

It is the time for Consummation. Jackal One pricks up his ears and turns his head this way and that, and the congregation sways and sighs in the viewing gallery. A sound, a scent, a movement. You can always trust Jackal One to sense the Arrival.

I shake the painful rushing wind and the seductive images of the veldt from my mind and concentrate on Here and Now. The Holy Officiators all bow to White Eagle, and Rosehip and Hen sway to the foot of the operating table and kneel down, eyes closed, lips mouthing the Preparation. The three Jackals move to the entrance doors and wait for the Sign. All eyes turn to the TV monitor that dominates the theatre, part of the high-tech security system that the Bastards are so proud of. The digital clock ticks the seconds away, and White Eagle's face fills the screen, his all-seeing eyes gazing into the eyes of the Priests and Priestesses.

It is my responsibility to ensure that everything to do with the Way is conducted in accordance with ritual, and in silence. Oh, yes, silence. This is because Monkey Boy finds it easier to control the wall-mounted TV cameras than the microphones that are set behind grilles. I am not sure why this should be the case, but Monkey Boy knows about such matters and says he is working on it. Meanwhile, we take care not to make noises that will attract the attention of the Bastards in the security centre.

White Eagle's eyes slowly close, and the massive head drops ponderously in the Nod of Assent. Jackal Two swings open the doors, and there's Lamb and Orchid engaged in a knee-trembler against the corridor wall with a stocky youth. The youth is heaving and rutting against Lamb while Orchid bites his arse and plays with his balls. Very erotic. Despite the lad's efforts, he is looking thoroughly shagged out, which is the whole point. Drained and satiated is how White Eagle likes them. Something to do with the pituitary gland, according to Monkey Boy, who knows all there is to know about pituitary glands. He's a clever one, that Monkey Boy, despite his looks.

Jackal Two and Jackal Three steam through the door and grab the youth round the throat. Jackal One stuffs the Rag of Silence into his mouth, then the three Jackals fight him to the altar and strap him down, all bulging neck veins and swollen eyes. The soothing sight of sheer panic! Not many are privileged to see such a thing.

Lamb and Orchid pull their robes back on and take their places, either side of the altar. White Eagle's eyes pierce us all, and he gives the Nod of Permission. Rosehip and Hen hold the youth's legs as Lamb turns the wheel that moves the chromed restraining bars into the delivery position. I lift my robe and step forward waiting for the Cut of Silence. Spiderlady is good at this. Jackal One clamps the youth's head with a hand over his mouth while she snicks a scalpel through his larynx.

Perfect. Hardly any blood: a good omen. The Rag of Silence is removed from the lad's mouth to release a soft whistle as he tries to scream, and I feel my penis stirring in response, feel the warm and wonderful ache in my gonads that will soon be released. How can I tell you what this is like? A fighting bull guided to a heifer by hands that stroke with a greasy lubricant and direct my penis into the waiting, writhing orifice.

The great wind hurtles though my head, but it no longer brings pain, only the explosive pleasure that is my reason for living. Then hands pull me back, and in the great peace that follows I watch the three Jackals take their Communion, then Monkey Boy and the Chosen Ones from the congregation. The Priests and Priestesses bring each other to climax up in the viewing gallery, helping each other to muffle the grunts and sobs of pleasure.

A very successful Consummation. But the best is yet to come.

TUTOR NOTES

With relatively few words, this student has created a vivid, almost believable world of fantasy, rich in metaphor and strange inhabitants. There is a deep vein of gothic horror, almost comedic in its exaggeration, but crying out for illustration. The grammatical constructions are weak in places, and the structure could be improved with more logic and discipline. All together, a very satisfying effort. I'm looking forward to seeing where this storyline will lead.

7

The note from Toby Jennings was full of the kind of information that a well-connected solicitor can quickly garner, but it was also discouraging from Ben's point of view.

> Dear Ben
> I decided to scout around. Maybe this stuff will help, maybe not.
> The key medic is the chief psychiatric consultant, Professor Hugo Koch. He is a founder of the Ziegland Foundation for Social Reintegration in Boston (Massachusetts, not Lincolnshire). This is a multi-disciplinary think-tank devoted to improvements across all areas of society. Mental health is just one of its interests. Their belief is that mentally ill people represent a microcosm of society, and this is why Lindisholm caters for so many patients, from the slightly dysfunctional to the raging homicidal.
> They also believe that the most effective kind of treatment must allow mental patients to operate within a fully functioning social environment, with a range of hierarchies and activities. This is the rationale of the four-cloister system and the hospital's focus on self-sufficiency.
> Another precept is that the mentally ill should maintain links with so-called normal society, which leads directly to this business of having low-risk patients mingling with chumps like you.
> Ziegland is the most respected organisation of its kind. Bursting with top people. The hospital's head of psychiatric medicine, Professor Petra Jonser, is a Koch disciple. Well respected. Dedicated. But a reputation for being too methodical. One article I enclose describes her as 'robotic'.
> Foundation people come from all parts of the political spectrum. No partiality. No law suits. Not a hint of impropriety.

CareCorp plc, the operating company and owner of Lindisholm, has established much the same reputation, which you'd expect of a security firm whose main income is from government and defence contracts. Its chairman, Lord Balacombe, is considered to be a bit of a character within City circles, but very astute. A possible exception to the whiter-than-white brigade is the founder of CareCorp, a chap called Keith Melton. He holds the position of chief executive and is the major shareholder. Military background. Entered the City after leaving the Army. Got a reputation for being a chancer, but he pulled off so many prestigious deals that the Establishment stamped him okay. He maintains his Army contacts through membership of various clubs, notably Cavalry and Guards and another place for ex-service chaps called Club 122. Bit of a shady place, I understand. Mercenary recruitment and stuff like that.

As far as the hospital itself is concerned, compared with the other UK high-security hospitals, it's cheaper to run and has a higher medical success rate by far. There are no cases of a Lindisholm patient being released back into society and recommitting offences. No whispers of anything untoward! In fact, the hospital has won a number of lucrative outside contracts for work considered suitable for its patients.

A little bird told me that plans might be afoot for developing commercial projects in the outside world, using ex-patients. The hot tip is organic farming. Forget the book and buy shares.

Ever yours
Toby

Ben respected Toby's opinion, and here was the third person advising him that there was nothing about Lindisholm that could turn a boring book into a compelling exposé. Reading the enclosures made matters worse. The hospital was inspired by the highest of principles, and it operated like a well-oiled machine to achieve outstanding results for the benefit of all concerned. A very worthy cause.

So why did Ben have a growing conviction that something was seriously amiss? Was it wishful thinking on the part of a writer searching for a new topic? Maybe the injured calf and the dead sheep had unsettled him. And having one of the patients working on his property was rather spooky. Particularly the way Wesley reacted when Janice was around. It wasn't normal, but then Wesley was being treated at Lindisholm precisely because he was not normal. Round and round in circles.

Ben thought a chat with Wesley would be a good idea. He found the boy stacking firewood in the barn. There were gaps between the slates in places, and rainwater dripped onto the dried-out logs.

'Hey, Wesley. Fancy a walk into to Tregaron? Couple of things I need to get from the shops.'

Wesley looked uncomfortable. 'I'd like to, Mr Kirby, but it's outside the perimeter. My tag would set the alarms off.'

'Not if we went out of the far field, it wouldn't. Your security people said there was a blank spot because we have no Ping Pole there.'

The boy looked even more uncomfortable. Once again Ben had to remind himself that this was no ordinary youngster.

'Tell you what. We'll go in the Shogun. If anything happens, I'll plead ignorance and apologise. You wouldn't get into any trouble. What do you say?'

'In the Shogun?'

'Absolutely. What's more, you can drive across the fields to the road, just so long as you don't flatten any of Mr Newson's sheep.'

'And I won't get into trouble?'

'If anyone gets into trouble, it'll be me. And I'll be all right, because no one told me we couldn't go shopping together, did they?'

Wesley shook his head, a slow smile emerging. 'And I drive over the fields?'

'Definitely.'

Janice thought it was a good idea to take Wesley on an outing. He was always shy and reluctant to be alone with her, but he was beginning to relax a little with Ben. In fact, the two of them had struck up what seemed to her to be a warm friendship, without ignoring the reality of the situation.

'Just as long as you take responsibility,' she said. 'We're running out of unsalted butter, and I could do with a new pan scourer.'

'Anything else?'

'Can't think of anything.'

Wesley drove across the fields cautiously but with confidence in four-wheel-drive mode. The grazing sheep moved idly away from them, and Ben encouraged him to push the vehicle a little harder until they were happily churning up the gravel by the river bank.

'When did you get your driving licence?' Ben asked.

'Ain't got one. Used to belong to a gang called the Tenement Terrors, until the residents got vigilante. Took any car we fancied and blasted it all over the place. Handbrake turns, the lot! The others used to total most of the cars, but me, well, it was cool to get them back in one piece.'

'Very considerate.'

Wesley's grin transformed his face. A normal youngster up to mischief. 'You know how it is. Deprived inner-city kids. We didn't have nothing else to do, did we?'

'You tell me!'

For a few seconds Ben had the feeling that Wesley was about to take him at his word, to open up about something in the past. Then the boy brought the Shogun to an expert broadsiding stop at the gate leading to the road.

'All yours, Mr Kirby.'

They collected the scourer and a pack of slightly salted butter from the grocer's shop. Ben noticed that people smiled at him but gave the green-clad Wesley curious looks. Not antagonistic, he thought, but definitely curious.

He decided to treat himself to a pint of beer and started walking towards the hotel in the town square, the Talbot.

'Can't go in there, Mr Kirby.'

Again that note of fear.

'Yes we can, so long as you don't have alcohol. Follow me!'

The Talbot was another good pub with splendid old rooms and a display of paintings by local artists. A polite welcome from people in the bar, but again that cautious curiosity about Wesley, who sat uneasily nursing a bottle of Coke.

'Do people from Lindisholm work on farms around Tregaron like they do around Penford?'

'Don't know. Don't think so.'

'It's just that I was wondering how far Mr Newson's tenancies extended.'

Silence. Ben took a deep swig of beer.

'What do you reckon on this cloister system of yours? Alpha, you're in, aren't you? Green for Alpha, but I saw a couple of people wearing blue overalls on the farm. They come from Beta Cloister, do they?'

Another silence. The sparkle had gone out of the boy. In fact, he was looking decidedly edgy, and Ben began to think that perhaps this trip wasn't such a good idea. Maybe it was generating stress, and God knows what effect that might have. Wesley was, after all, a hospital patient.

'Right.' Ben drained his glass. 'Let's get back to the Mill.'

And of course, the first person they met outside the pub was the tight-lipped Dr Nikki Congleton, Wesley's humourless counsellor. Sod's Law in full swing. She was wheeling a wicker shopping trolley, and Ben could see a large pack of lavatory paper sticking out of it. That figured! He imagined the rest of the trolley was filled with pulses, textured vegetable protein and peanuts.

'Dr Congleton. What a pleasant surprise.'

The flat blue eyes swivelled towards him and back to Wesley.

'Have you been drinking, Wesley?'

Ben was about to respond, but thought it best for Wesley to speak up for himself. Only he saw that the boy's face was beaded with sweat. No grimace or any expression an actor might use to convey fear. A frozen blankness. His body was rooted to the pavement, shoulders rigid, elbows clasped into his sides.

'Wesley had a Coke. He's helping me with the shopping.'

The eyes glanced at the almost empty carrier bag.

'Is Mrs Kirby with you?'

'My wife is back at the Mill, ploughing the fields and uprooting old fence posts with her bare hands, like a modern woman should.'

Ben would have liked to think that the thin lips twitched in an unwilling appreciation of his wit, but they didn't.

'According to Mr Newson's reports, Wesley is doing a fine job helping you around the Mill. Perhaps the time has come for him to redirect his efforts towards your wife's responsibilities. Shopping is a very good idea. Housework and cooking would be good also. If we are going to rehabilitate our patients, we must not ignore the domestic side of life, wouldn't you agree?'

'Absolutely. That is very agreeable. But if he's going to do any shopping on his own, I presume you'd clear that with your security people?'

'Naturally. I trust we can look forward to the positive results of your wife's interest in Wesley's activities, then.'

As she walked away, pulling the wicker trolley, Ben took Wesley's arm. 'Come on. Let's get home and have a nice cup of tea.'

They travelled back in silence, and as they approached Brianne Mill Ben said, 'She's right, isn't she? I mean, it's not for me to get involved in your case, but if they're trying to cure you of something then the more normal your life, the better. And life is not all about chopping logs and tearing round fields in a four-by-four, is it? We need to go shopping for loo paper, just like Dr Congleton. Maybe not as much as she does, but I expect she's into the kind of food that makes you shit a lot. We have to shop, we have to cook, we have to clean the house and make beds. Don't we?'

He sensed the slight nod.

'And it's probably my fault, making you help me all the time. I expect I was thinking of when you first came to the Mill, you know, and you felt uneasy around Janice. You don't still feel like that, do you – not after all this time?'

'Mrs Kirby is very nice,' Wesley whispered.

'Of course she is, and she would certainly appreciate a little help. How about it?'

A nod.

'Right! That's settled.'

The first few times Wesley arrived to help Janice it was all a bit awkward. She didn't know quite how to treat him, for one thing.

'It's like having a cleaner,' she told Ben. 'No matter how hard you try, you end up cleaning the bloody place before they arrive. And you never, ever ask them to do something you wouldn't do yourself, which defeats the whole purpose, doesn't it, because that's why you hired them in the first place.'

'Just let him watch you, and he'll end up doing the things you do, so you can get on with something else.'

'And that's another problem. He still isn't comfortable with me. You must have noticed. Watching me is still a problem for him. Plus, if he helps with the shopping, we're not supposed to give him money, are we, so how can that help?'

'Get the shop to send a bill, or pay the money first, whatever. Christ, do I have to do all the thinking?'

93

'Thanks a bunch!' She was very annoyed, but Ben felt too irritated to apologise.

'It's true, isn't it? Every fucking decision that we need to make together, I end up making.'

Which upset her even more, so by the time Wesley's next visit to the Mill was due Ben and Janice were hardly speaking to each other and finding it impossible to break the deadlock. It reminded him of a line he'd read somewhere: 'There's only one thing harder than climbing up a greasy pole, and that's climbing back down again'. Like many witty sayings, it did not bear careful scrutiny, but it somehow captured the flavour of the situation.

Wesley did his best to watch Janice working around the house, but she wasn't making things easy for him. Daydreaming one minute, then excusing herself to go to the bathroom the next. She made them both innumerable cups of tea while Ben stayed in his study or trimmed overhanging trees. In the end, it was Wesley who brought matters to a head. They were sitting by the kitchen window, and Janice was staring out of it, nibbling another biscuit.

'Maybe I should go and help Mr Kirby.'

'What?'

'Maybe I should go and help Mr Kirby.'

'Oh God, I'm sorry, Wesley. I'm not very good at all this, am I?' She sniffed. 'I should be letting you do all sorts of things, so you get a good report, and look at me, feeling sorry for myself. Let's chop up some onions.'

She went to the vegetable rack, but he got there first.

'I can chop the onions.'

Their fingers touched, and she was surprised at the smoothness of his skin. He was too busy grabbing onions out of the red net sack to notice, and without thinking she touched him again. Then he noticed. He started grabbing at more onions, desperately, until he was dropping them on the tiled floor and trying to catch them, and it might even have been funny if he had not been making such a strange, panicky noise.

'Never mind the bloody onions, Wesley. Just leave them, for Christ's sake.'

He stood there, flapping his arms dementedly, and she remembered a little too late that he was a mental patient, not just a young, attractive lad. But there was no insanity in his face, just a desperate, helpless misery, and she knew right then that there was no threat to her, not from Wesley. She took hold of him gently, firmly, and pulled him in close so that his face was buried into her shoulder. He began to sob, heartbreakingly.

'It's all right, Wesley, it's all right. We've no need to be frightened of each other, have we?'

It was the slightest of movements, but a definite shake of the head.

'And I'll tell you something you can believe with all your heart. Nothing that happens here will ever get back to that awful Dr Congleton or to anyone else at the hospital. All we'll tell them is that you work hard and that you are a good person. How about that?'

'I don't want to go back there, Mrs Kirby.'

'I know you don't, Wesley, and the quicker we can help you to get better, the quicker you can go home.'

He pulled away.

'I ain't going to get better. No one gets better.'

'Of course they do. Ben's got a report. The hospital cures hundreds of patients every year. He'll show you. Whatever is wrong, they'll find a way to help you.'

'They don't want us to get better. You don't understand. They want to keep us the way we are.'

The fear was coming back.

Was this part of his mental problem, she wondered? Paranoia? Could she reassure him . . . should she even try?

'I'm sure that's not true. You've got some of the finest medical staff in the world. Why should they want you to stay the way you are?'

Wesley made a huge effort to control himself, clenching his fists to stop them trembling, forcing himself to look Janice directly in the eye, just for a moment, willing her to believe what he was saying.

'I ain't just talking about the medical staff, Mrs Kirby.'

His naked fear filled the kitchen with a palpable, infectious horror, and then Ben walked in.

'Hello you two. What's with the onions?'

They lay in bed, in darkness, each knowing the other was awake, neither daring to make a move, fearful that it would be rejected. The wedge was forcing its way between them. How? Why? Someone had to deal with this.

'I'm sorry,' she whispered.

'Me too,' he said.

After a pause she said, 'You must write this book.'

'You changed your mind?'

'Yes.'

'How come?'

'There's something terribly wrong in that place.'

He gazed into the dark, listening to country noises from the trees and the animals in the fields. He thought she meant the economics of Newson's farming operation.

'Yes there is, and it's something to do with smiling Fred Newson and his deals with local farmers. Everything else turns up trumps. Not a corrupt medico in sight. No secret links with drugs companies. No inflated research reports. No illicit drug testing, as far as I can see. The place is squeaky clean. I've checked out everyone who was involved in setting it up. The Health Service, the Home Office, that organisation in America. I've ploughed through CareCorp, and I've checked out the medical staff. I've even taken a look at this organic farming venture that Toby Jennings said they were setting up. It doesn't seem to have anything to do with CareCorp. Not officially, anyway. The company was incorporated a year ago: Lindisholm Organic Foods Limited. Newson and a bloke called Searle are the only shareholders and directors. Newson is small-time, like I said, and Searle is the hospital's general manager. It doesn't add up to much.'

'Maybe you're looking in the wrong places for the wrong people.'

'What does that mean?'

'The patients.'

'The patients?'

She turned the bedside light on, sat up and plumped up the pillows so she could sit comfortably.

'Think about it. We both have this feeling that something is wrong. Where did it come from?'

He sat up too. 'What are you getting at?'

'Wesley, that's who. And Wesley is a patient.'

'I know Wesley is a patient.' He couldn't help the exasperated tone leaking into his voice. 'So what?'

'That poor boy is absolutely terrified, but it's nothing to do with the hospital itself. Well, not the medical staff.'

'That Dr Congleton would scare the shit out of anyone, wouldn't she?'

'Damn right, but it isn't anything to do with her. He told me.'

'What did he tell you?'

'He said they didn't want him to get better. In fact he said they didn't want "us" to get better, and I said, "Of course they do!", meaning the doctors, and he said, "I ain't just talking about the medical staff." Don't you see? He's frightened of the patients.'

What Janice said might be true, but it was hardly surprising. Many young men sent to prison had to contend with homosexuality and the drugs culture – enough to scare any youngster. On the other hand, Lindisholm was so tightly administered that Ben could not believe such abuses could exist there. In any case, the occasions when some prisons and mental hospitals had been taken over or abused by the inmates had been well covered in the media over the years, which ruled that out as a topic for his book. Ben needed a new angle, such as maladministration or malpractice, but the leads he had at the moment were not impressive. Newson was a smug, self-centred little demagogue, running his farm with an eye to the main chance, but that was hardly the basis for a feature article, let alone a full-length book. Wesley's counsellor might provide a story of sorts; she was hardly what you'd call a normal person. Socially dysfunctional, in fact. But as far as Ben was concerned, all psychiatrists were socially dysfunctional. No story there.

But what if Janice was right? Maybe Wesley was scared of the patients. Truly, deeply scared. Problem was, finding out why was going to be a hard one to crack. High-security hospitals were not called high-security for no reason. There was no way he could adopt a conventional approach against a system designed to stop people doing just that. It wasn't the same as investigating commercial firms, where security was always a compromise with open communications people could hack into. Where could he begin?

He knew something about Lindisholm's physical security system because he lived on its borders and had seen the electronic tagging system in action. He even knew where there was a breach in the boundary, but he didn't see how that helped.

And then it hit him. The Mill was inside the hospital's outer perimeter! In terms of getting himself into the place, he was already over the first hurdle. He could try checking things out with Wesley again, then get to know some of the other patients who worked at Newson's farm. Use Newson's little scams to his own advantage. Expand his existing role of peripheral involvement into something more substantive.

He thought about time scales. To keep up his momentum in the marketplace, he should deliver an outline and sample chapters to his agent in around three months. If he couldn't work things into a book form by then, he could probably sell his research to a TV documentary maker. Maybe Norman Shelling would be interested. The more he thought about it, the better it sounded. After all, they were already connected to the hospital through the tenancy agreement. All he had to do to speed things up was to get more involved, somehow, but this would hardly be a straightforward exercise. He needed cunning as much as investigative expertise. For one thing, it would be far better if it appeared that he was being pulled into more contact with the hospital rather than taking the initiative himself. In fact, he should play the part of the reluctant helper. Fortunately, this process has already started with Fred Newson's persistence in getting the new agreement. Janice appeared to like the little prick, so maybe she could help. Maybe Lindisholm had a League of Friends she could join, so she could get inside the main hospital building and suss things out there. Yes, he definitely needed her help. Would she go for it?

'How about a nice cup of relaxing tea?' he suggested.

'Might as well. Let me make it.'

While she went downstairs and clattered around in the kitchen, he spun ideas for developing his project. By the time she rejoined him, he had a plan mapped out.

'I agree with you about Wesley being scared of the other patients, and that's where I have to start.'

'With Wesley? You can't do that.'

'Why not? Where else do I have to go? And you can help. His counsellor is actually encouraging you to get involved with him. It's a gift.'

'Christ, Ben. If you start on him like you do when you get obsessed with something, you'll scare the kid even more.'

'Rubbish. Chances are I'll be able to help him. Once thing's for sure, no one else is doing that.'

Janice felt truly exasperated with her husband. Yes, he was

brilliant, but that very brilliance blinded him to certain obvious realities.

'Neither of us is qualified to know that. And we might both be quite wrong about Wesley being terrified of the other patients. He might be paranoid, mightn't he? And if he is and if you go sticking your nose in, God knows what damage you'll do to his chances of recovery. You want to take that chance?'

'Yes.'

And there it was. Ben at his most dangerous, careless of anyone's feelings in pursuit of his objective. That was the unseen germ that tainted their relationship, that her sister Eileen had sensed and warned her about. When *The Façade* had been published, at least five leading executives had been sacked by major companies because of its revelations, and there was more than a suspicion that another had committed suicide because of the book. Ben didn't seem to care, and Janice found that hard to take.

'You selfish bastard. You just don't give a shit about anyone, so long as you get to write a feature or a book or one of your selfish-bastard friends makes a TV programme about it. You make me sick.'

'I make you sick, do I? Well, I'll tell you what makes me sick. It's people like you who go round saying we must have press freedom and who go apeshit when people like me turn that fine concept into hard-nosed reality. And don't think I don't know what's at the bottom of all this. It's that stupid bastard who topped himself, isn't it?'

'Two days after your goddamn book came out, leaving a wife and three children under the age of ten!'

'And also leaving a dozen small firms bankrupt, because he delayed payment of their invoices for months so he could carry on fiddling his own expenses and getting his end away with a range of prostitutes every time his beloved wife turned her back. I didn't put all that in my book, did I? You tell me why I should feel sorry about a scumbag like that, and I'll lay off Wesley.'

'What about his wife and family?'

'Of course I feel sorry for them. Actually, I feel sick about it. But not about him, and before you ask, yes, I can separate the two issues. The crooked bastard wrecked his own family, not me.'

She finished her cup of tea and lay down, rolling away from him. 'I still think you shouldn't involve Wesley.'

99

'Wesley is already involved, and my job is to find out in what. And I bloody well will. I just thought you'd help, that's all.'

'Well, I bloody well won't. Not unless you find some other way.'

8

Dr Nikki Congleton scrolled down her computer screen, comparing her private files with her handwritten comments on her patients. She was not happy with her progress at Lindisholm. Part of the trouble was the redoubtable Professor Jonser, who ran the clinical psychiatry department like an automaton. Nothing escaped the professor's critical eye, and she demanded time-wasting explanations for the smallest variation from the norm: the norm being the results which hospital staff were expected to achieve with each and every patient. Over three thousand patients, with a mere five hundred staff to deal with them! Admittedly, most of the patients were in the low security Alpha Cloister, but even so the medical staff spent hours each day working simply to remain in the same place, never mind advancing their careers. 'A brave experiment' *The Times* had called the hospital when its plan was announced by the government. 'A brave experiment, founded on the most advanced thinking in modern medical treatment of mental illnesses – a society within a society.'

Congleton's private view of this advanced thinking would have earned her immediate dismissal, had anyone discovered her innermost thoughts. For one thing, when it came to insanity, you could never have enough staff. Automated security systems were all very well, but there's nothing like the hands-on approach for keeping unruly patients in check, and the more hands the better, as far as Congleton was concerned.

Paradoxically, it was this despised feature of the hospital that she planned to use for her own advancement. Dr Congleton had a theory. If she could prove her theory, she would be recognised as one of the great innovators in psychiatric medicine. What she had in mind was simple but revolutionary. Dr Congleton held the view that there was no such thing as insanity. There was no such thing as diminished responsibility. There was no such thing as the balance of the mind being disturbed. In short, mental illness was a meaningless label created by societies that could not bring themselves to face a harsh reality: all humans are capable of all forms of behaviour. As far as Congleton was concerned, what Charles Manson and Peter

Sutcliffe could do today, the kid next door could do tomorrow. All that was stopping him was lack of opportunity and fear of retaliation. Give him the opportunity and take away this fear, and little Johnny Toogood would rip and tear and rape with the best of them. Or the worst of them. Best, worst . . . it mattered not to Congleton. It was not a moral issue. It was nature in action, and until this was recognised and incorporated in the correct treatment of anti-social behaviour, society would suffer the consequences.

As she scanned through her private notes on her patients, Nikki Congleton knew she had been presented with a wonderful opportunity to demonstrate the error that had afflicted her profession for generations.

Name	Cloister	Comment
Rosalind McMichael	Alpha	Sponsor: Home Office. Violent attacks of hysteria. Diagnosis: schizophrenia. Pathetic and inadequate. Died in the hospital's market garden shortly after I arrived. Official reason for death: an aneurysm. I note that our pathology department has kept her file open.
Roland Melville	Gamma	Sponsor: Home Office. Schizoid killer; a bull of a man who turned on his family in a frenzy of violence. Care: standard treatment.
Harold Jenkins	Beta	Sponsor: Home Office. Bouts of hysterical and anti-social behaviour. Diagnosis: obsessive-compulsive. Also suffers from Hutchinson-Gilford syndrome. Atypical IQ of 190. Formed an attachment with the hospital's IT manager, Robert Dagby.
Christopher Leamington	Delta	Sponsor: no listing. No patient history prior to admittance to Lindisholm. Diagnosis: paranoid schizophrenia and anosognosia (also

Name	Cloister	Comment
		see Abbott). Although this patient is assigned to my list, Professor Jonser has informed me that he has been temporarily removed from Lindisholm by his sponsor. No explanation!
Dorothy Lampton	Gamma	Sponsor: Home Office. A plain and unremarkable woman who killed more than a dozen children for no apparent reason as she travelled the country exhibiting health foods. Diagnosis: psychotic compulsive-obsessive. Good reports from art therapy.
Benny Jacobs	Delta	Sponsor: Home Office. Gangster and torturer from the East End of London. Diagnosis: schizophrenia, melancholia. Meticulous observer of the Jewish religion.
Hamel Said	Gamma	Sponsor: Home Office. Conducting his own violent kind of jihad against selected Christians, also from the East End.
Peter O'Brien	Gamma	Sponsor: Home Office. A schizoid killer. Practising Roman Catholic. Born in Ireland but lived in the East End for many years. Recently recloistered from Delta.
Jennie Booth	Gamma	Sponsor: Home Office. Common prostitute who took to killing her clients. Diagnosis: psychotic. Standard treatment.
Geoffrey Abbott	Delta	Sponsor: no listing. No patient history prior to admittance to Lindisholm. Diagnosis: paranoid schizophrenia and anosognosia (also see Leamington). Always

Name	Cloister	Comment
		co-operative. Obsessed with physical fitness. Non-standard results on usual IQ and psychometric testing, but I suspect high intelligence. Part of a special treatment programme to which I do not have access!!!
Noel Chard	Gamma	Sponsor: Home Office. Male model, transsexual, mutilator of homosexuals. Diagnosis: psychotic.
Derek Howard	Beta	Sponsor: Home Office. Sado-pederast. Multiple convictions for child abuse.
Alice Jones	Gamma	Sponsor: Home Office. Self-harmer and potential suicide. Diagnosis: manic depressive.
Joan Corbett	Gamma	Sponsor: Home Office. Poisoned three husbands. Standard treatment, however she could respond to ECT.
Janie Dolstead	Alpha	Sponsor: Home Office. One of the youngest patients at the hospital. Habitual liar. Too fond of lighted matches, particularly where her school was concerned.
John McWeeney	Alpha	Sponsor: Home Office. A totally dysfunctional young man with a mental age of six. Obsessive-compulsive.
Wesley Freeman	Alpha	Sponsor: Home Office. Would-be rapist and abuser of women. Diagnosis: manic depressive. Previous counsellor thought he was suffering from hysterical amnesia. More likely a convenient memory loss.

As far as Dr Congleton was concerned, every one of these patients was, like all others in the hospital, fully responsible for his or her own behaviour and should be treated accordingly, not as if they suffered from something that could be cured. She believed that, whatever the fine details of each case, the patients would be treated more appropriately in a cloister category higher than the clinical review board had set. Alpha Cloister was a superfluous waste of space and effort. Alpha patients should be moved to the more disciplined and secure Beta Cloister, Beta patients to Gamma Cloister, Gamma patients to Delta Cloister. Delta Cloister was the nearest any secure hospital could get to total control. It had the highest staff-to-patient ratio and the most comprehensive array of surveillance, patient tagging and security systems in the world. Laser beams, load cells, infra-red scanners, iris and hand-print recognition units and, of course, the omni-present tagging bracelets and transponder boxes fitted along every passageway in the building and on a network of masts around its perimeter. The security team could pinpoint each Delta patient to within a few millimetres on their 3D mapping system at any time of the day or night. They joked that the biggest thing that could leave Delta Cloister undetected was a hydrogen atom.

Movement of staff and patients between the cloisters was strictly controlled. Some of the staff, such as the security people, had total access; others were restricted to certain areas. As part of the hospital's belief in natural social intercourse, the less disturbed patients were allowed to move deeper into the cloister system to help influence those with more severe illnesses, while the more disturbed patients were occasionally allowed to move outwards for a few hours as a reward for improved behaviour and, in some cases, as preparation for a permanent downgrading of their threat potential.

As far as Congleton was concerned, it was a fundamentally flawed system based on wrong assumptions, but she could play the game with the best of them, biding her time and preparing the ground for the publication of her paper: *The Fallacy of Mental Illness – Case Studies from UK High-security Hospitals*.

To achieve her objective, Congleton was putting pressure on selected patients to assist the review board to upgrade their security status. In this, she had to be extremely careful. Professor Jonser had almost caught her out when she first interviewed Wesley Freeman. So the pressures had to be very subtle. Like making sure that Noel

Chard spent more time with male patients than with females in the hope that the homosexual element in the hospital would eventually counteract Chard's medication and spark off his violence; or like putting temptation in the way of the over-sexed and violent Freeman in the form of Mrs Janice Kirby.

Chard had already responded by beating up two male patients, for which transgression he had received several sessions in the electro-convulsive therapy clinic. Congleton was a fervent advocate of ECT, and in her opinion the unit was seriously under-utilised. It had certainly pacified the aggressive Mr Chard.

Unfortunately, Freeman did not seem to be rising to his particular bait, but Congleton was sure things would work out the way she wanted. Her thesis was based on the premise that people did what rewarded them and avoided what caused them pain. Freeman sought his reward in sexual contact with older women. Sooner or later, he would make his move with Mrs Janice Kirby. He would not be able to help himself. It would be his reward, after which he would receive the appropriate pain.

The idea that she was placing Janice Kirby at risk was not a matter of concern to the dedicated Dr Congleton.

LION TAKES COMMUNION

I, Lion, sweep my gaze around the Omega Cloister, aware of the attention my noble demeanour creates in this place of worship. The burning ache in my loins is a distant memory, replaced by a glorious warmth and the joy of anticipating Communion.

I step forward and lift his arms, feeling the sleeves of his robes slither and slide deliciously over my skin. High Priestesses Lamb, Hen, Rosehip and Spiderlady position the drip stands with their empty containers and needles at the ready: one for each arm, one for each leg. Amazingly the Offering is still struggling. The Beaters have picked a good one this time – strong – and his strength will pass to the worshippers.

With neat, surgical precision, Communion begins. Four needles are slipped into four veins, and the empty plasma bags lowered to the floor for the first time. We usually need to perform the Letting twice. Fourteen pints. Around seven two-litre bags.

When no more blood flows into the second group of bags, the Offering is hauled upside down, Spiderlady stabs deep into its neck, and a few more fluid ounces trickle into the waiting kidney dish.

The ceremony slips into overdrive. The Jackals assist the High Priestesses to dismember the Offering with scalpels, saws and cleavers, as the congregation shuffles forward to sip and to chew and to fill their Holy chalices with the Body and Blood of White Eagle so that they, in turn, can administer Communion to their own Flocks in the cloisters beyond Omega. All so secret. All so efficient. All under the watchful eyes of the Bastards and their automated surveillance system. When all is done, the Priestesses clean and sterilise the equipment, the congregation files out and the lights dim. I permit myself a shiver of anticipation. Maybe next time the Beaters will bring a woman. A lioness. A worthy mate for Lion.

Sometimes I move outside the Place, free to hunt, free to sink my fangs into succulent, living flesh in the comfort of darkness. One day

I will free myself from the bondage of the Place, but for the moment I must stay, so that I can look after my People and do the Lord's bidding.

TUTOR NOTES

A third contribution from our imaginative friend. Slightly over the top with his metaphors, but very powerful, nevertheless. I have not been asked to report or comment on the content of any student's work, but how many times do we hear of deranged people putting their dreams into reality? Maybe someone should cast an eye over this.

9

Ben researched his new project with typical single-minded intensity. Although he was tempted to pump Wesley for information, Janice's warnings of the dangers involved were difficult to ignore, so he decided on another tack. According to the landlord of the Blue Lion, Harry Price, Fred Newson's labourers from Lindisholm Farm had helped several farmers in the area to refurbish outbuildings over the past few years, all at very little cost to the farmers concerned. Ben would let Newson know that he and Janice were turning the barn into a studio for her pottery. This would require the removal of the roof slates, followed by the installation of a waterproof membrane and reslating, plus some repairs on the woodwork. Lots of labour-intensive activity. Would Newson rise to the bait?

He revealed his plans when Newson was enjoying a pint of beer with his drinking pals.

'There's a company in Tregaron that can handle most of the things that need doing. And there's space at the far end of the building we could turn into animal shelters. That could come in handy for you during the lambing season.'

'Sounds like a good idea,' Newson said. 'But there's no need to go to any trouble on my account.'

'It's no trouble. Like Alan said weeks ago, you're a good tenant, so anything we can do to help . . .'

'Tell you what, let me come along and give the site the once-over before you commit yourself to any final plans.'

Newson arrived at Brianne Mill two days later, and Ben showed him what he had in mind.

'Very good,' Newson said, 'but I can't have you forking out for this, just to help me.'

'That's incidental to the main work. And don't forget, we'll be increasing the asset of the Mill.'

'Sure you will, but why pay market prices when I can sort things out another way? I can get my people involved in this, and all you have to pay for is the materials. We can probably supply some of the wood you need at cost, and I'm sure we have some spare roofing felt lying around somewhere. What do you say?'

'I can't let you do that.'

'Rubbish! I'd only be returning your generosity. Where is Mrs Kirby, by the way?'

'Janice is sweating over her sketch pad. Waiting for the creative muse to flash down from potters' heaven to inspire her to produce another masterpiece.'

'It's just that Roy Ormley spotted one of her exhibition cards in London the other day,' Newson said. 'He thinks she's brilliant.'

'She is brilliant. Decidedly brilliant. In fact, she makes me feel completely inadequate.'

'You're pretty good at what you do, seems to me,' Newson said. 'I can't imagine how you managed to get all that material into print without ending up hanging under London Bridge like that Italian banker chap. Big companies can be lethal if they need to protect themselves. Bloody good book.'

'Very kind of you.'

'So, what do you say, Ben – can we help out on this barn of yours?' Newson persisted.

'Sounds great, but let me talk it over with Janice, just to make sure. I'll give you a call tomorrow.'

Hook, line and sinker. The bastard had fallen for it, and he thought it was all his own idea. Perfect.

'I don't need a new roof.' Janice was really angry with Ben over this one. 'I can think of a dozen things higher on my priority list than a barn roof, for Heaven's sake. I'd like the floor replaced, for one thing.'

'The roof is not the point.'

'So, what is the point?'

'I get access to several more patients, that's the point. Christ, the project will take maybe two or three weeks, start to finish, and we'll both have an opportunity to watch what goes on. If there's anything odd about Lindisholm, we'll suss it out together. What do you say?'

'What about Wesley?'

'You were right. I'll leave him out of it.'

'You mean that?'

'Absolutely. Maybe he'll open up of his own accord, but I won't push it. I promise.'

Janice knew how important this project was to Ben, knew what an effort he was making to take this line.

'All right, then. If Fred Newson wants to help, that's okay by me.'

The following Monday at eight o'clock in the morning a small convoy drove into the courtyard outside the barn: Newson's pick-up truck, a Ford Transit van and a lorry with a rubbish skip. When the vehicles rolled to a halt, Newson assembled several uniformed hospital patients and a young lad wearing jeans and a T-shirt into two lines, military-style. He rang the doorbell and waited until Ben and Janice came out.

'Good morning. Here we are, all present and correct. You know Wesley, of course. Peter O'Brien here is team leader.' He pointed at an older man with a thin face and a prominent Adam's apple, who stared impassively at them. He was wearing the yellow overalls of a Gamma patient. 'This is a very special day for Peter, who has been showing remarkable progress, according to his counsellors. He'll be working under my direct supervision, of course. Our young friend Donny over there is on hire from the farming agency. Peter thought this work would give him some useful building experience, and I agree. If we need anything we haven't planned, one of the team will ring the front doorbell. They are all under strict instructions not to go into the main house under any circumstances. With a bit of luck, we'll clear the slates over the next couple of days and start felting by the end of the week. If we find any dodgy timbers, we'll replace them as we go. Apart from a few knocks and bangs, you won't know we're here. We'll work until five each day, then you can check that all is well before we leave.'

'Sounds good to me.'

'All right, everybody,' Newson said to his team. 'Let's show Mr and Mrs Kirby what Lindisholm people can do, shall we?'

Ben and Janice started to go back into the house, but O'Brien held up his arm.

'Before you leave us, perhaps you'd be good enough to join in a prayer for our work today.'

His request caught them both off guard, but Janice decided that there was no way she or Ben should be involved in anything like this.

'I'm sorry, Mr O'Brien. My husband and I are not believers, but you go ahead by all means.'

'It is not necessary to be a believer. My people would appreciate your presence. It is a small thing we ask.'

Before she could reply, O'Brien lifted up both arms and tilted his thin face to the sky, while the other patients and the young labourer stood with their heads down. Newson stared straight ahead, clearly another non-believer.

'Let our work with earth and water, wood and stone be blessed. Let the trees that grow on this holy ground and the river that joins it to the Place be blessed. Let the people who labour and dwell here be blessed. Let the power of the Lord flow down to this place through the flight of the great white eagle, his servant. Amen.'

'What a weirdo!' Ben said, once they were safely back inside.

'He seemed very intense about this religion thing. Maybe that's what's scaring young Wesley.'

'I doubt it. Your average religious nutter is harmless enough, and that guy would never get out of the hospital if they thought he was a threat to anyone. Still, if his great white eagle delivers the goods, we'll end up with a nice new barn roof.'

'That's not the reason we're doing this, remember.'

'Only kidding. I fancy some toast. How about you?'

Janice nodded. 'How are we going to keep an eye on them without looking suspicious?'

'We'll wander around pushing wheelbarrows and mowing the grass, like people do on their own property. Tonight we'll compare notes.'

By midday, the patients had removed half the roof slates and stacked them neatly against the barn walls. Some of the roof timbers were rotten, and the lad called Donny came to the door and asked if they could burn them in a safe area.

'We'll have to hire another skip, otherwise,' he said in a broad Australian accent. 'The wind's in the right direction, and we'll keep an eye on it.'

Ben noticed that Newson's truck was missing, and he was about to ask Donny where the farm manager had gone when he saw it returning along the road and down the drive.

'Just popped along to Alan Walters with some of our organic flour,' Newson said. 'If Mrs Kirby bakes, I could bring some for you tomorrow.'

'No thanks. We're strictly ready-made pastry people.'

Newson looked at the young labourer. 'Everything all right, Donny?'

'I was just asking Mr Kirby if we could burn the old timbers when I've finished my job in the barn.'

'Good lad.' Newson turned to Ben as Donny walked off. 'New boy. Very responsible.'

'You said you'd be on-site.'

'Well, they're working under my supervision, but there's no need for me to be around all the time. The patients are under their usual medication, and if any of them did become distressed, there's always warning signs.'

'That's not the point.'

'I can understand your concern, but I've been handling teams like this for years. There's never been a single problem with patient behaviour. They've too much to gain and too much to lose.'

'I'd appreciate it if you'd stay here while they're working, all the same.'

Newson sighed. 'I can try, but I act a bit like a gaffer. If we need any tools or materials we haven't got with us, it's me that goes and gets them.'

'And that's hospital policy, is it?'

'Of course not. Not officially, anyway. Every one of my people has been checked out by their consultants as being no threat to anyone, and as far as absconding is concerned, forget it. The system takes care of that automatically.'

Ben was about to press the point, when he realised it would be to his advantage to play along with this sloppy procedure. If anything went awry, it would be grist to his writing mill.

'Well, if you're sure,' he said. 'By the way, you remember that sheep we found, up on the mountains by your place?'

'I certainly do, why?'

'You said that your pathology people would be examining the carcass.'

'That's right. Sorry. Should have told you. They think it was savaged by two or more large dogs. Certainly not a fox or a wildcat.'

'What about its ribs, and that business about the heart being missing?'

'No idea. Mind you, some of the hippie communes keep Rottweilers. Christ knows what they train them to do.' Newson smiled reassuringly. 'So, how's everything proceeding? Shall we take a look?'

When they went into the barn, everyone stopped work. O'Brien stood stiffly to attention while Newson examined what had been accomplished so far.

'Good progress, Peter, very good progress.' Newson turned to the lad in jeans who was standing waist deep in a hole he was digging by a cornerstone.

'And what are you up to down there, Donny?'

'Peter reckons there might be a water course under here, Mr Newson,' the boy said. 'Seemed sensible to check it out, just in case.'

'Excellent,' Newson said. 'Don't you think so, Ben?'

'Very thorough.' Ben looked over to Wesley, who was sitting astride a cross beam in the roof, but Wesley avoided his eye.

'If the Lord Beltane wills, we shall have the felting in place by Di-Jou,' O'Brien said. 'The slates will take longer to replace than you thought because the Devil has broken so many of the fixings.'

'Di-Jou, Peter?'

'Our Lord's name for Friday.'

'Fine, splendid,' Newson said. 'I know you'll do your best. That's why I chose you to lead the team.'

'The Lord chose me, Mr Newson,' O'Brien said, stone-faced.

'Of course he did,' Newson said soothingly. 'I just gave him a helping hand.'

Ben wondered what O'Brien was talking about. Lord Beltane? Di-Jou? It sounded like some kind of Druidic reference. Very peculiar – but the man was, to say the least, very peculiar!

And so the day passed. There was nothing weird, apart from O'Brien's religious mania. Nothing untoward, until the late afternoon, when Janice opened the kitchen window to let the wind take care of the smell of cooking as she prepared the evening meal. The trees were waving around and making quite a noise, but underneath the rustling of leaves and branches there was another sound. A murmur of sorts, pulsing in and out of the wind. Ben was wandering somewhere outside with his wheelbarrow, so she wiped her hands, made her way to the barn and looked inside.

At first there was only the sound, a monotonous hum and a peculiar scrabbling. It took a moment for her eyes to adjust to the dim light, and she was startled to see the patients lying face down around the far corner of the building where someone in yellow overalls was standing with his back to her. O'Brien. Swaying back and forth. And he appeared to have feet growing from his neck. When she moved forward to see better she tripped over one of the patients, who jerked upright and shouted, 'Help! Oh my God, help!'

Next minute, they were all shouting and screaming for help, louder and louder, until she was surrounded by hysteria. O'Brien turned towards her, and she saw that he was holding the young labourer upside down by the legs. He stared at her with a satisfied smile, nodding happily.

'Help,' he whispered. 'Young Donny's hurt himself.'

He began pulling Donny out of the hole, far enough for Janice to see the gaping wound in the lad's throat and the blood pumping steadily from it. When Ben rushed in to see what the noise was all about, Janice was screaming as hysterically as the rest of the patients.

At Lampeter police station, Detective Sergeant Jennifer Matthews was about to go off duty when the duty officer took the emergency call.

'Say again,' he said into the phone, looking at her. 'Right. We'll get someone from CID down there as quickly as possible.'

'Brianne Mill,' he said to DS Matthews. 'On the mountain road. You know the place. You went there after the owner was reported for growing cannabis in his greenhouse.'

'Well he was, wasn't he! Only by the time I got there it was all glowing merrily on his bonfire. What's he up to now?'

'He's long gone. The new owner just called an ambulance. His name is Ben Kirby. There's been an accident involving Lindisholm patients.'

* * *

By the time Jennifer arrived at Brianne Mill, the ambulance from the general hospital in Carmarthen was on the scene, and its driver was arguing with the driver of a private ambulance sporting Lindisholm Hospital livery. Several people wearing the distinctive Lindisholm overalls were sitting vacantly in a white Ford Transit, and a good-looking young man with blue eyes and a slightly broken nose was holding the hand of an attractive woman with blonde, short-cropped hair who was slumped in a chair, looking pale and shocked.

'Mr Ben Kirby?'

He nodded.

'I'm Detective Sergeant Matthews. What's going on?'

'What's going on? A fucking pantomime is what's going on.'

'Now, sir, that's not going to help, is it?'

Ben took a deep breath. 'My wife saw a young man bleeding to death, surrounded by patients from that damned hospital. I called that ambulance over there, but before it got here those two bastards from Lindisholm Hospital arrived and started jabbing everyone with sedatives, including the poor little sod who is injured. They even tried to jab my wife.'

Jennifer looked down at Janice. No one had thought to wrap her in a blanket, so without a word she opened the trunk of her car, took out her travelling rug, handed it to Ben, then went to the ambulances and showed her warrant card.

'DS Matthews, Lampeter. What's the problem?'

'There's no problem,' the Lindisholm driver said smoothly. 'The accident involves high-security patients, and we are equipped to deal with this kind of situation.'

'That's just it,' the Carmarthen driver said angrily. 'According to Mr Kirby, the lad who's been injured isn't a hospital patient. We took the call, and it's our responsibility to take the boy to Carmarthen. This idiot won't even let us see him.'

'I take it you have no objection to letting me see him.'

The hospital driver nodded towards his ambulance, and Jennifer swung the door open and looked inside. A male nurse was sitting next to a mobile stretcher on the left of the ambulance adjusting a plasma drip into the arm of a young, very white-faced youth with bandages round his throat. He did not appear to be breathing, so she went inside to take a closer look. A patient in yellow overalls was strapped into the other stretcher.

'For God's sake, he should be in intensive care, not lying there while you argue about who's responsible.'

'We've stitched the wound, and his condition is stable, although he needs blood, ASAP,' the hospital driver said. 'I'd be obliged if you could clear a path for us.'

'We've got Haemaccel and other IV kit on board,' the Carmarthen driver insisted. 'He also needs oxygen. He's our responsibility.'

'Have you got all that?' she asked the other driver.

'We've got saline drips, yes . . .'

The Carmarthen driver glared at him.

'The amount of blood he's lost, he needs Haemaccel, and he needs it now.'

'Right! Shift him to this vehicle immediately or I'll arrest you for obstruction. Do it now!' She went back to Ben. 'Can you show me where the accident happened?'

'Sure, but can you keep an eye on Janice for a minute?' Ben strode to the Ford and tapped on the driver's window. 'Where's Fred Newson?'

'Last I saw, he was making for your barn, Mr Kirby.'

Ben went back to Janice. 'You all right for a minute?'

She nodded tiredly, so he beckoned to DS Matthews, and she followed him to the barn. Fred Newson was standing by the hole in the corner, holding the curved brushing hook. When he heard them coming he turned and held it up.

'He must have slipped and fallen on this, poor little bastard. It's razor sharp. Farmers round here call them slashers.'

'Mr Newson from Lindisholm Farm, isn't it?' Jennifer asked.

'That's right. And who might you be?'

'Detective Sergeant Matthews,' she said flatly. 'And you shouldn't be wandering around like this.'

'Only trying to help.'

'I'd be obliged if you'd put that down, and please don't touch anything else until I've had a look round.'

Newson placed the brushing hook on the pile of earth that Donny had excavated.

'What were they doing here?' she asked Ben.

'Helping to refurbish the barn.'

'Part of their therapy,' Newson interjected. 'Work in the community.'

He sounded defensive, she thought.

'What's the hole for?'

'The lad who was injured was digging it,' Ben told her. 'He said the patient called O'Brien thought there might be water there, so they were checking the foundation. Janice says it was O'Brien who was holding him after it happened.'

Jennifer shone her torch into the hole. 'Looks like he was right. It's pretty wet down there.'

'It was dry earlier on,' Ben said. He reached down and dipped his fingers in the liquid. Sticky, and, when he held his hand towards the light, dark red. 'Oh Christ!'

'Right,' Jennifer said. 'I want this barn clear until I can get an incident team here. Probably won't be until the morning. I'll be arranging for everyone to give statements.'

'I take it you won't need me,' Newson said. 'I arrived after Mr Kirby called for assistance.'

'I don't know what happened here, Mr Newson, and I most certainly will need a statement from you. We can contact you at the hospital farm. I take it you have no problem with that.'

When they got back to the house, the Carmarthen ambulance was pulling out of the drive, its blue lights flashing. Jennifer went to the Lindisholm driver and stared at the patient lying in the straps. He was rolling his head from side to side, flecks of spit dribbling from the corners of his mouth.

'Is this Peter O'Brien?'

'O'Brien plus 150 milligrams of chlorpromazine.'

When Jennifer crouched over him he stopped moving and gazed at her blankly.

'Mr O'Brien. Peter. I'm Detective Sergeant Jennifer Matthews. Can you tell me what happened in Mr Kirby's barn today?'

He grinned, and dribble ran down his chin. 'Lord Beltane called us from the skies through his servant the white eagle to teach his people the ancient crafts.'

'Can you tell me what happened to Donny?'

'Donny, Donny, Donny. Poor Donny.'

'Yes, poor Donny. Can you tell me what happened to him? Were you teaching him one of the ancient crafts?'

O'Brien cackled, a sharp, unexpected sound that made Jennifer flinch. 'Poor Donny was not one of his People. No, no, no. Not poor Donny.' O'Brien blinked furiously a few times. He seemed to be making a huge effort to focus on what he was saying. 'Fell on slasher. Fell on slasher. Poor Donny.'

'You won't get any sense out of him, Sergeant,' the ambulanceman said over her shoulder. 'We had to treat all the patients to get them settled down. As far as we can see, they found the lad lying in the barn and began calling for help. Mrs Kirby came to see what was wrong, and her husband dialled the emergency services.'

Jennifer climbed out of the ambulance and took out her notebook. 'If you'd kindly give me your name . . .'

When the two hospital vehicles had moved off down the drive, Jennifer Matthews asked Ben and Janice if they were prepared to make their statements while events were still fresh in their minds. Several cups of coffee later she left Brianne Mill with two sheets of paper. One told how Ben had heard the noise of shouting from the barn and found everyone inside shrieking for help. The other said how Janice had done much the same thing, but she could not remember what had happened between hearing noises from the kitchen and the first ambulance arriving. Too shocked, which was not unusual. Nothing conclusive, but things seldom were. Plenty of questions, though. For one thing, why were high-security hospital patients working on a farm building in the first place?

Roy Ormley's computer screen bleeped, and a new e-mail flashed onto his screen. It was from Alex Searle, the general manager at Lindisholm Hospital:

For Your Information

Farm manager reports an incident at Brianne Mill involving one agency labourer and nine hospital patients from a work-in-the-community project. Labourer taken to hospital in Carmarthen. All patients returned safely. Local press might pick up the story, but no sign yet. Official reaction to possible press enquiries: hospital patients on standard rehabilitation programme were not directly involved in the accident. The local police have been informed.

A. Searle

It was, on the face of it, routine notification of an incident by a senior company executive to the directorate. No further action necessary. Had it not been for the location, Ormley would have filed it for automatic archiving after the statutory ninety days. But this concerned Brianne Mill – subject of Fred Newson's recent report about Ben Kirby, investigative writer and potential public relations problem. Home of Janice Kirby, beautiful, lonely and possibly responsive. Ormley nibbled the top of his ballpoint pen and decided it was time he paid Lindisholm Hospital a visit.

The police incident team arrived at the Mill at eight o'clock the following morning. Neither Ben nor Janice had slept very well, and Ben felt decidedly scruffy when he opened the door in his dressing gown to find DS Jennifer Matthews looking neat and cool in her business suit.

'Good morning, Mr Kirby.'

'Just got up,' he explained, unnecessarily. His head felt as if he'd got the worst of a bottle of Ouzo.

'Sorry to bother you so early, but there's a thing or two on Mrs Kirby's statement I'd like to check. Is she available?'

'She's not feeling too bright this morning. I was going to take her some toast and coffee. Would you like some?'

'Thanks all the same, but I haven't long had breakfast.'

'It's Java. Freshly ground.'

'All right, then. My colleagues are setting up in the barn, if that's okay. I'll see how they're doing.'

'What's the latest on the young lad?' he asked. 'Donny.'

'Still on the critical list. Lost a lot of blood, and the injury to his throat is serious. The blade cut though his vocal cords.'

'Bloody hell! How did he manage that?'

'That's what we hope to establish, Mr Kirby.'

'Ben,' he said.

'Maybe Ben over coffee.' She smiled. 'I'll be back in a moment.'

He could hear Janice taking a shower when DS Matthews knocked on the kitchen door some minutes later. All this bloody activity had woken her up. The percolator began to bubble as he let Jennifer in.

'Just in time. Milk and sugar?'

'On its own, thanks.'

She took off her jacket and hung it over the back of a chair. She was almost the opposite to Janice in looks, height, build. At least three inches shorter. Dark hair, not blonde. Compact rather than willowy. But there was the same aura of physical energy, the same direct gaze. She looked as if she might laugh a lot, when she wasn't being a police detective.

He splashed the coffee onto the table, and a few drops splattered over her skirt.

'Shit! Sorry!' A dash for the dishcloth.

'Don't worry. I do it all the time. It won't stain.'

'Bloody clumsy.'

He had a feeling that she agreed with him, and that made matters worse. She pinched the patches with the damp cloth and gave them a brisk rub.

'It'll be all right.' She sipped the coffee. 'This is nice. What did you say it was?'

'Java. We get through quite a lot.'

'I'm not surprised.'

Ben wondered if she was being friendly because of the coffee or because of the job.

'What's the problem with Janice's statement?'

'I'll have to discuss that with Mrs Kirby, I'm afraid. But I would like to ask why you had Lindisholm patients working on your property.'

'There's nothing wrong with that, is there?'

'Not as far as I know. High-security hospitals operate within the health service, not the Home Office, so the police authority has no direct involvement. However, we are always concerned if there might be a public order problem. If any of the patients had wandered off and then committed an offence, for example. Or if they committed an offence on your property and under your supervision.'

'They weren't under my supervision.'

Ben had a growing suspicion that her reason for taking coffee was not because of the coffee.

'Who was supervising them?'

'The chap who manages the hospital farm.'

'Mr Newson. And was he here all the time?'

No he bloody well was not.

'You'll have to check that with him. I was in my study most of the afternoon.'

'What were they doing here in the first place?'

'Helping to fix the roof on the barn. As far as I know, it's primarily a matter of therapy. Keeping them in touch with normal society. Part of the cure. Plus it's part of the agreement with the landlords that Newson has arranged around here. He rents some of our fields, for example, and the deal is that he arranges for selected patients to do odd jobs. The hospital maintains responsibility for them, of course. It seems fair enough.'

'As I said, all we are interested in is public order matters. Whether a crime is committed, or about to be committed.' She smiled. 'This really is good coffee. Any left?'

He poured her another cup, very carefully. Her hand and wrist were bronzed. The cuff of her blouse very white. Short fingernails with a touch of nail varnish. A hint of perfume. Beaudelaire?

'Thanks, Ben.'

He had to remind himself that this was a career policewoman sitting in front of him.

'Glad you like it. We get it from a shop in Aberystwyth. The Mecca.'

The noises from upstairs suggested that Janice was up, and about to put in an appearance.

'Yes, I know the place.'

One of the police investigation team tapped on the window, and Ben opened it.

'Just had a call from the hospital, Jennie. The young lad has fallen into a coma. Seems pretty serious.'

'Right. How's it going out there?'

'Bob's through with his photos, and we've got samples of the blood and a few of the things around the pit. Not much to go on, far as I can see at this stage. My guess is that the brushing hook was lying on the ground, and he tripped and fell on it. Unless someone deliberately cut him, but that wouldn't make any sense in the light of what Mr and Mrs Kirby tell us. It's pretty dark in that corner, and there's all kinds of rubble lying about. Evan's trying it for prints, just in case.'

'In that case you'll have to get prints from that farm manager too. He got hold of the bloody thing yesterday. Let me know if you come up with anything.'

Jennifer leaned across Ben to close the window, and Janice came into the room. Stopped dead.

'Any of that coffee left?'

Ben peered inside the pot. 'I'll make another one.'

'Don't bother. I'll have tea.'

'Detective Sergeant Matthews would like to go over your statement.'

'Is that right?'

'Just a couple of points, Mrs Kirby.'

'Fine. Ben, why don't you take a shower while we do that?'

It wasn't so much what she said as the way she said it. Janice
was utterly, truly pissed off. When he was standing in the bathroom
waiting for the shower to heat up, he sniffed under his armpits
and groaned. Not the way to create a favourable impression with
a detective sergeant wearing Beaudelaire!

Jennifer Matthews stayed silent while Janice boiled water and
poured it over a Lady Grey teabag in a mug. Even in jeans
and an old sweatshirt, Janice Kirby looked stunning. She also
looked very uptight, which was understandable, under all the circumstances. Jennifer wondered which particular circumstance was
making her most uptight: the accident in the barn; getting up too
early because a pile of working coppers had descended on her;
settling into a new home? Not for a moment did Jennifer think
it might have anything to do with another woman sitting cosily
in her kitchen drinking *their* brand of coffee out of *their* mugs
at *their* time in the morning. Leaning over *her* husband. She
took Janice's statement out of her case and put it next to the
statement.

'I just need to check one or two things.' She took her notebook
from her bag and put it on the table.

'Such as?'

'Your husband says he heard shouting and screaming while he was
on the far side of the house. He recognised your voice calling for him.
On the other hand, you stated that you heard noises coming from the
barn while you were in the kitchen. If that's true, then he couldn't
have heard your voice in all the shouting. Not at first, anyway. So
when did all the shouting and screaming start – before you went into
the barn or after?'

Janice frowned. Things were still very hazy. 'I'm not sure. Can I
see?'

Jennifer passed her the statement. Memories plucked, and she
shuddered.

'I was cleaning vegetables, and there was a kind of moaning noise.

124

Not a loud noise, I thought it might be the wind. Then I realised it was coming from the barn, so I went to see.'

'So you didn't hear shouting at first, like you said originally.'

Janice shook her head. 'I don't think so. Moaning, not shouting.'

'You hear moaning, and Mr Kirby hears shouting, with your voice thrown in for good measure. Which means that the shouting must have started somewhere between you leaving the kitchen and arriving at the barn.'

'Oh God,' she said. 'They were letting him bleed to death. They were all lying on the floor like some kind of ritual was going on while that awful man in the yellow overalls held him over the hole. The woman was holding the sickle thing. God Almighty.'

Janice began to shake. Jennifer thought for a moment that she was becoming hysterical, but she took several deep breaths and forced herself to calm down.

'There was a woman patient?'

'Yes. I heard Fred Newson call her Joan when they were getting back into their van. It was absolutely horrifying. I didn't remember it yesterday. I'm sorry.'

Jennifer scribbled notes, remembering all the cautions about the vagaries and unreliability of witness statements. A woman going into a dark barn where an accident had happened. Who knows what tricks the mind can play?

'If what you say is true, there are serious implications, aren't there? You have to be very sure about this.'

Janice recalled O'Brien's face. The leer. The knowing nod of the head. The whisper.

Help! Young Donny's hurt himself.

'I'm very, very sure.'

DEATH OF ANTELOPE

There she is, working her way down the potatoes. Antelope. Large doe-eyes restlessly flitting this way and that, as well they might. Danger is ever-present. Especially for someone who blabs secrets into the unclean ears of a Bastard, and the Bastard annotated these words in her digital recording and sent e-mails to the supervisors and asked her other patients about Omega Cloister and White Eagle, which was why the People knew about Antelope, which was why Bull and Spiderlady were slowing down as they neared the far end of the row of runner beans in the market gardens that surrounded Lindisholm so that Antelope could catch up with them as she moved along her row of potatoes.

Lamb and Jackal Three are already there, and for a moment or two there is a jumble of bodies with Antelope at the bottom, held still so that Spiderlady can insert the hypodermic needle deep into Antelope's anus and discharge the cocktail of sedatives, tranquillisers, amphetamines, nerve blocks and corticosteroids and other stuff deep into her lower bowel where no needle mark will show up, and from then on it is like a royal performance of Swan Lake or some such other balletic shit, with Antelope spinning this way and that, wondering what happened and what this numb feeling is that keeps giving way to manic impulses to jump and shriek with pleasure and pain that amplifies to ecstasy and agony. And we all begin waving our arms towards the surveillance cameras and shouting, Help! Help! But by the time the Bastards arrive Antelope has already broken her own back in one last, supreme muscular spasm, with everyone yelling and wailing helplessly, and the Bastards looking guilty, because this isn't supposed to happen, and they assume it must be their fault.

Everyone is splitting up for evening counselling and medication, and the Bastards are all subdued on account of Antelope. What on earth could have gone wrong, they'll be asking themselves? Who on earth could have got it wrong? How on earth can we sort it out?

Not too difficult for them. There are more qualified doctors in the Place than you could shake a death certificate at. They'll think of something suitable. A fit. A seizure. An aneurysm. A thrombosis. A coronary. Take your pick, oh ye Bastards. Antelope probably died of them all. The Lord's Will be done!

TUTOR NOTES
Another contribution from 'Lion', and I must say he has an extra-ordinary ability to create a situation in which the reader is drawn into his phantasmagorical world of horror and evil. The thought occurs that the student might be basing his story on an actual event. Must check this.

12

Alex Searle stared at his screen distastefully. The message informed him that Roy Ormley was arriving on the midday train that terminated at Swansea station and expected to be picked up by a limousine and booked into the Royal Hotel in Lampeter. It wasn't the extra work involved in having a CareCorp director on site that was worrying Searle; it was the possible repercussions. People like Ormley didn't lift a finger unless they had a hidden agenda. He decided to pay Newson a visit at the farm.

'Quite frankly, Fred, this is the last thing we need. People like Ormley are bad news.'

'I quite agree, Alex, but we're stuck with it. He's probably worried about the Brianne Mill incident. From a PR point of view, can't say I blame him.'

'That's all very well, but he could stick his nose into all kinds of things, like you-know-what.'

'Ormley's only here to make sure all the shots are covered. You know how paranoid London can be.'

'The latest report says the lad's critical. What if he pegs it? The shit'll hit the fan, that's what!'

'Take it easy. Donny Talgarth works for the labouring agency, not the hospital. I only take people on who haven't any family strings. New Age travellers, New World rovers. Drifters who need cash-in-hand and no commitments on either side. They come, they go, and no one gives a damn. Works perfectly, so don't worry.'

Newson was right. Roy Ormley didn't give a damn about Donny Talgarth's accident. As far as he was concerned, there had been a minor cock-up. Nothing the local management couldn't handle. But Lindisholm was a vital part of the CareCorp empire. Lindisholm was a flagship enterprise, a jewel in the CareCorp firmament. It was the prototype for a chain of similar enterprises across the developed world. A foolproof and cost-effective way of dealing with society's fuck-ups. Best of all, an ethical investment, while ethics still commanded a significant place in the investment markets. None of the key market movers knew about the plan, of course, and Keith Melton wanted it to stay that way until he was good and ready to let a few clues slip in the right places. Ormley's job was to keep the communications lid on anything that might threaten the success of this billion-dollar venture. And if a threat appeared, he had to find out who was involved, why, and what to do about it. That was his job, but it was not the only reason he was stepping distastefully out of the Pullman onto the platform of Swansea station, with its hubbub of backpacking students, provincial mums with collapsible baby carriages, and dull-eyed sales representatives with laptops in plastic briefcases. It was all too stultifying for words, but Ormley was motivated by something that transcended the banality of the provinces: the possibility of a new sexual conquest. He had taken everything a large metropolis had to offer in this respect and found it deeply wanting. The bored career girls, the proficient and expensive hookers, the randy housewives, the sexually starved and the sexually satiated. It had become a formula. He knew how they worked, and they knew how he worked, and in the end nothing worked. It all became mechanical, and then – occasionally – something, someone, blew away the filth and made him feel alive again. Janice Kirby had done that, just with her voice and her photograph. Ormley was in a state verging on mania and panic: he had to meet this woman, even if it might prove to be yet another disaster.

There was only one way to find out, and that was why he was looking for the peaked cap of a chauffeur holding up a cardboard sign with 'Lindisholm Hospital' scrawled on it in black letters.

Young Donny died an hour before Ormley's arrival in Swansea, just as the police team at Brianne Mill was about to put away the ribbons, the specimen jars and the fingerprint powder. The surgeon in charge of the case said it was probably a blessing in disguise. His brain had been starved of oxygen for too long. If he had regained consciousness, chances were he would be in a vegetative state, hooked up to nutrients and waste bottles for the rest of his life. Poor, poor Donny. So the police team left the black-and-yellow plastic barrier ribbons round the hole in the barn, in case the coroner wanted a more detailed forensic examination, and everything jerked into a new gear. Suddenly people were talking about accidental death and inquests, but beneath the talk there were suggestions of something other than accidental death. Ben wished he knew how these rumours began, how they were promulgated. Then Janice dropped her bombshell.

'You did what?'

'I changed my statement. That appalling bastard in the yellow overalls was trying to kill him, and he bloody well succeeded.'

'You can't be serious. The hospital says that O'Brien was trying to pull him out of the hole, and when you arrived they all panicked.'

'O'Brien didn't panic. He smiled at me.'

'For Christ's sake, Janice, it was too bloody dark in there to see anything that clearly.'

'I saw enough to know that no one was trying to save him. They were all lying on the ground like a bunch of noviciates in the Vatican. When I arrived, they realised the game was up, so they all started shouting and screaming to confuse the issue.'

She was staring at him, white-faced. Was she in some kind of shock?

'The issue? What issue? The poor little sod had an accident, and they were trying to help him. Why on earth would they want to kill him?'

Janice was close to tears. 'Jesus Christ, Ben. For weeks you've been blitzing my brain about something being wrong at the hospital, and now you're face to face with this you're full of crap. I saw O'Brien's face, and O'Brien was trying to kill Donny. That's all there is to it.'

'Yes, something is bloody well wrong, but it can't have anything to do with Donny. It doesn't make any sense.'

She took hold of his shirt in both hands and said very quietly, right into his face: 'Sense? We are dealing with criminally insane people here, and you're coming at me with sense?'

'Even insane people have some kind of logic.'

'Exactly. And your job is to find out what that logic is and write your fucking book.'

Despite yesterday's ordeal, despite her obvious distress, she was looking him right in the eye and laying it right on the line. This was Janice at her best. This was why he had fallen in love with her, married her. She cut through the shit and laid it out for him to see. They were growing apart, and she still did it. And he still loved her. It was crazy.

'Okay!'

'Right,' she said. 'And there's one more thing I'd like to know. Do you fancy her?'

For a split second he was tempted to ask who, but there was only one 'her' in the frame.

'No,' he said. 'I don't fancy her at all.'

She stared into his eyes, searching for some kind of verification. Maybe she found it, just before he realised that he did fancy Jennifer Matthews.

'There's one more thing. Wesley was there. He knows what happened. The gloves are off with Wesley, as far as I'm concerned. If they let him come here again, you ask him what the hell is going on.'

13

The Lindisholm chauffeur glanced at his passenger in the driving mirror. The big shot from CareCorp. Word was, he was up here to deal with public reaction to the accident in Penford. Probably going to kick someone's arse. Well, he was going to need a pair of very heavy boots now that the kid was dead. Ormley probably didn't know yet. Maybe he should know. But common sense prevailed. Never volunteer anything, especially bad news. The chauffeur overtook a tractor pulling a hay wagon. Nice car, the Lexus. Plenty of power when you needed it. Not that this London bugger was taking any notice of his driving skills. Too busy trying to use his mobile. The chauffeur watched him for a while, then decided to tell him the problem.

'Hand jobs are no good in the mountains, sir. Try the car phone. It usually picks up signals round here.'

It did. Ormley got out his pocketbook and began looking for numbers.

'Star-one gets you the hospital switchboard. Star-two is a direct line to the general manager. Star-three is the main CareCorp switchboard in London.'

'Thanks.'

Ormley pressed the button that raised the glass screen to cut off the man's babble. He had been burning to make this call. Would she sound the same?

'Brianne Mill.'

Shit. It was the husband.

'Mr Kirby?'

'That's me. Who are you?'

'Roy Ormley. Perhaps you remember . . .'

'Oh, yes. Thanks for all the bumph. Very helpful.'

'Sorry it took so long.'

'No harm done. What can I do for you?'

'I'm visiting the hospital on business, and I wondered if you and Mrs Kirby might be free to join me for lunch or dinner over the next couple of days. There's something I'd like to discuss with you both.'

'Like what?'

Like, when will you be out of the way, so I can make a straight play for your wife?

'I'd prefer not to go into it over the phone. You know how it is.'

Ben did not know how it was, but he was intrigued and concerned. Had this smooth-talking bastard got wind of his writing project?

He needn't have worried. Ormley was thinking on the hoof. Right this minute the only thing he wanted to discuss with anybody was Janice Kirby. But not with her husband.

'We're actually quite busy at the moment. I'd ask you over for a coffee, but the place is still swarming with the Pit Bull family.'

'Pit Bull family?'

'The Police Incident Team. P-I-T, Pit. Pit Bull. You know. They're trying to figure out how this young lad died.'

'Sorry? You're breaking up. Police what?'

The line was crackling, like it does just before contact is lost.

' . . . Incident Team. They're investigating how that young worker could have cut his own throat like that . . . Tragic. I suppose that's why you're up here . . . Hello? Sorry, can't hear you any more . . .'

'Who was that?' Janice asked.

'That bloke from CareCorp. The one who screwed up getting their annual report to me.'

'Roy Ormley?'

Janice remembered the laugh. Deep. Knowing. Exciting.

'Right. He's here visiting the hospital.'

'And . . . ?'

'And he asked if we were free for lunch or dinner. Says he's got something to discuss.'

It was like pulling teeth!

'So . . . ?'

'So I told him we were busy. I'm poking into his business. I don't need him poking into mine.'

'That's charming. How about asking me what I think?'

'When did you ever want to meet some company shithead?'

'Since I moved here and got stuck with a husband who doesn't bother consulting me when someone asks us out to dinner.'

'Or lunch.'

'I'd prefer dinner, thank you.'
Jesus. He couldn't do right for wrong!
'Okay, okay, I'll call him back.'
'Don't bother.'
She really was pissed off again. Deeply, truly, pissed off.

14

Ormley tapped the phone, like you do when it's not working properly. He wasn't sure what Kirby had just said about the kid who was injured, but what little he had heard didn't sound too good. Suppose the lad died? There'd be coroner's courts, internal reports, external reports, the press and – worst of all – the awesome Professor Jonser sticking her heavily IQed brain into everything to make sure that nothing affected the smooth running of patient treatment. Of all the many notable people Ormley had ever met, Jonser was the only one who truly frightened him. She was an expert in everything that was designed to reveal what someone was thinking and not what they tried to present to the world. Body language? Jonser had written the definitive work on interpreting its convoluted choreography. Psychometric testing? Jonser did it on the hoof. No cumbersome forms, mind maps or charts for her, thank you. The ghastly woman was a walking lie detector. Ormley put the phone back in its cradle and lowered the glass partition. The chauffeur's eyes were switching from the road ahead to the driving mirror, which gave him a view of the passenger seat.

'You're Brian, aren't you?' Ormley always did his homework with staff names. It impressed the hell out of them.

'Yes, sir.'

'So, what's the gossip on the incident at Brianne Mill?'

'Gossip, sir?'

'One thing I've learned in business, Brian, is that you people in the car pool always know what's going on before the rest of us. What do you think happened over there?'

Brian knew very little, but a few whispers were drifting around, as always.

'The patients who were there are still in therapy. Seems the kid slipped into a hole he was digging and cut his throat on some kind of sickle. The patients tried to help him, but they all got too hysterical. Then the owners of the farm called the emergency services . . .'

Hysterical? Still in therapy? Digging a hole with a sickle? What the fuck was going on?

'How is the boy doing?'

Brian glanced in the driving mirror, a brief satisfaction that he knew more about something than a company director.

'He died a couple of hours ago.'

Ormley groaned to himself. More trouble. So he looked for a bright side, as he always did when things went wrong. The bright side was, it gave more reason for his visit to Lindisholm. More justification. Excellent.

Alex Searle had laid on afternoon tea for the head office arrival. The first time Ormley had visited the hospital, the cakes and scones and the way the Alpha patients who served him kept staring with their slack eyes made him feel sick. He was a confirmed Marks & Spencer prepacked food man, and nourishing organically grown, stone-ground, wholewheat flour and tasteless greengage jam was not his diet of choice. Not to mention the goat's milk in the herbal tea. Searle laid on the tea every time Ormley visited the damn place, and he had run out of excuses not to eat or drink anything. *Sorry, Alex; had something on the train . . . Sorry, Alex; a touch of the collywobbles.* So he nibbled and sipped and nodded at the patients.

'They always get a kick out of seeing someone enjoying their food,' Searle said seriously. 'And the medical team place great value on these things. A further step towards rehabilitation.'

'Good to make, good to eat, good to make, good to eat,' one of the patients babbled at them.

'That's right, Alice,' Searle said.

'Good to sow, good to reap, good to sow, good to reap. We sow, we reap, we make, we eat. He likes it, he likes it. Soon they will all like it. Gifts from the Lord, gifts from the Lord . . .'

'It's all right, Alice,' Searle said firmly. 'You can take Mr Ormley's plate to the kitchen now.'

Ormley never got used to this. Just how the fuck was a demented old bag like that ever going to be rehabilitated into normal society? He put on his most sympathetic smile.

'Thank you, Alice. Very nice.'

She began babbling again, and a male nurse in a white gown appeared through the door like a genie and led her away.

'So. Before I meet the others, tell me what the hell happened to this young lad?' Ormley asked.

'A genuine accident, Roy. Nothing for us to worry about.'

'There's always something for us to worry about. "When you're at the top of the tree in a gale, no publicity is good publicity,"' Ormley quoted from Lord Balacombe's extensive Mission Statement. He made his voice sound serious, as if he believed in all that homespun crap. 'Which patients were involved?'

Searle pushed a list towards him.

'A Gamma?'

'O'Brien's counsellor has been very happy with his progress. He was recloistered from Delta to Gamma status before this happened. He's been quite badly traumatised. They all have.'

Once again, faint warning bells rang for Ormley. Gamma patients were, in the main, psychotic, and as far as he knew psychotics were not noted for faint-heartedness. Their medical condition was not, of course, his responsibility. But getting all the facts absolutely right was essential for any public affairs director. You could lie all you wanted to, but you had to know exactly what you were lying about. Most of the people that Ben Kirby had pilloried in his book had failed to observe that simple truth.

'Have the police been here?'

'You bet. One of Lampeter's finest turned up shortly after the lad was injured. She wanted to interview the patients involved, so I sent her to Professor Jonser to put her straight.'

Ormley nodded. A secure hospital meant just that. Secure for the public, but also secure for the patients. In any case, someone sectioned under the Mental Health Act is by legal definition not competent to give evidence. Still, Searle and his colleagues seemed to have things under control. Only one more question.

'How are the Kirbys taking it?'

'Quite a shock for them, especially Mrs Kirby, but Fred Newson assured them that the hospital assumes total responsibility for any repercussions.'

'Splendid. Bert will need your report by close of play today.'

Bert Cook was Ormley's press manager in London. He did the leg-work with the media after Ormley had decided whose strings to pull.

'Not a problem.'

*   *   *

137

For the rest of the afternoon, Ormley had meetings with the heads of departments. This was largely cosmetic; they all submitted monthly reports by e-mail, and Ormley scanned each one to make sure nothing was out of line. No surprises lurking to upset Keith Melton's secret development plan. The only discordant note came from the hospital education officer, Sheila Sallis. Once again, self-sufficiency was the aim. Some of the hospital patients were qualified teachers and others had qualifications in trades and professions, but they still needed outside teaching help, and Sallis organised classes inside the hospital in conjunction with the local education authority. This teaching programme had a practical value and it also looked good on paper. Some patients were entered for public examinations each year, and Ormley gained a great deal of positive publicity in prestigious publications from their exam results. More importantly from CareCorp's point of view, Lindisholm ran testbed facilities for computer system development, not only in the treatment of mental health but also in cognitive research and education. The contracts were worth a great deal of money and were not controversial, unlike conventional drug research.

'We can deal with most of the academic subjects up to GCSE level,' Sallis was saying, 'but we're very weak on the creative and cultural side. It's a pity, because some of the patients show considerable potential.'

It was after six o'clock, and Ormley was only half listening. He had to phone the Kirbys again. Maybe he could persuade them to have dinner, despite Ben Kirby's claim that they were too busy. How could they be too busy in the middle of the country, for God's sake?

'Maybe you could get one of the local schools to lend you an art teacher.'

'I thought of that, but their budgets hardly allow for their own requirements, let alone anything extra. We offered to pay, but they saw that as competition. I interviewed a post-graduate student to start a creative writing course, but he couldn't spell, never mind write poetry.'

'Right,' Ormley said, standing up. 'Keep up the good work, Sheila. We're relying on you to help us get some more stories into the press. Now, I wonder if I might use your phone?'

She realised that he was dismissing her from her own office, but the smile made it worthwhile.

'Of course, Mr Ormley. I'll just get my things.'

When he dialled the Kirbys' number his fingers were shaking. Some people go to pieces over alcohol, others over cannabis or cocaine. With Ormley it was sex. It wasn't that he had a direct problem with his fixation. Sex was wonderful, necessary. It was the side-effects that gave him grief. The time, the expense, the unwanted emotional entanglements, the feeling at the end of it all that he had lost something. After each encounter he swore to himself with deep sincerity never to do it again. Sometimes he could go for days, working happily at being a highly paid CareCorp director, only to find his eyes trapped by a female shape or his nose reeling under the onslaught of a provocative perfume. Or a voice on the telephone.

'Brianne Mill. Janice Kirby speaking.'

'Hello, Mrs Kirby. This is Roy Ormley. I spoke to your husband a while ago, but we lost contact.'

'Yes, he told me.'

'It was just that I was visiting the hospital, you know, all this unhappy business with the young lad you had . . . not that that's why I wanted to get together. I just thought it would be nice to link up.'

'Ben said you were wondering if we could all have dinner, maybe. Something you wanted to discuss.'

'It's very short notice, but I was wondering if that would be possible, yes.'

'We do have a couple of things arranged, but nothing that can't be postponed. When were you thinking?'

'Sooner the better, don't you think? In fact, I may have to get back to London tomorrow.'

'Looks as if it'll have to be tonight, then. There's an Indian restaurant in Lampeter. It's very good. The Shapla. Near the Post Office. You can't miss it.'

'Would eight thirty suit?'

'Eight thirty would be fine.'

Ormley requisitioned a company car to drive to Lampeter, booked into his hotel and arrived at the restaurant at eight. He secured a table for three and ordered a bottle of Indian beer. When the Kirbys arrived at twenty to nine he was halfway through the third bottle. He recognised Janice the moment she stepped into the room. Tall, short blonde hair as in the photograph. Model features, and eyes that would stop a locomotive. The man following was even taller. The husband. Alert. Irritated. Looked like a bloody rugby player. He stared around the diners, but she spotted Ormley in an instant and walked towards his table confidently. When he stood up she held out her hand.

'Good to meet you, Roy.'

'You too, Mrs Kirby.'

'Janice. This here is Ben.'

The two men shook hands and said hello.

'I really must extend my commiseration over this tragic accident, Lord knows how upsetting that must have been,' Ormley said.

'Is,' Ben said shortly.

'I beg your pardon?'

'*Is* upsetting. Not *must have been* upsetting.'

'Now, Ben,' Janice said. 'I'd really like to forget all that, at least for this evening.'

Their conversation was interrupted by the usual flurry of waiters taking coats and handing over laminated menus. Ormley ordered more beer.

'Not for me,' Ben said. 'Got to work when we get back.'

'Oh, come on, Ben,' Janice said. 'There's nothing worse than someone staying sober when someone else is getting drunk, is there Roy?'

'I wouldn't know. I'm usually too drunk to notice.'

She laughed. 'I doubt that. You don't look the kind of man who'd let a few alcohol molecules get the better of him.'

And that's how the evening continued. Janice and Ormley bouncing pleasantries off each other, causing Ben to become increasingly morose. But he did begin drinking, and after several bottles he also became belligerent.

'Okay,' he said truculently. 'What's this thing you wanted to discuss with us?'

The question took Ormley by surprise.

'What?'

'You said on the phone before we were cut off that you had something you wanted to discuss with us both.'

Ormley remembered his remark, made under pressure because he had been desperately wanting to speak to Janice, not this clown of a husband. He had to come up with something to save face.

'Indeed I do,' he said, wondering how to get out of the impasse. Then Sheila Sallis and her problem with creative classes came to the rescue. Of course. The perfect solution. 'The thing is, our education officer is finding it very difficult to get someone along to take classes in creative subjects. Your experience as a writer could be very helpful, and I know Mrs Kirby . . .'

'Janice.'

' . . . Janice is involved in art. I hope you don't think it presumptuous, but our Miss Sallis was wondering if either of you would be able to lend a hand, for an appropriate fee, of course. I think the idea has considerable merit.'

There was a silence while Ben and Janice looked at each other, faces blank.

'No more than once a week,' Ormley said hurriedly. 'I can't pretend that it would be like a normal teaching situation, but there's full supervision, and these classes always work extremely well.'

A little voice was telling him to shut up. He'd made his point. Got off the hook. Unhoisted himself from his own petard. And then, amazingly, this stuck-up writer turned the whole thing round.

'Sounds interesting, doesn't it, Janice?'

It didn't sound at all interesting. Unnerving. That was what it sounded like. Ben caught the look on her face and pressed her foot under the table.

'I mean we have friends who take classes in prisons in London. They say it's very rewarding, don't they, Janice?'

'Yes. Very rewarding.' She groped for something sensible to say. 'What kind of studio facilities are there?'

'Everything you need. Easels, canvas . . . paints.'

'I'm a potter, Roy. I use a potter's wheel, clay and slips, lots of water and a ten kilowatt kiln. I make a mess.'

She wasn't a potter. She was a goddess, and she was sucking his soul into her cool, grey eyes. He took a deep breath and managed to smile. He hoped he didn't look as strained as he felt.

'We also have facilities for sculpting and pottery, including kilns. Last year one of our patients sold a set of alabaster figures to an American collector for a five figure sum. Of course, most of the work is hardly what you'd call conventional or usable, but if anyone shows talent we try to turn it into a profitable activity, as we've done with the farm. The tragedy is, most of these facilities aren't being used, but with the right kind of tuition we might end up producing marketable pottery and publishable writing. What do you think?'

Janice didn't know what to think. She knew that Ben would be both astonished and excited. He would also be examining the possible repercussions. Was this a cunning double-think on the part of Roy Ormley? After all, Ormley was in charge of public relations for Lindisholm. For all they knew, he was thinking: Kirby could give us grief, so start controlling him. If that was Ormley's plan, he had a lot to learn about Ben Kirby. She was sure that Ben would go for it. Inside the hospital, working among patients – what better place for an investigative writer to be?

She was not so sure about her own role. It would be a good way to get back into her work, but teaching art was never easy, and teaching art to mental patients would be even more difficult. Horrendous, considering what she had seen in the barn.

'I don't really think I'd be up to it.'

'You're underestimating yourself,' Ormley said with conviction. 'It would be a great opportunity for the patients, and I have to confess I'd get good mileage out of it from a PR point of view, but that surely isn't a bad thing, is it? Mind you, I'll have to check all this out with Professor Jonser and her staff before we take things further. They always have the final say. I just need to know where you both might stand.'

The funny thing was, the more Ormley floundered on about teaching at Lindisholm, the more brilliant it sounded to him. If Jonser went for it, he could square things with the CareCorp board and stick a few more feathers in his cap. In fact, he would by-pass Jonser and go straight to Lord Balacombe. Why fuck about with the Indians when there's a chief? He was sure the old man would agree with his idea. Most important of all, he would be able to retain contact with Janice Kirby. She was looking at him. Was she feeling that incredible buzz too? How could she not? The electricity was flashing both ways – it had to be.

'I think you could say we are both interested in principle, Roy,' Ben said. 'How about we put the ball in your court and ask you to come up with a proposal? That way, we'd know exactly what we might be committing ourselves to.'

'Do you have a fax?'

'Sure,' Ben said, and gave him the number.

'You'll have it first thing in the morning.' Ormley paused, then his eyes lit up as another possibility to see Janice presented itself. 'It so happens that I've got an appointment with Prof Jonser tomorrow afternoon. Maybe you'd like to come along and have a look round the hospital while I'm still up here. You could meet Sheila Sallis at the same time.'

Ben drove back to Brianne Mill feeling very good about their evening with Roy Ormley. What had at first promised to be a boring chore had turned out to be a surprise opportunity, even if Janice found the idea too disturbing.

'I wish you hadn't told him we both could be interested,' she said. 'People still aren't taking me seriously about that bloody business in the barn. How do you think I'd feel, walking into that place knowing I might meet those dreadful people?'

'If they've done anything dodgy, don't you think they'd be banged away somewhere very safe? There's no need to worry.'

'Very reassuring!'

'Of course, we have to judge everything against the fact that the guy has the hots for you,' Ben said as they turned into the drive.

'Don't be stupid.'

'It was written all over his lascivious face.'

'He's not bad-looking, actually.'

'Really? Well, just so long as you haven't got the hots for him, that's all.'

'Don't be bloody silly.' She reacted a shade too quickly, but Ben didn't seem to notice.

'Bit odd, though, putting us in the frame for creative teaching.'

'The man's probably good at his job, and he sees a potential benefit for his company.'

'Maybe, but don't tell me they don't know what I do.'

'They know what you do, all right. What they don't know is that you're trying to do it to them.'

Ormley checked his watch and picked up the phone. Eleven fifteen. His turn to call Lord Balacombe. From ten o'clock to midnight every evening, each director had a ten minute slot to contact the chairman and report on the day-to-day issues of the company. That way, the old man kept his fingers very firmly on the pulse.

'Good evening, Roy. How's the situation at the hospital?'

'Good evening, sir. We've got no problems. Unfortunately the lad died before recovering consciousness, so no one will ever really know what happened.'

'That's too bad.'

The old bastard actually made himself sound sincere.

'Yes, sir. However, something positive may come out of my visit, but it needs your blessing. The education officer here is having a problem with her creative classes, and I believe we have found a solution. If Professor Jonser agrees, I'd like to invite two local people to come in and give art and creative writing classes.'

'That's a hospital management decision, Roy.'

Meaning, why is a board director getting involved?

'I'm thinking of Ben Kirby and his wife. They recently moved into the area.'

Ormley listened to the sound of his chairman thinking.

'Isn't Kirby the chap who wrote that book, *The Façade*?'

'Yes, sir. But if we put that to one side, he's ideal. Having an established author give writing classes would be a real PR plus. Same goes for his wife. She's a well-known potter, and we already have all the equipment in place, so cost will be minimal. There's huge publicity mileage to be gained out of this, especially if any of the patients turns out to have talent.'

'Roy, you cannot seriously be suggesting this.'

It was moments like this that Ormley relished. His fast thinking had once again led him onto dangerous ground and the adrenaline began to pump round the system. It was all or nothing, the business equivalent of an aerial dogfight. Melton and his City lackey Balacombe had a lot hanging on the Lindisholm project. Any error of judgement, any mistakes, and Ormley was facing a terminal career situation. It was time for Ormley to be bullish.

'I am suggesting it very seriously indeed, sir. Look at it this way. Apart from confidential patient records, we have absolutely nothing to hide from Ben Kirby. Quite the contrary. We have everything to show him. Imagine how it will look to the outside world: CareCorp opens its doors to the author of *The Façade*. Investigative writer and wife give classes in high-security hospital.'

Ormley paused, then threw one of Balacombe's homilies back at the man. '"Knowing thine enemy is not enough. Get him inside, and get him on-side."'

'You know, Roy, I sometimes think you're too clever for your own good.'

'Can I take that as a "Yes", Lord Balacombe?'

Balacombe allowed himself a smile of self-congratulation. He had picked a good fellow in Roy Ormley. The chap could be played like a frisky trout. He made another annotation in the notes he would relay at the end of his evening phone calls to the man who ran CareCorp, Keith Melton, the founder and major shareholder.

LION'S REVELATION

Drugged to the scrotum with lithium salts and an intraventricular infusion of dopamine and norepinephrine, I was confined in a straitjacket and propped up in a chair in front of two senior clinical Bastards who asked me a bunch of questions along the lines . . .

'Okay, Geoffrey, we've done an RA trace and a chemical footprint analysis, and the drugs we found in Rosalind McMichael came from the same batch as the ones we gave you. Any idea how?'

And.

'Have you any idea what she meant by "White Eagle" and "The Place"?'

And.

'You do realise, don't you, that you will stay in Lindisholm only for as long as we believe there's a chance we can cure you, otherwise it's back to your Army chums!'

RA trace? Chemical footprint analysis? Who the fuck did the Bastards think they were kidding? Everyone in the Place gets drugs from the same fucking batches, don't they? Everyone knows the Bastards aren't here to cure anyone. They are here to make money by dosing the People so they can monitor side-effects and set up commercially profitable enterprises using slave labour. Well, Antelope's demise has given them some more clinical data – how much strychnine it takes to make a person break their own back when acting in conjunction with muscle relaxants. They should be handing out weekend passes, not giving a person a hard time!

But Lion knows how to play their game.

'I wish I could help, but I was all drugged up, wasn't I? Maybe she was hallucinating, you know, dreaming about white eagles in high places. I do that. Sometimes I think I'm a lion, you know, king of the jungle, moving effortlessly over the veldt. It helps me to get through the day. And I know what you mean about getting cured, really I do. I'm doing the best I can. You've got to believe me.'

That was cool, telling them about Lion. Very cool. I could see that I was creating a good impression, all trussed up in Velcro and Kevlar but acting like I was in a job interview.

It was at this precise moment of cosmic time that I received my true conversion. For a split second it scared the shit out of me. I thought that I'd already been converted, but compared to this, compared to this . . .

I smiled with mega benignity at the Bastards while the wonderful conversion filled my brain and body with awesome power. So complex, and yet so simple.

I – Lion – can do absolutely everything I want to do, and there is nothing they can do to stop me, apart from sticking me in this fucking straitjacket, which is no big deal, because they eventually get tired of lugging you to the crapper.

At this glorious moment, I received my vision, direct from White Eagle. It felt like he was standing right beside me, breathing his wisdom into my ear.

All I have to do to achieve perfection is to beat the drugs. Fight them every inch of the way. Battle against them. Counteract their wicked influences. Transmute. Mutate, like the mosquitoes that mutated against DDT. Think of it! No matter what they pump into my arm or force down my throat or how they foul my water, I, Lion, will remain dominant and perfect.

And having achieved perfection, what then?

Before my conversion, this problem would have thrown me into a towering rage of jagged frustration. But for the first time in my life I was content not to know an answer, because I knew with all the certainty in my being that White Eagle would tell me, when the time is right. I leaned forward towards the Bastards and nodded assuringly.

'I have seen the white eagle, and he tells me that I will be cured within the walls of the Place.'

God Almighty, I'd done it again! I had uttered words that were not to be spoken. White Eagle. The Place. Just like Antelope had done, but so cunningly that they were unaware of my accomplishment.

At that point I began to laugh with sheer joy. They tried to carry on the interrogation, but every time I tried to say anything, another laugh came roaring out of my throat. They couldn't handle that, either. Stupid bastards!

147

TUTOR NOTES

It seems to me that Lion is blending fictional events with real experiences. It is impossible to sort out which is which. Of course, this is not my responsibility, but under the circumstances, I have mentioned the situation to Professor Jonser, and she is not unduly concerned.

15

As Ben and Janice drove past Lindisholm Farm and down the narrow road into the valley, it became apparent that Newson had not been exaggerating when he described the hospital's security. The so-called Ping Poles were situated on every vantage point, and as they approached the hospital through acres of carefully tended market gardens they could see that the perimeter was surrounded by arc lights and a thick privet hedge, behind which was another fence of ribbon wire. There was only one way in and out, a sleekly modern security unit with a weighbridge for goods traffic and separate channels for passenger vehicles and pedestrians. Disconcertingly, patients were walking through the gates with no apparent check on their progress. Most were wearing green and blue overalls, with a few yellow and one or two red-clad patients among them.

Dominating the scene was the hospital building itself. From the approach road it seemed as if a gigantic space wheel had crashed from the heavens and come to rest on its side, white, glistening and strangely disturbing.

'There's your target,' Janice said quietly.

A security guard came towards them.

'Mr and Mrs Kirby?'

'That's right,' Ben confirmed.

The guard spoke into his mobile phone, and a stocky man with a pugnacious expression came out of the entrance building, hand outstretched.

'Good morning. I'm Tim Johnson, head of security. Welcome to Lindisholm. There's a couple of formalities, so if you'll come inside . . .'

'Inside' was a miniature version of a NASA space centre. Banks of TV screens were laid along the back wall, and an operator was sitting in front of a large curved display of the hospital and its immediate environs, with green, blue, yellow and red dots moving slowly around. A sculpture of concentric rings was installed in the wall above the equipment, green, blue, yellow and red stone, with the Greek letters alpha, beta, gamma and delta assigned to the rings and inlaid with gold leaf. As a symbol of Lindisholm Hospital and its four cloister system, it was very impressive.

The only other person in the room was a patient wearing blue overalls, a tiny figure with a wizened face and large bright eyes that watched them both intently.

Johnson pushed a flat box towards them.

'Just write things out with the stylus, like you would on paper,' he said. 'Capital letters are best.'

Ben was aware of most of the new technologies involved in the reception area, but he had not seen them integrated before. This was a direct entry system for handwritten information, and he wondered how efficient it would be. He found out five seconds after he signed his name, when a flap opened in the counter and a tag bracelet emerged. A minute later, another one issued forth for Janice.

'We have to secure these on your wrists for the duration of your visit,' Johnson explained. 'Reprogrammable Dual Discriminating Tag Technology. Polycarbonate casing. Kevlar and carbon fibre straps. Tamper-proof and practically indestructible. State of the art! We remove them when you leave.'

At that moment, Roy Ormley appeared. Ben presumed the system had informed him of their arrival.

'Good morning to you,' Ormley beamed, seizing their hands in turn. 'Janice, Ben. On behalf of our chairman, Lord Balacombe and the staff, welcome to Lindisholm. I trust Tim has been looking after you properly.'

'Impeccably,' Ben said.

'Jolly good, jolly good. Perhaps we could prevail on your further services, Tim, to give our guests a hint of what you and your colleagues can achieve from this unit.'

'Certainly, Mr Ormley.' In what was obviously a well-practised routine he turned towards the TV screens. 'What you see up there is a selection of key locations within the hospital buildings. Each is covered by a controlled video camera. I can change the selection or zoom into any one section using voice commands. Be so kind as to watch the screen with the red cabinet in the centre row. Charlie-Echo-zoom-in-five . . .'

The image on the screen immediately enlarged from a general view of a long room with several beds to a close-up of the central corridor.

'Charlie-Echo-turn-right-three.'

The remove TV camera responded instantly, to show a single bed with a patient lying in it.

'Charlie-Echo-turn-up-two-zoom-in-two.'

They found themselves staring at an elderly woman, skin stretched tight over her features, mouth moving as if she were chewing on something tasty.

'Angie Ultman, an Alpha patient, rest period.'

A tall, imposing woman with Slavic features and short dark hair had come quietly into the control centre.

'Ah, Professor Jonser.' Ormley sounded slightly disconcerted. 'I believe our appointment is set for three o'clock.'

'So it is, but I was passing by.'

'In that case, allow me to introduce everybody.'

Ben had read up on Professor Petra Jonser. First-class degree from Heidelberg. Postgraduate work in Berlin. Before she had accepted her appointment as Head of Psychiatric Medicine at Lindisholm she had been Head of Psychiatry at the Maudsley Institute and an adviser to the European Commission. She was also a board member of the Ziegland Foundation for Social Reintegration, the US charity whose strategies had been incorporated into the structure and operation of the high-security hospital.

'I understand Lord Balacombe has given your appointments his blessing,' she said to Ben.

There it was again. The supreme arrogance of those who believe that working for their particular organisation is the life-long ambition of everyone they meet.

'Lord Balacombe has a reputation for excellent judgement.'

The corner of her mouth twitched in the tiniest hint of a smile; so at least the woman had a sense of humour.

Tim Johnson was standing stiffly, almost at attention.

'I'm sorry to have interrupted your demonstration, Mr Johnson,' Professor Jonser said. 'Please carry on.'

'Thank you, Professor. I was just about to invite one of our guests to try and repeat my system instructions.' He turned back to the screens. 'Reset Charlie Echo.'

The image on the central screen returned to the long view of the ward.

'Start with "Charlie Echo", Mrs Kirby,' he said to Janice. 'That identifies the camera.'

'Right,' she said. 'Let's see . . . Charlie Echo zoom-in-five.'

Nothing happened.

'Mr Kirby?'

Voice recognition: an added level of security, Ben realised. He wondered if the operating program was set up at the default level. They usually were, to make life easier for the controllers.

'Charlie Echo zoom-in-five.'

Again nothing.

'There we are,' Johnson said with obvious satisfaction. 'Unless it recognises who is speaking, it will not respond. I will now demonstrate our search facility. Over to you, Simon.'

The guard at the central console nodded. 'Any suggestions?'

'Excuse me,' Janice said. 'Can you find out where any of the patients are with this thing?'

Johnson nodded. 'We can get a hospital location or a GPS readout – that's our Global Positioning System – and we can also get an actual image, if the patient is in range of a camera.'

'Can you find a young patient called Wesley?'

'Sorry, we go by codes, not names,' the guard at the console told her.

'That would be Wesley Freeman,' Professor Jonser offered. 'Alpha 99-52-7301.'

Ben wondered if the professor had memorised all the patients' names and codes. She probably had the brain power.

'Search Alpha 99-52-7301,' Simon said.

One of the thousands of green dots on the large display began to flash, and a scrolling legend informed everyone that patient Alpha 99-52-7301 was attending a maths class in lecture theatre F3.

'Charlie-November Alpha search close-up,' the guard said, and a screen to the right of the console zoomed and panned to show Wesley sitting attentively at a desk, pencil in hand. 'We can try for sound, if you want, but it's not always possible to synchronise audio with visual because of the location of the mikes.'

'No, that's fine, thanks,' Ben told him. 'Really, very impressive.'

'Right,' Ormley said. 'Let's show you round.'

Before they could move, the wizened patient in the blue overalls stood up with a determined look on his face.

'Wesley is my friend.'

'That's right, Harold,' Professor Jonser said. 'You've made lots of friends here, haven't you?'

'I know what mikes are for, don't I?'

'Of course you do, and Mr Johnson says you're a great help to his staff, isn't that correct, Mr Johnson?'

'A great help indeed, Professor. I don't know how he does it, but if any part of the system crashes, Harold can usually sort it before the backup systems kick in, can't you, old son?'

'Mr Dagby is my friend, too. He knows everything, and he told me everything.'

Janice shivered slightly. This kind of conversation was surreal, disturbing. An image of the appalling scene in the barn flashed into her mind. Christ, were they really considering getting involved in all this?

'As far as is practical, we encourage patients like Harold to take an active interest in the running of the hospital,' Professor Jonser told them. 'It helps to provide a stable emotional base if they can understand why things are the way they are.'

'Is Wesley your friend, too?'

Janice was unnerved to find Harold staring at her. 'Yes,' she said. 'I hope so.'

'Wesley doesn't like it here.'

'That'll do, Harold. Our visitors have a lot of things to see before they leave,' Professor Jonser said firmly.

Ormley had arranged for them to meet the education officer, Sheila Sallis, over lunch in the main restaurant. One of the hospital principles, he explained, was that the low-risk patients shared as many facilities as possible with the staff. Eating and recreation were included, so they sat among mainly green- and blue-uniformed patients who ate in a strangely regimented way, keeping their eyes on their plates but occasionally glancing over to the visitors' table.

Ms Sallis was a brisk, no-nonsense woman who clearly enjoyed her work. 'Only a fool would call it easy, but you'll find it hugely rewarding,' she said as they stacked their used plates on a moving belt which slid them quietly and efficiently into the kitchens. 'The difference between our classes and, say, a good comprehensive school's is that we have a far wider spread of intelligence, ability and achievement here. In a typical Lindisholm class you'll have some students who aren't going anywhere while others are capable of out-stripping the tutor. Our tutors get tremendous job satisfaction . . .'

'We're running a little late, Sheila,' Ormley said, looking firmly at his watch. 'Tell you what. Why don't I take Mrs Kirby to the art studios while you show Mr Kirby one of the classes? We can meet back here at, say, two thirty for a coffee and a chat.'

Ben caught Janice's eye and gave her his told-you-so look. She kept her face expressionless.

'Good idea, Mr Ormley. Two thirty it is. We have to go through that access point over there, Mr Kirby.'

'Call me Ben, please.'

As he accompanied her through the space between two upright chrome rods, he realised why Newson and his colleagues used the phrase Ping Poles. A soft 'ping' sounded as he passed between the rods, and his bracelet responded by emitting a single high-toned 'bleep'. The same thing happened when Sheila Sallis followed him.

'That's just monitoring our whereabouts. You don't notice it after a while,' she said. 'Not unless you try to pass into an area you aren't supposed to be.'

'What happens then?'

She smiled and took out a mobile phone.

'Simon? Hi. Sheila Sallis here. I'm about to demonstrate the exclusion signal to Mr Kirby in Alpha Cloister, Sector 12. Can you let Tim know, as well? Thanks.' She put the phone back and said, 'Why don't you go through that access point?'

She pointed to a corridor that had a sign saying Beta Cloister over it.

It reminded Ben of the security checkouts in retail shops that buzz if you wandered into the street without paying for a tagged item. 'Sure,' he said, 'so long as you're here to bail me out.'

He walked over to the corridor entrance and passed between the rods. His bracelet immediately began emitting high-pitched bleeps, and a gong above his head chimed quietly. He began to move back into Alpha Cloister, but Sallis motioned him to stay were he was. After a few seconds the sound of the gong grew louder until it echoed into the restaurant and along the corridors. The patients who were sitting at the tables fell silent and stared at him, and those who were walking past stopped and stared. Even though it was just a demonstration, it was eerily disturbing. Then a woman patient in a yellow uniform came up and took his arm.

'Back to Alpha, back to Alpha. Must go back to Alpha,' she smiled benignly. 'Back to Alpha immediately, or no communion for you, my lad, no communion for you . . .'

'Thank you, Alice,' Sallis said. 'And well done. Now, Ben, let's go and see the English language group at work.'

'So the internal security is self-regulating, then?' he commented.

Sallis looked blank for a moment. 'Oh, I see. Yes. The security staff only come if the patients can't sort things out for themselves. Over the years they have developed their own system of reward and punishment. We call it the Treatment. It seems to work very well.'

'Seems?'

'As far as we can tell. It's become an integrated part of the therapy, so it's difficult to judge because so many other factors are involved. The clinical staff monitor everything very closely, so if it didn't work I'm sure they'd think of something else.'

'What's this communion I wouldn't get if I didn't behave myself?'

'No idea. I imagine they just make things up, like parents do for children.'

Janice followed Ormley along the outer corridor of the Lindisholm complex, which curved continuously to the right, with work areas of various kinds alternating with open plan offices on each side. The general impression was of a busy, well-disciplined factory, with every patient engaged in a task. One or two white-coated men and women walked among them, stopping occasionally to talk and move on.

Ormley noticed her interest.

'We undertake light assembly work for companies as far afield as Birmingham and Plymouth. The product tasking has been chosen primarily for its therapeutic benefits, but also because the products compete with foreign imports. Good for the economy as well as the patients.'

'Are those Christmas crackers?'

'Absolutely. We have ten fabrication rigs and a packing machine, which provides employment for several dozen patients throughout the year, plus a significant income for the hospital.'

155

'What about those people ... the ones using computers and telephones?'

'Believe it or not, that's a call centre for information technology clients. Certain categories of patient are ideal for dealing with problems arising from new computer hardware and software. Your husband may well have had his queries directed here, if he's ever used a technical helpline in his work.'

Janice was still pondering this when Ormley took a left-hand turn and entered a rest area with several doors leading off it. He opened one, and they went inside a large studio with shelves full of painting materials, chairs, easels and several paintings hanging on the walls. Some were garish, with chaotic, violent use of primary colours. Others were enormously detailed, even delicate in their execution. The styles ranged from figurative to abstract, and one or two showed considerable accomplishment.

'Some of this work is very good indeed,' she said.

He closed the door, took her arm and guided her further into the room. Ordinarily, she would have felt threatened, perhaps removed his hand, but he let go before she could react.

'We have three patients who have been exhibited in London and New York. The patient who produced those oils of children has five paintings hanging in a Cork Street gallery, as we speak. Three have been sold to private collectors at what I believe are handsome prices.'

'What happens to the money?'

'Technically speaking, all patient earnings are the property of the hospital authority, but in the case of works of art we place any income in a trust fund for the patient concerned and charge a management fee. Lord Balacombe insisted that they had this facility.'

'The chairman of CareCorp?'

'That's right. An extraordinary man, Lord Balacombe.' Ormley conveyed a totally hypocritical air of respect for his boss. 'Very far sighted.'

Janice sighed and looked around. 'I don't know about this, Roy. You'd be far better off getting someone who has direct experience of water colours and oils.'

'We have tried very hard, believe me. Talking about pottery, the workshops for sculpting and pottery are over there. Would you like to see?'

'I don't think so. I can see everything is well organised here, but you have to understand how I feel about what happened in our barn.'

'It must have been very distressing for you.'

'Distressing? Christ, you PR people know how to make understatements.'

Ormley did some fast back-tracking. 'You're right. Unless I'd seen the accident myself, there's no way I could understand how you feel. I do apologise.'

Janice stared at him. He really looked contrite, and it was obvious that he had no idea that she had given the police a statement accusing the patients of a deliberate killing. It was then that she realised only Ben and the police knew about her statement. She was so close to the event that she'd assumed everyone else would know. Stupid. And maybe she was being stupid about Donny Talgarth. Maybe Ben was right. The barn had been very dimly lit. Maybe she had imagined what she'd seen and heard. The security and discipline she was seeing in the hospital made it very hard to believe that any of the patients could behave so outrageously. Everything about the place was so efficient. She took a deep breath.

'Apology accepted. I've been a bit jumpy lately.'

'Great,' he said. 'Let's have a look then, shall we?'

As she expected, most of the sculpting facilities were based on the use of clay as the main material used by the patients, but she saw some wood and stone chisels and mallets in a locked cabinet. There was a set of pedestals to the side of the pottery kiln, over half a dozen of them, holding busts of young men and women, modelled in clay and slightly larger than life size. She wandered over and touched them gently, tilting them over so she could see their bases.

'These are remarkable. Who's "GA"?'

'I suppose it's the artist,' Ormley said. 'You think they're good?'

'The proportions are beautiful. Not too sure I like the finish, but GA has a great sense of drama. Lots of emotion.' She stepped back and looked around. 'This is very serious stuff. Very impressive.'

'Lindisholm is a flagship enterprise.' There was a note of pride in Ormley's voice. He wished he could tell her about CareCorp's expansion plans. Too confidential, of course, but he could boast a little. 'We're setting the agenda for other high-security hospitals in Britain, and overseas. "What Lindisholm achieves today, the others strive for tomorrow." That's the motto.'

Janice gazed around the facilities. She had not taught classes since university days, and she had no formal qualifications in many artistic techniques. But she wanted to support Ben's writing project, and this seemed like an ideal way to do that.

Ormley was staring into her eyes. He was excited about this project, and his excitement was infectious. She liked his enthusiasm and the peculiar air of worldly-wise cynicism he generated.

And then he said, 'Maybe it's not such a good idea after all.'

He had not meant to say it, but something had happened to Roy Ormley, standing in the hospital's art studios close to the woman he had targeted as his next conquest. He did not know what it was at first, because he had never been in love before. He simply felt a sense of panic, and a revulsion of the fact that he was using her.

Janice was bewildered. 'I'm sorry? I don't understand.'

'I think we should get back to the others. I mean, at least we should sleep on this. It's a big step, and you might not like it here.'

Bewilderment changed into irritation.

'Let me get this straight. You phone us up, drag us out to dinner, frog march us into your bloody hospital, offer me this work, and now you want to sleep on it?'

Not for the first time in his life, a woman was making Ormley wretched, but this was one of the worst instances he had experienced, and he suddenly figured out why. Before he could stop himself, he put it into words.

'I'm in love with you.'

She knew he fancied her. Even Ben had seen that. And, to be perfectly honest, she liked him. Nothing physical – but she felt a kind of flattered warmth, a boost to the old self-esteem. She recognised the womaniser in the man, of course. He loved women as a libertine loves women. Couldn't get enough of them . . . used them. And yet she knew with an unerring instinct that all this had fallen apart. When Roy Ormley said he was in love with her, he was speaking no less than the truth, and it obviously frightened the hell out of him. It also frightened the hell out of Janice.

'You're right. We should definitely sleep on it.'

On their way back to the restaurant, a Gamma patient who was wrapping a small plastic spinning top into a purple Christmas cracker suddenly screamed and threw the part-assembled cracker into the air. Her screaming intensified, a gut-wrenching siren of deep unhappiness that froze Janice into startled immobility, expecting medical staff in white coats to come rushing to the rescue, waving tranquillising syringes like they did in TV movies. But no white-clad figures appeared, although Janice noticed two observation cameras turn towards the patient. The other patients stopped work, and one of them picked up the paper wrapping and the plastic spinning top and stood patiently by the woman's work station until the screaming subsided as suddenly as it had begun.

'How many of us would just love to do that every now and again,' Ormley murmured. 'I sometimes wonder if we're not the insane ones around here.'

'This is going to work out fine,' Ben said, when they met for coffee. 'There's a great reference library, and the hospital has its own website. The potential is incredible.'

He sounded genuinely enthusiastic, which upset Janice even more than Ormley had done. How could Ben sound so genuine, when his entire purpose in being here was to shaft everyone and everything connected with the place?

'Roy thinks we should sleep on it.'

'Sleep away, old girl. I've talked everything through with Sheila Sallis, and if Professor Jonser gives us the thumbs-up I start classes next Monday morning at ten o'clock.'

WHITE EAGLE

What do you expect of me, oh you Bastards? I rise above your shit on wings of pure energy. I am, yet I am not. You created me, yet you know me not. Only my People know me, and through my People you will know me.

For I am all-powerful and all-pervasive.

I see the evil you have caused, and I will destroy it.

The land that you profane, I will make pure again.

The rivers and the seas that you foul, I will return to health.

The air that you pollute, I will clear of filth.

The animals and the plants that you adulterate, I will cleanse of poison.

When this is done, I will come among my People and rest, and we will fear no evil. For I am with you. My rod and my staff will comfort you.

> *'Soul, since it was the Lord himself that blessed me,*
> *It should be well for thee, matter possessed thee.'*

White Eagle
Omega Cloister

TUTOR NOTES

A strange development. Someone is now using one of the characters created by the class as a pseudonym. Very apocalyptic, this. It's a mite biblical and 'New Age', but powerful thinking, and powerful writing. The final two lines are a quote. From where, I wonder?

16

Only when Ben walked into the lecture room and found himself the focal point of thirty pairs of brightly interested eyes did he fully realise what he'd let himself in for. True, there had been a build-up of panic at Brianne Mill over the weekend, when he failed to find some of his old books on grammar and the structure of poetry, plays, novels and other forms of writing. A scan of the Internet brought over half a million references into his study, and all the search refinements he could think of still left him with over two thousand web pages to visit. He was convinced that thirty seconds into his class he would be subjected to deeply probing questions on the merits and techniques of Geoffrey Chaucer, William Shakespeare, Harold Robbins, John Grisham and Uncle Tom Cobbleigh and all.

'Don't be silly,' Janice said practically. 'You'll be too busy getting over stage fright and trying to remember their names to worry about Chaucer. Just remember what you're really doing there.'

What am I really doing here, he thought, as Sheila Sallis introduced him to the class?

'This is Mr Kirby,' Sallis told the assembled patients. 'He is a famous writer, and he is going to help you to develop your writing skills.'

'Good morning, everyone,' Ben said.

The brightly interested eyes stared at him intently.

'I want you all to be on your best behaviour,' Sallis continued. 'Your counsellors have gone to a great deal of trouble in selecting you for this class, and I want you to show Mr Kirby the respect that you would show to any other member of staff. To make things easier for him, you should be wearing first-name tags. Geoffrey, would you stand up, please?'

A huge, bald man with a bland, characterless face stood and looked blankly at Ben. He was wearing the red uniform of a Delta patient. Red for danger.

'Geoffrey can be a tower of strength, Mr Kirby, when he puts his mind to it. You will help Mr Kirby all you can, won't you, Geoffrey?'

The huge man's mouth widened into an expression faintly resembling a smile.

'Everyone can rely on me. You know that, miss.'

'Thank you, Geoffrey. Now, class, before I leave Mr Kirby in your tender hands, let's remind ourselves of the Lindisholm way, shall we?'

The class stood up.

'We are all here to get better and better,' they said in a sing-song chant. 'We are all here to help each other. We are all here to respect each other and the hospital staff who help us.'

'Good,' Sallis beamed. 'I'll leave you to get on with it, Mr Kirby.'

Tim Johnson had explained to Ben that the room would be under constant surveillance, that automatic security systems were in place, and that a trained member of the security team would be into the room within sixty seconds of any untoward occurrence. There was also an automatic barrier that would operate if anything moved from the auditorium to the lectern. Nevertheless, as he gazed around the class, Ben felt a recurrence of his weekend panic. He counted one red and three yellow uniforms. Four patients with the two highest security gradings. What had they done to qualify for their elevated position in the Lindisholm cloister system? Ben's mind boggled.

'Please, sit down.'

There was a single, flowing movement.

'I don't know about you,' he said, 'but I believe in being absolutely frank and honest. I'm nervous being with you today, but I hope we can agree on one thing. We are here because we are interested in writing. Am I correct?'

The brightly interested eyes stared at him unwaveringly.

'We would like to know what you mean by writing,' the man called Geoffrey said. 'Do you mean writing as in calligraphy or writing as in a means of communication?'

'Good question, Geoffrey,' Ben said, and immediately had the bad feeling that he had been too patronising, but Geoffrey's expression never faltered. A polite, technical curiosity. 'I mean writing as a means of communication, but more than that. Writing as a means of expression and as a means of recording human thought and achievement. The ability to translate the spoken word into a permanent record of our thoughts. It's something that sets mankind above his fellow animals, this ability to mark and record our own history.'

'Yes.' The big man nodded thoughtfully. 'Even the cleverest animals can't write, can they?'

'Or plants. They can't write, either.' This from one of the women dressed in yellow. She looked familiar, and he peered at her name tag. Joan. God, yes. The woman who had come to help with roofing the old barn. And then another recognisable face sprang into focus: Peter O'Brien. The man who Janice swore had deliberately cut Donny's throat. The hospital authorities were clearly not paying any attention to her allegations, or they surely would not have entered him into Ben's class. He took a deep breath to steady himself.

'That's right, Joan. Although animals and plants can communicate with each other and do some pretty wonderful things, they can't write.'

'As far as we know,' Geoffrey said.

'If the Lord wanted animals to write, He would so decree,' Peter O'Brien said solemnly. 'If He wanted his People to know about it, so He would also decree.'

It dawned on Ben that if Janice were right about O'Brien and also right about Wesley saying he was frightened of the other patients, Ben could be standing in front of the very patients who were frightening Wesley. And this fear – or at least the cause of it – was what he planned to reveal in his book. The thought helped him to get back on an even keel.

'Not necessarily,' Geoffrey was saying to Peter. 'He has given us free will, has He not, so we can find things out for ourselves?'

'We will not find out anything that the Lord does not wish us to find,' O'Brien stated dogmatically.

'"The Lord giveth and the Lord taketh away,"' someone said, and then several voices were raised, quoting and misquoting from the Bible and generally adding to a growing babble.

'Excuse me, ladies and gentlemen,' Ben interrupted. 'I'd like to get on with the class, if that's all right with you.'

Everyone immediately fell silent, and the eyes began looking at him intently again.

'I thought we'd start by touching on what grammar is all about, just so we can agree on a few basic rules of writing.' He went over to the blackboard and delved into a box for some chalk. 'Can anyone tell me one of the essential parts of writing – one of the forms of speech . . . ?'

When Ben got back home after having lunch and a debrief on his class with Sheila Sallis, he poured himself a large whisky, sat on a settee with an exaggerated sigh and then held his head in his hands.

'Bloody hell!' he said with great feeling.

'Pupils give you a bad time, did they?' Janice asked.

'They sure did, but not the way you might think. There are some very bright people in that place. At least half a dozen of the class know a damn sight more about English grammar than I do. And the ones who don't catch on very fast.'

'They've probably given you the best of the bunch.'

'You think so? Well, how about this: two of the bunch were the ones you say were holding young Donny over that bloody hole in our barn. Peter O'Brien and the woman who Newson called Joan. How does that grab you?'

Amazement.

'I don't believe it! That's outrageous. What the fuck do they think they're doing, putting those people in front of you? Weren't you scared?'

'That's the funny thing. I wasn't. There's the security, for one thing. If any of the patients tried to move from the auditorium to the lecture desk, a protective screen would drop down, plus security guards can get there in under a minute. Apart from that and the coloured uniforms, it's just like a straightforward adult education class.'

'Except for the fact that they are all certified nutters.'

He sipped the whisky. 'Sure they are, but the main thing is that I'm inside that hospital once a week. What more could a guy ask?'

'So, what's next on the creative writing agenda?'

'I set them homework for next week: "What is your favourite story, play or poem? And say why in not more than a hundred words." That should start some kind of ball rolling.'

'Sounds as if you actually enjoyed yourself.'

'That's another funny thing. I did. They all seemed so, so – *interested*.'

'I suppose if you were banged away in a sterile environment like Lindisholm for an indefinite period, you'd be interested to break the routine.'

'Probably. I just wonder what's going to come out of all this, from their point of view. You keep hearing of people in mental hospitals coming up with enormously creative things, particularly painting. Take Van Gogh.'

'You take Van Gogh. I think his poppies stink.'

'Poppies was Renoir. Van Gogh was daffodils.'

'Wordsworth was daffodils,' she said. Then, after a pause, 'Do you think I could handle it, Ben?'

'Giving art classes? Sure. It's all a bit weird, but I think it'll be very rewarding. Plus we get another set of eyes and ears inside the place.'

Members of the psychiatric staff of Lindisholm Hospital were also discussing Ben's first creative writing class, via the statutory e-mail system. The teaching session had been recorded on video, and the recording had been promulgated to the consultants involved in the patient list for the class. Professor Jonser asked for comments, and all but one of the responses were ladled with self-congratulatory assessments: excellent conduct by all patients, due to keen evaluation of patient potential and efficient selection of the class members. The one exception was Dr Nikki Congleton:

> The reaction of these patients to the class conducted by Mr Ben Kirby was atypical of normal class behaviour. This is the only class on record in which bizarre behaviour and chronic symptoms of the diagnosed illnesses for the patients concerned were absent; no dysfunctionality, no erratic or anti-social symptoms. The impression gained is that each member of the class was in control of his or her behaviour, which gives rise to the question: how accurate are their clinical diagnoses? Furthermore, if patients can control their behaviour in this way, as seems to be the case, why do they not control their behaviour on a 24-hour-a-day basis? This class behaviour supports my thesis that current psychiatric practice based on the work of Freud and successive workers in the field is seriously flawed.

Naturally, this was not the report Congleton submitted to the e-mail network. It was handwritten in her private notebook, an activity comparable to a Roman Catholic Cardinal secretly using the Vatican library to compile a verification of the Koran. Her official report said: 'Mr Kirby's creative writing class was an unremarkable and unstructured event. We must wait and see if and how his class develops in terms that have beneficial (or otherwise) effects on the patients.'

Professor Petra Jonser looked long and hard at Congleton's contribution. Her new member of staff had a cynical attitude to the activities within the hospital. In itself, this was no bad thing. It is all too easy to accept everything without question; therein lies the way to lazy governance and the eventual collapse of any institution. But there is constructive cynicism and destructive cynicism. As yet, Jonser did not have enough information to decide on which side of the dividing line Congleton was working.

The following Monday, Fred Newson called at Brianne Mill while Ben was conducting his second class. When Janice opened the door, she was surprised to see him looking embarrassed. He was not, in her opinion, the kind of man who was embarrassed very easily. She did not invite him in.

'I've called because I feel personally very bad about what happened. Quite apart from anything else, we've left the roof unfinished.'

'Ben has been in touch with a building firm about the roof,' she told him. 'They're coming to give an estimate on Friday.'

'That's understandable. I'd do the same, under the circumstances. However . . .' he paused, searching for the best way to explain. 'I'd like to complete the work for you at our expense and without using hospital patients. We have three people with building experience working at Lindisholm Farm at the moment. They reckon it won't take more than five days to replace the slates, complete with new battens and felting. And it won't cost you a penny. It's the least we can do. Promise me you'll think about it.'

Her first reaction was that she wanted nothing more to do with this man or his bloody farm people. As far as she was concerned, he was responsible for what had happened to Donny, whether it was an accident or not. Newson had promised to be on site, and he'd left the premises at least twice.

'I really do not think that would be appropriate.'

'They've done work on several farms round here,' he persisted.

'Alan Walters, Tom Attwood, and Gwyn Evans, for example. They'll all be happy to give references.'

'I don't want to discuss it. In any case, I'd have to talk it over with Ben. I'm sure you understand how we feel.'

'Of course I do. Just think about it, that's all I ask. And there's another thing, I'm afraid.' She waited as his embarrassment intensified. 'It's Dr Congleton. She asked if you'd be willing to have Wesley back.'

'You must be kidding.'

'The thing is, he seemed to be progressing well while he was working here, so she felt she ought to ask, in Wesley's interest. I can guess how you feel, but I have to support her on this. Whatever else you must think about Lindisholm, the patients come first.'

The temptation to tell Newson to remove himself at top speed was almost overwhelming, but she knew that Ben might take a different view. After all, finishing the roof themselves would be expensive, and this thing with Wesley might provide Ben with much needed information.

'I'll talk it over with Ben,' she repeated.

Wesley sat in front of Dr Congleton, eyes lowered to a spot on the floor by her feet, which he could just see under her desk. Although she was always very polite and formal, he sensed her dislike. Even her efforts to make sure that he had his share of community experience seemed flaky. It was not anything tangible. He simply did not trust her. Plus, he had this problem: if Dr Congleton decided that he had overcome what the psychiatrists had diagnosed, back he'd go to court, and the whole thing would start all over again. There was no way he was going to talk about the incident in the school sports pavilion. No way.

'You seem to be making progress, of sorts, Wesley,' Dr Congleton said after she had absorbed the information on her screen. 'We are particularly pleased that you have formed friendships here. How do you feel about that?'

'Don't know, miss.'

'Take your friend Harold, for example. It says here that you first met him when you went to computer classes and that the two of you often spend free time together. Harold is not exactly the kind of person you'd meet in your local pub, is he?'

'No, miss.'

'So, can you tell me how you feel about him?'

'He makes me laugh, miss.'

'You mean you laugh at him?'

'No, miss. He says funny things.'

'What kind of funny things?'

Wesley thought hard. It was true that Harold Jenkins was funny, but it was not easy to explain why. Certainly not to someone as uptight as Dr Nikki Congleton.

'He makes up things, miss.'

Dr Congleton had infinite patience for this kind of conversation. It was being recorded, and if necessary it would show her colleagues in psychiatric consultancy how hard she worked to get to the heart of a patient's problem. It was the length of the interview and the development of communication that mattered. Wesley's actual answers were not important.

'What kinds of things?'

'He gives the others names, miss.'

'Such as . . . ?' she encouraged.

'Well, there's a big man in Delta Cloister who Harold calls Lion. He says that lions hunt in the jungles, and then he walks around like a lion, which is funny. And there's the jackals, and someone he calls Spiderlady. Harold says they have some kind of special place where they go and when I ask where, he says, Nowhere. He makes me laugh.'

'Why does he make you laugh, Wesley?'

Wesley laughed because he was terrified of Lion and the three jackals and the others who walked around Lindisholm with cold, staring eyes, so he laughed like you laugh when you're in church or when your teacher is a right bastard and you get the giggles, and then you can't stop laughing even though you could get into big trouble. But there was no way he was going to explain that to Dr Congleton, was there?

'It just does, miss.'

'Good, Wesley, that'll do for today. One more thing. I've asked Mr Newson to contact Mr and Mrs Kirby to see if they'll have you back at Brianne Mill. I believe you were making considerable progress there until that unfortunate incident in the barn.'

She paused and watched to see if there was any reaction. There was.

Wesley's expression hardly changed, but his face became a sickly grey and a sheen of sweat appeared on his forehead.

'Do you have a problem with that?'

A whisper. 'No, miss.'

Congleton felt that she might be experiencing a breakthrough. The over-sexed Wesley had obviously been resisting the attraction he felt for Janice Kirby, but the strain must have been enormous. Now he would have to carry on the resistance – or succumb to the temptation and help to prove Congleton's theory.

'Good,' she said. 'The sooner the better.'

Wesley went back to his bed for a rest period before starting a work shift carrying cardboard cartons of Christmas crackers to the hospital loading bay. They were keen on rest periods at Lindisholm. Daily medication followed by thirty minutes of rest, during which the medical staff in the control centre made at least two visual checks on their monitors. Wesley learned soon after he arrived not to move around, or twitch, or make any other sign of disturbance. If he did, a nurse would appear and increase the dose of whatever medication they were giving him. So he lay there, willing himself not to move. But he could not stop the thoughts that swirled unwanted and unwelcome into his mind. Always the image of his teacher moving towards him, her perfume, her touch, the warmth, the softness . . . And from there, the approach of the groundsman Joe Carver, the violence, the police, the court . . . Lindisholm . . .

'Hello, Wesley. Are you still my friend?'

He opened his eyes, and there was little Harold Jenkins – otherwise known as Monkey Boy – staring down at him. It was impossible to know what Harold was thinking, because his expression never changed. But he was the one person in the entire place that seemed to care.

'Right on, Harold. Best mates.'

Harold nodded. 'Mr Dagby is my friend, too. He lets me watch the computer, and I watch my friends. I am suffering from progeria, and I am sometimes a very bad person. That's why I'm here, isn't it?'

Wesley sat up. 'I don't think you're bad, Harold, no way. Not like the others.'

'Not like the others,' Harold agreed. 'Some of them are very bad. I watch them, as well. They do bad things. I don't like bad things.'

'Stay away from them, or they'll do bad things to you. So will Dr Congleton if she sees you in here while I'm resting.'

'She can't see us. I told the computer not to look at you today.'

'Are you kidding?'

'I can tell the computer anything I like. That's why the others won't hurt me. I tell the computer not to look when they go into Omega Cloister and do bad things. If I did not tell the computer not to look, they would do bad things to me as well.'

'I'm scared, Harold. They're always staring at me, and I'm scared.'

'They watch everybody. They want to see if you can help them.'

'I just want to get better and go home.'

'You can't get better, because you're not ill, are you? You can't go home, Wesley. You can never go home. That's what White Eagle said. "We are all here to serve the Lord," he says.'

'That's crap, man. We are here to get better. That's why they built this place, to make people like us better, and that's a fact. All this stuff about White Eagle is crap.'

'No it isn't,' Harold said seriously. 'I asked the computer, and it told me. It said that White Eagle lives in Omega Cloister, and sometimes Lion makes me go there with him and the others. They do very bad things there.'

'There ain't no Omega Cloister in here, and that's all there is to it.'

'Yes there is,' Harold said solemnly. 'The computer knows.'

17

Dr Nikki Congleton looked dispassionately at the new, clean bandages on Joan Corbett's arms. The nurses had cleaned and bandaged the self-inflicted wounds and brought her straight to the counselling suite, where she sat, eyes downcast, face set in an uncommunicative grimace. That was all right with Congleton. She neither expected nor wanted a communication.

'You are very lucky the nurses found you so quickly, Joan. You might have been lying there for ages, bleeding into your sheets. You might even have died.'

Fat chance of that. Not many self-harmers delivered a lethal cut. It was always a slice or two into the subcutaneous tissues, like tapping into a rubber tree. The blood leaks out, harmlessly, a crimson, messy cry for help from someone who simply cannot be bothered to live a normal, responsible life. Congleton thought of them as self-indulgent-harmers. She despised them, and she despised those who doled out love and sympathy to them even more. What they needed was a swift jolt of therapeutic reality. She scribbled out a prescription and handed it to the nurse.

'I'm starting you on a course of ECT,' she said. 'We'll begin straight away so you can get the maximum benefit. We'll start with daily treatments for one week, and if you're a good girl we'll reduce this to two a week until you're better.'

That got a reaction, all right. The expressionless face was transformed into a look of animal terror.

'No, no, no,' Corbett babbled. 'It hurts, it hurts.'

'It certainly does not hurt, Joan,' Congleton said firmly. 'It will make you feel better. You'll be able to relax, and the bad things you think will go away. I'll come with you now to make sure we get off to a good start, and I'll see you every day, so we can make sure everything is progressing well.'

The ECT equipment in Lindisholm Hospital was hardly ever used, because Professor Jonser and most of her colleagues believed that the wide range of drugs now available for psychiatric disorders presented a more effective and safer means of treatment. What they were overlooking, as far as Nikki Congleton was concerned, was the sheer punitive aspect of the treatment. Descriptions of the process seldom included reference to the unbearable headaches, the terrifying disorientation suffered by the patients, the panic of being strapped onto a table and having electrodes clamped to the temples. The sickness. The memory loss.

The word passed through the hospital like a sorrowing wind.

Dr Congleton is giving Spiderlady ECT. Poor, poor Spiderlady. Can Lion help our sister?

O my People, as Spiderlady suffers so do we all suffer. Let us cherish our sister and surround her with our love so that she can overcome the pain. And fear not, for I will release you from the Bastards so that you can fulfil the wishes of the Lord Beltane.

SPIDERLADY

The phantoms whisper her name.
Child, you survived,
But now you must die.
Your time has come.

The knives beckon.
A silvery smile of sharpened teeth.
There is no going back.
What has been learnt has been learnt:
The questions put, and recognised.
A wily enemy making gestures
To comfort and advise.

The knives beckon and glint, kindly,
Knowing what they know.
Reds, scarlet, crimson and vermilion
Wait
For the artist to begin to create
A painting of a life, without answers or hope.

TUTOR NOTES
From a technical point of view, I don't think anyone can fault this,
bearing in mind it was produced in a continuous stream of writing,
with no alterations or corrections. Dark thoughts, indeed, but once
again an awesome energy and insight into something deeply hidden.
Sounds painful. I wonder what triggered it off.

18

Roy Ormley was feeling good and bad. Good, because he had convinced Lord Balacombe that the Lindisholm operation needed his full-time attention in the run-up to going public on the development strategy. Bad, because he had no idea how he could capitalise on this development in terms of his feelings for Janice Kirby. He had agonised over every remembered word, phrase and nuance of their conversations together, trembled at the raw breakdown of his emotions in the hospital's art studio. Most of all, he was terrified that his madness would impinge on his work, show up as a professional deficiency for which there could be only one outcome: farewell CareCorp PR director. And that would be ironic, indeed, now that Janice had decided to take up the hospital's request to start art classes. In that sense, it had all worked out as Ormley had originally planned. What he had not planned on was his absolute infatuation with the woman – and this strange feeling that he had called love, right to her face, the first time he had used the word with any woman. It was all very disturbing.

He rented a cottage on the outskirts of Lampeter, a half hour drive from the hospital and eighteen and a half minutes' drive from Brianne Mill. He knew it took that long, because he had averaged it over the five journeys he had made from the cottage to Brianne Mill at various times of the day and night. On the fifth drive he was stopped by a local police car, breathalysed, and asked what he was doing on that particular stretch of road at four in the morning.

'I'm here on business, officer,' he told the young constable. 'This is the western boundary of my company's security area, and I'm checking the response times of the transponders we've installed here.'

'And what company would that be, sir?'

'Lindisholm Hospital. I am a director of the holding company, CareCorp plc.' He added the last bit in the hope it would impress the fellow.

'Probably best if you did this kind of thing in the daylight, sir. We tend to stop vehicles after midnight. Just in case.'

Bumptious little sod.

'I quite understand. Thanks for the advice.'

He followed the police car back to Lampeter, working it out in his head. A total of ninety-four minutes, thirty seconds. Divide by five. Equals eighteen minutes, thirty seconds. Exactly. That's how far away she was.

As he lay in his newly installed king-size bed, he wondered what Janice would be doing. Almost midnight. Probably in bed too. Next to that supercilious husband. Or maybe she couldn't sleep, either. Perhaps, just perhaps, she was thinking of Ormley. Why not? An attraction like this must surely be mutual. That's how Nature worked. Compatible pheromones. Mutual attraction. Maybe she didn't want Ormley as badly as he wanted her, but she had to feel some damn thing. He wondered how he could get her to visit his temporary home. *Hi, Janice. Roy Ormley. I'm having a house-warming get-together. You and me, getting it together, like no one ever got it together before.*

Ormley was right about one thing: Janice was not asleep. She and Ben were discussing Newson's request for them to have Wesley back.

'I don't have any problems with that,' Ben said. 'Do you?'

'Not really, except that I'm sure he knows what happened in the barn to that boy Donny. He was sitting up in the rafters like some bloody lookout.'

'Let's not get into that again. It was dark in there. I'm not saying I don't believe you, but the police haven't come up with anything that backs up what you're suggesting. Let's try to keep an open mind.'

'I've got an open mind. I took it into that barn and I brought it back out again. It tells me that those bastards were happily murdering that boy for whatever crazy reason. I don't care what the police found or did not find.'

'If Wesley does know, I'm all for having him back here. Like you said, the gloves are off. I'll ask him straight out who he's so frightened of, and why.'

'Fine. I'll let Fred Newson know in the morning. He can do a few chores, then drive the Shogun around. He likes doing that.'

There was a long silence as they lay side by side in the dark. He put a tentative hand out to touch her, but she pulled away.

'I'm really tired.'

'Sure,' he said. 'Me too.'

Wesley turned up on his mountain bike at nine o'clock on the following Wednesday morning, overalls tucked into his socks like a school kid. He was quiet and withdrawn, avoiding eye contact. They gave him a cup of tea, and Ben asked him to split some logs. He had a knack for splitting logs, seldom taking more than one swing of the axe for each one. By midday he had stacked enough to last a month. Ben gave him a hand piling them in the woodshed, then sat him down in the kitchen while Janice tidied the bedroom.

'We're both glad to see you back here, but there's a question I need to ask you.'

Wesley stared at the floor.

'You know that Mrs Kirby and I are giving classes to some of the patients?'

The boy nodded.

'Okay, my question is this: is there anything we should know about these people that their consultants can't tell us?'

'I don't know what you mean.'

'You know exactly what I mean, Wesley. You told my wife some weeks ago that you were frightened of the patients. So tell me – which patients, and why do they frighten you?'

'I never said that, I never.'

'Not in as many words, but that's what you meant. So, what's going on? What happened to Donny? You were there. You saw what happened. How the hell did he manage to hurt himself like that?'

'I didn't see nothing. I was working in the roof. Donny hurt himself, and the others tried to save him.'

'Mrs Kirby doesn't remember it that way. She says they were lying on the ground, chanting, while Peter O'Brien held Donny over the hole he had been digging. Upside down.'

'No, no, no . . .'

Ben knew he either had to back off or push things to the limit. He took hold of Wesley's arm firmly. 'Wesley, I don't believe you. Why won't you tell me what happened?'

'Please, Mr Kirby. You don't know what it's like. They know everything that goes on.'

'Who knows everything? If you tell me, I'll be able to help.'

176

'They'll kill me.' A despairing wail.

'Who'll kill you? O'Brien . . . the woman who was with him . . . who?'

'The people in Omega Cloister. Leave me alone!' Wesley pulled his arm away, shrank into a corner, covered his head with his arms.

'Omega Cloister! What is Omega Cloister, for Christ's sake, Wesley?'

'That's where they live. It belongs to them. That's where they take you, and no one sees you no more.'

'Look, Wesley – if you want to get out of that bloody place, you can't afford to get involved in anything weird, and Donny's death is weird. In any case, how could anyone possibly know what you tell me here?'

Wesley looked up. Ben had never seen anyone in a state like this. Sheer panic.

'If I tell you, you'll ask questions, and they'll know.'

That was fair enough. But Ben intended to ask questions anyway, sooner or later. On the other hand, maybe this was the way through Wesley's problem.

'I appreciate that, I really do. But the chances are that I could blunder along and ask the wrong people the wrong questions, and these people might think it was you that started the ball rolling. If I know who they are and what they're up to, I can avoid that.'

He could see that this made Wesley think. Maybe here was a way through the terror, whatever it was.

'There's nothing wrong with me,' the boy said desperately. 'Not like they said at the trial. Now they've put me inside, and that Dr Congleton hates me. She's never going to let me out, and if I talk to you those people will kill me.'

'I'm sure Dr Congleton would not let her personal feelings interfere with her professional judgement. But she's on staff. What I want to know is, who are the patients you're having problems with?'

'I don't want Dr Congleton to know if I tell you anything.'

'Of course not.'

'I'm already helping all I can,' Wesley said.

Ben suppressed a sigh. Perhaps it was time to back off.

'Okay, Wesley. I'll be careful anyway, and if I do everything by the book I don't see how anything bad can happen to you.' He tossed the Shogun keys across the table. 'You've done a bloody good job this morning. Go and have a little fun before we all have some lunch.'

Wesley caught the keys like a tree frog grabbing a fly. Nothing wrong with his physical reactions.

'Can I take her down to the muddy bit by the river?'

'So long as you keep her on all four wheels and hose her down afterwards!'

Janice heard the engine revving as Wesley performed miracles of skid control across the mud.

'Good God, what's he up to?'

'Letting off a little steam, I hope.'

'Did he tell you anything?'

'Not much. He thinks Congleton hates him, but she probably hates everyone. One thing is absolutely clear, though: he's scared shitless by something in that damn hospital. He called it Omega Cloister.'

'But there isn't an Omega Cloister.'

'He says some of the other patients go there, and that doesn't make sense. No one can go anywhere in that bloody place without the staff knowing.'

19

Professor Jonser agreed to schedule Janice's art classes on Monday mornings to coincide with Ben's creative writing classes, so that the Kirbys could travel to the hospital together. On Janice's first day, Tim Johnson the security chief checked the studios with her before the patients were allowed inside.

'This is one of the few places where we can't stick to our standard protection programme,' he told her. 'With everyone mingling about, we can't use drop barriers, and there's a lot of potential weaponry lying around. I'm afraid you'll have to put up with at least two members of my staff being present at all times. Just a routine precaution, of course.'

'Don't worry. I'll be glad of the company. This is all a bit new to me.'

'You'll be okay. Although some of the class will come from the high-security cloisters, they'll be here as a reward for clinical improvement. We get very few problems.' He handed her a set of keys. 'These are for the cupboards. If you'll just sign the logbook . . . everything has to be checked in and out, including the keys. My people will look after the things the patients use. All I ask is that you stay alert and report anything that seems peculiar. Don't worry if it's a false alarm. Better to be sure than sorry.'

Janice scrawled her name in the appropriate box and took the keys. 'They're not labelled.'

Johnson smiled. 'Another security ploy. You have to learn which key opens which cupboard. If the wrong person gets hold of them, they'll spend ages finding the one they want.' He looked at his watch. 'Right! You've got some time to get used to the place before the class kicks off. Eleanor Jones and Howard Tolbright will report here in ten minutes. All duty staff wear white overalls with coloured name-tags. Security is black. You'll soon get used to the system. There'll be twelve patients in the class. They will address you as Mrs Kirby. You should use their given names, which are sewn into their overalls.'

After opening cupboards and checking the contents, it was clear to

Janice that although the studios were well stocked, the organisation of tools and materials was a mess. Spatulas designed for clay modelling were mixed up with wood chisels and paint brushes, and watercolour tablets were jumbled up with tubes of oil paint. As there was no time to sort things out, she decided that the first lesson would have to be very simple. There were plenty of charcoal sticks, a shelf full of sketch pads, and two large bins in the corner contained clay. Several plastic aprons were hanging on a row of hooks, and above each hook was a name label holder. The first thing she would ask them to do would be to cut their own name-label out of the pages of a sketchbook and write their names for the hooks. Then she realised that she would have to issue them with scissors, which didn't seem such a good idea, so she decided to cut the labels out herself. Halfway though this process, the door opened and two fit-looking security staff came in.

'Good morning, Mrs Kirby. Eleanor and Howard reporting for duty,' the woman said. 'Is there anything we can do to help before the class arrives?'

Eleanor was short and dark, with an intense, determined expression. Howard had the sort of fair, good-looking face that always reminded her of Scandinavia.

'Good morning. Yes. There is, actually. Perhaps you could distribute twelve sketchbooks and sets of charcoal sticks around the work benches.'

'Certainly,' Eleanor said, 'although I think you'll find it simpler if we start with one sheet of paper and one charcoal stick. They have to sign for everything they use. It's part of the therapy more than anything else.'

'Sorry. Should have realised.'

'How could you?' Howard said pleasantly. 'Takes all of us a while to learn the ropes.'

Eleanor held up her watch and began an exaggerated countdown. 'Five, four, three, two, one . . .'

The door opened and the class filed in silently, except for a soft 'ping' as each one passed between the sensors.

'The computer knows that each of them is scheduled to report here at ten thirty. They have two minutes to check in, otherwise the system generates an exception report. It then scans the establishment to find them. If it can't, a manual check takes place,' Howard whispered. 'But that's hardly ever necessary. The place runs like clockwork.'

Eleanor held her hands up, and the class shuffled into two lines of six. 'Good morning, everyone, let's tell Mrs Kirby the Lindisholm way, shall we?'

'We are all here to get better and better,' they said in a sing-song chant. 'We are all here to help each other. We are all here to respect each other and the hospital staff who help us.'

This was it! D-Day! Now she knew how Ben must have felt, facing his writing class for the first time. She took a deep breath.

'Good morning, everyone. I am Mrs Kirby.'

'Good morning, Mrs Kirby.'

'I hope we are all going to get to know each other over the next few weeks, but the important thing is, we are all here to enjoy ourselves by trying to paint, or make models or draw things, or whatever kind of thing we like to do.'

Her voice sounded to her as if someone else was speaking, and it sounded like a load of crap. But it continued . . .

'And so Eleanor and Howard will give you all a sheet of sketching paper and a single stick of charcoal. First, you have to sign for these things, and then I want you to use them to draw whatever you want, whether it's as simple as a circle or as complicated as a vase of flowers. Just have a go.'

Eleanor held up the logbook, and the class filed up to her and collected a piece of charcoal and a sheet of paper, then they all stood, gazing at Janice. All except one. An elderly, grey-haired woman stood in front of the oil paintings of children Janice had admired when Roy Ormley was showing her around. Her name-tag said 'Dorothy'. She had tears running down her cheeks, and the others were watching to see what Janice would do about it. She glanced at Eleanor and Howard, but they had settled on chairs, one at each end of the room, and appeared totally unconcerned.

'Hello, Dorothy. Is this your work?'

Dorothy nodded. 'They have taken my children away.'

'Mr Ormley tells me that some of your work is in London, where lots of people can see it. But these are beautiful, too. There's not much I'm going to be able to teach you about painting, is there?'

'I want my children back. I want them back.'

Dorothy's distress was painful to see, and Janice searched for some way to help. 'I'm sure we can arrange that. You don't have to sell your work if you don't want to. We'll get the paintings back here for you.'

Dorothy turned to her, face absolutely blank, but the words she breathed were full of hate and disgust. 'Not my paintings, you fucking idiot. I want my children back. My children. My children.'

As she repeated herself over and over again, her voice rose slightly, and the other patients began to move forward. They were watching Dorothy now, not Janice, who stepped back alarmed. Eleanor and Howard remained relaxed, sitting on their chairs.

Gradually, Dorothy's demented whisperings subsided, and she went to stand by one of the sheets of sketching paper. The others followed her, watching Janice again.

'Right. Where were we? Good!' She desperately tried to think what to do next. 'What I'd like you all to do is draw me a ball on a beach.'

They gazed at her blankly, and she wondered if they understood what a ball on a beach was all about. This was a bloody mental hospital, after all. Maybe some of them had never seen a ball, or a beach. Christ, she hadn't bargained for this.

' . . . or maybe you would like to draw Howard or Eleanor sitting on their chairs . . .'

Eleanor and Howard took notice of this, all right. And the patients turned to look at them. One or two began giggling.

'If you need any help, please call out. Meanwhile, I'll just wander around to see how you are coping.'

Ten minutes before midday a buzzer sounded, and the patients put down their stumps of charcoal and stood still while Eleanor checked the remains and the sketch sheets against the logbook. Janice beckoned to Howard.

'I've cut small wedges of modelling clay for them to work on for next Monday. That'll be all right, won't it?'

'I don't see why not. We'll have to let their counsellors know, of course.'

Janice explained to the patients how to work the clay until it was soft and malleable. 'Once you've got it into a shape that you like, set it down somewhere out of harm's way and bring it along next Monday.'

When everything was properly logged, the patients filed out as efficiently as they had entered. Howard nodded to Janice.

'Good timing. Midday, on the dot. How do you feel?'

'Bloody shattered. I don't think I've ever worked quite so hard.'

'We all feel like that at first. It's because we have to concentrate on every small detail, but you did fine, Mrs Kirby.'

'Thanks, that's very reassuring. By the way, who should I see about Dorothy's paintings? She seems a little confused, but very keen to get them back.'

'Don't worry about that.' Howard glanced at Eleanor, who was out of earshot. 'Like she said, it's not the paintings she was on about. She wants her children back.'

Janice had visions of a young Dorothy unable to cope with some kind of tragedy involving the death of her children. Maybe a house fire, or a car accident.

'That's really sad,' she said. 'I don't how anyone could ever get over losing their children.'

'It's wasn't like that.' Howard lowered his voice. 'In the late eighties and early nineties, Dorothy Lampton was a registered childminder. She murdered thirteen children. Worst case of serial infanticide since Herod the Great.'

'Okay, everyone, we're finished here,' Eleanor called. 'Back to your assignments, and well done. You'll all have a positive report today.'

20

'God Almighty!' Ben said when Janice told him about Dorothy Lampton. They were driving up the mountain road, away from Lindisholm. She searched through the sketches.

'Here. This is hers.'

'I can't see, unless you want us to roll off the road.'

'Sorry, but it's very good. She chose Eleanor, and look what she's done. A nursing mother and child. And it's a spitting image, right down to the chair, and her overalls. Some of the other patients did good stuff, too.'

'I should imagine they've given you people with a range of abilities. That's what I think they did with my class. Makes sense, when you think about it. Keeps the tutor on his toes.'

'On her toes.'

'Right. So you liked it, then?'

'Y'know, I haven't stopped to think. Yes, yes I did like it. Very much. I took your tip and gave them some homework. They've taken a lump of modelling clay to do whatever they want. I checked it out with the security people, and they seemed happy about it.'

'Jolly good,' Ben said. 'Be interesting to see what they come up with.'

When they arrived home, Ben took the batch of writing from his briefcase and settled down at his desk with a glass of whisky, looking forward to what he would read next. In the four weeks he'd been giving his classes, the students seemed to be heading towards a crazy kind of group novel, the kind where one person writes a section, then another, then another. It was not always coherent, of course, but you'd expect that under the circumstances. Even so, it was fascinating how the writers were blending the reality of their lives together in the hospital with a spooky world of almost sinister fantasy. Certainly a bloody kind of fantasy, but Ben imagined that the use of violence in their fiction might well be an instinctive means of releasing mental pressures. That would make sense. He had also woken up one night after a dream in which the patients really were performing acts of sacrifice and cannibalism. He would try to discuss this with one of the psychiatric consultants, or maybe with Professor Jonser.

The first manuscript out of the current pile of work was written in the neat but cramped style he recognised as belonging to Peter O'Brien:

I AM JACKAL TWO

I was angry at first, being offered a chance to join this writing class. I come from a nation of writers, so what did I need this for? But Lion and the others think it is a good idea to commit to paper the precious thoughts and actions that flow from the Place. For the future generations, Lion said. Our bible. Our chronicle. That seems sensible.

Parables are good for this kind of thing, because they let us teach others and guide them towards the Way. I will begin with the Parable of the Mill:

'One day White Eagle called his People and told them that the time was arriving when the Word of Lord Beltane would be carried from the Place and into the World Outside and that we would need to prepare for this in many different ways.

'The manner in which the Word will be carried has been preordained and is not to be divulged until it is time. Suffice it to say that our preparation involves the blessing of the Earth and man's structures thereon in the manner of the Old Ones.

'And so the People took their sacrifices unto those who dwell below the Place, and they did bless the Earth and the buildings thereon with the blood of the sacrifices, that the Earth and the buildings and the enterprise of the People would be blessed until all eternity.

'And all was proceeding according to the Plan until those who dwell in the Mill below the great mountain did wickedly interrupt the Holy work of the People and cause it to be halted so that the People suffered great pain and anguish.

'Woe be upon the evil doers!'

Ben put down his pen and stared at the handwritten pages. More pagan Druid rubbish! But O'Brien's mention of 'the Mill' was a little too close for comfort. He searched back in his student file until he found Lion's references to Spiderlady. Then he checked Spiderlady's poetry, with its preoccupation with knives and death. Spiderlady's real name was Joan Corbett, and Joan Corbett had been standing next to O'Brien holding the brushing hook that Donny had fallen on to cut his own throat, 'accidentally'. Then he remembered Wesley's frightened comment about Omega Cloister and turned to previous contributions from Lion, and Jackal One.

'Oh, shit!' Ben said softly.

21

Professor Jonser's office was the height of high technology. Not a bookshelf or magazine in sight, but dozens of CD-ROMs lined in carousels above a line of computer equipment and communication cables. When Ben went in, she waved him to a chair and stared at him for a few moments. When he had phoned her to set up this meeting, she had not asked why he wanted to see her. Faced with her steady gaze he got the uncomfortable impression that she already knew.

'When I was at university in Heidelberg, Mr Kirby, we were told about the paperless office of the future. I decided that this would be one of my tasks, and as you can see I have succeeded. Everything I need to read is either in these computers or available on networks. Everything I write is dealt with in the same manner. I like to think I have contributed in a small way towards halting the world's deforestation.'

'I should think you've saved at least one entire forest all by yourself.'

She gave that tight, corner-mouth smile. 'You writers are prone to a certain exaggeration.'

'I guess we are, but not, I hope, on matters of fact or substance.'

'And did you want to see me on matters of fact or substance?'

Good question. The answer was, of course, no. Everything he wanted to talk about was supposition and coincidence. There was only one way to tackle this woman, and that was head on.

'Some of the things the class members write about are disturbingly realistic. They describe events that I've been assuming are fictional, but they weave in things that have actually happened. They also keep referring to Omega Cloister. Is there such a place here that you don't tell anyone about?'

'Why are you interested in Omega Cloister?'

'It seems to play a pivotal role in their stories.'

There was a silence. Then the tight smile raised a corner of her mouth again. Ben wondered if it were, perhaps, not a smile at all, but some kind of nervous tick.

'Some of my colleagues were against having you and your wife working here amongst us. They argued that you in particular might believe you could uncover something that would show Lindisholm in a bad light. That is, after all, your profession. Others, myself included, argued that if our work is as effective as we believe, your presence would not harm us; in fact, having you here might even be to our benefit, from what our administrative masters call "a public relations point of view". Whether this is true remains to be seen, but in one thing we were all correct. You are a very effective researcher.'

'Thank you. So what about Omega Cloister?'

Jonser reached for her computer mouse and opened a video file. It showed a patient, a huge, bald bulk of a man, hunched over a desk carefully writing on the kind of lined paper on which Ben's students submitted their stories. The camera zoomed over the man's shoulder until they were both able to see his words:

I AM LION

I look around majestically as the sun appears over the eastern horizon to send long dawn shadows across the darkened veldt, with its brown grass and teeming herds, feeling the shiver of anticipation as the final stage of the hunt begins. The Offering is still trying to satisfy the demands of Lamb and Spiderlady out there in the corridor. What a way to go! Perhaps, next time, the Beaters will bring a young female, so that I can sow my seed into her womb as she lies on the altar. It has been weeks since that happened, a long time, and my head is full of the howling, rushing wind that drowns the unclean world in pain. But this young male Offering will help. Better than nothing. First me, then the Jackals, then the others. I wonder what pleasure White Eagle gets out of all this, sitting there in Omega Cloister, cut off from the world; but that gaunt, blank face gives nothing away.

'Fascinating,' Jonser said. 'I look forward to the next episodes, as I'm sure you do yourself. I too am intrigued by the way the students weave reality and imagination so convincingly.'

Ben had been making the assumption that the patients' work would be for his eyes only. Certainly no one had asked him for copies, and now he knew why – they already had them. And Jonser seemed to have come to the same conclusion as Ben had done, initially at least. The stories were a blend of fact and fantasy.

But Jonser's air of unruffled calm was all very well! Wesley's terror had started Ben believing that there was more fact than fiction in the work. Not just Wesley's terror, either. There was Donny, and the hole, and the blood. That was real, and that was what Jackal Two had just been writing about. Fact and fiction, but where did they meet, and where did they part?

Jonser was keeping pace with his thoughts – or some of them, at least.

'I can imagine your concern, Mr Kirby, and I appreciate the trouble you have taken in coming to see me. However, I assure you that these stories are figments of the considerable imagination of your students, and so is Omega Cloister.'

'You mean they got together and invented a fantasy place for themselves?'

'In a manner of speaking.'

'Isn't that bizarre, bearing in mind we're talking about mental patients?'

'Under ordinary circumstances it would be, but Lindisholm is an extraordinary facility. We focus on developing a community spirit. People who would normally be dysfunctional work together and play together for considerable periods of time. Small wonder that they create novelties such as Omega Cloister. I dare say they have developed other constructs within the cloister system.'

'So you aren't worried about all this?'

'Far from it. I gave instructions that their creation should be developed as part of their therapy, using our computer's virtual reality capability. There is a considerable expertise in this kind of technology among the patients, and they have developed Omega Cloister into their own simulated environment. We check it from time to time and add the information to patient case notes for periodic evaluation.'

Professor Jonser's reaction was convincing, but many of the senior people Ben had pilloried in *The Façade* had provided him with convincing explanations of events. Ben was not going to accept Jonser's apparent sincerity at face value. Cynicism was what his work was about, after all.

'Maybe you can guide me as to what is real and what is virtual,' he said. 'What about the death of "Antelope", for example? Is it a fact or fiction that someone died in the market gardens, and if so is it a fact or fiction that the patients killed her, or what?'

'It is not hospital policy to comment on individual cases. As one of the policy formulators, I can hardly breach my own rules. However, you surely know that writers take real events and conjure fantasies around them.'

'Fair enough, but I assume that if someone died there a death certificate would have been registered in Carmarthen.'

She smiled again. Or was it a twitch?

'Look under the entries for April last year, if you must. I trust your fears will be allayed and that you will carry on your good work. We would hate to lose such a talented tutor.'

The register of deaths in Carmarthen Town Hall showed that Rosalind Mary McMichael had died at Lindisholm during the afternoon of Friday, the twelfth of April. The post-mortem indicated that she suffered a massive dilation of the aorta artery, which led to a fatal heart attack. Internal bruising of organs and a broken spinal column were also recorded. There were no external bruises from other injuries, apart from those consistent with a body falling. No date had been set for an inquest. Was someone holding things up?

Janice was not impressed with his day's work.

'You were sitting right in front of the woman, and you didn't ask her about Wesley or Donny! I don't believe it.'

'What would that have achieved, apart from alerting her to the fact that Wesley is a source of information and that you are convinced that Donny was murdered? I was there to sound her out, not parade my wares . . . "Hi, Professor, my wife thinks that your patients murdered Donny Talgarth, and young Wesley Freeman is terrified about some people who live in Omega Cloister – which you say is a virtual therapy unit – and on top of that we think your patients are indulging in a sacrificial ritual involving gang rape and cannibalism." Jesus, they'd lock me up, too.'

'Talking about locking you up, that policewoman phoned. She wants to see you. Again!'

'Probably something to do with your statement. I mean, that's what is hurling the shit into the air-conditioning unit.'

'She asked for you, not me.'

'For Christ's sake, Janice. You make it sound like there's something going on here.'

'You mean there isn't?'

'No more than there is between you and that tailor's fucking dummy with the Hollywood teeth and the heart-warming laugh. Christ, it's like watching a Tom cat stalking a bitch in heat.'

'You're mixing your metaphors.'

'Yeah? Well, we writers are allowed to get away with that every now and again.'

'Listen to us! Maybe we should never have left London. This place is making us act like Taylor and Burton.'

'God forbid.'

'It's true, Ben. There's hardly a day goes by when we aren't hacking at each other. What's going on?'

He had no idea. He loved Janice to distraction, but she was also driving him to distraction, and he was doing the same thing to her.

'Maybe it's the seven-year itch.'

'That happened three years ago. We got over it, remember?'

They had both indulged in wild but inconsequential flings with other people's partners. It had just happened, without any arguments or back-biting. Janice's sister Eileen had been scandalised, but there had never been any question of their relationship being faulty or seriously threatened. Not like now.

'I'm scared, Ben. I'm scared of losing you, and I'm scared of staying with you.'

Ben returned Jennifer's call, and she asked if it would be convenient to see him in Lampeter when she finished duty that afternoon. They met in a café where the owner served an excellent bowl of cawl, rich vegetable soup based on lamb stock. Just the thing for a cold autumnal day.

'I need a quiet chat,' she said when they settled down. 'Informal. Hope you don't mind.'

'All depends. I have to keep reminding myself that you're a police officer.'

He had not meant to say it, and she looked amused.

'Should I take that as a compliment?'

'More sensible to take it as a storm warning. By the way, is it Ben and Jennifer, or Mr Kirby and Detective Sergeant Matthews?'

'I'm off duty, Ben. At least, I'm about to come off duty. I'd like to discuss your wife's statement.'

'Ah! I thought that was *verboten*. Off limits.'

'Strictly speaking, it is. But we're having problems, and I need to make quite sure that her recollections are reliable.'

'You want me to comment on my wife's reliability?'

'I know it's out of line, Ben, but if she's right all hell could break loose. We've already made an application to interview the patients concerned, and although the hospital gives the appearance of helping we're getting absolutely nowhere. They insist that the patients involved are in no fit state to be interviewed.'

'If my wife says that she saw O'Brien and his lady friend holding that lad over a hole so he could bleed to death in front of half a dozen wailing nutters, then that is what happened. There was no panic or shouting until she walked into the barn, and O'Brien smiled at her.'

'I didn't mean to upset you.'

'What the hell did you expect?'

'I'm sorry.' She looked sorry. In fact, she looked really fed up. 'I have to be honest, Ben. This is new to me. In normal circumstances we would have arrested Peter O'Brien and Joan Corbett within hours of getting your wife's revised statement. We still could, in theory, but advice from counsel is to leave things alone until we get the co-operation of the hospital, and they are going strictly by the book. Unless I get a warrant, any decision to allow access to patients rests with the medical staff, and they aren't obliging. If there's the slightest doubt in Mrs Kirby's mind about what happened we need to know now. Otherwise she could end up facing some very aggressive questioning by a defence counsel at a preliminary hearing. So will you, because your statement doesn't tally with hers. And after we've been through all that, the case will be kicked out because the defendants are unfit to stand trial.'

'Let me get this straight. You seem to be saying that Janice's statement doesn't count for much one way or the other.'

'You could put it like that.'

'That's the way *you're* putting it, not me. As far as I'm concerned, if those two patients are fit enough to attend my creative writing classes, they're fit enough for you and your colleagues to interview them.'

'They're doing what?'

'Attending my writing classes. And you should see the stuff they're handing me. In fact, you definitely should see it.' He stood up.

'Now?'

'Why not now? You can also ask Janice about her statement. But do me a favour. Ask her after you've read O'Brien's contribution.'

Jennifer read the paper headed 'Jackal Two' and then shuffled quickly though the pile of stories that Ben had collected over the past few weeks, while Janice and Ben watched with interest as her expression changed.

'This reads like a horror story.'

'It is a horror story. The problem that Janice and I have is whether it's a true horror story or something that some very sick people have conjured up together.'

'It can't possibly be true.'

'Isn't that what you're saying about Janice's statement?'

'I'm not saying that,' Jennifer protested.

'Hoping, then.'

'We just don't believe that any useful purpose will be gained by proceeding down that route, but if Mrs Kirby stands by her statement we are obliged to carry on.'

'I think it's called the pathway to justice,' Janice said. 'I saw what I saw, and that monster O'Brien did what I say he did, and here you have his bloody confession. What more do you want?'

'Unfortunately this would not last a second in a court of law. It was written for a creative writing class, after all. Can't you see what a problem we're facing?'

'That's what you get paid for,' Janice said unsympathetically. 'You, the judge and everyone else. For Christ's sake, we were told that O'Brien was only let out because he was responding so well to clinical treatment. If you don't all do your bloody jobs, he'll be let out again. You want that on your conscience?'

'Of course not. But my opinion isn't the point, I'm afraid. The advice we've been given doesn't take feelings into account. Only matters of proof and evidence, and this is not evidence.'

'I don't want to do your job for you,' Ben said quietly, 'but there's a line of enquiry you might find instructive.' He pointed to Jackal Two's story:

And so the People took their sacrifices unto those who dwelt below the Place, and they did bless the Earth and the buildings thereon with the blood of the sacrifices, that the Earth and the buildings and the enterprise of the People would be blessed until all eternity.

'When O'Brien came to Brianne Mill to work on the barn roof he ranted on about "Lord Beltane".'

'He said it to me, too, when he was strapped into the ambulance,' Jennifer remembered.

'It rang a bell, so I looked it up. Beltane was – or maybe I should say is – an ancient Celtic fire god.'

'All that means is that O'Brien isn't a Christian religious nutter,' Janice said. 'He's a Celtic religious nutter. So what?'

'I'm afraid I don't get the connection, either,' Jennifer said.

'When the ancient Druids were involved in an important building, they dedicated it to the gods through a human sacrifice. If O'Brien was killing Donny, like Janice believes, maybe that's why.'

'How does this lead to a line of enquiry?' Jennifer asked.

'Because Fred Newson assured us that his workers have helped to build or repair several barns and other buildings round here. He even offered references. All you have to do is dig up the floors and see what's underneath.'

'That's all?'

'Yes.'

'Have you any idea what that would involve?'

'Sure. You'd have to get search warrants, but maybe the farmers will let you have a look without a warrant.'

'Mr Kirby . . . Ben . . . this is ridiculous.'

'Read those stories again. Read my wife's statement. Add the fact that Donny bled into a hole in our barn . . .'

'No, no, no!' Jennifer stood up. 'Stick to your statement by all means, Mrs Kirby, and we'll plod through the procedures, but I seriously advise you to keep this speculation to yourselves.'

'Ben has a point, sergeant,' Janice said. 'At least it's something that can be followed up.'

'If Ben has a point,' Jennifer answered, 'why have we had no reports of any missing persons?'

*　　*　　*

194

They both felt tense after Jennifer Matthews' visit. Ben decided to cook one of the few dishes he could manage without burning everything in sight: penne arrabiata – lots of garlic, herbs and chillies. Janice opened a bottle of white wine, poured out two glasses and settled down with a magazine.

When the meal was ready, Janice took her first taste and nodded. 'This is very good.'

'Thanks.'

'I mean it.'

'I know.'

'She has a point, though, doesn't she?'

'No. Just because no one is reported missing doesn't mean that no one is missing. Donny is missing.'

'No he's not.'

'Yes he is. He's lying in the mortuary, and no one has come to claim the body. And if you hadn't interrupted that bastard O'Brien, young Donny would probably be stuffed under the floor of our barn and covered by rock or concrete. And no one would have come to claim the body then, either.'

'So you do believe me.'

'Of course I believe you. For all I know Jennifer Matthews believes you as well, but there's nothing she can do about it.'

There was another long silence.

'Fred Newson will know if any of his workers have vanished,' Janice said.

'Sure he will, but can you imagine that slimy little shit getting himself involved in any kind of investigation?'

'Worth tackling him, though.'

Ben went to stand by the window and gazed into the gathering darkness, across the stones on the riverside hillock, towards the mountains and Lindisholm Hospital.

'What the fuck is going on over there?'

Janice took his hand. 'That's what we've got to find out, isn't it? Despite Detective Sergeant Matthews.'

'And despite CareCorp's anti-publicity machine.'

'You mean Roy Ormley? For my money, he knows exactly what's happening. Maybe I should do my Mata Hari bit. You know, pillow talk. It used to be a perfectly honourable activity.'

'I hope you're joking,' he said.

She looked across the field at the mound of ancient stones. 'Of course I am.'

Ben decided it was time to have a chat with Newson.

'Ben Kirby, Fred. Is it convenient to talk?'

'Yes, of course. Always ready for a chat with the landlord.'

'I'll be passing your place shortly. I was hoping I could interrupt you for ten minutes or so.'

'Of course. Come for tea, or something stronger.'

'Tea would be fine.'

The thin girl who had been at the farm when Ben and Janice first called on Newson served tea and cakes. What was her name? Not dissimilar to Janice. Janie.

'Thank you, Janie,' Ben said. He was rewarded with a darting glance and a quick smile.

'I suppose that's all part of a writer's paraphernalia, being able to remember names like that,' Newson said when the girl left them alone.

'If only it was. Her name's like Janice, that's all. Mostly I have to write everything down, or I forget.'

'Me too.'

'Glad to hear it. In a way, that's the reason I wanted this chat.'

'Sounds very mysterious.'

'I hope not. It's just that I was wondering about the agency labourers you employ. You mentioned that it was sometimes difficult to keep track of them.'

'Isn't that a fact,' Newson sighed. 'They come, they go. Fortunately, there's a ready supply, so in the long run it doesn't matter.'

'That's exactly what I was wondering about.'

Newson looked blank.

'The bit about it not mattering,' Ben explained. 'Surely you need to keep tabs on everyone, for tax reasons if nothing else.'

'Good God! That's the last thing we need to get involved with. They're all self-employed, otherwise we couldn't afford to use them.'

'Still, if any of them took off before a job was finished, you'd remember, wouldn't you? I mean, for one thing the agency would owe them money.'

'It can happen,' Newson said evasively. 'Why do you ask?'

'Come on, Fred. Donny Talgarth could well have vanished if Janice hadn't gone into the barn when she did. You said your people also helped some of our neighbours. Did any of them disappear on those jobs?'

Newson's eyes bulged. 'Jesus Christ, Ben, what the hell are you getting at?'

'You know exactly what I'm getting at. And while I'm at it, I'm wondering about that dismembered sheep, and how a calf can gash its throat so deeply on barbed wire.'

'I already told you. The sheep was probably killed by hippie dogs. The calf cut itself on ribbon wire we used for some of the fencing. It's been replaced now.'

'Hippie dogs and ribbon wire. Great! And what about our brushing hook and Donny's throat? Let's try again, shall we? Did any of your other people vanish before a job was finished?'

Newson stood up, trembling with anger. 'I'm trying to run a bloody farming enterprise. Have you any idea how hard that is? Sheep get killed and calves get stuck on fences. How dare you come round here like this, making suggestions, sticking your nose into things!'

Ben stood up too, equally angry. 'Listen to me, you little shit! You're up to your slimy elbows in something that stinks, and now you're spreading it all over Brianne Mill. My wife is worried sick about what she saw, and I've got the police on my back asking all kinds of questions. I'm bloody well pissed off with all of it. Now I'm going to ask you one more time – did any of your workers disappear before these jobs were finished?'

'Of course they did! You don't imagine the shiftless little bastards have the decency to finish a job of work before they piss off to the next magic mushroom party, do you? For Christ's sake!' Newson was suffused with righteous and convincing outrage.

'If that's the case, all I can say is you're running a bloody shambles, and I'd like to know where the fuck all this profitability comes from.'

'Janie, Janie! Come and see Mr Kirby back to his car, will you.' Newson's voice trembled with rage.

The girl appeared in seconds and escorted Ben though the farmyard. As she kept the Dobermans from growling at his trousers, she mumbled something.

'Sorry?' Ben said.

'There were three besides Donny,' she whispered. 'Far as I know.

Three. Here today, gone tomorrow. Mr Newson doesn't care, as long as he gets the money.'

Ben took a chance.

'Janie, what the hell is going on in the hospital? What is Omega Cloister?'

'Nothing. I don't see nothing. I don't know nothing about Omega Cloister. I work hard here, and Mr Newson gives me good reports.'

She clanged the gate shut behind him and ran back to the farm-house.

22

CareCorp's contact in the Ministry of Defence was a Colonel Henry Clarke. Each month, Keith Melton was obliged under the terms of the CareCorp contract to furnish Colonel Clarke with reports of the progress of the two Army patients committed to Lindisholm Hospital by the Ministry, Sergeant Geoffrey Abbott and Major Christopher Leamington. The medical brief was deceptively simple: effect the rehabilitation of the patients from active service to normal civilian life. No details were given, and the presumption of the medical and psychiatric staff was that these two men are suffering from the 'trained to kill, now what?' syndrome that affects many front-line soldiers. There was also a suspicion that they had experienced some kind of extraordinary trauma that might lead to suicide, a problem that was causing increasing concern to the government. Why else would the Ministry of Defence select them for such specialised and expensive treatment?

And so, on the first Monday of each month, Melton accessed LISA and prepared two reports. Abbott's was easy enough. Leamington was another matter. Against all logic and reasoning, Leamington had disappeared, and Melton had to find some answers. Meanwhile, he began extrapolating and interpolating Abbott's monthly report into a believable report for the missing Leamington. There was no reason why he shouldn't be able to keep this going until the launch of the Lindisholm franchise. After that, he wouldn't need to give a shit.

23

As the next phase in his creative writing classes, Ben decided to encourage his students to develop the themes they had introduced into their class work to see what else might be revealed. At least, that was his plan. But when he began his next class a subtle change had taken place in the students. They seemed nervous, and kept glancing over their shoulders towards Geoffrey Abbott in his customary seat at the back. Peter O'Brien, Jackal Two, was particularly out of sorts, refusing even to look at Ben, never mind answer any questions.

'Maybe we should play word games,' Ben suggested. 'It's always useful to improve the way we use words to express ourselves. For instance, can anyone think of a three-letter word that adds on the back of "sauce" and the front of "cake" to form two new words?'

The silence grew.

'Come on, now. It's not hard. How about you, Pedro?'

Pedro Sharez shrugged and doodled into his notebook.

'I'll give you this one. "Pan". See? Saucepan and pancake. Let's try another.'

He turned back to the board.

'Can we forget all this for a minute?'

The voice was calm, assured. Geoffrey Abbott.

'Of course. If there's something else you'd like me to cover . . .'

'Just a small point. We'd like to know why you are taking these classes.'

It was said in a very mild voice, but the impact was alarming. With uncanny accuracy, Abbott had thrust a spear into the heart of things.

'I'm not sure what you mean, Geoffrey. The hospital needed two tutors, and my wife and I were invited to take classes.'

'It's just that things don't stack up. For instance, I have just finished reading our library copy of your exposé of big-business practices. Now, here you are in Lindisholm Hospital, encouraging us to write all sorts of things for you. Is there a purpose to this, I ask myself? Invited or not, are you engaged in a similar exposé in Lindisholm?'

It was all low-key and matter-of-fact, but Ben felt an enormous undercurrent of malevolence. He began to wonder about the efficacy of the protective screen that Tim Johnson assured him would prevent any physical contact between himself and his students.

'The only purpose I have here is to help everyone in this class to improve their writing skills. I hope I'm succeeding in that.'

'It is indeed important for us to be able to express ourselves,' Abbott told him, 'but apart from a few grammatical points we do not get any meaningful feedback from you. It's as if you're using what we write for your own ends.'

The round eyes stared at Ben out of that moon face, bland, completely emotionless. So why did Ben feel out of his depth, threatened? The answer was simple: Abbott was right. Somehow he sensed that Ben had a hidden agenda. Ben played for time to gather himself, to defuse the suspicions.

'What kind of feedback do you have in mind?'

'Take Peter's last contribution. He showed it to me, and it is very imaginative. But you haven't mentioned it to him. You haven't taken him to one side and given him the benefit of your constructive criticism. The same is true for most of our work. You'll have guessed we're trying to collaborate on a story that you will find creative. We thought this would be in the spirit of the class. We would like to know what you think of our work. That's not too much to ask, is it?'

Ben felt sweat trickling down his back. Tension. 'Of course not, and I must apologise if I have caused any offence. I've written tutor summaries for every piece, but these summaries are for my own consumption, a kind of shorthand for keeping up with what you are contributing. I'll be happy to extend this to a personal appraisal.'

'We're glad to hear that, Mr Kirby,' Abbott said. 'Would it be too much to ask if you could start things off by explaining how you feel about Peter's parable of the Mill?'

Once again, Abbott brought the burning glass to a cruelly sharp focus, and despite his mild tone Ben felt that any hesitation or weakness he showed would precipitate some kind of crisis. He launched himself into a distinctly top-of-the-head critique.

'Not at all. I'm sure Peter won't mind if I begin by pointing out that he is clearly a deeply religious man. As such, his aim in writing his parable is almost certainly to convey complex thinking in a way that others will find it attractive. In this, he succeeds. He writes forcefully and directly to the reader. Of course, most parables have a hidden meaning, and it's not so much the writer who is under scrutiny here but the reader. What I mean is, how should the reader interpret the parable? This aspect of the work is beyond my remit as your tutor, but for what it's worth, I believe Peter is expressing very powerfully a deep dissatisfaction with today's society and pointing out that solutions to our problems might be found in earlier societies than our own. There are many who would agree with him.'

Abbott gazed steadily at him. 'Are you one of them, Mr Kirby?'

'Geoffrey, I'm doing the best I can with the writing. You can't expect me to get involved in debates about my personal views. We'd never get anywhere.'

To his relief, the giant nodded slowly, and the class settled back in their seats.

On the way home, Janice chatted animatedly about her own class, not noticing that Ben was unusually quiet.

'Some of them have taken extremely well to clay modelling. The first time they tried, most of them turned up with not much more than wiggly snakes, the kind of thing that children roll between their hands. Now they're becoming a little more adventurous. In fact, I'd go so far as to say risqué. You remember those statuettes in the cathedral shop in Portugal? You know, on the shelf at the back, those phalluses . . . well, guess what they seem determined to make . . . Ben, are you listening?'

'Sorry?'

'Christ, you're miles away, and I've been blethering on about what I've been doing. How did your class go today?'

'In a word,' he said, 'scary.'

'Scary?'

'Very scary. I think I understand how Wesley feels.'

'What on earth happened?'

A good question. What had happened in that class? A mental patient with the highest possible security grading had cut right through the shit and practically accused him of investigating the place. He'd placed Ben so firmly on the spot it hurt, and in a flat, neutral manner which made the episode even more chilling.

'They put me through the Lindisholm equivalent of the Third

Degree. At least, that Delta patient I told you about did. Geoffrey Abbott. He complained that I hadn't given them any feedback. He then suggested I was working there for my own reasons. I got the impression that this would not be very popular.'

'You're kidding.'

'I wish I was. Abbott went out of his way to mention that their writing is make-believe. Created out of real situations, but make-believe. Jonser thinks the same, of course, but I'm convinced they have a hidden agenda. It's got something to do with this stuff about Lord Beltane. They want to write a kind of chronicle, to record what they do. They need my help, but they don't want me getting into the act. My guess is, they've been documenting things that really happened, but they got a little bit too enthusiastic and let too much out of the bag. Abbott was probing to see how I was reacting to it all. It was a damage limitation exercise, as far as he was concerned.'

'Is he still suspicious?'

'No idea. I think I made the right noises. All I can do is carry on and see if anything develops. He did raise a valid point about feedback, though. I need to concentrate on tutoring them. It can't do any harm.'

24

Professor Jonser had a list in her private files which she used to help to gauge the progress of Lindisholm with respect to matters that would never appear in the annual report, or any other kind of report. These were the unofficial and undesirable activities used by older and more experienced inmates in secure institutions to indulge themselves outside the official regime and also to exert control over the younger and more vulnerable patients. Her list comprised: tobacco; alcohol; homosexuality; violence; protection; pornography; drugs; patient visits with unauthorised conjugal intercourse; and paedophilia. Against each item for each cloister she had a three-star code. One star meant that, as far as she could ascertain from staff reports and her own observations, the cloister was free from that particular activity. Two stars meant that it existed, but was confinable. Three stars meant she had to take remedial action to get it back to one star.

Professor Jonser never thought religion might rate a place in her system. Religion was something that drifted in and out of the hospital on Sabbaths and holy days, along with the Salvation Army, the Women's Institute and the Friends of Lindisholm Hospital. There was a chapel, a synagogue and a room accepted by the Islamic community as the closest thing to a mosque they were likely to get. Religion was something that existed within her institution in the same way as air-conditioning. So, when she began checking the contributions made by the patients to Ben Kirby's creative writing class, with their pseudo-religious overtones, it did not occur to her that she might be witnessing the development of something real, pernicious or harmful. It was not remotely possible for patients to bring outsiders into the cloister and conceal what they were doing from security. The nearest they could get to that kind of behaviour was by using the interactive environment of Omega Cloister. Jonser's job was to maintain the highest standards of psychiatric treatment and not to become involved in matters outside her remit. If the media had reported an outbreak of missing persons, she might have taken a closer look. Even more to the point, the police were not making enquiries in that direction. As far as Jonser's orderly mind was concerned, that was an end to the matter.

Because of this, Lion, Spiderlady, Rosehip, the three Jackals and their fellows were able to worship happily and securely – and to extend their influence, radiating through the cloisters in a vigorous programme of conversion and worship, in the long tradition of other missionaries, evangelists and proselytisers. Which is why Wesley found himself confronted by an attractive woman patient called Jennie Booth one day during a library period. Jennie had been a prostitute, and she had received five life sentences for murdering clients. She was in Lindisholm because two doctors came to the professional conclusion that she was suffering from a treatable obsessive-compulsive psychosis. She had also given them the best sex they ever had in their lives. Quid pro quo.

'Hello, Wesley. I'm Lamb,' she said.

This was what Wesley had been dreading. This is what his friends Harold and Pedro Sharez had told him about.

'They come up to you, man,' Pedro said, 'and they get you involved.'

'How come they never got you involved?'

'You joking? No one never got Pedro Sharez involved in nothing he didn't want to get involved in. They leave me alone, man, but guys like you, guys like you ...'

Wesley had drifted into many a nightmare with Pedro's words ringing in his head.

Now it was here. This woman he had seen with some of the others they'd told him about was staring at him with big black eyes, shining, like they were on fire. She was looking at his crutch and licking her lips. Jesus!

He ignored her, carried on looking at the bookshelves, but suddenly there were two other patients in front of him, standing like they were giving him the Treatment. Then three of them, four, five, until he was surrounded. Security wouldn't take any notice, because they'd assume he had committed a small transgression which was being dealt with by his peers. Reward and punishment. There was nothing he could do, and all his fears of the past few months crystallised.

Lamb was standing in front of him again.

'It's all right, darling. We want you to be one of us, that's all.'

* * *

Monkey Boy was crouched in the corner of the security room, ignored like a piece of familiar furniture, watching the monitors. He heard the console operator call out, 'Check Echo Foxtrot, Tim. Someone's getting the Treatment in the library.'

'Can you see who it is?'

The operator zoomed in and checked the register. 'One of the kids from Alpha Cloister. Freeman. One of the Gammas is there.'

Tim Harding checked the screen. 'He's okay. Probably got himself wrong-zoned. It happens.'

The operator watched the group swaying around Wesley for a moment, then switched away, bored.

Wesley's knees collapsed, and they held him up, while Lamb cradled his penis in her fingers and slid her mouth round his glans. His orgasm made her feel as if she was receiving a blessing direct from the Lord, and she swallowed his sperm greedily before standing up and leaning against him, reluctant to let go of such a magnificent staff.

'Your babies are inside me, Wesley. It's almost like we are man and wife, don't you think?'

Suddenly they were all walking away, leaving him staggering, trying to find his balance. There was a whispering.

'You are in Omega Cloister now. One of us. One of the People.'

When the night nurse wheeled the treatment trolley round to Wesley's bed that night, she found him lying with his eyes open, trembling, face covered in sweat. She was authorised to tranquillise any Alpha and Beta patient without referring to the doctor-in-charge, so she did. He fell into a deep, exhausted sleep.

Monkey Boy sat next to Wesley at breakfast, his little fingers picking at his food as he glanced around the tables. No one was nearby that he need worry about.

'They want you to take some charms to Mr Kirby on Friday.'

Wesley kept his head down, eyes avoiding contact. 'I ain't taking nothing to no one.'

'They can make you. But there's no need to worry. They like Mr and Mrs Kirby. They want to make sure they have good luck, that's all.'

'I don't want no part in this, man.'

'I can give you something to take, too.'

'What?'

'Something from the computer. Mr Kirby will like my something. It will help him.'

'This is bad, Harold. You're all putting me on the spot, man.'

'You'll be all right. But you must do everything they say. They can do very bad things.'

The next night, Wesley dreamed about Lamb and what she had done to him, and the dream became reality. When he woke in the morning and felt the damp sheets, his fear was compounded by shame. He spent the day in an agony of fright and bewilderment, although no one took any notice. No one except Monkey Boy, who looked at him with bright eyes without being able to move his face into an expression of any kind. But Wesley knew that Monkey Boy was on his side, and that meant everything to him. Even Pedro Sharez was trying to be supportive, letting Wesley win the games they played in recreation periods, when everyone knew Pedro was a fiend for winning. So it wasn't as bad as it otherwise would have been, not until the People made contact, later in the afternoon as he tended to the cloister gardens.

It was a small bag made out of some kind of leather, its opening sewn up to secure the contents, pressed into Wesley's hand by an old Beta crone with straggly grey hair who whispered, 'Hide it in Brianne Mill tomorrow, hide it, for the Lord has spoken. It will protect His People.'

Lindisholm overalls had no pockets, so he fiddled with his trainers and stuffed the leather bag into his sock. It didn't seem such a big deal, and he found himself wondering why he'd been so fearful of it all. He could hide the bag where he had put the notes he had been writing for Mr Kirby. They said it was a good luck charm. That was all right by Wesley. Maybe all this stuff about the People wasn't as bad as Monkey Boy and the others said it was.

By bedtime, he had forgotten about Harold's promise to send the Kirbys something from the computer, until the lights went out and he snuggled into his pillow. There was something small, flat and hard touching his fingers. Breathless with excitement he pushed his hand further along the mattress until he could feel all round it. A floppy disk!

For the first time since he had been taken to this dreadful place, and despite his reservations about the People, Wesley Freeman felt that something positive was happening. Tomorrow he was taking good luck to a man he was learning to respect, plus something that Harold had said would help them. He had no idea what it was, and he didn't care. He'd hide that away, too, where Mr Kirby would find it without knowing for sure who had put it there. Better safe than sorry. And it felt good to do something that people like Dr Nikki Congleton didn't know anything about.

25

Roy Ormley had a number of duties to perform during his visit to Lindisholm, and one was to broach the subject of Lindisholm Organic Foods Limited with its two directors, Alex Searle and Fred Newson. Like other large companies, CareCorp had a policy that dealt with staff inventions, patents and intellectual property rights. In this case the situation was straightforward. Two employees had formed an independent company without informing CareCorp lawyers of their intentions. They had broken no law, but they were in breach of their contracts with CareCorp. Company policy was to approach such cases with a view to assessing what CareCorp could gain or lose. A company search revealed that the only shareholders and directors were Searle and Newson. A deeper probe showed that Newson had been acquiring options on tracts of farmland throughout England and Wales. The lawyers also knew about Newson's agricultural labouring agency which was supplying workers to Lindisholm Farm. Their assessment was that he should be allowed to continue, pending further investigation, because the agency was supplying labourers at discounted rates, and therefore the company was enjoying an overall benefit. Not only that, Newson had established links with the Patients Rehabilitation Foundation, a charity that found employment for ex-mental patients and prisoners. After discussing the situation with Keith Melton, Lord Balacombe had instructed Ormley to make his assessment of what seemed like a promising commercial venture with a view to adding it to the CareCorp portfolio – with or without Searle and Newson. At the very least, this meant a thorough update on Newson's management of Lindisholm Farm was called for.

Ormley knew about the Dobermans and had brought some scraps of meat along to distract them, so when he arrived at the main gate and they appeared, growling, tongues lopping out, he was pleased to see that they lost all interest in him at the chance to gobble down some titbits. He parked the Lexus outside the gates, and the dogs trotted along beside him wagging their stumps as he made his way towards the main farm building where Newson had his office.

'Roy, good to see you.'

'Morning, Fred. Hope you don't mind the impromptu call.'

'Not at all, delighted, in fact. It'll give us a chance to catch up with each other. Things are going extremely well here, and I know how keen you are to gain favourable publicity. Come and have some tea.'

This meant another organic food ordeal, with the thin girl acting as waitress. Janie, Newson called her. Skin and bone. Ormley was wondering how he could drain his cup of disgusting fennel tea into one of the pot plants when the phone went.

''Scuse me, Roy . . . Hello, Newson speaking . . . Yes, I know . . . Absolutely . . . Really? . . . Yes, I think so . . . Well, thanks for the call . . .'

He put down the receiver. Searle had belatedly alerted him to Ormley's visit. Searle had also informed him that someone had been making enquiries about their land options. Several of the vendors' solicitors had phoned Searle to check if they were still interested, implying that another possible purchaser had appeared on the scene. Ormley's visit was too much of a coincidence. Time for risk assessment. Maybe a spot of crisis management. Pity, though, if CareCorp was making enquiries. Their venture needed another three months of consolidation before it could survive an attack from that quarter.

'Problems, Fred?'

'Just reassessing our kelp requirement. We've taken over more land to the south of Lindisholm, and we'll need to increase the stock.' He rubbed his hands briskly. 'Right! Where should we start? If you've no objection, I recommend we take a trip to the mills. I've been working on something I think you'll like.'

That's right, keep everything nice and ambiguous, Ormley thought. The oleaginous little shit must be desperate to know how CareCorp had caught onto his scam with Alex Searle – and what they intended to do about it.

'Excellent. I haven't been there since the grand opening.'

'Many improvements to show you. I think you'll be impressed.'

'May as well go in my car. I'll be coming back this way later, so I can drop you off,' Ormley said.

'Paying the Kirbys a visit?'

Newson's voice was offhand, but he was wondering how Ormley was coping with the desirable Mrs Janice Kirby.

'Yes, and we owe you a vote of thanks, Fred. Had it not been for your e-mail alerting us to their arrival in the area, we would not be enjoying the luxury of having two very talented tutors in our education initiative.'

'How's that going?'

'Professor Jonser is very impressed. It seems we may also have a budding novelist in our midst. Maybe even a poet. We've always had talented artists on site, of course, and Mrs Kirby seems to have started her classes very positively.'

Was Ormley fucking her yet? It would be very useful to get something solid against the head office bastard, especially at a time like this.

The mills at Lindisholm were situated at the head of the valley where several underground mountain springs merged to form the River Brianne at the site of former mine workings. The amount of water power during all but the dryest of summers was considerable, and Newson had arranged for teams of patients to refurbish the leats and the wooden mill wheels, so that cereal crops grown on the farm could be stone ground in the traditional manner. The energy was free, so the process was cheap. More to the point, it fitted in with the organic philosophy of the hospital farm.

Newson directed Ormley along an old drovers' road, which made him wish he were driving Janice Kirby's Shogun rather than the low-slung Lexus.

'Pull in here, Roy, and you'll be able to get everything in context.'

The car was at a vantage point that allowed them to see the mills, slightly beneath and to their left, with the river tumbling steeply over rocks before winding its way south through the relatively flat acreage of the market gardens, skirting the hospital cloisters and disappearing into the far reaches of the valley.

'You'll remember that we are limited as to the amount of cereal crops we can grow,' Newson said, 'so we use any over-capacity here to offer a milling service to local organic farmers on a quid-pro-quo basis. We take a percentage of their produce as payment. We also keep the wheat and barley husks to supplement our animal feeds. The system works very well. The unit I mentioned is in the building to the far right.'

'The one with the new mill wheel?'

'Yes. Guess what we produce!'

Ormley had no idea, and he didn't give a damn. This was truly boring.

'Bone meal!' Newson exclaimed with satisfaction. 'Best source of farming minerals you can get.'

'You add it to the cereal husks for animal feed, do you?'

'Christ, no. We use it on the market gardens. It's incredibly good for the soil, and the patients get a big kick out of applying it. I guess they respond to the natural cycle involved. You know the kind of thing. We kill to eat, so we must give something back to nature. Primitive, but therapeutic. At least, that's what the consultants reckon. Like having pets.'

'Pets?'

This was getting worse.

'You must have seen the reports – how stroking cats helps to calm disturbed people. It's a primitive instinct. Like organic farming. Of course, we can't have pets in the hospital, and gardening is the next best thing.'

'I'll take your word for it.'

Ormley, fighting yawns by the minute, was making a valiant effort to see if Newson's developments could be put to use by the CareCorp publicity machine. He did not hold out much hope . . .

Mental hospital grinds fertiliser bones with water power . . .

He shuddered. It was not exactly the headline to grab the attention of a busy news editor.

'Come on,' Newson said. 'We can ford the river above the mills to get a better look.'

Ormley looked pointedly at his watch and started the engine. 'Bit behind schedule, I'm afraid.'

Newson looked genuinely disappointed, and for a moment Ormley wondered if he had been judging the man too harshly. Maybe Newson was more committed to his work than it had seemed. The moment did not last long.

'Tell me about Lindisholm Organic Foods Limited,' he said suddenly.

'Good heavens! That's the very thing I wanted to talk to you about.'

A typical Newson response. Nimble. Dissembling. It was the last thing the man wanted to discuss.

'I thought you just wanted to show me this new mill of yours.'

'That's all part of the strategy.' Newson paused. The next few moments were crucial, and very tricky. Ormley had the power to make or break his fledgling enterprise. 'Look, Roy, I know I'm out of order from a company viewpoint, but it's always like that, isn't it?'

'Always like what, Fred?'

This would be interesting. Newson wriggling on a hook of his own making.

'Innovation! You begin by working your balls off for your company, and somewhere along the line you get a bright idea, one that just might work if only you could check out some of the basics. But when do you inform your employer . . . what's the best time? You tell me, Roy.'

'When you incorporate a limited company?'

'You're right. I should have done it then, but there are so many variables, so many unknowns.'

'Our corporate people could have helped with all that.'

'But don't you see – the fun is doing it yourself. That's the challenge. That's why I haven't told the company until today.'

'Come off it, Fred. You're only telling me because I already know, for Christ's sake. What you and Alex have been doing is using CareCorp time and facilities to build up your own business. Jesus, you're even using a registered CareCorp trading name.'

Ormley was wrong. CareCorp had registered Lindisholm Hospital, not the name Lindisholm. If push came to shove, Newson could win a court case, but that was the last thing he needed. What he did need was breathing space.

'You're right, Roy, and I apologise for the secrecy. I'm just hoping you and the board might see the benefits of this approach.'

It took all Ormley's control not to laugh at that one.

'Benefits?'

'Absolutely. We already have pilot schemes up and running. In two months we'll have opened up our first four commercial farming ventures. Two in East Anglia, one in Cheshire and one in Lincolnshire. In six months we can increase this to twelve. They'll be registered organic within two years of trading, but they'll be making a profit within one year, because we have already lined up premium retail outlets for our label. They'll be run by professional farm managers and – get this – they'll be staffed mainly by ex-patients of Lindisholm Hospital.'

'I hope you're joking.'

'Think about it. They have experience of our farming methods because of their time in Lindisholm. So we have zero recruitment and training costs. On top of that, it validates and extends the whole idea of Lindisholm's back-to-the-community policy – and in a controlled environment. Some ex-patients will need after care, and guess who'll provide it, and guess who'll provide physical security. Guess who'll provide fleet transport and distribution. Christ, CareCorp could even get into organic food retailing. It's a real win-win situation, Roy, I'm telling you.'

Ormley was thunderstruck. Five minutes ago he had been relishing the thought of sticking this smug little arsehole firmly up shit creek. But in one burst of fervent talking, Newson had opened up a vision that took his breath away. It made sense. It was brilliant. And Newson was only talking about the UK. He had no idea that CareCorp itself was close to a world launch for the Lindisholm franchise. Was there something in this for Roy Ormley?

'How are you financing it?'

'European grants, deferred payments on property and capital goods, low interest loans . . . you name it! Alex and I have ploughed most of our savings into this, and the timing couldn't be better. With over-production in intensive farming and all this set-aside, there's a million acres of land going begging out there, and we can beat foreign imports because the organic market is so emotive to a growing number of consumers. They're an articulate bunch of people who don't see why the UK can't grow what they want. Well, the UK can grow what they want. I tell you, Roy, we cannot lose, believe me.'

Ormley did believe him. The market signs were that many consumers wanted purer foods and were willing to pay premium prices. It was a growth market, and a venture like this could make millions.

'I don't know, Fred. This is something I should refer to the board.'

Newson banged his fists on the car fascia, one hundred per cent focused on convincing Ormley to leave things alone.

'Jesus Christ, Roy, that would ruin everything. Can you imagine that gang of fuck-ups getting hold of this before we've put everything in place? Can't you see?'

'I don't know, Fred. I just don't know.' Ormley sighed heavily. 'You're putting me in a very difficult position.'

Newson's penny dropped. The son-of-a-bitch was blackmailing him. If Newson had been carrying a shotgun, he would have used it and dropped the body down the nearest disused mine shaft. How much did the bastard want?

'Stop the car for a minute, Roy. I need to take a piss.' He did, too.

Ormley watched the steam rise from the rocks. Quite a bladder capacity!

'How much?' Newson asked when he was back in the car.

'What?'

'How much do you want to keep quiet?'

'Good Lord, Fred, it's not like that.'

'What is it like?'

'My bet is you've been doing all this on a shoe string. You're seriously under-financed. The first sign of a cock-up, and you'll have so many carpets pulled from under you, you'll end up in the basement. I don't want to take money out, I want to put money in.'

It was Newson's turn to experience the jaw-dropping routine. 'Do what?'

'I want to buy in. I'll need to see every damn thing you have, of course. The real stuff, not the crap you show to the bank. If it stacks up, I can whack fifty big ones into it. Maybe more.'

If Ormley was serious, and he sounded very serious, there had to be a snag, but Newson couldn't think what it could possibly be – apart from the share-holding implications. But why . . . ?

'But why?' he asked.

Ormley couldn't possibly tell Newson the real answer to that. It turned him on. It was a gamble. And what a wonderful gamble. Neither Newson nor Searle was aware of all the implications, and there was no need for them to know. And the beauty of it was, Ormley could not possibly face any insider trading investigation, because there was no corporate or financial link between CareCorp shares and Lindisholm Organic Food shares.

'Because it's a brilliant concept. If it works, you'll have to go public. You and Searle could become millionaires. I want in, Fred. But there's no way we can achieve critical mass in a venture this

215

big on our own. I have all the City contacts we'll need to make this work.'

We can achieve . . . On *our* own . . . ! The cheeky bastard. A third partner would wreck Newson's control of the company. Alex had long ago agreed that Newson should be the majority shareholder and overall boss man. An investment the size Ormley was suggesting would turn that on its head. But Ormley was ahead of him, and said the one thing that clinched it.

'I don't want voting shares, Fred. You're running this thing fine without me. We can draw up an agreement that gives me my capital back with a suitable return over an agreed period. The only stipulation is that the company does go public, but you shouldn't worry about that. It will make you for life – and Alex.'

As Newson absorbed this, Ormley was already anticipating setting up the equivalent of Lindisholm Organic Foods in any country that took the Lindisholm Hospital franchise, but Newson and Searle didn't need to know about that, either. Christ, this was the opportunity of a lifetime!

When Ormley drove to Brianne Mill on the off-chance of seeing Janice Kirby, he was drunk with elation. He nodded and waved happily to the Lindisholm patient in green overalls who was cleaning the henhouse and rang the door bell. He saw it was an Alpha patient, but he hardly registered the fact. When Janice opened the door, it took the last vestige of his restraint not to grab hold of her and waltz around the courtyard.

'I was just passing. Thought I'd call on the off-chance, so we could chat about your classes. See if there's anything I can use from a publicity point of view.'

'I'm afraid Ben's out for the afternoon.'

'That's a shame,' he lied.

His energy was incredible. He was looking at her with those luminous eyes, making no attempt to leave, and she took a small step down a very slippery slope.

'Why don't you come in, now you're here?'

She led the way to the kitchen, thinking that a cup of coffee would be a good thing.

'Listen,' he said. 'What I told you the other day, you know, when we were in the studio. I'd like to apologise.'

She should have laughed it off, said, no need to apologise, think nothing of it. Instead, she took another step. 'Why? It was the truth, wasn't it?'

She knew. She understood. Surely to Christ she felt the same way. He wanted to step forward and take hold of her, but he couldn't move his feet. Passion was swirling with terror. What if she turned him away? He couldn't catch his breath, and for a moment she thought he was going to faint. Then he gasped and whispered: 'Sweet Jesus, help me.'

She took a final step and let him lean against her, and then they were kissing like drowning people sucking oxygen. They fumbled and stumbled their way upstairs with ugly, unbalanced, desperate movements, arriving naked at the bedroom, and she didn't give a shit that this was the marital bed, that he was pressing inside her, and there was no way she could contain the scream that he forced from her. Elemental, wild and totally explicit.

Wesley heard the sound of her orgasm as he spread new straw for the hens, and it paralysed him. As it swelled and throbbed, large tears formed in his eyes and ran uncontrollably down his cheeks. He finished patting the straw into place, making little depressions where he knew the hens liked to settle. Then he straightened up, brushed the loose straw from his green overalls, and began walking.

Janice lay trembling. What the hell had she done? Why?

Ormley deluged her with aftermath. 'Oh my God, holy shit, that was utterly fantastic! Christ, how I love you. What an incredible day. This is a new beginning for both of us. No, really, I *really* mean it. Just wait 'til I tell you what's happening. I'm lining up a deal with Fred Newson. He's developing a chain of organic farms that will make a fortune. It could make me a millionaire. Just think of it, I won't have to take any more shit from that sanctimonious old bastard Lord Balacombe or that scrotum Keith Melton and his indescribable Army friends. No more brown-nosing the fucking media . . .'

'I think you better go,' she said tonelessly. 'It's four o'clock. Ben could be back any time.'

His mind spun on and on. Ben? Ben? Who the fuck was Ben?

Yesterday's man. The no-hoper. The one-book wonder. Let him come back. The sooner they dealt with this the better. On the other hand, they needed time to prepare.

Janice rolled out of bed and collected her clothes, keeping her back to him. He didn't notice.

'Sure,' he said. 'Christ, it'll take us both some time to get used to this. Best to let things take their course for a while, but it's agony when I'm not near you. You know that, don't you?'

He caught hold of her and held her close, breathing the smell of her hair.

'I must go to the bathroom.'

'Right. Look, I'll let myself out. I'll call you tonight and come round, you know, to talk about the classes. I need to do that, anyway.'

She went carefully through the house to make sure Ormley had left nothing behind, that there was no sign of his visit. She stripped the bed and carried everything to the site of the bonfire behind the barn, emptied a can of petrol over it, threw a match in, careless of the blow-back. When the bedclothes were ashes, she raked the embers until they were reduced to unrecognisable powder.

Ben arrived home at six o'clock, by which time Janice had taken a very hot shower, scrubbed herself raw and fried several cloves of garlic. The house was permeated with the fumes. Cleansed.

'Smells good,' he said. 'Where's Wesley?'

'What?'

'His bike's still outside. I thought he must be having a tea or something. Bit late for him, though.'

'Maybe Fred Newson picked him up. I don't know.'

'Are you okay?'

'Yes, I'm okay. Why?'

'You seem a little vague. I mean, if Newson had called for Wesley, he'd have let you know.'

'I doubt it, not after your row. He probably doesn't want to speak to either of us again.'

'You're right. God, I'm hungry. What are you cooking?'

'Cooking?'

He saw that she was looking strained and tired. Not surprising. considering everything she had been through in the past few weeks.

'The garlic. Smells very good!'

'Yes. I thought maybe we could have a stir-fry, but I got behind with things. Sorry.'

'That's all right. Let me start chopping the veggies.'

26

Ben was still chopping when Fred Newson phoned to ask if Wesley had left Brianne Mill yet. Ben took the call, and the two men were icily polite to each other. Half an hour later Newson arrived in his pick-up, his face stiff with concern. They looked in and around the outbuildings as the autumn night closed in, calling Wesley's name. At eight, Newson asked to use the phone and reported a missing patient to the duty security officer at the hospital, Mervyn Jessell. Following the standard routine, Jessell initiated a scan of all patients, followed by a video check that started in Delta Cloister and worked outwards through the Gamma, Beta and Alpha cloisters. Only five patients out of three thousand were not where they should be. Three were indulging in an impromptu sex session in a bedroom, one had fallen asleep on the lavatory, and one was Wesley Freeman, whose absence had been logged by the security system, but ignored by the guard because Wesley was only an Alpha patient, and he'd been late once before because of a puncture.

Jessell informed the police, and a routine visit was made to the location of the last sighting. Only the visit was not really routine, because the place was Brianne Mill and the duty CID officer was Detective Sergeant Jennifer Matthews. Two incidents involving young people from a mental hospital within a few weeks of each other at the same location was enough to make any police officer more than slightly interested.

Jennifer asked them if anything was missing, like money or clothes. No, there wasn't; nothing they could see, anyway. Her colleagues conducted a door-to-door enquiry and discovered that Tom Attwood had seen the green-clad Wesley walking through the Kirbys' field towards the river crossing at half past three – and, yes, he was sure because he arrived home just in time to miss the beginning of the three thirty sports bulletin. Mervyn Jessell remembered that the Ping Pole in the southern field at the Mill was out of action, so Wesley could have waded across the river and set off down the road without triggering the alarm system. That set a road search in motion.

At eleven o'clock, a police helicopter was made available, and Jessell gave the pilot the transponder code for Wesley's bracelet tag so he could search the surrounding countryside, in case Wesley had left the roads. The pilot soon got a reading but dismissed it as an aberration. It came from Brianne Mill. After several unsuccessful sweeps of the area, the aberration was still there, so he alerted the forces on the ground and set his helicopter down, near the riverbank where Wesley had danced in the mud with the Shogun.

A torchlight search led to the discovery of Wesley's clothes, neatly folded on the ground under a willow tree. He had placed three other things under the tree: an axe that he had taken from the tool shed, his tag bracelet, and his left hand.

A police dog handler found Wesley, a few feet away downstream, lying in the reeds as though he were asleep. He was an experienced officer. Seen most things. But this tragic little scene got to him. His dog started whining, unable to understand his master's reaction. The helicopter pilot called in the result to police headquarters, asked for an ambulance and took off, showering the sad group of police officers and security staff with spray from the river. Janice appeared from the house with a clean white sheet. She waded into the water and began wrapping it round the body, and no one told her that they hadn't finished taking photographs yet. Two young constables helped to bring Wesley to the bank, collecting reeds and grass to arrange underneath him so he wouldn't have to lie in the mud. Janice knelt there, sobbing, and when Ben tried to ease her away she clung to Wesley's body.

'My fault,' she moaned, like a child might confess to her father. 'My fault.'

'Don't be silly,' he whispered. 'How could it possibly be your fault?'

27

Detective Sergeant Jennifer Matthews discussed the situation with Inspector Cliff James, her boss in Lampeter. The Donny Talgarth case was still creating headaches, and both Ben and Janice Kirby had refused to give statements concerning the death of Wesley Freeman.

'The only question we have to consider,' Inspector James said, 'is whether you believe they are obstructing us in our enquiries.'

'Not really. I suppose they are still sensitive about our reaction to Mrs Kirby's statement concerning Talgarth's death, and maybe that's why they are reluctant. On the other hand, Mr Kirby is arguing that as neither he nor his wife saw anything of Freeman after lunchtime, there's no point. Mrs Kirby is genuinely upset.'

'How upset is genuinely upset?'

'Come on, sir! She's just had two violent and unusual deaths dumped on her doorstep.'

'The point is, we need their statements. And we need statements from the neighbours. Everyone is talking suicide, but why would that kid go to those lengths all of a sudden, mental patient or not? We have to keep our options open.'

'Maybe he just decided to opt out of the system.'

'You're probably right, but let's get everything down on paper, shall we? Go and see the Kirbys again. Talk with the neighbours. Something might crop up that will give us an explanation.'

Tom Attwood confirmed that he had caught a glimpse of Wesley in his green overalls walking across the Kirbys' field towards the river at three thirty. Ben reluctantly supplied a few words about providing an opportunity for a Lindisholm patient to take part in a back-to-the-community therapy programme. Janice flatly refused to say or sign anything. And then a farmer's wife, Marion Lewis, told the police she had seen a large shiny black car leaving Brianne Mill as she was driving home after picking the children up from her sister's house after school. She said the time was just after four o'clock. No, she did not know what make it was, but she was sure she had seen it parked in the evenings in Lampeter, near the Royal Hotel. It was a Japanese-looking make of car, she thought.

Roy Ormley was astounded to receive a phone call from Detective Sergeant Matthews obliging him to attend an interview at Lampeter police station. When he arrived, she was downright aggressive. A car similar to the one he was using had been seen leaving Brianne Mill at four o'clock on the afternoon Wesley Freeman had drowned. Did he call at Brianne Mill, and if so when did he leave? Why did he go there? Did he see Wesley Freeman? Did he talk to the boy? How did he seem? What was Ormley doing at precisely three thirty, the time that Wesley was seen walking towards the river? But, if he had been in the kitchen having a cup of coffee with Mrs Kirby, he would surely have seen Wesley, because there is a clear view of that particular field from the kitchen window . . .

Is this a statement, sergeant, or are you conducting an interview? I am taking a statement, sir, at this juncture . . .

Back to Janice Kirby. Can she at least confirm the times of arrival and departure of Mr Ormley? Thank you, Mrs Kirby. And perhaps you might have caught sight of Wesley from the kitchen window at around three thirty. He would have been in full view. No? Well, if you say so.

Janice took a panic-stricken call from Ormley.

'The shit has really hit the fan over this Freeman business. How am I supposed to keep the press out of a thing like that? Plus, I've just had that bloody detective woman asking me to confirm that I visited you yesterday afternoon. Christ, Janice, I actually saw the little bastard round where you keep the hens. I waved to him. I told them I called round to discuss your art classes, but I'm not sure they believed me. She said they'd probably want to interview me again. What the hell am I going to tell them?'

'Tell them the truth,' she said, and hung up.

Ormley stared at his phone in disbelief. Maybe they'd been cut off. He was still jiggling the connect button when the incoming call from Lord Balacombe came through. His Lordship did not sound pleased.

'Keep a lid on this, Roy. That is non-negotiable. You've currently got four news editors to deal with. Say we are seeking their co-operation on not releasing details until the next-of-kin have been informed. Tell them you'll give them a full briefing as soon as this is done. After that, ask yourself why I'm telling you how to do your job.'

'I'm on top of it, sir.'

'I sincerely hope so. You should be here in London, not gallivanting round the damned countryside. However, our founder and CEO – for reasons that elude me – wants you to stay there.'

Ormley got the details from Bert Cook in London and called the editors back, asked what were their deadlines, how could he assist, did they need any background information, could they stick to the basic facts until the inquest when he could give them the complete inside story?

They agreed to restrict their reporting to a simple statement of fact: *The body of a young man was discovered yesterday on a farm near Lampeter. Police are withholding the identity until the next-of-kin have been informed. Foul play is not suspected.*

From a PR point of view, it was a routine matter. So why did Ormley feel that his world was falling apart?

28

The rain started shortly before Wesley's body had been taken from the river, and it fell steadily throughout the next day and the next until everything was soaked. Outside doors swelled and jammed. Earth turned to mud. Wheel tracks in the mountain lanes became rivulets, rivulets in the hedgerows became streams, streams in the fields became rivers, and rivers overflowed their banks to turn fields into lakes. At first everyone was saying how good all this was for the reservoirs. They put up with the ceaseless putting on and taking off of mud-caked rubber boots. They resignedly hung sodden pullovers and jackets over pumping radiators. They stumbled out of bed in the middle of the night to put buckets under rafters where broken slates were letting in water. They put up with it, but in the end, everyone became thoroughly depressed at the dull, wet greyness of it all. Which is probably why Ben exploded.

To be fair, he had taken four phone calls from Roy Ormley that were the most asinine communications he had ever had the misfortune to receive in his entire working life. Janice refused to answer the phone, and she would not take over from him when Ormley said he would like to discuss her art classes.

'Why is this guy phoning us up all the bloody time?' he yelled after slamming down the receiver for the second time that day. 'Next time *you* can talk to him.'

'No.'

'No? What the fuck do you mean, no? He wants to talk about the art class, so talk about the bloody art class, will you! I'm sick of the sound of his bloody voice.'

She walked out of the room.

'Janice, for Christ's sake, what's wrong?' he called.

Stupid question. What wasn't wrong? He picked up the telephone and dialled a London number.

'Eileen, it's Ben.'

'Ben. This is a surprise. How's Janice? How's the bathroom coming on? We haven't talked for ages. Is everything all right . . . ?'

He cut short the deluge. 'How soon can you get over here?'

'What?'

'I said, how soon can you get over here?'

'Well, this is a bit sudden. What exactly do you mean, how soon?'

'I mean, how many hours to pack, get in that bloody car of yours, and get that arse of yours over here?'

A long silence.

'I'd like to speak to my sister.'

'So would I.'

'What have you done now, Ben?'

'For Christ's sake, Eileen, I haven't done a damn thing, which is part of the problem. Janice needs help. Your help.'

Another silence.

'I can set off in three hours. How long is the drive?'

'Give yourself five hours.'

'I'll be with you around midnight, then. Tell me how to get there.'

Ben knocked gently on the bedroom door and went in. Janice was curled up on the bed, her back to him. Awake. Silent. He sat on a chair.

'Some shitty things have been happening. I thought we were dealing with them, but I guess two deaths take some handling.' He could tell she was listening, but he could not understand why she wasn't responding. No matter how bad things might get between them from time to time, they had always been able to talk. 'I haven't been much help, either, have I? I mean, all this crap about my next book, and getting you involved in that bloody hospital. Pretty stupid.' A pause. 'So I asked Eileen to come over. In fact I insisted. She'll be here around midnight.'

29

High in the mountains above the Lindisholm valley the underground streams, swollen by the rainfall, jetted from the mountains like monstrous hydrants, pouring through the leats to the refurbished mill, powering the hammers and turning the wheels that smashed and ground the bones from the hospital slaughterhouse.

Sedated for the night, in his metal cot, deep within Delta Cloister, Lion sensed the grinding and the hammering beneath the hum of the hospital. He brought his wrist tag slowly up to his nose and breathed in the odours of high technology that included the faint, tell-tale smell of marzipan. Lord Beltane had ordained Lion's martyrdom. Strange. He had thought about the deaths of many others, never his own. When the time came, would he be worthy?

Lion smiled. Either way, what did it matter? The ancient gods were calling him, and he would answer their calls. He would guide the People into the paths of righteousness. He would smite the enemies of the Lord and grind them into dust so that they could be reborn as the flowers, as the grain, and as the beasts of the field; for he was the chosen of the Lord.

30

Ben took a tray of tea and sandwiches upstairs and found Janice preparing the guest bedroom with towels and fresh linen.

'Thought you might like this.'

'You could have asked me first.'

'It's avocado and crispy bacon. Your favourite.'

'Not the sandwiches. Eileen.'

'But I thought you wanted her to come and visit.'

'I do. It's just that you could have consulted me first.'

'For Christ's sake, you haven't been talking to me, have you?'

She rubbed her hand across her eyes tiredly. 'Sorry. You're right. It will be great to have her here. Thank you.'

Eileen dropped everything to journey quickly to Brianne Mill, and she arrived at ten thirty, greeting Ben with her usual frosty reserve. Ben wondered once again how sisters could be so different. Eileen, short, dark and plump, hugging the lithe, sensual, fair-skinned Janice. Not a hint of family resemblance between them. And once again he marvelled at Eileen's deft ability to shut him out. By the time he brought her cases from the car and carried them to her room, she had settled Janice at a corner of the kitchen table where there was no space for anyone else, refusing his offer of tea or coffee.

His 'I'll just pop along to the pub, then, and leave you two to catch up on things,' was rewarded with a look of disapproval. As far as Eileen was concerned, he could do nothing right, and Janice always seemed oblivious to the fact.

'It's rather late to be out pubbing, isn't it?' Eileen asked, pointedly.

'Things are more civilised round here,' he told her. 'They keep pulling pints as long as we keep drinking them.'

The bar was quite busy, and several people looked up and stared when he walked in. Tom Attwood and Mary Drover were sharing a table with Alan Walters and the farmer Gwyn Evans.

'Evening, Ben,' Walters said. 'What can I get you?'

Ben saw that their glasses were almost empty and insisted on buying a round.

'Quite a kerfuffle at your place,' Attwood commented when he settled down.

'That poor boy,' Mary sighed. 'What a dreadful thing! You must be terribly upset, both of you. How is Janice taking it?'

'It hasn't been easy. I asked her sister Eileen over, you know, to give a hand. They're having a good old chinwag, so I thought I'd leave them to it.'

'If there's anything I can do to help, just let me know.'

'Thanks, Mary.'

'It must be quite an ordeal, what with the police tramping around, asking questions,' Walters said. 'Have they figured out exactly what happened?'

'Maybe Ben doesn't want to talk about it,' Gwyn Evans said.

'That's all right. I think we're all pretty sure what happened. The real problem is why.'

'Let's not forget where the lad came from,' Attwood observed. 'Could be all kinds of reasons.'

As they pondered this, one of the young farmers at a nearby table stood up and walked unsteadily towards them, before stopping in front of Ben.

'Is it true what they say about his hand, then? Cut off, was it?'

'Now, John, let's not bother Mr Kirby with questions like that, shall we?' Gwyn Evans said.

'Then there's that young lad Donny Talgarth. Ritual killing, someone said it was. Could be someone cut off this other lad's hand the same way. Ritual.'

'All right, John. That's enough.'

'No it ain't. We've got a bloody right to know what's going on round here.'

'There's nothing going on that you need worry about,' Alan Walters told him.

'Nothing going on?' The young farmer leered at Ben. 'I dunno about that. My Aunty Marion seen that flash bugger from London driving into your place right about when that lad is supposed to have drowned himself. That's what she told that detective, anyhow.'

Ben stood up, fists clenched.

'He's drunk, Ben,' Walters said quickly.

Gwyn Evans took the farmer's arm and pushed him firmly back to his table. 'Let the man enjoy his pint, can't you?'

But the beer had turned very sour in Ben's mouth.

First thing in the morning, before Janice or Eileen were awake, Ben called Lampeter police station and asked to speak to Jennifer Matthews.

'Detective Sergeant Matthews is out on a call,' the clerk told him.

'Could you tell me when she will be back?'

'I'm afraid not, sir. Can I tell her who called?'

'Ben Kirby. I'm coming into Lampeter, soon. I'll call in to see if she's back.'

When he replaced the phone, Eileen was standing at his study door. 'I take it you're trying to see that female detective who Janice told me about. Do you think that's wise?'

'Do you think that's any of your business?'

'Anything that upsets my sister is my business. She seems to think you fancy the woman. I certainly wouldn't put it past you.'

He glared at her, exasperated, fighting the familiar red mist. 'You know, Eileen, your concern for Janice is the one thing that's kept you from pole position on my shit list.'

'Charming. When you get back I'm going to give you a real piece of my mind. You're behaving like a piece of shit yourself. But then that's not so unusual. I wish Janice had never met you.'

When he called at the police station, Jennifer Matthews had not returned, so he sat in his car, brain spinning at a frenetic speed. Questions about Janice and Ormley, the need to produce another book, the suspicions and speculation about Lindisholm, the menacing Geoffrey Abbott, the deaths of two young men on his – their – property, the ingratiating Fred Newson and his scams with the farmers, the unbearable Eileen. One thing was sure: he had to separate the Lindisholm project from his domestic life. But everything seemed welded to everything else.

He was making a real effort to relax, to let his mind slow down, when Jennifer Matthews tapped at his window.

'Hello,' he said. 'I was hoping to have a chat.'

He looked tired. It took the hard edges away.

'Sure. Let me dump my things in the station, and I'll buy you a drink.'

Jennifer got to the bar first and ordered two pints. She was so bloody capable. He wondered if she ever behaved irrationally, if she ever screwed up.

'Thanks.'

'Pleasure. What's the problem?'

She guessed what the problem was. On top of all the trauma, he had probably found out that his wife had had a visitor she hadn't told him about. There weren't too many conclusions you could draw from that kind of scenario. She reminded herself that this was a material witness in two recent deaths and that the coroner had yet to pronounce on the probable cause. Sometimes material witnesses became suspects.

'I just want . . .' Suddenly he wasn't sure what he did want. 'Everything is in a bloody mess. I need to know what's going on.'

'Fair enough. We're still not sure about Donny Talgarth, but Wesley is a straightforward suicide. His fingerprints are all over the axe, and his lungs were completely filled with river water. He probably blew out all his breath and sucked in a lungful. It's quick and painless, so I'm told.'

'Apart from the amputation of his hand, you mean.' He rubbed his eyes wearily. 'Jesus Christ!'

'I'm sorry.'

'Why are you sorry? Janice keeps telling me it's her fault, because she thinks she could have stopped him, somehow. Maybe it's my fault. We kept forgetting that Wesley was a mental patient. We don't even know why he was there. Maybe we could have helped him. Who knows?'

'You were helping him by letting him work on your property.'

'We were using him.'

She thought he was referring to the work Wesley was doing around the farm. 'It was all part of his therapy, wasn't it?'

'I don't mean that. As we got to know him, we realised that Wesley was frightened of something. Janice thought it had to do with the other patients. That's why she was so freaked out by that business with Donny. I think she has a point.'

Jennifer sighed. 'Let's not go down that route again.'

'It's all right for you, but I have to live with this. I have to live with a lot of things. Like what was Roy Ormley doing at my home when Wesley died – fucking my wife or killing a patient?'

Some of the customers glanced at the source of the raised voice, then looked away quickly when he glared back.

'The fingerprints . . .' she began.

'Are you telling me you can't fake fingerprints onto something? Plus, suicides who drown themselves often tidy their clothes up first. So Wesley goes for a walk, Ormley follows with the axe wrapped in plastic, chops his hand off to make it easier, holds him under the water, then does the tidy clothes ploy to help make it look authentic.'

'Why would Ormley do that?'

'Why would Wesley do it?'

'Maybe we'll find out from the hospital, if we ever get to interview the right people. But I can tell you one thing. Wesley took his clothes off by himself. Only his footprints were by the tree. He piled his own clothes tidily, then he found a log, put his left wrist on it, and chopped his hand off with one clean blow. Then he drowned himself.'

'No, I don't buy that. He was happy working with us. It doesn't make sense.'

'Like you said, let's not forget Wesley was a mental patient,' she reminded him. 'It probably made sense to him. Who knows?'

Ben looked utterly dejected.

'You liked him, didn't you?'

'We both did. We had become very fond of him. I think he liked us, as well.'

Jennifer stood up, looked at her watch. 'Got a moment to add some of that to your statement?'

'I haven't said anything significant, have I?'

'Just to flesh things out a little. It all helps. It won't take a minute.'

Inside the police station, she took him into an interview room and closed the door. Then she opened her briefcase and pulled out a file.

'So, you're working on all this, are you?'

'On all what?'

'As a writer, you're working on something concerned with the hospital?'

'What makes you think that?'

233

'I'm a detective, for heaven's sake. Here we have an investigative writer, his professional curiosity aroused by the UK's premier high-security mental hospital, getting himself and his wife involved in tutoring inside the place. How would you add all that up, Ben?'

'No comment.'

'Ah, well. It's none of my business. Excuse me for a moment.' She smiled and left the interview room, closing the door firmly.

The file she had left on the table was headed, 'Wesley Freeman'. It contained the dossier on his arrest at Elm Park Senior School in Wolverhampton, the charges of attempted rape and grievous bodily harm, the weeks at Brinsford remand centre, the reports of the social worker and psychiatrists, the court records, the commitment to Lindisholm Hospital. Ben scribbled notes frantically. By the time Jennifer returned he was sitting relaxed, his notebook back in his pocket.

'I think we're about through,' she said.

'Thanks.'

'Don't worry, Ben. I have a feeling you might be able to repay the favour, with interest. By the way, Wesley's mother is due to make the formal identification tomorrow morning at nine thirty in Carmarthen. The hospital mortuary.'

Janice saw Ben arriving back from Lampeter from the bedroom window. She had been gazing towards the henhouse. It was about a hundred feet away, and the window had been open when Ormley was in the room . . . in the bed. And Wesley had been tending to the chickens, when . . . when she had climaxed, cried out . . . Was that why Wesley had gone to the river? Could such a thing drive a young man to commit suicide?

Ben took a deep breath, called, 'Hi!' and came up the stairs into the bedroom. 'Where's Eileen?'

'I asked her to go back to London.'

'Why on earth did you do that? I thought you'd be glad of her company.'

'So did I. But there's something we have to sort out, between us. We couldn't do that with Eileen here. You know what's she's like. Anyway, I heard what she said to you. She had no right to speak to my husband like that.'

She sounded very calm, and he remembered one of his friends

234

telling him that people who committed suicide through stress often behaved normally at the end, as if their decision had solved all their problems. He felt a surge of panic.

'What's the mattress doing downstairs?'

'We need a new one.'

'That is a new one.'

'No it's not. We need a new one.'

She was telling him about Ormley, and he didn't think he could handle it. But he could see that she couldn't handle it, either. He moved towards her, and she shrank back.

'It's all right.'

He was forgiving her. That made it worse.

'It's not all right.'

How could she possibly tell him about the orgasm, the love cry that had carried across the fields? She knew with absolute certainty that her elemental sound had led Wesley to his final act.

'We must get over this,' he said. 'Ormley, Wesley . . . We have to talk.'

'I know, but it's so hard.'

'Let me tell you about Wesley. He was a very disturbed boy long before he came to Brianne Mill. DS Matthews let me see his file. He was charged with sexual assault on his teacher and physical assault causing actual bodily harm on the school groundsman. Christ knows what really happened, but that's not the Wesley we came to know, is it?'

She shook her head, blinded by tears.

'His mother is due in Carmarthen tomorrow for the identification. I'd like to be there. I'd like us both to be there.'

There were two people in the hospital mortuary viewing area when Ben and Janice arrived, a young clerk from the coroner's office and a woman in her mid-forties wearing a dark suit and hat, strained, making a big effort to retain her composure. Mrs Freeman. The clerk glanced across as they came into the room, but Wesley's mother just stared at the viewing window, which was obscured with a purple curtain. No one said anything. At nine thirty, two young mortuary attendants pulled the curtain aside to reveal Wesley lying on a bier, carefully draped in a linen shroud. His arms were crossed over his heart, with no sign of the injury, and someone had put a large daisy in his fingers. His face was smooth and peaceful, with no hint of the fear that clouded it so frequently.

The clerk murmured something to Mrs Freeman, who nodded, then whispered, 'Yes, that is my son. That is Wesley.'

The clerk made a note on his clipboard.

'I need you to sign this, Mrs Freeman.'

She managed to scribble a signature.

'Can I go to him?'

'Of course.'

One of the attendants opened the door, and she went to Wesley, standing over him, upright, fighting tears. Then she gently took the daisy and put it in her purse, leaned down and kissed his forehead.

'The inquest will be held next Wednesday,' the clerk said when she rejoined them. 'We can release your son to you immediately afterwards, if you let us know what arrangements you would like to make.'

'I want my boy to come home.'

'Yes, madam.'

She took a deep breath, and only then did she notice Ben and Janice. She stared at them, puzzled, and Ben went over to her.

'I'm Ben Kirby, Mrs Freeman. This is my wife, Janice. We're so very sorry.'

Her face cleared slightly. 'Yes. Wesley wrote about you. He said you were very kind to him. Thank you.'

She was making an awesome effort not to collapse, and Janice went and took her hand.

'Would you like to see where he ... where he left us? It's very beautiful.'

'I have to catch the bus soon. I have to be home this evening.'

'We can take you to Aberystwyth station afterwards. There are trains direct to Wolverhampton from there. It'll be quicker than the bus, anyway.'

'I don't want to put you to any trouble.'

They took her to the river and let her stand by herself with her thoughts, gazing across the valley and listening to the shrill keening of kites and buzzards and the calls and twittering of dozens of smaller birds. She took the daisy from her purse and tossed it into the water, then walked back to them.

'It is beautiful. He must have been happy, at the end, mustn't he?'

'I guess so,' Ben said.

They all three knew it wasn't true.

'We've got time for some tea,' Janice told her.

Ruby Freeman hesitated. 'Is it far to that place, where he was?'

'The hospital? No more than twenty minutes,' Ben said. 'Would you like us to take you there?'

She nodded.

'Tea first,' Janice insisted. 'We could all do with a cup.'

Ben checked his large-scale map and discovered the drovers' track which Newson had used to show Ormley the mills. The rains had gone and the clouds had lifted, so there was a clear view down the valley to the concentric circles of Lindisholm. Ruby stared down.

'My son died because of that place,' she said softly. 'It is evil. Evil. He knew. He was very sensitive. Can't you feel it?'

Ben glanced at Janice. Was it evil that they were feeling?

'It's down there,' Ruby said, 'and it's breeding. He is down there.'

'Who is?' Ben asked.

'The evil one. Satan. The one who took my boy from me. I'd like to go home now, please.'

'Poor woman,' Janice said that night. 'I wonder why her husband didn't come.'

Ben remembered the social worker's report in Wesley's police file.

'No love lost between stepfather and son, apparently.'

'Still, you'd think he'd have been here!'

'You were great, today,' he said, and was rewarded with a small smile.

'Was I, Ben?'

'Yes, you were. It was very kind to ask her back. I'd never have thought of that.'

'She seemed so lost.'

'I'm going to the funeral,' he decided suddenly. 'Do you want to come?'

Janice shook her head. 'No, but you go. I have plenty to do here. Keep my mind off it all.'

'Okay.' He paused. 'What are we going to do about these bloody classes on Monday?'

'Haven't thought about it.'

But she did think about it then. And the answer came back clearly. Every whiff of Lindisholm or anyone connected with the hospital carried a stench; from the fear they sensed in Wesley, to those dreadful stories that Ben's patients were piling on him, Donny's death, the religious maniac O'Brien, Wesley's suicide ... And then there was Newson's organic farm chain that Ormley had boasted about. If anything smacked of corruption, that did. To cap it all, they had Ruby Freeman's reactions. Okay, so Ruby was probably a church-going lady using biblical language, with all her talk of the evil one, but she had sensed something bad down there in the valley, too. Surely so many people couldn't be suffering from an overwrought imagination. Surely there was something terribly wrong at Lindisholm Hospital.

'Wesley's mother seems to be a good judge of right and wrong,' she said. 'I think we should carry on. Both of us.'

32

The international development of the Lindisholm Hospital concept included a financial exit route for Keith Melton that would create a vast personal fortune. Nothing and no one would be allowed to get in his way. In particular, not those two lunatic bastards Leamington and Abbott. When the hospital authorities had alerted him to Leamington's disappearance, he explained that the Army had moved the major to a secret treatment centre and that no one was to be informed of the details for reasons of national security. This kept them off his back, but he knew that he could not keep the Army out of it for very long. At the very least, he needed to know what had happened, so that he could provide some kind of explanation.

He stared at Jamie Batson's report. Apart from the man's bed and personal cabinet, no trace of ex-Major Christopher Leamington had been discovered during the search of Alpha Cloister. Not a hair. Not a red corpuscle. Not a single double helix of DNA. Leamington had escaped from Lindisholm Hospital, and Melton had to know how. He had to discover the fault and fix it, otherwise his plans would be ruined. This put ex-Sergeant Geoffrey Abbott in a very hot seat indeed.

It put Lindisholm's computer manager Robert Dagby in the line of fire as well. Leamington could not have escaped without Abbott's assistance, but neither could he have done so unless the security system had a flaw. Melton sent Dagby an encrypted e-mail, instructing him to investigate the basic level of computer instructions, the machine code, to see if there was anything out of line.

Melton had other problems. Routine, perhaps, but they had to be dealt with nevertheless. There was this young fool getting killed, closely followed by the first suicide of a patient in years, and both on an unofficial work placement scheme at the same bloody farm. To add to the grief, the grapevine carried rumours that his PR director was distracted by the randy wife of a nosy journalist. He also had to deal with the unauthorised business venture of Lindisholm's general manager, Alex Searle, and the Lindisholm farm manager, Fred Newson.

He needed some kind of activity that would pull the idiots together, to make them work like a team, instead of behaving like a bunch of dribbling farts. Melton looked at his diary and picked up the telephone.

'Roy Ormley.'

'Keith here, Roy. We're having an open day at Lindisholm on November the first. I'm faxing the guest list to you. I'd like your recommendations by nine o'clock tomorrow morning.'

He put down the phone.

Ormley stared into his mouthpiece in horrified disbelief. That gave him less than three weeks. It was impossible. He turned the phone off and took several deep breaths. Calm down, Roy. This is the kind of thing that gets the old adrenaline flowing. This is what you're good at. Think about what Melton said. An open day, but he was sending Ormley a guest list. Everything depended on that list. Ormley opened the drinks cabinet and poured himself a large whisky. He was halfway through it when the fax machine began purring.

Christ! Three government ministers, half the CareCorp board, the hospital architect, representatives of several embassies and consulates – the kind of people who had full diaries for the next two years.

It suddenly struck Ormley that something was missing from the list. No journalists. No local dignitaries. This was not an ordinary open day, in fact not even an open day. It was a sales day. These were all people who stood to benefit when CareCorp launched its overseas sales drive for the Lindisholm franchise. Maybe things were not as bad as they had first seemed. But he would need a great deal of expensive professional help to deal with the arrangements.

33

There are few places more melancholy than an inner-city crematorium in autumnal rain. Grey, dulling drizzle, drenching slabs of anonymous high-rise apartments that provided a sombre background to the featureless chapel buildings and the squat spire that camouflaged the chimney and fooled nobody. Ben arrived as people were leaving from the previous service, and he looked around to identify Wesley's other mourners. The only people he could see were two girls in their late teens, holding small bouquets of roses and carnations. As the time approached to go into the chapel, no one else appeared, so he followed the two girls inside, where a middle-aged vicar stood waiting to greet them. Ben took a chair in the middle row of seats, and the girls sat behind him. The vicar glanced at his watch several times, and then nodded to someone sitting behind a curtain, and hymn music throbbed from an unseen organ.

The vicar was halfway though his second prayer when the door banged open and a family row exploded into the chapel.

'You get back out here, woman! He disgraced the family, you hear me. You got no place in there, and neither has he . . .'

The doors swung shut and drowned out the ranting, and Ruby Freeman walked to the front of the chapel, upright, expressionless, and somehow heroic. She nodded to the coffin lying on the chrome-plated rollers.

'Is my son in that?'

The vicar looked stunned, then managed to say, 'This is the service for Wesley Freeman.'

Ruby walked to the coffin and placed her hand on it, then crumpled to the floor.

'Wesley, Wesley, what have we done to you?'

Ben left his seat and put his arm under hers.

'Come on, Ruby. Sit with me.'

She looked up at him. Tears. Lost. Empty.

'Oh, Mr Kirby. What have we done to my boy?'

When they went outside, a tall, thin man standing by an old Nissan Bluebird lurched forward, fist upraised.

'I told you, I told you . . .'

Ben stood between them, anger boiling up dangerously. 'Take it easy.'

'Take it easy? And who the fuck might you be, telling me to take it easy in front of my wife?'

'This is Mr Kirby,' Ruby said, tiredly. 'He was Wesley's friend.'

'Wesley's friend, was he? Well let me tell you something, Mr interfering Kirby. That boy brought shame and disgrace on his mother.'

'The way you're bringing shame and disgrace on her right now?'

The man swung a blow, and Ben caught his wrist. Held it tight.

'I don't know why you're so angry,' he said. 'My wife and I got to know Wesley well, and he was always a perfect gentleman. Maybe you should try to act like one yourself.'

The man glared at him, then looked away and got into his car.

'Thank you for coming, Mr Kirby. I'd ask you to my home, but . . .' Ruby shrugged and turned to the two girls who were still standing in the doorway of the chapel and gave them a brave smile. 'Thank you for coming too.'

The Bluebird coughed into life and the man hooted the horn. Ruby hesitated. 'I think I should let you see this, Mr Kirby. But please let me have it back. It's all I have left of my boy.'

She handed Ben an envelope and joined her husband in the car, which vanished down the driveway, trailing blue smoke.

The girls turned to walk after it, and Ben called, 'Can I give you a lift somewhere?'

They stared at him, wary of strangers offering lifts.

'You really Wesley's friend?' the one called Beth asked.

'I'd like to think so.'

'Come on, Jackie. He's okay.'

They clambered into the back seat of the Shogun.

'This is nice,' Jackie said as they moved off. She prodded the CD controller. 'Got any Spliff-Rot?'

'Spliff-Rot?'

'Behave, Jackie, will you,' Beth scolded. 'It's her fave band. She's mad about them.'

'Oh.' Ben arrived at the crematorium gates. 'Which way?'

'We've got to get back to work, so you better turn right, then left at the lights.'

As they slipped into the traffic, Ben asked, 'Were you at school with Wesley?'

'That's right,' Jackie said. 'We liked him, didn't we, Beth? Beth went out with him for weeks and weeks. He was your longest steady, wasn't he?'

'Yeah. He wasn't like the others.'

'Wasn't like them in what way?'

There was a pause.

'Well,' Beth said thoughtfully. 'He never pushed it. If you said no, he'd lay off. Mind you, we didn't always say no, did we, Jackie?'

Jackie giggled.

If you said no, he'd lay off!

Seven words that stood the whole Wesley Freeman issue on its head. How could a young lad who 'never pushed it' end up beating his school teacher and attempting to rape her? It did not make sense.

'Did anyone ask you about that kind of thing when Wesley was arrested?'

A surprised silence.

'Like who?'

'His solicitor, his social worker . . . the police?'

'Turn left at the chip shop,' Beth said.

'Bloody police – are you kidding?' Jackie answered. 'All that lot want to do is lock you away, isn't it? Why don't you ask that Miss Squires what happened?'

'Right,' her friend said. 'Ask that Miss Squires. She had the hots for Wesley, didn't she, Beth?'

'Hot and creamy. She went all to pieces if he looked at her. Poor cow.'

Ben recalled Anne Squire's statement. *. . . early evening . . . felt suddenly ill, and Wesley got me a cup of water, then all of a sudden he got hold of me, and I pushed him away. I am not sure what happened next. I remember Wesley hitting me, and then Mr Carver came in, and I think Wesley hit him as well . . .*

Something was very badly wrong.

'Here we are,' Beth said suddenly. 'Thanks for the lift.'

They were outside the gates to a factory. Cracker Knitwear. Packers wanted: apply within.

'You're welcome.'

34

A visit to Elm Park Senior School while Ben was still in Wolverhampton seemed like a very good idea after his chat with Beth and Jackie, but most schools had upgraded their security, so you couldn't wander into the grounds and chat to the pupils. Ben needed an appointment, or at least a reason for going there. He stopped at a pub and got the school's telephone number from directory enquiries.

'My name's Kirby. I'm in Wolverhampton for the day, and I wonder if it would be possible for me to call later this morning to collect a prospectus,' he asked the secretary.

'Of course, Mr Kirby. You can collect one at the school office any time up to four thirty. You'll find the main entrance opposite the fire station in Pollard Road. There's a visitors' car park to the right. You can't miss it.'

He arrived as the pupils were switching lessons, an apparent chaos that swelled, filled the open spaces with a mass of bubbling humanity, and then subsided as quickly as it had started. Ben made his way to the school office, a large room with half a dozen staff sitting at computers, sorting files and dealing with pupils.

'Ben Kirby. I called a short time ago,' he told the girl who came to the service window.

'Oh yes, you'd like a prospectus. I got one out for you.'

'Is there anywhere quiet where I can read through it?'

She looked at him and smiled. 'We're desperately short of space, but you can grab a chair in the headmaster's line-up. Willie! Move over so this gentleman can sit down, would you?'

Ben took his place on a small wooden chair among a group of pupils who were waiting to be seen by the headmaster for one reason or another. He opened the prospectus and thumbed through pages which told him how the school was funded, how it had grown in numbers and in stature over the past five years and how it was beginning to take its place in the scholarship listings. It showed pictures of the new science and language laboratories and the new gymnasium, and here Ben stopped and peered incredulously at the teacher who was helping a pupil to haul himself up a climbing rope. An attractive woman with short blonde hair and a willowy, well-proportioned body. 'Our head of sports gives a young climber a helping hand.'

It could have been Janice standing there, holding the rope steady. The similarity was startling, and Ben suddenly realised how Wesley must have felt, confronted with the double of the teacher he had been accused of attacking.

'Good morning. Are you waiting to see me?'

Ben looked up. Horn-rimmed spectacles, cropped red hair and a chubby smile.

'I'm Charles Grettley, headmaster of this mayhem.'

Ben struggled up from the small chair. 'Ben Kirby. I just popped in to see your prospectus.'

'Welcome to Elm Park. Can I help in any way?'

Ben was on the verge of telling the headmaster a string of half truths to gain his confidence, the kind of thing he had done all his working life. What could be easier than saying he was moving to Wolverhampton; that his son was very athletic; so what facilities did Elm Park offer, and could he meet the sports teacher, please? All of a sudden, that was not an option. No more deceit or subterfuge.

'I'm researching a book that involves an ex-pupil of Elm Park Senior School.'

'Good gracious! Has one of our old boys achieved some kind of fame, Mr Kirby?'

'He died a few days ago, headmaster. Wesley Freeman. I've just been to his funeral.'

Grettley's smile faded. 'You are writing a book about Wesley?'

'No, not about Wesley, but it will certainly involve him. I'm in Wolverhampton to get a feel for things, to see if I can understand what happened here.'

'You'd better come into my study.' Grettley led the way, telling the secretary to stop all calls as he passed the office. 'Sit down, Mr Kirby. Would you like a cup of tea or coffee?'

'Black coffee, no sugar, would be fine.'

Grettley poured out two coffees from a machine behind his desk. 'You are, I assume, hoping to meet Miss Squires.'

'Yes.'

'And you appreciate that I cannot possibly countenance such a meeting. She is still extremely distressed by what happened.'

'I could always wait outside until she finishes, or track her home. But I won't do that. I would simply appreciate meeting her here, while you are present.'

'Why?'

Ben was not sure how best to answer. Should he summarise the tragic sequence of events leading to Wesley's suicide which had begun in this school, with Anne Squires, the woman who, according to two recent pupils, had the hots for a handsome youth who always respected the word no? Should he mention Lindisholm Hospital – not so much the futuristic way forward in the treatment of mental illness as a lethal web of medical malpractice and worse, if even a fraction of his suspicions were correct?

'Do you know where Wesley spent the last few months of his life?'

The headmaster nodded. 'That new high-security mental hospital in Wales, Lindisholm Hospital. The local education authority sent us reports until his eighteenth birthday in case he came back to school.'

'It boils down to this. If Wesley did everything the police charged him with, then a central plank of my story goes up the creek, and Lindisholm will retain its reputation as a shining example of mental health treatment. On the other hand, if Wesley didn't do these things, I may get a chance to prove that the company behind Lindisholm is one of the most dangerous and corrupt organisations in the country. And I have to tell you that everything I have learned about Wesley makes it impossible for me to believe he attacked Miss Squires. She did withdraw her statement, after all.'

'Joe Carver didn't, and Wesley assaulted him too.'

'The groundsman. I know.'

The two men stared at each other. Grettley picked up his phone.

'Betty, would you ask Anne Squires to come here right away? Thanks.' There was a long silence, then he looked out of his window at the pupils making their way across a playground. 'Would you believe that I became a teacher because I wanted to share the joy of mathematics with young and eager minds, Mr Kirby? Now look at me. I've become an administrator, an accountant, a social

247

worker, a public relations manager . . . and now this. How should we pigeon-hole this kind of exercise, I wonder?'

A quiet knock, and Grettley's door opened. In the flesh, Anne Squires' resemblance to Janice was even more astounding than in her photograph. Except for her eyes. Blue instead of grey. And without the fire. Less assertive.

'This is Ben Kirby, Anne. He's writing a book, and he wants to know about Wesley Freeman. I decided to introduce you, but it's entirely up to you whether or not you want to discuss the matter with Mr Kirby. Whatever you decide, he has promised not to make contact with you outside school. I believe Mr Kirby is a man of his word.'

The blue eyes hid behind clouds.

'I have to put all that behind me, Mr Grettley. I don't want to talk about it.'

'That's understandable, Miss Squires,' Ben said. 'I certainly don't want to upset you in any way, but I need to understand why Wesley did what he did and particularly why he refused to give evidence. Maybe you can help.'

The cloudy blue eyes became evasive blue eyes.

'They sent him to a mental hospital, didn't they?'

'Yes, they did.'

'Well, then.'

There was a silence. Grettley glanced at Ben, wondering why he wasn't telling her about Wesley's funeral.

'Sorry,' Ben said. 'I don't understand.'

'They sent him to a mental hospital. I would have thought that gives you your reason, Mr Kirby.' She was near to tears. 'I don't know why he hit me, I really, really don't.'

He believed her. Of all the things Wesley had done or had been accused of doing, attacking his teacher was the most perplexing. It was uncharacteristic. There was no reason for it.

'Okay, Miss Squires. I'm sorry I've upset you like this. But I'd like to have a look at the sports pavilion, headmaster, if that's possible.'

Grettley glanced at his watch. 'I can spare a moment or two. I'll take you there. Thank you, Anne.'

The pavilion was a modern, clean, but well-used building overlooking extensive playing fields and an athletics track. There was a front lobby with cold drinks and snacks dispensers, and doors leading to separate facilities for male and female pupils. Several boys and girls were sipping drinks and nibbling chocolate bars. The headmaster clapped his hands for attention. 'Okay, people. My guest and I would like a few moments, if you don't mind.'

There was a shuffling of feet and a dragging of school bags, and suddenly they were on their own, as Wesley and Miss Squires would have been, on that chilly November afternoon, almost a year ago.

Wesley got me a cup of water.

There it was. The cold water dispenser, at the back of the room. She's feeling ill. Wesley gets the water, turns, probably waits while she drinks it. Then something happens. She's got the hots for Wesley. She grabs hold of him? He grabs hold of her? All of a sudden, he's beating the shit out of her, and before you know it the groundsman, Joe Carver, comes along and gets involved.

As Ben stared through the window, Anne Squires appeared on the path leading to the pavilion door.

What did the police report say? Buttons from a woman's blouse scattered on the floor . . . torn pants and bra . . . Wesley's trousers round his feet, underpants round his knees.

And there's Joe Carver striding towards the door, just like Anne Squires was doing now . . . Five, four, three, two, one . . .

Of course!

She came inside and pushed away two girls in sports kit who were trying to follow her.

'The *Express* phoned me at home last night. They want to know how I feel about Wesley's suicide.'

'How do you feel?' Ben asked.

'I feel . . . dreadful. I feel responsible.'

'You're not responsible. I don't think for one moment that you did anything wrong.'

'Neither did Wesley.' She was crying openly, and her eyes had lost that cloudy, evasive look. An acceptance of guilt, bringing the twin reactions of sorrow and relief. 'I let him down, didn't I?'

Ben knew without any doubt that Wesley had attacked his teacher to save her reputation, because the groundsman was about to come into the pavilion, and that he had remained silent because he could not tell the truth and he would not tell a lie.

'We all let him down, Anne,' he said gently. 'Everybody in the bloody system let Wesley Freeman down.'

*   *   *

He had forgotten about Ruby's envelope until he was driving south on the M5, so when he pulled into a service station for diesel he went to the cafeteria for a coffee. The letter was handwritten, and the ink had been smudged in places.

> Dear Mum
> My friend said he can post this without them knowing. Don't tell no one you got it, only I had to let you know. Mum I'm scared. I do the best I can, but it ain't no good. They want me to do things that are wrong. I can't tell you what. I'm all mixed up Mum. The doctors don't know what is happening. They are stupid so I am writing it all down as good as I can on bits of paper, and I got stuff from the computer and other stuff to hide on Mr Kirby's place for him to find. Mr and Mrs Kirby have been good to me Mum so if anything happens you can trust them all the way. I hope everything is good for you and that Steve ain't pestering you no more. He is a bad man Mum like some of the ones we've got in here only they are worse believe me so maybe he ain't so bad after all. Ha ha that sounds crazy don't it? But that's what I am so they say. I know I brought shame and disgrace to the family.
> I am so sorry Mum. I love you.
> Your son
> Wesley

'Are you all right, mate?'

A large lorry driver was staring down at Ben with a worried look on his face. Ben grabbed a paper napkin and blew his nose, hard.

'Thanks, yes, I'm okay.'

'You don't look okay.'

'How do I look?'

'You look like shit.'

'That would be about right,' Ben said.

Back on the motorway, he picked up his mobile phone and called Janice. 'How's everything down on the farm?'

'Productively speaking, fine. Three eggs, two courgettes and a potato. Not what you'd call intensive farming, but it's ours, and not a chemical fertiliser in sight. How was Wolverhampton?'

He was pleased to hear her sounding so upbeat.

'Wolverhampton was astonishing. I'll tell you all about it when I'm home.'

'Any idea what time?'

'Two hours. Maybe two and a half.'

'I'll have a libation ready and waiting. By the way, did you take your diary with you?'

'It's on the desk. Why?'

'I need to phone the vet. One of the hens is acting a little weird . . . It's not on the desk.'

'I left it by the computer.'

'Nope . . . Ah, it's on the mantelpiece. Great. See you later.'

He smiled. Janice could be truly scatterbrained at times.

35

Ben turned into the precipitous road that led to Penford across the Cambrian mountains. It was the kind of track that obliged someone to back up for several yards if two cars met. Not for the inexperienced or the faint-hearted! So when the lights of a motorcycle showed up behind him, there was little he could do to let the rider go past. A cliff down to the river on the left, cliffs up to the peaks on the right. Fortunately, the cycle stayed reasonably far behind, its headlights dipped in the gathering gloom.

His car phone chirruped.

'Ben Kirby.'

'Ben. Good to talk with you.'

'Who's speaking?' It was difficult to hear, because the motorcycle had caught up, and its exhaust was bellowing.

'Geoffrey Abbott.'

The large bland face swam into mental view: Lion.

'What can I do for you, Geoffrey?' Did they let Delta patients make phone calls?

'I just wanted to make contact. To thank you.'

'How do I deserve your thanks?'

Ben had to slow down as the Shogun lifted its front end over a sharply canted rise in the road.

'Don't be so modest. You are helping the People to fulfil their destiny. They can express themselves with more confidence. That's worth a thank you, isn't it? So how was your visit to Wolverhampton?'

'Didn't catch you. There's an idiot on a motorcycle trying to insert himself into my exhaust pipe.'

'Sorry about that. I said: how was your visit to Wolverhampton?'

It's funny, the things that can make your blood run cold. In this case, Ben wasn't sure whether it was Abbott's reference to Wolverhampton or the fact that the motorcycle pulled back several yards. Or both.

A mental patient from the top security cloister in Lindisholm was following him on a dark and lonely road and discussing the events of the day. What the hell was going on?

He slowed down at another hair-raising corner, and the motorcycle surged up again.

'It was so-so. I went to a funeral.'

'Poor Wesley. One of life's tragic victims.'

Ben discovered that sweat was running down his face and soaking his collar. He also discovered that he was driving far too quickly when the Shogun clawed its way round a narrow hairpin bend and ricocheted off an outcrop of rock.

'Steady, steady. Can't have you joining Wesley, can we now? According to Lord Beltane, it's not your time. You still have much to teach us. And we still have much to learn from you, but there's a conundrum, Ben, after you assured us you were only interested in helping us to write. Why is our tutor driving all the way to Wolverhampton for Wesley's funeral? Does this make sense?'

The road began twisting into a valley where the river looped backwards and forwards under several stone bridges.

'I love these mountains, don't you, Ben? So clean, apart from what the human race is doing to them, of course. I have to keep my eye on all that. Part of my job, you might say.'

'What do you want, Abbott?'

'I told you. I want nothing. You want to know why, Ben? Because I have everything. Those genetic incompetents in Lindisholm have, despite themselves, accomplished something wonderful for me during my sojourn there. They have freed me, Ben.'

'What?'

Another arm-wrenching turn in the road, and Ben slammed his brakes on. The motorcycle braked almost simultaneously, staying several feet to the rear. Abbott's reflexes were incredibly fast.

'I said, they freed me.' The smug voice continued as if nothing had happened. 'They made me immune to the system. I can do anything I want. Anything. And what can they do to me that they haven't already done? It's exquisite, isn't it?'

There was a farm near the river bridges. Maybe Ben could drive up there and get this lunatic off his back.

'Depends what it is you want to do.'

'I want to serve Lord Beltane. That is now the entire purpose of my life.'

The turning for the farm was coming up on the right, and Ben slowed down.

'I wouldn't go there, Ben. What'll it achieve? A dead farmer and a crippled writer. Stay on the road, like a good chap.'

Fear stabbed again. Very cold and numbing. He carried on, across the bridges and towards the pine forests on the mountain range up ahead.

'Tell me, what do you have to do to serve Lord Beltane?'

'I have to do everything I can think of in case that's what He wants. How's that for freedom?'

'It's insane.'

'Not at all. It's the ultimate sanity. Can't you hear how happy I am? Shit, I've never been so happy. I could break your neck, go and confess, and what can they do to me that they aren't already doing? I can do any fucking thing I want, and no one can touch me.'

'There's always someone who can touch you.'

'I take it you're thinking of the Lord Beltane, or maybe White Eagle. Why should they want to touch me, when I'm doing their bidding?'

Lord Beltane? White Eagle? What was all this shit?

'Not at all. Take me, for instance.' He slid the car round another blistering corner. 'If I can make you happy enough to deserve your thanks, what's to stop it working the other way? What's to stop me doing something that really pisses you off?'

There was a silence.

'Very cunning, Ben, very cunning. But when it comes to cunning, I think Lion has the edge. Just think of this conversation and ask yourself: how can Lion do this? Ask yourself what Lion will do if you make him unhappy. Ask yourself, what is Lion going to do next? Ah yes. What next? If I'm not mistaken, I can get from here to Brianne Mill at least twenty minutes before you, where your beautiful wife waits. A lovely woman, Ben. Quite lovely.'

The motorcycle engine gunned to high revs, and the large bike roared into the trees by the side of the road to emerge several yards in front of the Shogun. Ben felt sick. His mobile phone could not get a call signal, so he wrenched the car round, banging into trees and rocks, until he was driving at breakneck speed back to the farm by the river.

He interrupted the farmer's evening meal.

'Please,' he gasped. 'I must use your telephone.'

It seemed ages before Janice answered.

'You sound awful. What's the matter?'

He gulped several breaths.

'I want you to get in the car and go straight to Tom Attwood's place. If he's not at home, go to the Blue Lion and stay there. Do it now.'

'God, Ben, what on earth's wrong?'

He was almost in tears.

'For Christ's sake, please, just do it now. Forget your bag. Forget the bloody animals. Put the phone down now and get out of there. Go on, put the fucking telephone down NOW and go!'

There was a click and then the dialling tone. He looked up to find the farmer, his wife and three small children staring at him.

'I need to call the police.'

They kept on staring as he punched 999.

'What? What number am I speaking from . . . ?' Ben held out the phone.

'Two six one five nine five,' the farmer said into the mouthpiece.

'You got that? Now listen to me. There's a maniac going to my house on a motorbike. What? Ben Kirby, for Christ's sake. Brianne Mill. My wife's on her own. That's where he's heading, and I'm on my way there.' He slammed the phone down. 'Thanks.'

'I don't suppose you'd like a cup of tea?' the farmer's wife asked.

'A brandy?' her husband suggested.

One of the children began to cry.

He drove to Tom Attwood's house first, but it was dark and silent, so he swung the car towards the Blue Lion. As he sped towards the village, he passed a police car partly hidden in a known vantage point to catch unwary drivers who were speeding or not wearing a seatbelt. A few seconds later its headlights shone into his driving mirror, and its blue lights began to flash. He jammed his brakes on and leaped out of the car.

'Where's my wife? Is she all right?' he shouted at the young police driver.

The policeman got out of his car too. 'Are you aware that this road has a fifty mile an hour speed limit, sir?'

Disbelief.

'You what?'

'I have to ask if you have been drinking, sir.'

'Drinking? There's a bloody maniac on a motorbike trying to get to my wife, for Christ's sake. I called the emergency number.' Ben's voice trembled and rose up and down the scale uncontrollably. 'I'm on my way to find her.'

'I must inform you that I suspect you have been drinking, and I intend to breathalyse you, sir. Would you mind getting into the back of my car while I take your details?'

As the policeman opened the car door, Ben lurched forward and gave him a vigorous push.

'You stupid, stupid fucker!' he shrieked.

Minutes later he broadsided into the Blue Inn car park and careered into the bar. Janice was sitting on a bar stool, talking to Harry Price.

'Thank God!' Ben shouted.

She just had time to say, 'What in heaven's name is going on . . .' before the young police constable burst in.

If Ben thought his evening had been bad, the worst was yet to come. It was like slow motion.

'Right, sir. I am arresting you for assaulting a police officer. You do not have to say anything, but –'

'Listen to me, you stupid little fuck, there's a maniac threatening my wife, and all you can do is give me this shit!'

'Ben, calm down,' Janice warned.

'Calm down? I'll calm down when this arsehole apologises.'

'November Charlie one five. Do you read me? Over,' the policeman said into his radio.

That did it. Ben swung a fist, and the young policeman crashed to the floor where he lay twitching.

'We could say he slipped,' Harry Price said thoughtfully, 'but I don't think anyone will believe us.'

The police sergeant who arrived to sort things out was in no mood to compromise. He arrested Ben, drove him to the police station in Lampeter and locked him emphatically in the single cell, despite protestations that a madman had threatened to assault Janice. After a couple of hours to allow him to cool off, the sergeant got Ben in front of his desk and read the riot act.

'This is not the way we expect people to behave round here, but I'm told on good authority that you have been under a considerable amount of pressure. That is no excuse, of course, but bearing in mind that Constable Evans has generously agreed not to press charges, I am offering you the opportunity to accept an official caution and give me your assurance that this episode will not be repeated.'

'Absolutely,' Ben said. 'I'd like to apologise to the constable. Is he all right?'

'Tim Evans is prop forward in my village rugby team, Mr Kirby. He says you caught him by surprise. Reading between the lines, I don't think he would be very happy to let the world know he was put on his back by a writer, if you take my meaning.'

'Where do I sign?' Ben asked in relief.

36

Lindisholm's computer manager Robert Dagby checked the machine code listing for the tenth time, hoping that what his programmers had pointed out was a mistake. But no. There was the sub-routine that contained an incomplete compilation of hospital security codes. Any patient with a wrist tag set to a missing code would be able to walk through the system as if he or she were on a day trip to Brighton. Dagby did not know why Keith Melton suspected that there was something wrong with the system, and he didn't care. Melton's reputation for ruthlessness with his staff was legendary. He took a deep breath and picked up the phone.

'Keith, it's Robert Dagby. I believe we've found what you might be looking for. There is an exception error for some of the security codes.'

'Exception error?'

'That means something is excluded from the program that should be there. In this case it's a range of code numbers. This particular error nulls security for any patient assigned one of the missing numbers. Fortunately, these particular numbers are outside the range currently in use.'

Melton thought hard. Only Leamington and Abbott had been issued with security numbers outside the normal range, but no one knew that, least of all Dagby.

'You better e-mail me those numbers right away.'

'No problem.'

'How could this get into the system?'

'The program team thinks it's part of an early test cycle that stayed with the finished program. The alternative explanation is that someone managed to access the machine code and alter it. This would be highly unlikely in view of the firewall. It would take a genius with a lot of time and some luck to get through that.'

Melton grimaced to himself. Lindisholm was not short of geniuses with plenty of time. Luck was something else. Melton did not believe in it.

'What about program documentation?'

Dagby had been dreading this question. If only program compilers weren't so bloody lazy.

'There is no program documentation, I'm afraid. Explanations and notes were appended to the code as it was written. If anything goes wrong with the basic code, we'll have no references to sort it. We no longer write code like that, of course.'

To his amazement and relief Melton replied: 'Thanks for the call, Robert. You've solved part of a mystery. Good work.'

So Christopher Leamington could have avoided the Lindisholm security system. But Dagby's report created more questions. How come this particular patient's security number coincided with this gap in the security coding? How could Leamington have been aware of the gap? Someone must have assisted Leamington to escape, and one name was in the frame: Geoffrey Abbott. In any case, how would he have known about the gap? Then again, why had Abbott not escaped?

Melton was convinced about one thing: Major Christopher Leamington had done what many professional soldiers had done over the centuries: escaped incarceration and gone to ground. He probably had a small fortune salted away in various names and in various countries. Survival was not a problem for Leamington, at least not for the moment. Melton had the ultimate sanction against Leamington, should it ever be needed. Against Abbott, too.

37

Dr Nikki Congleton put down the phone and stared at it in surprise. Professor Jonser's instruction had been simple to the point of rudeness: *Come to my office now without fail.* It was also a break with the tradition of communication by computer. People went to people's offices when something very serious was up, or something very trivial, like a social meeting. Congleton had no social meetings. Neither did Jonser. So this must be serious. Jonser probably needed her help with a difficult diagnosis, or guidance as to how best to deal with a patient.

All this was on her mind when she knocked on Jonser's door and went inside, to find half the hospital management committee staring at her. It took a few seconds to realise that the stares were anything but friendly. Tim Johnson from security, Robert Dagby from information technology, and Alex Searle, general manager. There were also two of the men who had been involved with the recent maintenance work in Delta Cloister. Tough, smart, military-looking.

'We have a crisis,' Professor Jonser said without preamble. 'One of your patients is involved. Geoffrey Abbott. You recall my notation on his hospital records, I'm sure.'

Only too well. *Code Five applies to this patient.* Meaning: all consultations must be conducted in the presence of at least two security staff. Congleton had breached this regulation and seen Abbott several times in the past few months on her own. Abbott had always been – the word charming sprang to mind – but Congleton was too shrewd to let that fool her. Abbott was charming because he wanted something from her, and she had been trying to ascertain what that might be. She, in turn, wanted something from him. Like the others in Congleton's unofficial research he was subject to her pressures. Code Five meant that he was a particularly dangerous patient. Psychotic, anti-social, unpredictable and ruthless. Congleton therefore used her authority to place him in contact with other patients whenever she could, in the hope that he would snap and reveal his true colours. Ben Kirby's creative writing class had been an ideal opportunity. She had entered Abbott's authorisation for the class and also keyed in Ben and Janice Kirby's temporary staff ID to deal with the Code Five condition, but as yet Abbott had behaved impeccably. Until now, maybe. Congleton's heart gave a little jump. Was her research about to take a positive step forward?

'Anything I can do to help, professor,' she said.

'You can start by explaining this. It appears to be a plan for unauthorised patient research and the misuse of hospital funds and facilities.'

Congleton took the computer printout from Jonser. It was the synopsis of her research paper: *The Fallacy of Mental Illness – a Case Study from Two High-Security Mental Hospitals*.

'This is from my private files.' Congleton was outraged. 'How dare you!'

'Dr Congleton,' Jonser said, calmly. 'Only two weeks after one of your patients committed suicide, we have received an unconfirmed report that another patient, Geoffrey Abbott, has been seen outside the hospital. A third patient is the subject of police interest after the first unfortunate incident at Brianne Mill. Here we have three of your patients involved in high-profile and totally undesirable situations. Your treatment records indicate that you have been consistently placing many of them in situations where they might well encounter the wrong kinds of stress. My concern is to try to understand what you are doing to see if it will help us to contain this crisis. We can do without your tantrums.'

Congleton's outrage changed to bewilderment. 'Outside the hospital . . . Abbott . . . That's impossible.'

'I agree, but we have the report, and we have the fact of Freeman's suicide. We must assume that there is a flaw in our system, and I must know if you have any information that will help. I am particularly concerned to see your private notes.'

Nikki Congleton was damned if she was going to hand over her hard-won information. While Freeman's death was regrettable, it also tended to prove her theory. Too bad if the little thug couldn't take the pace. And, as far as Abbott was concerned, someone had simply made a mistake.

'You've accessed my private files, so you already know my views.'

'I'm trying to make this easy for you,' Jonser sighed. 'I want to see your handwritten notes and anything else that could throw light on the situation.'

'There isn't anything else.'

One of the two maintenance men stood up and walked slowly to stand in front of Congleton – right in front, his nose almost touching hers.

'Let's not fuck around, Dr Congleton. My colleague and I have the authority to strap you to one of your own beds and pump you so full of relaxants you'll be telling us when you last had it up the arse. So why don't you just give the professor what she wants and save us all a lot of trouble?'

It was not so much what he said as the small smile on his face when he said it that convinced Congleton. She pulled a folder from her briefcase and handed it to Jonser.

'Thank you. Is there anything else that might help?'

'There are copies of the work my patients have been doing in that creative writing class you set up.'

'Yes, I am familiar with this material. Have you read it?'

'I noted Kirby's assessments. He's not very good, and neither is the patients' writing.'

A small twitch developed in Jonser's left temple.

'Thank you, Dr Congleton. That will be all, for the time being. Meanwhile, I am withdrawing your authority to use the ECT suite. ECT is restricted to patients who show no response to pharmaceutical treatment, as you would have known if you had taken the trouble to keep up-to-date with current psychiatric practice.'

When Congleton left the room, Professor Jonser quickly scanned her notes and passed the file to the two men.

'Perhaps there's information here that will help you to ask Geoffrey Abbott the right questions, Mr Batson. For instance, there are references to a patient who died of an aneurysm in the hospital farm some months ago. We have investigated this episode, of course, but there is no concrete evidence that the patient's death was other than accidental. What we have in the other pages are flights of patient fantasy. "Lion" is Geoffrey Abbott's nom de plume. I should inform you that the police now want to interview him in connection with his alleged appearance outside the hospital. Needless to say, I objected.'

'We need to see him alone, and with your video system deactivated,' Batson said.

'Naturally.'

Jonser had no intention of turning off the surveillance system. She had a professional interest in all categories of interview techniques.

Geoffrey Abbott was doing effortless chin-ups in his cell, his fingers hooked into the steel mesh of an air-conditioning screen in the ceiling. When the door slid open he hung there, looking amiably at his visitors.

'Hello, Jamie. Hello Terry. Long time no see. How's the Unit?'

Jamie Batson pulled a snub-nosed pistol from his pocket and fired it into Abbott's thigh. It made a coughing sound. Abbott looked at the yellow flight sticking out of his leg.

'At least you didn't have to hide in a pile of Bosnian shit to get that into me like last time, you scrotum.'

Lion felt the weird sharp numbness of the drug travelling through the highways and byways of his body. Russian tranquilliser gun, so probably a derivative of that new stuff, 3-MF. No problem for Lion to deal with this. But let's not give the game away.

Abbott's eyes glazed and he dropped to the floor. Jamie kicked him in the crutch, and he wheezed in pain.

'You mother-fucking animal,' Terry said sincerely. 'Christ knows why the boss stuck you and Leamington in this fucking place. Waste of fucking time, if you ask me.'

'Well, no one did ask you,' Abbott wheezed.

Jamie kicked him again.

'For two pins we'd put you out of your fucking misery right now,' Terry snarled.

'Be my guest.'

Abbott made several attempts to get off the floor, so Jamie leaned down and jabbed another syringe into his leg.

'The old man wants a word.'

Keith Melton watched on his video link-up as the two men lifted Geoffrey Abbott's huge bulk onto his bed, so he was in front of the camera. He was gazing around erratically and trying to sit up. Most people would have been in a coma.

'Hello, Geoffrey. Tell me how you got Major Leamington out.'

Abbott swung his head towards the camera, spittle running down his chin, eyes rolling wildly. Jamie had probably used too much Big Three. Dangerous stuff.

'Tell me how you got him out,' Melton repeated.

Of all the questions for which Melton had ever needed an answer, this was surely the most important. A key patient disappears from the heart of a maximum security institution. A flaw in the programming, Roger Dagby said. Or maybe a cute trick thought up by Leamington and Abbott that the IT team had not anticipated. The two of them were clever enough. Getting in and out of tight situations had been their way of life, after all.

He was about to ask again, when Abbott managed to control his speech functions enough to say, 'The Lord Beltane took Chris into his bosom.'

Then he giggled like he had done the last time Melton had tried to interrogate him, a chilling sound coming from that awesome frame.

'Listen, Geoffrey.' Melton made his voice sound soothing. 'I know it's been tough, but it really would help me to know what happened. I could make your life a hell of a lot easier than you have it now.'

'What happened? The fact is, you got it wrong, didn't you? Tough shit!'

'I don't think we got anything wrong, but I would like to know why this writer thinks he had a conversation with you the other day. You know – Ben Kirby. He says you followed him on a motorbike. Did you get out the same way as Chris? How about it?'

No answer.

'Okay, Jamie,' Melton said. 'Push some caffeine down him and carry on. Get back to me when you're finished.'

It took half an hour, several cups of sweet black coffee and innumerable slaps in the face to get Abbott functioning so that he could talk coherently.

Lion was irritated, beset by two hyenas that he could kill with one sweep of his mighty paw. But that would spoil his plan. That would

*interfere with his holy work. It would anger Lord Beltane and his
son White Eagle. So Lion held back and pretended to let the drugs
and the beating sap his energy and his will.*

Jamie and Terry were skilled in the kind of interrogation that got fast
results in a live-fire situation. Brutal, effective. But this was the first
time they had come up against one of their own kind. More particularly, one of their own kind who had developed his inner resources
beyond their understanding. Their questions were accompanied by
pain, and Abbott's answers were delivered through spittle.

'What happened to Leamington? How did he know his tag wouldn't
trip the security screen? What about your tag, Geoffrey – have you
been walking in and out of here like some fucking tourist?'

'I like it here, why should I bother going outside?'

'We've been told that's exactly what you have been doing, going
outside. Waltzing around the hills, slaughtering animals, riding
motorbikes and doing Christ knows what. Come on, Geoffrey,
what the fuck are you up to?'

'I'd like to help, really I would, but I don't know what you're
talking about.'

'The hell you don't. If you don't come clean, we have authority
to cripple you.'

'Why would you want to do that to an old pal?'

'Old pal! Listen to the man. We hated your guts, Geoffrey, you and
Leamington. Everything you did put the Unit at risk, but you didn't
give a shit, either of you.'

Abbott managed a laugh. 'That's rich. The Unit was always at risk.
You were angry because we got better results. Made the rest of you
look like a bunch of choirboys.'

Even Lion couldn't stop the scream bubbling out of Abbott's
mouth as Terry's knife cut through the nerves in the back of his
right hand.

'Try wanking with that, you fucking animal,' Terry said.

'Okay, smartarse,' Jamie said. 'That'll be all for the time being. By
the way, Keith asked us to mention that he's closed the gap in security,
just in case. He also said to remind you about your Kidderminster tag.
It's been activated, so stay away from any unauthorised checkpoints
if you want to draw your Army pension.'

*   *   *

Professor Jonser saw her visitors off the hospital premises. She was not very impressed with their performance. The medical staff would have to stitch two of Abbott's tendons back together. Stupid, unnecessary and expensive.

'By the way, gentlemen, I need to know what medication you gave him. He is, after all, in my care.'

'Combination of chlorpromazine, scopalamine and trimethyl phentanyl. The Big Three. Never fails. If Abbott can get out, he would have told us. Definitely. We'll just have to see why this guy Ben Kirby thinks different.'

Janice was tending the pot plants by the front door when a dark maroon car came up the drive. Two men got out, clean-shaven, dressed in suits and shiny polished shoes. The shorter of them seemed to be in charge.

'Mrs Kirby?'

'That's right. What can I do for you?'

'My name is James Batson, Mrs Kirby, and this is my colleague Terence O'Malley. Is your husband at home?'

Despite their smart appearance, Janice did not like the look of them. Too cocky. Almost aggressive.

'Can I ask where you gentlemen are from?'

'Certainly. We're employed by CareCorp. We'd appreciate a word with Mr Kirby about the incident he alleges involving a hospital patient.'

'Incident? You mean the lapse in your hospital's security?'

'I wouldn't put it like that, Mrs Kirby,' Batson said.

'How would you put it?'

'As I said, we'd appreciate a word with your husband.'

Janice put her garden basket and gardening fork on a bench and stared at him. 'Do you get training in bad manners, or does it come naturally to you?'

At that moment the sound of a diesel engine roared from behind the trees by the ruined mill. O'Malley gave her an unpleasant smile, and the two men set off over the fields.

Ben was coming to terms with the idiosyncrasies of his second-hand tractor on wet grass when his cordless phone buzzed.

'Two of CareCorp's finest are making their way over to you,' Janice told him. 'Nasty-looking bastards. They are incredibly rude.'

'Rude? What do they want?'

'Something to do with your "allegation" about Geoffrey Abbott. I was within an inch of kicking them out, but they took it upon themselves to find you.'

Ben looked towards the house in time to see two men appear from behind the trees. 'You're right. They are nasty-looking bastards.'

He killed the motor, climbed out of the driving seat and waited for them.

'Mr Kirby, I take it? My name is James Batson and this is my colleague Terence O'Malley.'

'And what can I do for you, Mr Batson, apart from suggesting that you learn a few manners?'

'Oh dear. Have we upset somebody?'

'How about starting with me?'

'I sincerely hope we don't have to do that, Mr Kirby. All we want is to ask a couple of questions about the report you gave the police on Geoffrey Abbott.'

'I don't give a shit what you want. You were not invited onto this property. You are therefore trespassing, and I am telling you to remove yourselves by the shortest possible route.'

'The fuck you are,' O'Malley said.

Ben took out his phone and keyed in a number. O'Malley lurched forward, but Batson held him back.

'Let Mr Kirby make his phone call, Terry.'

They waited while Ben connected with the police.

'Duty officer? This is Ben Kirby at Brianne Mill. I have two trespassers on my property who have threatened me and refused to leave. Yes, they have identified themselves to me. Mr Batson and Mr O'Malley who claim to work for CareCorp plc. Fine.' He held the phone out. Batson took it.

'We are leaving right this minute,' Batson said, and he handed the phone back to Ben.

'We'd still like to know about your allegation. What makes you think Abbott followed you on a motorbike? Do you really think he could wander out of a high-security system and do that?'

'None of your business. Just get off my property.'

'We've checked your cellular phone account, and there's no record of any call being made or received at the time you stated.'

'You're a persistent little shit, aren't you?'

'You have no idea, sunshine.'

O'Malley gave his nasty grin.

Ben held out his arm invitingly and started walking towards the house. 'Why don't I lead the way?'

'We handled this all wrong,' O'Malley said to Batson as they followed him. 'We've been too fucking polite.'

'You think so? Why don't you be less polite, then?'

O'Malley quickened his pace and swung a punch towards Ben's kidneys. Ben side-stepped, and O'Malley slipped on the wet grass and fell into a pile of sheep dung. Ben kicked him in the crutch and turned to face Batson, expecting retaliation.

'Nice one, Mr Kirby. Couldn't have done better myself.' Batson helped his colleague back to his feet, holding firmly onto his arm. 'Calm down, Terry. Mr Kirby has a right to protect himself. Just make sure you wear boots next time you come to the country.'

'Bastard!' O'Malley muttered.

'On balance, Mr Kirby, we don't see how you could be right about meeting Geoffrey Abbott. But if you are right, he went to a hell of a lot of trouble just to have a chat, and that could be very, very bad news for you.'

'How so?'

'Geoffrey kills people. You wouldn't believe how much he enjoys doing that. The more pain, the better. It goes well beyond all this bollocks about sadism or psychosis. With Geoffrey, it's like a religion. Bearing that in mind, you can see how keen we are to check our security.'

'You go a funny way about it. Try being nice to people for a change.'

'We all have our methods, don't we? It would be in your interest as well as ours to clear this one out of the way, believe me.'

'All right. I'll tell you what I told the police, and then you can get the hell out of here.'

38

The visit from Batson and O'Malley was extremely unsettling. Ben felt as if he was being dragged further and further into something beyond his control, something he had not felt in all his years in journalism. Janice was simply outraged by their intrusion.

'Just who do they think they are?'

'They're obviously ex-Army, and not a particularly nice part of the Army,' Ben said.

'You mean like the SAS?'

'Doubt it. I got the impression that they were more high profile. The SAS mostly lie about in the dirt keeping out of everyone's way. They only go berserk if things go wrong. I got the distinct impression that these guys deal directly in the berserk business, whatever that might be.'

'Sounds horrid.'

'I don't like the way things are stacking up. I'm not any closer to figuring what's wrong at Lindisholm, and all of a sudden we have these idiots getting involved. It's like pushing water uphill with a pin. Mind you, that little creep Batson did say something interesting. They got hold of my cellular phone log. Apparently, there's no record of the call I got from Abbott on the mountain road. I better check that out.'

'Surely that's private information.'

'There's no such thing as private information. The phone companies supply the police with that kind of stuff every day of the week. Commercial firms can get hold of it quite easily, too.'

'So, what now?'

He sighed. 'No idea.'

'What about Wesley's letter to his Mum – didn't he say he brought something here?'

'Shit, I'd forgotten about that. He said he hid it somewhere he thought we'd find it sooner or later. Maybe it's in the barn. He was there a lot. Or the henhouse? You try there, and I'll look in the barn,' Ben said.

He searched the benches, poked about in the straw, moved tools and wheelbarrows to one side and then thought of the rafters where Janice had seen Wesley the day Donny was injured. He set a ladder against the barn wall and grabbed a torch. There was nothing obvious, but after a moment the light caught some scratching on the underside of one of the roofing slates. He had to turn his head awkwardly to see the letters.

'*THEY ARE KILLING DONNY. WF*'

'My God,' Janice said when he told her what he'd found. 'Poor Wesley. He must have seen everything. No wonder he was so frightened. The police will have to take my statement seriously now, won't they?'

'They'll probably suggest you wrote it yourself, just to convince them.'

'They wouldn't do that.'

'They might.'

'But his fingerprints will be up there, won't they?'

Ben sighed. 'Maybe. In any case, there must be more than a scratched message. Perhaps he put something in the house.'

'He was hardly ever there. Certainly not unless we were, too.'

They had the brainwave at the same time.

'The Shogun!'

Janice opened the passenger door and looked in the glove compartment and side pockets. Ben poked inside the spare wheel cover and then pulled the back door open and looked in the compartment where the jack was stored.

'Got it!'

'It' was a small leather bag with the opening stitched up, an envelope with several pages of notepaper, and a computer disk with 'LISA: Lindisholm Information System Access, Unit 7, Isis Business Park, Newbury' printed on the label.

Wesley's notes were attempts to explain why he was frightened, and they failed to throw any light on the problem because his fears were largely intuitive, intercepting a look here, a glance there, among people who by virtue of their very existence were behaving oddly. But one contained the observation that the patients who handed out the Treatment to other patients also took part in some sort of communion:

> They do this kind of religious service somewhere in the hospital then they go round like they've done confession or had communion. All smiles and happy faces when they do that and it's scary.

Ben remembered what the grey-haired woman had mumbled to him when Sheila Sallis demonstrated the security system. 'No communion for you, my lad.'

Another note explained why the leather bag was there and referred to the computer disk:

> They gave me the Treatment yesterday, and something else happened. I can't tell you what but they said I should hide this bag near you and it will protect the patients and bring you good luck. I hope it does. I'll put it there tomorrow before I do the henhouse. Harold is my friend and he gave me the computer disk. I don't know what Harold put on it but he said it was for you only don't tell no one else about it or maybe he'll get into trouble. I don't know if They know about the disk or not. You can't tell with Harold.

Ben folded the notes back into the envelope, then used a pair of scissors to unpick the stitching in the bag. When he prised it open and looked inside, a stale, nauseating smell seeped into the kitchen.

'Christ!' He held it out for Janice to see.

'I really do think we should show all this to that policewoman right away,' she said quietly.

'Not the disk. I need to see what that's all about first.' Ben sealed the bag and its contents in a plastic wallet and put it in the freezer.

The disk contained an executable program and a 'Readme' file. This told Ben that to use LISA he should type KeithMelton without spaces and the password ESREVINU. If he saw *Check Super Sysop ID* at any time, he should enter the password again, but reversed to UNIVERSE.

Janice peered over his shoulder. 'What does all that mean?'

'It looks like Wesley's friend Harold has given me the golden key to the Lindisholm computer system. I wonder why.'

'Wesley did say he was helping you. Presumably Harold is friendly with someone with access to this kind of thing. Let's see what it does.'

It was good to see that Janice was bouncing back into the spirit of things.

'I need to back up my work before using it, in case there's a virus on board. Let's tell Jennifer Matthews about this bag first.'

*   *   *

DS Matthews called round at nine o'clock the following morning, accompanied by the young constable Ben had floored in the pub. He fixed Ben with a steely look that spoke volumes.

'I'd like to apologise for the other day,' Ben said.

'Lucky punch.'

'Unlucky, more like it.'

The policeman suddenly grinned. 'If you've got any more like that one, we'll sign you up for the rugby team.'

'No way. That was the only punch in my repertoire. I really am very sorry.'

'Don't mention it.'

'What's all this about a message from Wesley Freeman?' Jennifer asked.

'It's in the barn,' Janice said. 'Right up where he was sitting when O'Brien and the others were killing Donny.'

Jennifer and the constable climbed up the ladder in turn to see the scratching. When they had made notes, Ben took them to the kitchen, opened the freezer and handed Jennifer the plastic wallet.

'What's this?'

'My best guess is, a human eye, ear, nose and other bits,' Ben told her. 'Wesley hid it in the Shogun. Apparently, some patients ordered him to hide this to protect themselves and bring us good luck. He put these notes there, too, but they don't throw much light on the situation. So now you have Janice's statement, backed up by the message Wesley scratched in the barn that your people missed, plus this bloody thing.'

DS Matthews checked the contents and grimaced. 'I'll have to send this to the pathology lab before I do anything.'

'How long will that take?' Janice asked.

'A few days, maybe a couple of weeks. I'll do my best.'

Jennifer turned to the constable.

'Why don't you look through the barn one more time, just to make quite sure we haven't missed anything else.'

'Sure thing, sergeant.'

'I've been checking up on Geoffrey Abbott,' she said when he'd gone. 'Here's the report, which I haven't shown you, of course.'

Ben opened the file and held it so Janice could see while he flipped through the contents. They looked at Jennifer blankly.

'That's right. Nothing. No police record, no arrest record, no psychiatric committal record, no employment record, no family record, no address, no nothing.'

'I don't get it,' Ben said.

'I have a friend in Central Criminal Intelligence. He says this kind of thing is usually something to do with the Ministry of Defence.'

'That would tie in with the two creeps who called here the other day,' Janice said. 'They looked as if they'd done their share of defence-mongering.'

'Two security men from CareCorp security,' Ben told Jennifer. 'Very military. They said that Abbott enjoys killing people. Your contact could well be right.'

'It doesn't get us very far, though, does it?'

'Christ, there's so much hanging in the air,' Ben said in exasperation. 'And I have a nasty feeling it's all about to come crashing down on our heads.'

'Don't worry,' Jennifer said. 'CareCorp has seriously beefed up security at the hospital, and we're running more patrols in this area, just in case you were right about meeting Abbott. As soon as we've checked out your little bag of tricks, I'll see how things stand for taking another look at the Donny Talgarth incident.'

39

The next evening, Ben settled down at his desk to see what was on the floppy disk that Wesley had hidden in the Shogun. Once he had backed up his working files, he clicked on the disk's program icon. After a few seconds a message appeared telling him that LISA had analysed his system and he could log in on a text-image basis but not real-time audio-visual. It asked him if he wanted to dial into LISA now, and he clicked the OK button. After the usual routine of clicks and buzzing from the modem, he was presented with a welcome screen which asked him to type in his user name and password.

KeithMelton . . . ESREVINU

Seconds later the message 'Super Sysop logged-in' appeared above a menu of options, starting with a direct link to CareCorp Strategic Centre with links to other computer systems in the group, including Lindisholm Hospital. Whoever created this disk had given Ben an open doorway to CareCorp. Perhaps it was because Harold wanted to help Wesley rather than Ben, but the result was the same. He had been given the power not only to access all the information held on the company's computer network but also to change and control the system from top to bottom.

Ben knew that the most efficient way to browse databases over the Internet is to take a steady, logical approach. He was itching to open a route into Lindisholm, but first of all he put the pointer on the CareCorp Strategic Centre icon and opened it. He was presented with a 3D view of a virtual reality building. Using his games joystick he moved along the corridors and into elevators to other storeys, zooming in to open-plan areas and doorways with CareCorp executive names on them. He went to the top storey and found offices for the directors and one for the company secretary which contained files of all the company board meetings, including legal activities, contracts and financial planning. Boring but necessary. Save for later. Have a look in Melton's office.

It was as if a burglar had managed to evade an entire company security system to find himself in the corporate treasure chest. In one file, Ben discovered the codes that the chief executive used to issue cheques and to transfer funds electronically from one account to another. In another he found copies of all personnel contracts of employment. In another were records of ex-gratia cash payments made to people in the countries where CareCorp had business interests.

Very interesting! Ben added a selection of these files to his hard disk too. When he clicked on a drawer marked CEO – Personal, a filing cabinet appeared containing drawers with typical headings: Assets; Bank accounts; Domestic; Health; House; Investments . . . He was about to skip to another area when he saw that the bottom drawer was labelled with the Greek letter Ω. When he tried to open this drawer, the message 'Check Super Sysop ID' popped onto the screen.

Ben typed in UNIVERSE and clicked on OK.

'Welcome to Omega Cloister,' a synthesised voice told him.

Janice brought a mug of coffee laced with rum into Ben's study. He didn't notice her as he clicked his way though a maze of images on his computer screen. Focused. Dedicated. It's times like this when you know, truly know, how much you love a person. She wanted to lean forward and kiss the nape of his neck, but it was too soon for that. Far too soon, after Roy Ormley. How very, very sad the world can be.

Ben couldn't believe it. His access to Omega Cloister took him into a world of crazy images, with on-screen help boxes explaining the significance of each one, with interactive links to Lindisholm and other sites. Some of the images showed a large, gaunt man sitting like a Buddha in austere surroundings and gazing into the camera, reminding Ben of Marlon Brando in *Apocalypse Now*. Another series showed an operating theatre, with the green, blue, yellow and red overalls of Lindisholm patients gathered round the table. Each image was captioned 'A scene from the patients' interactive development of Omega Cloister'.

The hair on the back of Ben's neck prickled. He was looking at images that had been described by patients in his writing classes, and everything was remarkably realistic. There was no way this was a simulation, as Jonser had suggested. Christ knows what he'd see if he accessed the system with a fibre-optic link and got full audio-video.

As he drilled down into the database, he came across a directory called 'The Unit: Leamington & Abbott'. It contained a file of Abbott's exploits, complete with photographs of horrifyingly mutilated young soldiers, that would have done credit to a medieval torturer.

This was the man who sat benignly at the back of Ben's writing class asking questions about syntax and the philosophical implications of expressive writing, the man who had followed him on the mountain road and intimated an interest in Janice, the man who had interrogated him on his motives for being in Lindisholm.

Major Christopher Leamington's folder contained similar material. At the end of both these files was a cross-reference to an MoD facility near Kidderminster. This turned out to be a covert unit for the manufacture of miniature, radio-activated, anti-personnel devices, and Abbott and Leamington had been issued with wrist tags that had been modified there. The cases contained a tiny detonator and enough Semtex to blow a man in half, with a microscopic radio receiver tuned to a high-frequency detonation code. Someone, presumably Melton, had ensured that these two men could be stopped in their tracks. Major cracks were beginning to open up in the squeaky clean Lindisholm Hospital, and here was all the proof he needed. The idea of a worthy book to succeed *The Façade* did not seem so far away after all.

Ben opened his computer organiser and jotted down some notes.

1. Major health institution shelters Army torturers.
2. What happened to Major Christopher Leamington?
3. Security breakdown allows dangerous killer(s) to wander free.
4. Check Abbott's 'cult leader' activity.
5. Check what the patients mean by Communion.
6. Abbott's hospital file is blank: implies unofficial arrangement between ministries. Check this.
7. Check civil liberty aspect of security tags.
8. How could high-security hospital patients run the institution under the noses of the authorities?
9. Omega Cloister: real or false??
10. What is the connection with Newson's organic farming activity???

Ben wanted to share his excitement with someone. Not Janice, because some of this information would be upsetting. Anyway, it was eleven o'clock, and she had probably gone to bed. Too late to phone Jennifer Matthews at home. If she wasn't on duty she might have gone to bed, too. On the other hand, this is why she had given him her phone number. Wasn't it?

'It's Ben Kirby,' he said when she picked up her phone.

'Good evening, Ben. I was going to call you tomorrow. I've got preliminary results from the path labs.'

'That's quick.'

'We can, occasionally, pull the stops out. The bag was made from a human scrotum. The tooth contains a filling of the type commonly used in Australia and New Zealand. The other items were, as you suggested, an eye and pieces of human organs. Each of them was taken from a different person, and there are indications that they were removed while that person was alive.'

'God, that's horrendous! So presumably you'll be able to arrest those damned patients, at last.'

'Hardly. The hospital authorities are still putting obstacles in the way of any police presence. The first thing they would do is deny that your little bag of tricks has any relevance to them or their patients. You don't have proof that it was Wesley who hid it in the Shogun – or even that it came from the hospital in the first place.'

'What will it take to convince you?'

'It's not me you have to convince. It's my senior colleagues, followed by the Crown Prosecution Service.'

'And I thought *I* was a cynic!'

'Well, that's my news, for what it's worth.'

'Thanks. Look, the reason I called is . . . I wondered if you fancied a late night coffee. There's something here you should see.'

'You're right about the late night. What is it?'

'I've got my computer linked into the CareCorp database. Don't ask how, but there are some things I need to show you.'

'It can't wait until the morning?'

'I'm saving what I get as I go, but I have no idea how long I have access to this. If one of their IT people notices the connection, I'll be cut off.'

A sigh. 'In that case, I'll be with you in about half an hour.'

'Great. See you then.'

When he put the phone down, he noticed a mug standing on the cork mat by his telephone. Cold coffee with rum flavour. He went to the kitchen to heat it up in the microwave. Everything was buzzing, as the significance of the computer disk became increasingly apparent. Even now he had almost enough material to write a hatchet job on CareCorp and its overseas connections, not to mention Lindisholm Hospital. He would have to be selective in what he showed to Jennifer. She was, after all, a working police officer, and she had made it very clear that this was her main consideration in life. He couldn't go far wrong if he restricted things to the Omega directory.

The video unit above Geoffrey Abbott's cot flickered into life and the face of the patient in charge of the hospital's IT helpline service appeared: Michael Jason – until his breakdown, the owner and managing director of a leading-edge computer software company.

'Wake up, Brother Geoffrey,' he whispered.

Abbott's eyes clicked open.

'Ben Kirby has accessed LISA. He is online as we speak. He is interested in deviations and errors. He has just made these notes . . .'

Ben's numbered list appeared on the screen.

'You were right to wake me,' Abbott said. 'Prepare my way to Brianne Mill, and I will pray to Lord Beltane for guidance. Thank you, Brother Michael.'

Jennifer's car rolled to a stop outside the front door, and Ben opened it before she could ring the bell and disturb Janice.

'Thanks for coming. I had to show you while everything's still linked up. It's incredible.'

He was like an excited schoolboy, animated, vigorous. She followed him into his study, and he showed her the images of Omega Cloister.

'That's exactly how things were described in the stories my students wrote. If we had a video link, I bet we'd see those bastards doing everything they described. They've got someone stretched out on that table. This can't possibly be a simulation.'

'I don't know so much. They're getting more and more realistic.'

'If this is real, though, it adds weight to what Janice says she saw.

If they are cutting people up on that table, then who's to say they didn't cut young Donny Talgarth's throat?'

'You're jumping to conclusions. Even if these pictures are what you think they are, we'd have to prove where they came from, and get corroboration. That wouldn't be easy.'

'Christ, that again!'

She sighed. 'Can I sit down, please?'

'Sorry, of course. Let's have a coffee. Or a brandy, maybe.'

'Coffee would be nice.'

They went into the kitchen. He poured coffee beans into the grinder, then stopped.

'Shit. This noise will wake Janice. How about a tea?'

'Fine. Weak, no milk or sugar.'

Lion sensed the life of the mountains. Streams pulsing underground. Sighs from the conifers as the breeze rippled through their needles. Smells rising from the valleys. Smoke fires as people warmed their homes. The sweet odour of grazing sheep. The lights of Brianne Mill shining over the ancient altar in the field by the river.

What was the scribe doing? Was he a boon to the Lord's People, helping them to chronicle their work, or was he a danger who must be removed? Lion was puzzled, for he had received no guidance from Lord Beltane. In the meantime it would be seemly to give the scribe a sign of the Lord's power. After all, what is the point of having power if you don't use it?

Lion saw the scribe through the slats in the blinds. He was sitting in the kitchen with a young woman who was wearing a dark business suit. What manner of person would be visiting near midnight dressed in such a fashion? Lion looked into her car and saw the communication equipment. A policewoman. And Kirby was probably still online to the Lindisholm system. How interesting.

Lion stared at the first floor window which he knew was the main bedroom. The light was still on. Perhaps the scribe's wife was reading in bed. The very thought made Lion's member stir heavily. How easy it would be. But he was on a holy mission. Maybe one day Lord Beltane would bless such a union. This thought led to another. He would deliver his warning to the scribe's wife while the scribe was entertaining one of Her Majesty's finest. That would be appropriate. And pleasurable.

Ignoring the pain in his injured hand, Lion picked the lock on the back door and soundlessly made his way up the stairs.

Janice heard the car arrive and watched through the curtains as Ben opened the door to Jennifer Matthews. She climbed back into bed feeling utterly miserable and rejected. Was this the end, when a husband made an assignment while his wife was still in the house? She would never have believed that Ben could be so cruel, despite everything that had happened. If she had felt even the merest flicker of anger she would have gone downstairs and confronted them. But there was no anger. Only guilt, and a deep sorrow. Imagination increased her misery. They were embracing. He was unbuttoning her jacket, slipping his hands inside, pressing himself into her . . .

She lay, trying to control the sobs, huddled into the pillows, oblivious to the opening and closing of the bedroom door.

The first sign she had of Abbott's presence was the numbing pressure of fingers on her neck and a heavy, naked body slipping into the sheets behind her. There was a feral smell, pungent, threatening. Someone's face nuzzled into her short hair, breathing in hungrily.

'Do you know who I am, Janice?'

The fingers eased a fraction, and she managed a slight, painful shake of the head.

'Come now. Your husband must have told you about me, about our conversation the other day. I'm Geoffrey Abbott.'

Janice felt his penis harden, and a new terror flooded into the room.

'You feel me rising? So beautiful. But Lord Beltane brings me here with his warning. I have no instructions about mating with you. Not yet. But this feeling is very powerful. Can you imagine my staff thrusting into your body, filling you with holy seed? Maybe that is our destiny. What do you think?'

His fingers loosened again.

'What do you want?'

'Ah, the question of questions. I want to serve Lord Beltane, to bring his power to the earth, to spread his word among the People, to release them from the bondage of the Bastards . . . I want to rise above the shit and see the destruction of the Bastards as they struggle against the irresistible truth . . . but above all, right this minute, I want to fuck you into another universe, to tear into you, stabbing, scouring, feeling you shudder and scream with pleasure and pain. The greatest fuck you will ever experience. Surely that holds some delight for you? Some joyful anticipation?'

Janice fought the gathering hysteria.

'You said you had a warning . . .'

'Ah, yes, the warning. Your husband must do nothing that will endanger Lord Beltane's People and their destiny. Lord Beltane chooses not to tell me if he is a force for good or evil, so I will bide my time, but he is wandering into the killing zone. Ah . . .'

The great penis was developing a life of its own, pulsing uncontrollably between her buttocks, but Lion must leave no trace of his visit. His huge hands turned her easily round and forced her head beneath the sheets, squeezed her jaws until they were locked open to receive him. Her efforts to breathe, to escape, increased his pleasure, and within seconds he was pumping sperm into her mouth. His final act was to hold her lips shut, so that everything was swallowed safely away.

'Remember, Janice. Ben must do nothing to harm the People in their holy work. I think you can imagine the consequences.'

Abbott squeezed the side of her neck with expert fingers, inducing a paralysis that would keep her immobile for several minutes. He slid noiselessly out of the bed, and through her pain she felt rather than heard the door open and close as he left the room.

The hen that Lion collected from the coop fluttered and cackled frantically before his fingers tore it into two pieces, which he jammed onto an iron hook by the back door. Take heed, you unbelievers, take heed of the Lord's word. He then began the loping run that would cover the miles to Lindisholm within the hour. Everything in Lion's universe was in harmony. He had made the right choices tonight. Lord Beltane would be pleased with his servant.

Eventually the pain subsided, and Janice managed to drag herself to the lavatory before the retching overcame her, violent, noisy.

'Janice, are you okay?' she heard Ben calling.

He found her huddled in the corner of the bathroom by the lavatory, waving her hands at him and screaming, 'Get away from me! Get away, you bastard!'

'Christ, darling, what's the matter?'

'Get away!'

Jennifer called, 'Is she all right?'

'You better come up,' he said distractedly. 'Janice, come on. Let's get you back to bed.'

'No, get him away.' She struggled to her knees and managed to turn the lever that flushed the lavatory. 'Get away, you bastard!'

'Janice, it's me, Ben. Have you been dreaming . . . a nightmare?'

'What's wrong?' Jennifer asked.

'Christ knows.'

'Get out of here!' Janice screamed. 'Get out!'

She slumped to the floor again and began wailing.

'Get away, get away . . .'

'God Almighty!' Ben felt the hair rise on the nape of his neck.

'Someone's been here. Geoffrey Abbott. That fucking animal has been in our home again.'

'Impossible. That hospital is closed tighter than Fort Knox. She's hysterical. It must have been a nightmare. I'll help you get her into bed.'

Janice struggled feebly to resist, but they managed to lie her down and cover her.

'You've been very sick, Janice,' Jennifer said. 'Did you eat anything that could have upset your stomach?'

'It's not her stomach,' Ben insisted. 'I'm telling you. That bastard Abbott has been here. Christ knows what he's done to her. I'm going to call our doctor.'

'Never mind your GP,' Jennifer told him. 'I'll call the duty police doctor.'

While Jennifer went to make the call from her car radio, Ben tried to comfort Janice, but she kept pushing him away.

'Dr Peerless will be here in about twenty minutes,' Jennifer told him quietly when she came back upstairs. 'He says she might have been hallucinating. It could be food poisoning. He says we have to keep her calm and try to get her to drink some warm fluids.'

The police doctor arrived looking slightly put out at the inconvenience of a late-night call. Ben and Jennifer went downstairs, and when he joined them some minutes later he looked puzzled.

'There's nothing physically wrong, as far as I can tell without a full examination. She is extremely distressed, and I can only suspect she has suffered a truly bad dream. They can cause hysterical reactions, on occasion. She seems half in and half out of consciousness. That in itself is not unusual, but it's a state that doesn't usually last more than a few seconds, minutes at the most.'

'Did she say anything that could give a clue?' Ben asked him.

'The main thrust is to keep someone away, presumably the person in the dream. May I ask if your wife is a religious person, Mr Kirby?'

'No, definitely not. Why?'

'She mentioned an abbot. I'm no psychologist, but it seems Mrs Kirby has been seriously disturbed by whatever was in her dream. She accepted a weak sedative, and my guess is that she'll be fully recovered by morning. Now, before I leave, could I have a private word with you, DS Matthews?'

'Certainly, Charles,' Jennifer said equitably.

Ben heard the doctor's voice, low and measured from the other side of the front door.

'There really seems to have been no need for bringing me here, Jennifer. This is a matter for her GP.'

'Ordinarily, I'd agree with you, but Mrs Kirby and her husband are involved in a number of incidents in which we have an interest. It seemed appropriate to keep this within our bailiwick in case it has a bearing on the cases concerned.'

'Has it?'

Jennifer had seen Ben's face change when Dr Peerless mentioned the word Abbott. Fear mixed with anger. She had felt an unaccustomed prickling of the spine, too.

'It might well do. I'll keep you informed.'

She came back into the house and stared at Ben.

'Could Abbott have been here?'

'Why not? It would explain Janice's condition, wouldn't it?'

'But why would he bother . . . what's the point?'

'The point is, he's a fucking madman. Ask *him* why.'

'If I get the chance, I will. Meanwhile, why don't you check Janice while I have a look outside?'

'Well, for Christ's sake, be careful. That bastard is capable of anything.'

She got a torch out of the glove compartment of her car and walked round the house, flashing it over the windows and doors. At the back door she found the hen, dismembered, stuck on a hook. She used her radio to call for a patrol car and then put a call through to the hospital security department.

'This is Detective Sergeant Matthews based at Lampeter. Who am I speaking to?'

'Mervyn Jessell, deputy head of security. What can I do for you, DS Matthews?'

'Well, Mr Jessell, I have reason to believe that one of your patients is missing.'

A silence.

'That's absolutely impossible.'

'Nevertheless, I'd be very grateful if you would check out Geoffrey Abbott. I believe he is assigned to Delta Cloister.'

'Abbott? If you insist.' A pause. 'I am looking at Geoffrey Abbott. He is safely tucked up in bed, where he should be.'

'Hang on, Mr Jessell.' She covered the phone. 'Abbott's in bed.'

'The fuck he is!' Ben shouted. 'Give me that bloody thing.'

She held him off.

'For Christ's sake, calm down . . . Mr Jessell, are you physically looking at Abbott?'

'He's on the CCTV, and that's live. He's definitely in bed.'

'Do me a favour. Could you please make a physical check and call me back? Thanks.' She gave him the number and rang off. 'Sit down, Ben, and don't worry. We'll sort it.'

Ben didn't answer, and she hoped fervently that she was right.

Here they come, to check out old Lion. But Lion comes and goes like a shadow, through the valleys and the mines, fast as lightning, he comes, he goes, slipping through their cloisters while they watch, unseeing. Good evening, Mr Jessell, sir. Old Lion can recognise your footfalls from a mile away.

The telephone call from Jessell was brusque and to the point:

'I have visited Abbott's room with two members of my staff, and he is in his bed fast asleep.'

'Thank you for checking, Mr Jessell.'

'You're welcome.' He rang off.

'Abbott is in bed.'

Ben looked at her. Didn't say anything.

'Janice will be all right, Ben. There's been a lot of stress.'

'What about the chicken?'

'Some louts from the hippie commune in the hills. They do things like that from time to time.'

'It was Abbott,' he said tightly.

'It's not possible.'

'Everything is possible. He's been here before. He looked through my diary. How else did he get my mobile number? And he was here tonight.'

'Not according to hospital security, Ben.'

'Fuck hospital security. Fuck nightmares. Fuck food poisoning. That raving monster went into our bedroom and terrorised my wife. Christ knows what he's done to her.'

'Even if he did come here, Dr Peerless said there was no physical damage.'

'So, the good doctor is an expert in physical damage, is he?'

'For God's sake, Ben, he's a police doctor. He's seen more grievous bodily harm and rape than you've had hangovers. Christ, look at the time. I'm on earlies.'

'I'm sorry, Jennifer. This has been one fucked-up night.'

She moved close and took hold of his hands. 'It's not your fault, okay? I'm going to have a serious talk with my guvnor about this hospital business. One thing is absolutely certain. You've been suffering far too many coincidences. I'll check in with you in the morning.'

A quick squeeze of his fingers and she was gone, leaving her perfume on his hands.

40

In the morning, Janice stayed in bed, exhausted and distressed. Whatever it was that had happened, she did not want to talk about it. Ben brought her tea which she didn't drink and snacks that she didn't eat. He asked if he should phone Eileen, and she shook her head. The only thing he could hang on to was the fact that the police doctor had said he had found no evidence of injury. No assault. No rape. But something dreadful had happened, and she was shutting him out of it, isolating herself. To try to take his mind off things, he went to his study and checked back through his notes to see what he could follow up without leaving her alone. Batson's comment about his mobile phone log was still niggling, so he put a call though to the company and asked to speak to someone in the technical department.

'Bill Watson,' a voice said.

'This is Ben Kirby, one of your customers.'

'What can I do for you, Mr Kirby?'

'I live in a mountainous area, and there's a particular road where no one can make or receive calls on their mobiles with any of the cellular companies. However, a couple of weeks ago I did receive a call. How could that happen?'

'If there's no repeater station in range, it couldn't. If you can give me your number and the date, I can run a check.' After a few seconds, he said, 'I can confirm that one call was made from your phone to a Penford number at four twenty-seven in the afternoon, and that's all.'

'That was to my wife when I was in the Midlands. The call in question was around two hours later.'

'Nope. Nothing there.'

'I definitely took one.'

'Do you know the calling number?'

'Sorry, but the guy who made it was following me on a motorbike.'

'Ah well, he could have been using a scanning radio transceiver. Not legal without a licence, but some models cover our frequencies.'

That sounded credible. It was also very interesting, bearing in mind the reference to radio transceivers in the Omega Cloister file on the Kidderminster factory.

'Is that kind of equipment easy to get hold of?'

'I shouldn't be encouraging you, but yes. Most good communication shops stock them. Tottenham Court Road in London is the best place. They do mail order, if you know what you're looking for.'

'Something covering the ten to twenty gigahertz range.'

'That's moving into satellite and military applications. Not my field, but I can give you a contact who might help.'

Ben noted the name and phone number and then called Mary Drover to see if she might be free to sit with Janice for an hour or so in the afternoon.

'Love to,' she said, 'if you can make it after lunch.'

His third call was to Tom Attwood.

'Tom. Ben Kirby. I need a real favour.'

'What is it?'

'I want to check the work that Fred Newson's people did in your barn.'

A silence.

'I'm not sure I understand. Check what, exactly?'

'Hard to explain over the phone. I'd like to call round with the detective from Lampeter who's been examining things over here. DS Matthews.'

'For Christ's sake, Ben, you can't be serious!'

Ben suddenly realised that Attwood and others in the neighbourhood could be a little sensitive to having anyone checking things that involved Fred Newson and his wheeling and dealing, not least a police sergeant.

'I am serious, Tom. And it's nothing to do with any arrangement you might have made with Newson.'

'Why DS Matthews?'

'She would be there simply as an observer. I need to check something out, that's all. More for my own peace of mind, really. Can't we at least have a chat about it?'

'If you're sure it's not going to drop all of us in the shit . . .'

Minutes after he put the phone down, Jennifer called to see how Janice was getting along, as she had promised.

'She's resting. Still pretty shocked.'

'This is a rotten thing for both of you.'

'More for Janice than me, I'm afraid. Christ knows where it's heading. There are a lot of question marks hanging around, which is I why I need your help.'

'If I can.'

'I'm going to see Tom Attwood this afternoon about the work Newson's people did in his barn. I'd like you to be there.'

'Your pagan sacrifice theory, I presume.'

'Yes. It's worth a shot, and if Tom goes along with it you won't have to bother with search warrants and all that stuff. What d'you say?'

'If half what we hear about Fred Newson is true, you're not going to make yourself very popular with your neighbours.'

'Can you be there?' he repeated.

She checked her appointments.

'I can make it after lunch, around three o'clock.'

Attwood met them at his gate, clearly disconcerted by their visit. He asked Jennifer if she would mind if he had a quiet chat with Ben.

'What is it you want to check?'

'There's no simple way of saying this,' Ben said. 'I'd like to dig up the floor to see if Fred Newson accidentally left one of his agency workers there.'

'I beg your pardon?' Attwood's face showed a mixture of astonishment and outrage.

'Let me take a wild guess,' Ben said. 'While your barn was being refurbished, one of Newson's people told you there might be a problem with underground water, right?'

'As a matter of fact, yes. They dug down by the corner and sorted it out.'

'In that case, I want to dig there too. It shouldn't be much of a disruption, and I'll make it good afterwards.'

Attwood sighed. 'I don't mind telling you that I called some of the others, and they don't think I should get involved. On the other hand, there's been a lot of trouble recently, and it's all seemed to land on you and Janice. If all you want to do is check things out, I don't see what harm it could do.'

Attwood walked over to Jennifer. 'Are you here officially, DS Matthews?'

'No sir, but in view of recent events I believe it would be sensible to see if Mr Kirby's fears are justified or not. It would save the bother of getting a search warrant if we could do this informally.'

'Well, if you put it like that, but only if Ben will confirm he'll put everything back the way it was and pay for any damage.'

'You've got it.'

Ben borrowed a sledgehammer, crowbar and spade and attacked the corner where the patients told Attwood there might be water. The smell hit them first, fetid, sickening. Attwood grimly took another spade. When he dug into something soft, they stopped digging and scraped away the earth to reveal what looked like a human pelvis. Ben felt a flood of sorrow for Janice. She had seen this happen at Brianne Mill, and no one had believed her. He was honest enough to include himself. He had even harboured the unworthy suspicion that she could have scratched the message from Wesley on the roof slate to support her version of events.

'What now?' Attwood whispered.

Jennifer was already in her car, using her radio to call a forensic team.

When Ben returned home he was pleased and relieved to find Janice still chatting animatedly with Mary Drover and enjoying afternoon tea. Despite looking understandably tired, she was able to smile and pour him a cup.

'We've chosen what we need for the bathroom,' she told him. 'Better send the bank manager one of your persuasive begging letters.'

'Thanks, Mary,' he said wryly. 'I've just spent several weeks distracting her from all that.'

'Think nothing of it,' she said. 'Can't have you neglecting your ablutions, can we? Well, many thanks for the tea, Janice. I'd better be off before I spend any more of your money.'

'It's really kind of you to come over,' Ben said. He hesitated. 'I ought to tell you what's happened before you see Tom. I'm afraid you need to hear this too, darling.'

'What do you mean? There's nothing wrong, is there?'

'Not with Tom, no, but something Janice saw in our barn happened

289

in Tom's barn as well, and it might have happened in other places. Someone is buried there.'

Janice stared at him, white-faced. 'Oh, God. Who is it?'

'We've no idea. There'll be a forensic team working on it.'

'Christ, Tom must feel sick,' Mary said.

'Yes. He's absolutely choked. I'm so sorry, Mary.'

'It's okay, Ben. We know you're one of the good guys. You just make sure you look after this wife of yours. She's been through more than any of us.' Mary paused. 'Ben, Janice told me about the other night. I know I'm more or less a stranger to be saying this, but she's going to need more help from you in the next few weeks than most wives need from a husband in a lifetime. You will tell him what happened, won't you, dear?'

Janice nodded. 'Yes. Thanks, Mary. You've been great.'

They said goodbye to Mary, and Janice wandered over to a bench seat overlooking the garden.

'It was Geoffrey Abbott, Ben. He came to warn you not to do anything that would interfere with the activities of some people. Their destiny, he said. He carried on about this bloody Lord Beltane. He said you were entering the killing zone. And then . . . and then . . . he made me . . . do things.'

Ben felt a surge of ice-cold rage. He put his arm round her shoulders. 'Hush, it's okay, darling.'

'He hurt me, Ben. He knows how to hurt people. He used me. And then you tell me that the bloody hospital insists he was there all the time . . .'

'They didn't say that. They said he was there when they checked. That was some time after the doctor arrived here, wasn't it?'

'Half an hour . . . an hour? What was he travelling in – a helicopter?'

'I don't know how he did it, and I don't care. The thing is, he assaulted you, and this time the police really do need your statement.'

She leaned her head on his arm.

'They'll get it, believe me. And then I want you to write your book. I want you to show up the bastards who run that place for what they are.'

'Don't worry, I will. The only problem I have is, exactly which bastards are running it?'

41

Within hours of the body being discovered on Tom Attwood's farm, the local magistrate issued warrants for the police to search six suspect sites with teams of forensic investigators, and four more inhumations were discovered. Fred Newson was arrested on suspicion of complicity in murder, but protested his innocence and ignorance of all wrong-doing. He gave the police his agency records, which were sketchy and of little help, and with no evidence to prove otherwise he was released on police bail. Two days later he was told that no charges would be brought against him. Meanwhile, based on the forensic evidence, queries were made at the Home Office to cross-check missing person reports from Australia and New Zealand, and dental records were compared with the remains.

Janice gave a full statement to Jennifer Matthews regarding Geoffrey Abbott's assault.

'Yes,' she said calmly at the end of her interview, 'I do wish to bring charges.'

Detective Sergeant Jennifer Matthews and several colleagues visited Lindisholm Hospital with a search warrant and authority to interview all the patients whom Janice had named in her new statement. When the police convoy arrived, Tim Johnson was on duty. He did his best to delay matters.

'We can't let you inside now. The patients on your warrants are under medication. Professor Jonser has given strict instructions –'

'I don't want to arrest you for obstructing the police in the course of an enquiry,' Jennifer told him, 'but that's exactly what I will do if you don't assist my colleagues to set up interview facilities and then get these patients over here. We'll use the visitor reception room, if that's all right with you.'

Johnson picked up his phone. 'Tim Johnson here, professor. The police are here with warrants to search the hospital and arrest some of the patients . . . Yes, I told them that, but they aren't having any . . . Very good. I'll tell them.' He turned to Jennifer. 'The professor asks if you can wait until she gets here. She points out that all patients admitted under the terms of the Mental Health Act are under the protection of the court and will require legal representation.'

'This gentleman is Mr Arnold Hopkins,' Jennifer said. 'He is a solicitor appointed by the court to be present during the interviews.'

Hopkins nodded to Johnson and scanned down his list. 'Geoffrey Abbott was not admitted under Section 1. The police can remove him from the hospital and hold him for twenty-four hours without charge, if they so wish.'

'Rather them than me,' Johnson muttered. He watched morosely as the police team unloaded their equipment from the vans and began bringing it into the building. 'It would be far easier to arrange this if you all wore wrist tags, otherwise we'll have to switch off security everywhere you want to go.'

'I don't think that will present us with any problems,' Jennifer said. 'The forensic team need to examine your operating theatre to begin with.'

While Johnson was issuing the police with security tags, Professor Jonser arrived, not bothering to hide her anger.

'Who is in charge of this investigation?'

'Detective Sergeant Matthews.' She held out her identification.

'I must object in the strongest possible terms to this intrusion. I have contacted our legal representative, and he has informed me that no patient can be interviewed without legal representation. I would be obliged if you wait until he gets here.'

'They've brought a solicitor with them,' Johnson told her.

Jonser's irritation visibly increased. 'That is of no interest to me. I insist that you wait until our Mr Bradley arrives.'

'There is no need for that,' Hopkins said. 'The legal requirement is fulfilled by the presence of any solicitor. We are all officers of the court.'

'This is outrageous. These people are patients, I would remind you. I must at least insist that myself or their own psychiatric counsellors are present.'

'That's not a problem,' Jennifer said. She held out the warrant for Peter O'Brien. 'Would you please arrange for this patient to be brought to the reception room?'

'I strongly recommend that you use a patient interview room,' Jonser said. 'The reception room has no security installation.'

'That won't be necessary. My colleagues have set up our tape recorders, and I'd like to get on with things.'

'Very well. Mr Johnson, please arrange for your staff to be on standby. And ask them to bring Peter O'Brien here. I'll phone his counsellor.'

O'Brien arrived, bracketed by security men and followed by Nikki Congleton, who looked irritated and also slightly uneasy. After Jonser made the introductions, Jennifer showed O'Brien the arrest warrant.

'Peter O'Brien, I am arresting you for the murder of Donny Talgarth. You do not have to say anything, but it may harm your defence if you do not mention when questioned something which you later rely on in court. Anything you do say may be given in evidence. Do you understand?'

O'Brien smiled. Just with his lips. 'Of course.'

'And are you willing to give a statement to us now?'

'Of course.'

'This gentleman is a solicitor. His name is Mr Hopkins. He has been appointed to represent you, but you have the right to choose your own representative. Do you wish to exercise that right?'

'Mr Hopkins will do fine.'

PC Evans switched on the dual tape recorder. 'This interview with Peter O'Brien takes place in the presence of Detective Sergeant Jennifer Matthews, PC Tim Evans, Mr Arnold Hopkins, solicitor, and Dr Congleton, a psychiatric counsellor. Now, Peter, I'd like to ask you some questions about the work you did on a barn belonging to Mr Ben Kirby of Brianne Mill in the village of Penford. Do you remember this work?'

'Oh yes. Mr Kirby's barn. Yes. We had to mend the roof.'

'And during this work, were you accompanied by other people?'

'That's right. Other people. The Lord's people.'

'And was one of these people a young man called Donny Talgarth?'

'Young Donny. Yes, I remember him. But he was not one of the Lord's people. He was merely there at the Lord's bidding.'

'Can you tell us what happened to Donny?'

'Donny was taken away by the Lord.'

'Can you explain what you mean?'

'He was there at the Lord's bidding, and the Lord took him away.'

'Peter, when you were lying in the ambulance at Brianne Mill, do you remember me asking you questions?'

He shook his head.

'You have to speak it, for the tape recorder.'

'No.'

'You told me that Donny had fallen on a blade.'

'I don't remember.'

'We have a statement by a witness who says that you were holding Donny upside down over a hole and that you said Donny had hurt himself. Is this true?'

'The Lord bid Donny to stay behind and look after Mr Kirby's barn.'

'What do you mean, stay behind?'

'The Lord said if Donny stayed behind he would be taken up into Omega Cloister and live in peace with the others who stay behind to do the Lord's bidding. Praise be to the Lord. Praise be!'

'I think that's enough,' Nikki Congleton said.

'Would you like to pause for a while, Peter?'

'Satan speaks through her thin lips. She is doomed. Are you here on the Lord's work, sister?'

'I hope so, Peter,' Jennifer said.

'I hope so, too. The Lord calls everyone to his bidding eventually. It's only a matter of time. You carry on. I'll help you all I can.'

'I would like to know the truth about Donny. His throat was cut. How did that happen?'

'Happen, as in truthfully happen, as in the actuality of happening, as in the meaningfulness of happening?'

'However you want to put it.'

'If his throat was cut, that was also the Lord's bidding.'

Jennifer knew she was getting nowhere with O'Brien.

'One more thing. You have stated that Donny would be taken to Omega Cloister with the others. Which others do you mean, and where is Omega Cloister?'

'That's two more things. Are you sure you are not Satan?'

'I'm sorry. That was two more things, wasn't it? Let's start with who you mean by the others.'

'They were brought into Lindisholm by the beaters to give their bodies and their blood to the Lord. White Eagle, whom the Bastards called Christopher Leamington, was the first. He gave his body and his blood to the People, that they might live. Then, as far as I recall, there was Joyce Anslett, Stephanie Goodchild, Kenneth Malkins, Evan Williams and Gordon Neave.'

'May I consult with my client, detective sergeant?' the solicitor interrupted.

'Of course. Interview suspended at the request of Mr Hopkins at ten twenty-seven.'

'I must advise you, Mr O'Brien, that you are under no obligation to answer questions that do not relate directly to the matter with which you have been arrested.'

'The only obligation I am under is to Lord Beltane, Mr Hopkins. I will answer until the Lord bids me otherwise.'

Hopkins took Jennifer to one side. 'It is apparent that my client is not in a fit condition to make a statement that will hold up in court.'

'I realise that, Mr Hopkins, but bear with me. He knows what happened to several people who were killed and others who may be missing. It's not a matter of incriminating him. I'm trying to find out what has been happening.'

'I understand, but if I think you are leading him in a manner that is inimical to his interests, I will stop the interview.'

Jennifer nodded, and PC Evans started the tape recorder again.

'This interview with Peter O'Brien continues at ten thirty with the same people present as before. Peter, who are the people whose names you gave me?'

'No one in particular. We send beaters into the farms to select someone suitable and bring them into the hospital. We can give them anything their hearts desire. Sex, booze, drugs. How can they resist?'

'Surely that's impossible. They couldn't get past security.'

O'Brien tapped his nose. 'There's ways and means.'

'What ways and means?'

'The Lord's ways and means.'

'Where did all this take place?'

'In Omega Cloister, with the Lord.'

'And where is Omega Cloister?'

This time his smile reached his eyes, as he lifted his thin face to the ceiling.

'Omega Cloister is wherever you want it to be. Praise be to the Lord.'

Jennifer terminated the interview, and the custody team released O'Brien back into the care of the hospital.

'I don't see how any of that helps you, detective sergeant,' Hopkins said. 'It's gibberish.'

'Not all of it. At least we've got some names that we might be able to link with the bodies.'

When Geoffrey Abbott was escorted to his interview, Jennifer arrested him for assault and cautioned him. He stared at her across the table, relaxed, at ease, two large security guards sitting on each side. A cuddly giant with guileless eyes, incapable of harming a living creature. Jennifer supposed he was massively dosed with tranquillisers. He agreed to answer questions about the accusations made against him by Janice.

'Mrs Kirby has accused you of breaking into her home and assaulting her, Geoffrey. Do you deny that accusation?'

'Absolutely.'

'Is there any way you can support your denial?'

'I don't have to, do I? She has to support her accusation.'

'That's right, but it would help your case considerably if there was something germane to your defence.'

'Look at the security log. What is it they say about Lindisholm? "Not even a hydrogen atom can get out of here without being traced!" Ask Tim Johnson. Ask Mervyn Jessell.'

'Mrs Kirby is very sure about what happened.'

'Flat earthists are very sure. Mrs Kirby is suffering from delusions planted in her mind by Satan. You can hardly blame him for trying. Satan has to gather what crumbs he can, now that Lord Beltane is in the ascendancy.'

No police training technique prepares for this kind of thing. A hugely powerful mind rushing off at tangents. A friendly giant who kills for pleasure. Jennifer looked at her notes.

'I'd like to turn to another matter, Geoffrey. I understand that some of your fellow patients refer to you as Lion, or Brother Lion. Is this true?'

'It is indeed.'

'In the light of statements that have been made to me, I must ask if you have participated in any act of violence on any person either here in Lindisholm or outside?'

Abbott's equitable expression changed to one of surprise, amazement. He opened and closed his mouth a few times and began to laugh. Each time he tried to control himself, he set off again. Peal after peal of helpless, genuine convulsions. The security guards looked at each other, wondering if they should do something to stop him, but eventually he calmed down.

'Well, DS Matthews, the answer is in the affirmative. Why on earth do you think I'm here?'

'What I am trying to establish, Geoffrey, is not what you did before you came to Lindisholm, but afterwards.'

'Ah! Afterwards. Acts of violence, you say. Let me see. No, I don't think so. Not as such.'

'What do you mean?'

'Well, violence implies a certain loss of control. Going over the top. Losing one's cool. I don't think I can be accused of that. Well, not a lot. In any case, it's arguable that no one acting on behalf of the Lord can be violent. Assertive, firm, even ruthless, but not violent.'

'Why do I have this feeling you are playing games with me?'

'A sensible question. Rhetorical, but sensible. That is exactly what I'm doing. Playing games in the service of the Lord. Is there any reason I shouldn't?'

'Try "conspiracy to pervert the course of justice".'

'You have to admire the legal profession. They have such a splendid turn of phrase.'

'I'm glad you approve, Geoffrey.'

The warmth of his smile was almost tangible.

'And I'm glad you're glad. But what now? What happens next? Will you take me from here to one of your cells?'

'There's no need for that. We will submit the evidence to the Crown Prosecution Service for them to decide what action should be taken.'

'That sounds reasonable,' Abbott said, reasonably.

42

Jennifer met Ben and Janice in the Blue Lion that evening to tell them about Lindisholm. They settled in a corner of the bar with a bottle of wine.

'So, how did things go?' Ben asked.

'In a word, weird. You were right. That Peter O'Brien is completely off his trolley, and Geoffrey Abbott isn't far behind. Not to mention the staff. Professor Jonser is almost as scary as he is. Of course, Abbott denied everything, but O'Brien came up with some names that might help us with identification.'

'What happens next?' Janice asked.

'We bailed them into hospital custody. I doubt if it will get as far as a court hearing. Two minutes into it, their barristers would be arguing that they are unfit to plead or diminished responsibility and back they go to Lindisholm under Section 1. Everything will carry on as normal, except I don't think there'll be any more outside work parties.'

'As far as you are concerned then, it's all wrapped up.'

Jennifer sipped her wine, thoughtfully.

'I used to think all that stuff about a copper's instincts was a load of crap. Yet something is yelling that nothing is wrapped up, that it hasn't even started.'

'I feel the same way,' Ben said. 'No one has owned up to any breaches in security, and no one has said anything about improving things. If something has been going pear-shaped, what's to say the same things could not happen all over again?'

'Don't say that.' Janice shuddered. 'If I thought for one minute that Geoffrey Abbott could get out of that place, I'd bloody well emigrate.'

'I shouldn't think there's anything to worry about on that score,' Jennifer said. 'There are security guards all over him, and he's so shot full of sedatives he's almost out on his feet.'

'Thank Christ for that,' Ben said sincerely.

'What are you going to do now?'

'Carry on researching my book. They're having an open day for a bevy of visiting dignitaries, and we got a letter asking us to take part. I presume they don't know it was me who started the body count at Tom Attwood's farm, not yet, anyway. There's no way Janice will do it, but I'll get a chance to see who CareCorp is wooing, for whatever reason. Should be very interesting.'

43

At eight o'clock on the morning of Lindisholm Open Day, Roy Ormley had a meeting scheduled with Keith Melton in the hospital boardroom. Melton's face was composed into a friendly smile. But the atmosphere was not friendly. Ormley felt as if he had been strapped into an electric chair, waiting for the volts.

'Good morning, Roy. I'd like your assessment of the state of play.'

Time to be positive. Time to rise to the challenge.

'Good morning, Keith. Things are well in hand, now that the police have made their enquiries. Not a peep out of the media, apart from a few column inches in the inside pages. Mind you, that earthquake in France was a timely diversion.'

'Well in hand?' Melton turned to gaze out of the window and took a deep breath. 'We've got bodies all over the place. Half the patients have been arrested for murder and Christ knows what, and you say things are well in hand? What the hell's been going on here?'

'Only one of the patients was arrested for murder, Keith. Another was arrested for assault. And yes I do say that, bearing in mind all the circumstances. There's absolutely no evidence, so the whole thing will disappear down the legal drain. The media has to be very careful about things at this stage, otherwise they could get on the wrong side of the contempt laws. We can ride this out.'

'You make sure you keep the lid on it, that's all.'

'That's what you pay me for, Keith.'

Melton raised his eyebrows.

'Thanks for reminding me.' He slid a file across the table. 'This came through, from that PR firm you appointed,' Melton said. 'You know, the account director with the big tits.'

Melanie Parker. Yes. Another well-endowed young lady who had given her all to bring her company to Ormley's attention. Melton's expression gave nothing away, and Ormley wondered if his CEO knew about the event. Probably. Melton seemed to know everything that was related to his business interests, the bumptious little shit.

MEMORANDUM

TO: Keith Melton, Chief Executive Office, CareCorp plc

FROM: Melanie Parker, Account Director, Active PR Associates Ltd

SUBJECT: Open Day, Lindisholm Hospital

Dear Keith

I attach the final draft for your Open Day address.
Key guests who have confirmed attendance include Lord Balacombe, Chairman of CareCorp, and Lady Balacombe; Roland Keane, Secretary of State, Ministry of Health; Geraint Edwards, Secretary of State, Home Office; Sir Norman Castlemaine FRIBA, Architectural Consultant; Professor Hugo Koch MD, Chief Psychiatric Consultant; Brigadier Hartley Harrington-fforest, Ministry of Defence; 22 guests from prospective franchisee nations.

Please let me know if there is anything further we at APRA can do.

Best regards
Melanie

Keith Melton: address to guests

'Lord and Lady Balacombe, ministers, Sir Norman, Professor Koch, ladies and gentlemen . . . Welcome to Lindisholm. My name is Keith Melton, Chief Executive Officer and founder of CareCorp plc, the company responsible for operating Lindisholm on behalf of the Department of Health, working in close association with the Home Office and other ministries.

'The key to understanding Lindisholm is to note that the hospital is a community. A microcosm of our society. A social entity that exists to take responsibility for members of society who, for one reason or another, cannot live in peace with their fellows and who – in the opinion of two leading practitioners of psychiatric medicine – suffer from a treatable mental condition.

'When I use the word community, I give you another clue about the nature of Lindisholm. Our patients' skills and qualifications in a wide range of professions and crafts bring many benefits into the Lindisholm community. Thus, as the residents of our community benefit by being with us, we, in turn, benefit by this association.

'To put this two-way principle into practice, the hospital is organised into four cloisters, Alpha, Beta, Gamma and Delta, into which our patients are graded.

'Patients whose condition remains on a plateau provide us with a unique opportunity for study in a controlled environment, and the knowledge we gain is cycled back into the system. In this way we improve our operational skills and our remedial targets.

'Patients whose condition improves will progress through the cloisters until they can be released safely back into society.

'In this respect, we follow Pope's dictum: "Hope springs eternal in the human breast".

'Ladies and gentlemen, the mark of civilisation is that we must never give up hope, and neither must those in our care.

'As for the financial aspects of establishing and maintaining the hospital, it is our proud boast that our cost-per-patient has averaged up to thirty per cent lower than the most cost-effective of traditional Government-run institutions, an achievement that our overseas guests will no doubt find of interest.

'We are set to improve on this excellent record. This is down to a combination of factors, starting with Professor Koch's strategies for psychiatric treatment and rehabilitation, through Sir Norman Castlemaine's award-winning architectural design for an ultra-secure complex, right down to our profitable 2000 acre organic farm.

'Needless to say, it also includes the extraordinary abilities of Professor Jonser and her team, good management and good housekeeping by every member of staff.

'And now it is time for you to see for yourselves how the facility has been designed and equipped for the treatment of patients – some of whom have been labelled by the media the most dangerous people in our society – and how you can apply the Lindisholm concept to your own mental health care programmes.

'On your return to reception, our catering staff will serve you with light refreshments, and then we will answer questions before taking you round the farming complex which is a major contributor to Lindisholm self-sufficiency.'

'It's an excellent piece of work,' Ormley said. 'Unless there's anything you'd like to add, it covers all the shots.'

There was plenty that Melton would like to add, but not in public. Such as how the Chinese could double the productivity of their manufacturing gulags using Lindisholm principles, or how a military government could test new procedures for interrogation under rigorously controlled conditions. That was where the big money lay. The civil use of the establishment in the UK had merely been to convince world funding agencies to support international expansion. CareCorp would clean up on the sales of security systems, and Melton's shareholding would start an exponential zoom upwards.

'Yes, it's acceptable. Is everything on schedule?'

'Final staff briefing at ten. The guests arrive an hour later.'

'And you've got everything else under control?'

'Absolutely. Professor Jonser reports that the patients have settled down completely after all that rubbish with the police. They've been put through the routines so many times they're doing it in their sleep.'

'Just so long as nothing goes wrong, Roy.'

Again the careful smile. Again the sudden chill.

'Don't worry, Keith. Everything is contained. What could possibly go wrong?'

44

Ben set off for Lindisholm, negotiating the switchback road with accustomed ease. Janice tried to persuade him that she was well enough to run her art class, but Ben insisted that she stay at Brianne Mill and once again asked Mary Drover to keep her company. As far as his own feelings were concerned, he was not sure how he would react to seeing people in his class whom he now knew for certain had butchered an innocent young man, and more besides. He hoped he would rise to the occasion like a professional. One thing was for sure: he would never get another chance to see Lindisholm at such close quarters. This was an experience any journalist would relish.

Punctual to the second, his class came through the students' door and filed into their seats: Hen, whose name he knew to be Dorothy Lampton; Jennie Booth, who wrote her class assignments as Lamb; Rosehip, otherwise called Alice Jones; and Spiderlady the poet, Joan Corbett. Ben saw with relief that Geoffrey Abbott and Peter O'Brien were missing. He presumed that was because they were under close supervision in their cloisters after the police visit.

Today he had decided to take his tuition in poetry further forward. He started by commenting on the power of poetry and then introduced the notion of poetic structure, starting with rhyme and moving on to form and rhythm. Once that was over, he asked the class to write down any string of words that came into their heads, to see what they would produce. His students responded well whenever they were given a free rein, and today was no exception. Down went the heads, and thirty or so pencils began waggling over sheets of paper.

'Hands up when you finish,' Ben told them, and up shot the arm of a young lad from Beta Cloister, Pedro Sharez.

'Would you like to write it on the board, Pedro, so everyone can see?'

Sharez took his paper to the display board at the front of the auditorium and slowly transcribed his work, tongue sticking from the corner of his mouth.

> *I seen a krokodyle at the zoo*
> *Wot looked just like you.*

'It doesn't scan, does it, Mr Kirby?' someone shouted.

'It fucking rhymes, is what matters, you arsehole!' Pedro shouted back.

'Grammar, grammar, grammar!' someone else yelled.

Ben was quite relaxed about this. They let off steam from time to time, but they never took matters beyond being vocal. Not until today, of all days. Today, Pedro Sharez got mad at all the abuse he was taking. Gibbering with rage, he wrenched his seat from its steel brackets.

'I'm gonna trash this fucking place, you fucks!' he yelled.

Before Ben could move, the seat was hurtling in his direction, and before he could flinch away the protective glass barrier dropped into position. There was a loud clatter as the seat bounced off the screen and then the sound of polite clapping from the lecturer's entrance. One of the guests had arrived, a Chinese delegate accompanied by a security guard who began speaking urgently into his radio. There was absolute silence from the patients.

'I was informed this was a creative writing class,' the visitor said in impeccable English.

'That's right,' Ben said. 'We were discussing the structure of poetry.'

'An ancient tradition in my country too, although not one normally to excite such passion. Was it about your well-known William Shakespeare?'

'No, it was not!' Sharez shouted. 'It was about Pedro Fucking Sharez, and it rhymed, which is more than you can say for William Fucking Shakespeare. "To be or not to be . . ." Where does he get off with that kind of crap?'

'Would you please calm down, right this minute.' Ben hadn't intended to raise his voice so much, but it rang above the hubbub.

To his amazement and relief Pedro stopped shouting and sat down. The ensuing silence was almost as unnerving as the previous chaos.

'Your security is very impressive indeed, Mr Kirby,' the Chinese visitor said as he turned to continue his tour.

He had hardly done so when two security guards from Tim Johnson's department rushed into the room.

'Is everything all right, Mr Kirby?'

'Everything's fine. Bit of a misunderstanding, that's all. Nothing to worry about.'

The guards glared round the lecture theatre, but everyone was sitting motionless, staring straight to the front. One of them went up the steps to Pedro Sharez, who was perched uncomfortably on the remains of his seat.

'Where do breakages come from, Pedro?'

'They come from out of my pay packet, Mr Tolbright.'

'That's right, so watch yourself, or you'll be leaving here bank-rupt.'

He swiped his ID card through the security console and jabbed a code number into the touch pad. The protective screen hummed its way back into the ceiling.

'You lot behave yourselves,' the other guard said as they left.

Ben sighed and picked up the seat. 'Here you are, Pedro. See if you can get it back in place.'

Sharez took it from him and tried to slot it into the brackets. After a minute one of the other students began to help. Then another joined in. After a while, Sharez looked at Ben with a grin and sat down.

'Good,' Ben said. 'Perhaps we can carry on now.'

'What about my poem?' Sharez asked.

'You were absolutely right. It rhymed.'

As he was about to carry on, a large shape filled the students' entrance, and Geoffrey Abbott came in, dressed not in the distinc-tive red of a Delta Cloister patient but in the white overalls of a hospital nurse.

'Good morning, Ben. Do you know what day it is?'

Ben stared at him in astonishment. This was all wrong. Abbott was supposedly under strict surveillance, but he couldn't see any security guards. What the hell was going on?

'It's November the first. Open Day.'

Abbott beamed. 'Indeed it is. It is also the festival of Samhuinn, beloved of Lord Beltane. Quirk of fate, you might say.'

Quirk of fate. Christ. This was very, very bad. Thank God for the protective barrier, but could it work twice in such a short time? He had to stay calm. Ice calm.

'It's good to see you, Geoffrey. Have you changed classes?'

'I've changed cloisters. I'm in Omega Cloister now. That's where Chris Leamington is, where Lord Beltane is, where we all will be, sooner or later.'

'We were discussing poetry. Would you like to join us?'

'Other things to do, I'm afraid. Mr Cheng was quite impressed, wasn't he? He's in charge of moral regeneration in Xeneng Province. Moral regeneration means taking non-conformist people into custody and exacting a few thousand yuans' worth of production out of them before turning their carcasses into medical amulets and animal feed. Waste not, want not, as you might say. Very worthwhile.'

'You're very well informed, Geoffrey.'

Abbott must have been plundering the CareCorp computer system, too. If he had access to LISA at the same level as Ben, that would explain how he was able to wander about at will. He could simply remove his code from the system or reschedule events to suit himself. But he would need the assistance of a computer expert to do that. Maybe the same person who had given Harold the disk, which Wesley had hidden in the Shogun.

'Information and communication are vital to any successful enterprise. You of all people know that.'

The voice was friendly, but Abbott was looking at him with an expression that made his blood freeze. A snake sizing up a rabbit. The class members were staring too, still silent, but somehow all part of Abbott's presence. The atmosphere reminded Ben of a congregation at worship.

'Under other circumstances, Ben, I could get to like you. You think quickly, and you have a wonderful way of expressing yourself. We would have much to talk about. Unfortunately, you are also a conundrum. I hate conundrums, but Lord Beltane chooses not to explain this to me. Not yet. When he does, I'm sure we'll get together again. All three of us. Meanwhile I have work to do.'

Abbott backed through the entrance, still smiling. The class continued to watch Ben. All three of us. Janice. He remembered the panic button under the desk and slid his hand along until he could press it. The two guards arrived less than half a minute later, looking bemused to find no sign of a disturbance.

'What's up now, Mr Kirby?'

'We have just received a visit from Geoffrey Abbott from Delta

Cloister. I assumed he'd been withdrawn from the class. Now he's wandering around in white overalls without any supervision.'

The first guard took out his radio. 'Tim, it's Howard. I'm with Mr Kirby in Lecture Room 5. He says that Geoffrey Abbott is wandering around without supervision, wearing a nursing outfit. Can you check that, please? Are you sure? Okay.' He turned to Ben. 'Abbott assaulted a nurse earlier this morning. He is heavily sedated and is now strapped in his bed.'

This was unreal, a repeat of Abbott's assault on Janice. Ben kept his voice calm with some difficulty.

'He was here a minute ago, and he just left. Ask them.'

Howard stepped in front of the patients. 'You heard what Mr Kirby said. Did any of you see Geoffrey Abbott just now?'

They began shaking their heads.

'For Christ's sake, he was standing right there behind you,' Ben shouted.

'If he was behind them, they could hardly have seen him, could they, Mr Kirby?' the second guard said.

Howard keyed his radio again. 'Tim, it's Howard again. We have a problem in Lecture Room 5. Can you send back-up?'

'They bloody well heard him,' Ben snapped at him. 'Ask if they heard him.'

The door flew open, and three more security guards rushed in.

'What's going on?' the leader demanded.

'Keep this lot happy until the class finishes, then make sure they get to their next assignment. Mr Kirby has just made a serious allegation, and we need to check it with Tim Johnson.' He turned to Ben and pointed at the door. 'Let's sort this, shall we?'

Feeling like a schoolboy marching off to see the headmaster, Ben was escorted towards the reception area, occasionally passing Open Day guests who smiled and nodded and generally gave the impression that they were happy with what they were seeing.

Monkey Boy sat quietly by the operating console in the security control room, testimony to the flexibility of a system that allowed such a patient to develop skills in line with his aptitude. How were the visitors to know that he was watching everything that was going on – his photographic memory recording the keyboard strokes made by the operators as they entered the system with their IDs and encoded passwords, effortlessly logging everything into his abnormal memory to make sure nothing had varied from the routines he had passed to the hospital's technical helpline unit over the past few weeks, making sure that Lion was clear to move unrestrictedly throughout the hospital premises?

Dr Nikki Congleton was explaining the side effects of new anti-psychotic agents to a naval officer from Argentina when a priority message flashed on her computer screen: Professor Jonser requires you in Operating Theatre 1.

' . . . so you have to be careful with the dosage, otherwise the patient suffers a wide range of painful extrapyramidal symptoms,' she concluded.

'Thank you, Dr Congleton, that was most informative,' the naval officer said politely as he left her office.

Congleton made her way into the operating theatre, wondering why Jonser had interrupted her schedule. As the door clicked shut behind her, she saw the professor in the viewing gallery looking down at her, so she lifted her hand in greeting before moving towards the stairs. There was no response.

'She can see us and hear us, but that's it. Three hundred milligrams of curare are enough to keep an elephant nice and quiet, let alone the good professor.'

Congleton was startled to see Abbott standing behind the operating table, smiling benignly at her.

'What are you doing here, Abbott? And what's all this nonsense about curare?'

'Don't worry. I'm not going to give any to you. I need you with all your systems in working order.'

'Professor,' she called. 'Are you all right? What did you want to see me about?'

'She doesn't want to see you about anything. I sent the message,' Abbott said.

'That's not possible.'

'Of course it is. Everything is possible, if Lord Beltane wills it.'

It finally dawned on Congleton that this was a real emergency, that she was in danger. She darted to the nearest alarm button and hammered her fist into it.

'Immobilised, I'm afraid. So are the cameras. We even managed to get to the microphones, at long last. No one can see us or hear us unless we want them to. Isn't that splendid?'

She tried to pull the door open. Locked.

'We're going to play doctors and nurses,' Abbott said soothingly. 'I'll be the doctor, Professor Jonser is the nurse, and you are the patient. Why don't you take your clothes off for me?'

'Open this door at once.'

He closed the space between them at remarkable speed and caught her upper lip in an agonising grip between his forefinger and thumb. His other hand ripped her jacket, blouse and bra open in one bruising movement.

'We haven't got all day, my dear.'

Her skirt and pants were torn off with equal ferocity, before he carried her effortlessly to the operating table and strapped her into place.

'The People usually help at this stage, so you'll have to forgive me if I get some of the procedures the wrong way round. Now, according to your personal file, the first problem I have to cure is frigidity. You'll be delighted to learn that I have a one hundred per cent success rate in this operation.'

'Let me go, you bastard!' Congleton shrieked at him.

'Ah, yes, I forgot something.' He groped in the instrument tray for a scalpel. 'We call this the Cut of Silence for reasons that will become obvious. Apart from anything else it will spare me the sound of your prattling.'

The blade sliced painfully through her larynx, and her shouting was reduced to a bubbling whistle.

'Now, where's that surgical lubricant? It's not you I'm thinking about, it's good old King Dick down there. If you're as dry as everyone thinks you are, you could do him some damage.'

He smeared the jelly deep into her vagina and then plunged inside her, rutting and ripping like a bull.

'Not bad, not bad,' he panted. 'Let's put you into overdrive.'

He dug his thumbs into the nerves above her pelvis, and she began twisting and lurching demonically, spraying him with a mist of blood from her throat. His climax began slowly, ponderously, growing in great shuddering gulps of air and ending in a bestial roar as he collapsed over her.

'An excellent Consummation, my dear,' he gasped. 'Who would have thought it?'

As she lay twitching, he went to the washbasin to clean himself.

'You have to understand about Lord Beltane,' he said over his shoulder. 'I didn't believe Chris at first, but everything he said would happen has happened, so I began thinking, what if it were all true about the ancient gods? Apart from anything else, Lord Beltane brings respectability to what we do. Look at Communion, for example. We do it in the name of the Lord, just like the Christians. If we didn't, you would call us cannibals and savages, wouldn't you? Talk about pots and kettles! I mean, your behaviour isn't exactly without smudges, is it? Look what you did to poor Spiderlady, and Noel Chard, not to mention young Wesley Freeman. Christ, you people are arrogant. You fill this place with talented, gifted people and expect them to behave to order. Look where it's got you. Fortunately, Lord Beltane has provided His People with a way forward, so none of the shit you deal out matters to us.'

He dried his hands on a paper towel and leaned over her.

'I like this part best of all. After all, there's no reason why religion shouldn't be fun, is there?'

She summoned her last reserves of energy to resist as he pulled one of her breasts into his mouth and bit into it as though it was a melon.

'Very sweet. You are a surprising woman, Nikki. I imagined these would be all dried up.'

As his teeth tore into her other breast and then started on her face, the whistling somehow transmuted into a shrill scream, thin and piping, like steam escaping from a high-pressure valve. In less than three minutes, he reduced Congleton to a quivering mass of bloody contusions and broken limbs.

He went back to the basin and washed the mess away.

'I hope you're taking this in, professor,' he called up to the gallery. 'It's what the Unit was set up to do by the British taxpayer. Battle-shock, Unit-style. Create fear, alarm and despondency in the enemy ranks. It's a hell of a lot cheaper and more effective than an artillery barrage. And to answer the question that is no doubt uppermost in your very active mind, no, I'm not going to kill her. That's the whole point of the battle-shock business. Leave them alive for maximum impact. The only ones we kill are those who become a threat to us. Like Ben Kirby, for instance. You're a logical woman. You must see the sense in that.'

45

Tim Johnson stared at Ben, not bothering to hide his dislike. Here he was, in the middle of the busiest day the hospital had faced since start-up, listening to this air-brain. He had far better things to do.

'If it were up to me I'd revoke your contract and kick you out of here. I knew you'd cause trouble. What I can't understand is why you're doing this, you and that wife of yours. Giving the police all that crap about our patients. Trying to build up a story, are you?'

'If you'll stop ranting for a minute, I'm telling you that Geoffrey Abbott is wandering about your precious hospital as if he owned the bloody place. If you can't see that on your beloved system, then your beloved system is a load of shit.'

'Oh, really!' Johnson's voice shook with anger. 'For your information, Geoffrey Abbott is sleeping off a bout of bad temper. He assaulted a nurse.'

'Is the nurse dead?'

'Of course not. He helped to sedate Abbott, and he's over there now keeping an eye on him.'

'If Abbott assaults someone, they usually die.'

Johnson glared at him.

'Tango November, scan Delta Cloister, Bay 6, Cot 5.'

The nearest screen showed Abbott's bed, three straps firmly holding down the immobile occupant. There was an empty chair alongside with an open newspaper on it.

'He's probably gone for a leak,' Johnson said.

'For Christ's sake, can't you see something is wrong?'

Johnson looked at the screen again and sighed.

'Howard, keep Mr Kirby here while I check this.'

After he left there was an uncomfortable silence, then the guard asked, 'Is Mrs Kirby feeling better?'

'You know my wife?'

'I'm usually on duty in the studio when she has her classes.'

'She's feeling a lot better. Thanks for asking.'

'No problem. She's a nice person. The patients like her.'

'That's good to hear.'

Howard hesitated. 'I shouldn't talk about this, but some of them don't seem too happy about you for some reason.'

'What do you mean?'

'It's just little things. The way they stiffen up when you walk past them to your classes or when they hear your name mentioned. I've been in this business a long time. I just think you should keep your eyes open, that's all.'

'Thanks again. I'll do just that.'

Johnson and two nurses appeared on the Tango November video screen, and Howard tracked them as they went to Abbott's bed and pulled the sheet away.

'Oh shit,' Howard said. 'That's Phil Coleman.'

Johnson's voice crackled through the speaker.

'Howard, request Keith Melton and Alex Searle to the control centre. And check Abbott's location. We might have a Code Red situation.'

'What's Code Red?' Ben asked.

'Delta patient escaped. It's our equivalent of a nuclear attack.'

Howard looked seriously shaken. He went into the operations room and put out a call for Melton and Searle, then told the duty controller to locate Geoffrey Abbott.

She typed the name into the system and entered the code to zoom in on his security number. Nothing showed up.

'He's not on site, Howard.'

'That's impossible. Mr Kirby was talking to him less than ten minutes ago. You better get Harold back to his quarters.'

'Okay, Harold, you heard Mr Tolbright. Back to Beta Cloister, and thanks for your help with Open Day.'

'Is Brother Abbott doing bad things, Miss Wright?'

'That's nothing for you to worry about, Harold.'

'Brother Abbott is in Omega Cloister. Your sensors don't work in Omega Cloister.'

'Yes, I know,' she said soothingly. 'Now, off you go.' She turned nervously to Ben. 'The things they think of!'

When Melton and Searle arrived in the control centre, Johnson briefed them about the nurse's death and Abbott's disappearance.

'Christ,' Searle said. 'I'll get the visitors back to reception.'

As he reached for the microphone, Melton grabbed his arm.

'No need for that, Alex. We can contain this.'

Johnson looked uncertainly at Searle.

'We have to follow procedures, Keith,' Searle said.

'Fuck procedures! There's too much hanging on this, including your salaries.'

Before Johnson could protest, one of the guides burst into the room.

'Can someone come to Operating Theatre 1 right away?'

'No someone bloody well can't,' Melton snarled. 'We have a crisis here, or hadn't you noticed? Who are you supposed to be with, anyway?'

'The Chinese gentleman.'

'And you left him in Theatre 1?'

'He's outside the door. We couldn't get in. Professor Jonser's in there, and I think something's wrong.'

'Get Theatre 1,' Melton snapped.

The operator brought it up on the big screen.

'She's in the viewing gallery,' the guide said.

The image shifted to bring Professor Jonser in view, hunched against the viewing window and gazing down.

'I banged on the door and she didn't take any notice. I think she's ill.'

'Rubbish,' Melton said angrily. 'Can we talk to her from here?'

'Sure thing,' the operator said. 'Here's the mike.'

'Professor Jonser, this is Keith Melton. Can you hear me?'

There was no response from the professor, but they could all hear another sound, a kind of bubbling as if someone was boiling sugary water. The operator panned the camera again, and they saw the naked body strapped to the operating table, blood-splattered legs dangling crazily over the chrome delivery bars. He zoomed in.

Melton knew exactly what had happened to Nikki Congleton. Abbott was playing Unit games. He grabbed an emergency microphone.

'This is Keith Melton. Will staff with Open Day visitors please accompany them to reception. I repeat, will staff with Open Day visitors please accompany them to reception. We have a change in our schedule.' He clicked off transmission. 'I want all visitors out of here immediately. Tell them we reconvene at the Royal Hotel in

Lampeter after lunch. I want all off-duty security staff recalled. When they are in place, we go manual. I want the IT team to remove every authorisation sub-routine from the system and build it back up from scratch. That fucker Abbott is playing silly buggers with me, and it's got to stop.'

Johnson was fidgeting unhappily.

'Christ, that'll take hours to set up. Shouldn't this be a Code Red?'

'Are you fucking crazy? No one's escaped, have they? We just can't track Abbott, that's all. Code Red would ruin everything.'

Then he caught sight of Ben in the doorway of the reception area, listening.

'Who the fuck's that?'

'That's Ben Kirby,' Tim Johnson told him. 'Our creative writing tutor.'

'Jesus Goddamn Christ Almighty!' Melton bellowed. 'Get the son-of-a-bitch the hell out of my fucking hospital!'

Before anyone could move, Abbott came into the room, beaming at everyone. At the same time a red dot on the security screen began blinking, belatedly informing the operator that Delta Patient 98-765-45 was situated in the operations room.

'Hello, Keith. What's all the excitement about? System acting up again, is it? And there's Ben. I told you I could do anything I liked, didn't I? Lord Beltane gave me free will, and I will serve him all my days.'

46

As Ben drove back to Brianne Mill he could not shake off the feeling that Geoffrey Abbott was moving alongside, hidden by trees, short-cutting across hills. By the time he arrived, he was verging on panic, flinging open the front door, shouting, 'Janice, where are you?' at the top of his voice. He was relieved to see two startled faces peering down the stairs.

'We're up here, Ben,' Mary Drover said. 'I brought some interior-design magazines round. We're planning how to spend even more of your ill-gotten gains, I'm afraid.'

'Is anything the matter, darling?' Janice asked. 'I didn't expect you home this early.'

'That nutter Abbott's only gone round butchering people, hasn't he? One dead nurse and a mutilated counsellor. That Dr Congleton. Plus he seems to have turned Professor Jonser into a zombie. It's a bloody shambles in there. No more Open Day.'

'My God! Where's Abbott now?'

'That's the funny thing. He just strolled up to the security people as if nothing had happened and let them put him in a bloody straitjacket. He was smiling as if it was all some kind of crazy picnic.'

'This is absolutely dreadful,' Mary said. 'You must feel shattered.'

'Nothing a stiff drink won't fix.'

'I'll get us all one,' Janice said. 'What'll you have, Mary?'

'Tempting, but no, thanks. I've got a WI meeting this evening. Wouldn't do to turn up breathing fumes all over the place. Give me a call if you need anything.'

'It must have been absolutely dreadful,' Janice said as Ben gulped his way through a large rum and Coke. 'How on earth could he do things like that, right under their noses?'

'The same way he gets out and mutilates animals. The same way he gets in here. Their security system is like a bloody sieve.'

'You mean like that useless Ping Pole thing out there?'

'It's more than that. He's got someone in there who knows how to deal with computer systems. If I knew more about that disk Wesley gave me, I might even be able to do the same as Abbott.'

'Shouldn't you tell someone at the hospital?'

'Don't see what good that would do. Anyway, if Abbott does manage to fiddle his way out again, I might have found something that could stop him. I'm hanging on to it for the time being.'

Janice shuddered. 'I hope they set him in concrete and let him bloody well rot.'

'We should be so lucky.'

'Is he still prattling on about this Lord Beltane thing?'

Ben nodded. Quite apart from the failure of CareCorp to manage the affairs of the hospital, they were witnessing the activities of a very scary pagan cult, with all kinds of Druid and Celtic mythologies jumbled into it.

'I still can't figure out what's behind it,' he said. 'This "Lord Beltane" seems to have his origins in an ancient Assyrian god called "Bel". White Eagle is obviously the name they've given to Christopher Leamington. He seems to have started the whole thing. Abbott may be a raving lunatic, but he's a horribly logical raving lunatic. He's working his way through some kind of plan. It might have something to do with pollution. You know, spoiling the earth. That kind of thing keeps cropping up in the writing they gave me.'

'It might have something to do with the Earth Mother,' Janice commented. 'Lots of pagan weirdos are into that, aren't they?'

That sounded plausible. Ben thought of Fred Newson and his organic farming. Was that connected to Abbott in some way?

That evening after Janice went to bed, he used Wesley's disk to access the CareCorp system again and navigated his way to the file about the secret MoD facility at Kidderminster and the wrist tags that had been issued to Abbott and Leamington. Effectively the tags had been booby-trapped, designed to detonate if they were tampered with or if they received a five-digit coded radio signal sent over a particular range of frequencies. A device like that would stop even Abbott in his lunatic tracks. Unfortunately, the files did not contain the codes for the two units that had been issued. Even if Ben did acquire one of the scanning radio transceivers that Abbott had used to phone him on the mountain road, it could take hours to plod through all the variations before he hit the one that activated the man's tag. He wondered if the specialist mentioned by the mobile phone technician had any ideas.

'Harry Feldman.' The voice had a slight accent, but Ben couldn't place it. Maybe East European.

'My name is Ben Kirby, Mr Feldman. Bill Watson at my phone company said you might be able to help me.'

'I know Bill,' the voice said. 'Help costs money, Mr Kirby.'

'I appreciate that. I'm hoping to find some equipment that can solve a problem for me. If it exists, maybe I could buy it through you.'

He explained the problem – at least part of the problem. He omitted to say he wanted to activate an explosive. Feldman was ahead of him, and he didn't sound too perturbed.

'Sounds like you want your signal to scan into one of the new XHF miniatures and hit its detonation code.'

'Can I do that?'

'Sure. Are we talking defence or offence?'

'What's the difference?'

'You can put a zero to the right of your costs for offence. You'd need everything miniaturised to make it portable. Defence is much simpler.'

'Defence.'

'Fine. How far away will you be from your target?'

Christ, it was all getting disturbingly realistic.

'No idea. Up to a hundred metres, maybe more.'

'You'll need a computer with my software installed. I can download that over the Internet and talk you through the operation. You'll also need a scanning transceiver with one of my dongles fitted to a parallel port. Once you've set it up, a complete scan of five digits will take about four minutes to broadcast. All you have to do is switch off any maintenance programs and leave it running. The higher it's situated the better the range.'

'What's a dongle?'

'Are you technical, Mr Kirby?'

'No, I'm not.'

'Then don't ask.'

'Okay, but how do I know it'll work?'

'I'll include a reusable test miniature. The kit will set you back three grand. I take the major credit cards.'

'How much?'

The phone clicked off. Ben redialled.

'Don't waste my time, Mr Kirby. You want it, or not?'

Ben thought of the times Abbott had simply walked out of Lindisholm, despite all assurances that he had not, could not, have done so. He thought of Nikki Congleton bubbling on the operating table. He thought of Abbott looking at him in the lecture theatre. Most of all he thought of Janice, crouched in the bathroom. Spending three thousand pounds made him feel sick. Abbott made him feel sicker.

'Yes.'

When he had given his card number, Feldman said, 'The gear will be with you by courier tomorrow. Get back to me when it arrives.'

Ben knew he was taking a hell of a chance dealing over the phone with a stranger, but he reassured himself with the thought that Bill Watson had no reason to pass him to a shyster, and Feldman certainly knew what he was talking about. Suddenly there was a glimmer of hope in an otherwise blackened sky.

Maybe it was this that led him to the keyboard to start outlining his book. How an innocent boy from Wolverhampton led to the unravelling of a rotten and corrupt institution. How arrogant directors and incompetent managers allowed an evil man to indulge his savagery. How patients flocked to follow the pagan brutality he created. How even the farm that supplied wholesome organic foods was part of the corruption. The ideas flowed in a continuous, seamless sequence. It was a good feeling.

He would not have felt so good to know that the disk prepared for him by Abbott's computer guru had installed a program on his hard disk that called the LISA system at five o'clock every morning to download all the work he had done during the previous twenty-four hours.

47

Feldman had a sense of humour. The reusable target played a continuous tape of Bugs Bunny every time it was activated by the scanning radio transceiver. Ben installed the kit on a spare computer in the loft and linked it to the main computer in his study. He could reset the five-digit target code, place the target anywhere on his land and within four minutes of turning on the transceiver he got a result: *Bang . . . Ugh, you got me, Doc. Lay me down and let me die . . . Bang . . . Ugh, you got me, Doc. Lay me down and let me die . . .*

The only place it didn't work was on the far side of the ancient mound of stones, presumably because the rising ground provided shielding from the high-frequency broadcast.

Once he was sure everything worked, he explained it to Janice and gave her a demonstration.

'I can't believe they're incompetent enough to let him get out again, but if he does we'll be ready for him.'

'But are you sure about his wrist tag?'

He hadn't been at first, mainly because the man was creating havoc and Melton could stop him dead. Then he analysed everything he knew about Abbott's actions and put himself in Melton's shoes. The last thing the CareCorp boss wanted to do was blow up one of his patients. It would raise too many questions and jeopardise the Lindisholm project. As far as Ben could see, the tags issued to Leamington and Abbott represented a last resort, the ultimate sanction for an irretrievable situation. From what he had seen of Melton, the man clearly did not believe that such a situation had yet arrived. God alone knew what it would take to make him change his mind, but that was not Ben's or Janice's concern.

'I'm absolutely sure. If Abbott ever comes within range of this lot, he's history.'

48

Tim Johnson had been right when he told Melton how long it would take to make the change-over in security from automatic to manual. Even with a full complement of staff they could not cover all the necessary check points, so the system was left running and the extra people were deployed at key points in the system. This did not include the barriers through which the river flowed at the northern and southern perimeter of the cloister complex. Only salmon and trout could swim through those bars and along the fifty foot pipes. In any case, security sensors were in place.

Lord Beltane revealed the truth about Ben Kirby when Abbott's video link from the hospital's technical help centre showed how Ben was planning his book. Between the physical checks Abbott issued instructions to the People for his exit from Lindisholm to take place immediately after the midnight duty nurse had checked he was in his bed. He had to deal with the sedation by himself, of course, clearing his body and brain of its pernicious influence. He could not break the Kevlar restraints, but the bedframe was another matter. He simply bent the steel tubes enough to slip lengthways onto the floor. By then the control room guards were watching recordings of his cubicle that showed he was safely tucked away, and the security barriers had been reprogrammed to ignore his passage through the hospital. Of course, the difference this time was that the Bastards would know he was out of his bed once the next inspection took place, but by then he would be through the cloisters and climbing the rocks on his way to his victim.

His plan suffered a slight setback when he saw the extra staff at the hospital entrance: far too many for him to slip past unseen. The Bastards had even placed two people outside the control room by the vehicle barriers. Abbott smiled. He could have X-ed them without any trouble, but that would merely let the Bastards know that he had left the cloisters. Far better to leave a doubt in their minds.

He padded like a shadow towards one of the farm sheds and jerked the padlock and hasp out of the door. Seconds later and armed with a five-foot crowbar, he pushed the hasp back in place and headed for the river. It would take at least three hours to float and swim his way downstream to Brianne Mill, but he was not in a hurry. Plenty of time to enjoy his freedom and suss out the lie of the land when he got there. Maybe he would stay in the hills and do a little hunting first. Then he would deal with the Judas.

49

The Kirbys learned of Abbott's escape when Jennifer Matthews called round and woke them in the morning. After offering her some refreshment, Ben excused himself and climbed into the loft to activate the scanning system. It made him feel a lot better. When he got to the kitchen, Jennifer was telling Janice what had happened.

'He was sedated, strapped into his bed. He was under constant video surveillance. And on top of that he was physically checked every fifteen minutes. It takes some believing.'

'Everything the bastard does takes some believing,' Ben said. 'He'll come here, you know.'

'They are still denying that he's left the hospital. They're conducting a search, but there are hundreds of places he could be hiding.'

'All the stupid bastards have to do is ask themselves why a man like Geoffrey Abbott would escape out of his bed just so he could hide somewhere, for Heaven's sake. Whatever else he's up to, he'll come back here.'

'You're probably right, which is why I took the liberty of stationing four of our people out here as soon as we heard.'

Ordinarily, that would be reassuring, but Abbott had been trained by the best the world could offer. He would kill without compunction. He could live off the land. He had eluded the world's most sophisticated security system. He had been treated by the most advanced psychological techniques. And he had beaten them all. If they sold the Mill and settled somewhere else, Abbott would find them. Their hope and trust lay with Feldman's equipment, not a police guard.

'If he's got us down as targets you could put a hundred police officers out there and it wouldn't make any difference, except there'd be more dead bodies. The only weak spot he has is that someone might know more than he does. That's what I'm working on.'

The last thing he needed was a bunch of coppers lurking around when Abbott's wrist tag turned him into pot roast. According to

Feldman's notes, the blast could take out three or four people if they were too close.

'We'll keep officers here round the clock,' Jennifer insisted. 'At the very least they can raise an alarm.'

'I strongly advise that you do no such thing. Let me handle Abbott.'

'That's crazy,' Jennifer said. She turned to Janice. 'Can you talk some sense into him?'

'I'm on Ben's side. He thinks he can stop the bastard, and I believe him.'

'For God's sake, Ben. The man is a death machine. Unless you object in writing to my guvnor, I'm posting a team here, whether you like it or not.'

'Okay. But tell them to call for reinforcements if they see anything suspicious. And if they want to stay alive they have to stay awake and alert. Abbott won't offer second chances.'

Abbott's disappearance was, according to the security system, impossible. It was also impossible to keep the story out of the news, although Roy Ormley managed to contain it to a simple statement which was broadcast several times during the next twenty-four hours and repeated in national and local newspapers with a black-and-white photograph.

A patient has disappeared from a high-security hospital in mid-Wales. The man, is tall, well built and bald. Police urge members of the public not to approach the man, who is believed to be extremely dangerous. Householders in the area are warned to lock all doors and windows and to report anything unusual or suspicious to their local police station.

50

Ben was not too surprised to get a phone call from Norman Shelling that afternoon.

'This Lindisholm fiasco. There's all sorts of rumours flying around. We think it's a suitable case for my programme, and there you are – our man on the spot! How does co-producer sound? It's worth two big ones.'

'It's a nice thought, Norman, but no thanks. I'm working on a book.'

'Three?'

'Sorry. Right now, I've got more than enough on my plate.'

'Fair enough. Would it be in order to see if you can confirm a couple of things? Non-attributable, if you want.'

'Sure, if I can.'

'I heard that CareCorp is negotiating Lindisholm franchises with China, Argentina, Chile, India, Germany, France and the USA. True?'

'Where the hell did you get that list?'

'I twisted the arm of a PR lady with great tits and got the schedule for the Open Day. I also see you held a creative writing class as part of the demo. I guess that's one way of getting inside information.'

Ben smiled into the phone.

'I can't help much. All those countries had representatives at Lindisholm, but I've no idea if any of them are following up. I could poke around, if you like.'

'Thanks. Is it true that the patient who escaped killed a nurse?'

'It's true that a nurse has been killed, and it's also true that the hospital authorities can find no trace of a patient who they have described as being extremely dangerous.'

'Come off it, Ben. You sound like one of those bastards in *The Façade*.'

'Don't take this too seriously, Norman, but I'm beginning to know how they felt when someone asks these kind of questions.'

Shelling chuckled. 'Poacher turned gamekeeper?'

'Not exactly. Can I tell you something off the record?'

'Go ahead.'

'The patient concerned is called Geoffrey Abbott. He's in Lindisholm on some kind of Ministry of Defence remedial programme. He should be lying in a vat of sulphuric acid. The world would be a much safer place, and I would be a much safer person.'

'Bad as that, is it?'

'Yes. We are talking about a psychotic killer who makes Vlad the Impaler look like Mary Poppins. He seems to have got me in his sights, and my home is surrounded by well-meaning but utterly useless police guards. I'd feel a lot happier with a battalion from Twenty-two Regiment.'

'Can I bring my camera crew round?'

'Ha ha!'

'Seriously, are you in danger?'

'You could put it that way.'

'Anything I can do?'

'If Abbott has me lined up, you're better out of it, believe me.'

'I'll wish you good luck, then. Get in touch if you change your mind about the documentary.'

'If I have any mind left to change, I certainly will.'

51

At eleven thirty that night, two of the police officers assigned to protect the Kirbys at Brianne Mill were sitting in their car with the radio tuned to the local music station. Every fifteen minutes the broadcast was interrupted by the radio control centre asking them to respond. Every hour, they checked the premises on a two-man sweep basis, one moving forward while the other stayed in a secure location, and so on. It was a textbook operation. Trouble was, the textbook was based on the habits of ordinary criminals who were, by and large, ordinary people with ordinary intelligence and ordinary physiques.

Geoffrey Abbott slid out of the freezing river water and lay on the bank for a while to bring his heartbeat up from ten per second to its usual fifty. He opened his capillaries to increase his body temperature. He flexed his tendons and muscles to alert them to forthcoming activity. He was naked, except for a G-string and a belt with pouches containing everything he needed to survive for weeks in the mountains. He knew exactly how the two policemen would behave, and he knew exactly what he was going to do about it.

'Time for the two-step,' PC John Carver said, looking at the dashboard clock. 'Do you want to lead, or shall I?'

'Be my guest.'

Carver got out of the car and flashed his torch into the surrounding shrubs and trees.

'All clear.'

His colleague, PC Steve Taylor, slid out of his seat, padded over to the corner of the house and looked carefully round it. Thumbs up. Carver moved round the corner and over to the first of the outbuildings, checking forward, then back to Taylor. Thumbs up again. Taylor sidled round the corner of the house and died as a shadow detached itself from other shadows and broke his neck. The shadow sped past Carver to the next outbuilding and raised its hand to give the all-clear.

Just like old times, rejoiced Lion. Let the target see what it expects to see. Become what the target expects to see. Then X the target.

Carver moved forward to overtake Taylor, but he didn't make it.

In the bedroom, the air sighed and spoke of river water and sweat. Ben opened his eyes instantly, knowing that Abbott was in the room. His first thought was regret that he wouldn't be able to sue Feldman for the return of his money. Then the fear came. What in Christ's name had gone wrong?

'Hello, Geoffrey.' It took all the effort he could muster to get the words out. He hoped they sounded normal.

A deep chuckle.

'Ben, wide awake. Very good. We could have used you in the Unit.'

Janice grunted and turned over.

'Sound asleep,' Abbott said. 'That's nice.'

'Can we talk downstairs, Geoffrey? She's not part of this.'

'A moot point, but I don't see why not. I'll explain what I'm going to do.'

Abbott backed carefully down the stairs, his eyes locked into Ben's, that non-committal smile widening his mouth. Ben feverishly tried to remember what Feldman had told him. Had he missed anything out? Could he do anything, if he had?

'Things have changed, Geoffrey,' he said desperately.

'Nothing has changed. Lord Beltane has spoken to me of your plan. You are endangering his holy purpose. What was it you wrote? "A rotten and corrupt institution. An evil man indulges his savagery. Pagan brutality. Even the farm that supplied wholesome organic foods is part of the corruption." I'd say that sounds like a worthy successor to your last book, wouldn't you?'

Fear took a bound forward, along with sudden understanding. Wesley's disk worked both ways. Abbott or someone in the hospital now had access to his computer as well. No wonder things didn't work out with the wrist tag. They must have disabled Feldman's software. That was the moment Ben knew for certain that he was going to die. And Janice. He was going to die, and Abbott would then go back upstairs and . . . If only he could get to the computer. Maybe he could start the radio scan again. But how, but how?

'God, Geoffrey, you couldn't be more wrong.'

329

The big man stared at him, eyes narrowed.

'Ben, you are a very clever man. I am here to ensure that you can never harm the Lord's People, and that is what I must do.'

'Geoffrey, you are right about one thing. I am a threat. That's part of my calling, after all. But not to you and Lord Beltane.'

The large moon face was genuinely puzzled, genuinely interested.

'Not to Lord Beltane?'

'No. All that stuff you just quoted is about Fred Newson.'

Stop there. Don't explain. Let it sink in. He could feel sweat trickling down his spine, as if he were taking a shower.

'That doesn't make sense, Ben.'

'Think about it. Who has been stealing from Lindisholm and using farm labour to help his friends? Newson! Who has been using hospital patients to do his dirty work for him? Newson! Who has been involved in every single death on these farms? Newson! Certainly not you.'

'But Fred Newson is also doing the Lord's work. Can't you see that?'

Ben had no idea what Abbott meant, and he didn't care. All he wanted to do was get in front of the computer.

'Maybe so, but he is unworthy. I can show you.'

'Show me?'

'Yes. It's all in my computer. At the very least, you must not leave here without understanding.'

Abbott looked at him hard.

'No tricks, Ben. I don't like tricks.'

'How could I trick you? Where could we go if I did? All I know is that my wife and I are searching for our destiny, as you search for yours. We have faith too, you know.'

'Yes, I suppose you do.'

Abbott let Ben lead him to the study. They both stared intently at the computer. Its screen was blank, and the green light that indicated hard disk activity was flickering on and off at high speed.

Christ, of course!

Ben looked quickly at his wall clock. Twenty past four. At four every morning the disk maintenance program started. It over-rode all other routine activity. Feldman had warned him to disable his utility programs, and he'd forgotten. That's why the radio scanner hadn't worked. But it would carry on when the maintenance stopped.

Or would it? And how long did the maintenance take? Twenty-five minutes? Thirty?

'We'll have to wait, I'm afraid.'

A large hand reached out and iron fingers dug into his back, either side of his spine. Pain, such pain.

'Wait? What do you mean, wait? What the fuck are you up to, Ben?'

Maybe he should touch the mouse. That would stop the utilities program. Christ knows what would happen then. But he couldn't move.

At that point the green flickering stopped. The silence was intense. Then another program took over. The one that had been ticking quietly away when the maintenance routine started. The dialogue box for Feldman's software filled the screen. It showed a row of five numerals laid out like a fruit machine: 00150. Buttons above the numerals showed the words, 'Remote Scan interrupted by Main System Activity. Do you want to Reset & Continue? YES/NO. Do you want to Continue without Resetting? YES/NO.'

Abbott stared at it and a nerve began to tick in his forehead. Something was not quite right. He eased his fingers.

'What's this, Ben? You get me to come into your study, and you show me this shit? What's going on?'

Before Ben could say anything, and to his horror, Janice came into the study. She looked very pale, but very determined.

'It's a game I'm playing.' She casually reached for the mouse and clicked the pointer on the Reset & Continue button. 'There. That'll do the trick.'

The numerals flicked to five zeroes, then started racing into the tens and towards the hundreds. At the same time a message appeared: *Radio Scanning on Remote Computer Confirmed. Time remaining for this scan: 3 Minutes 40 Seconds. Frequency Range: 10–30 gigahertz.*

Abbott's face turned white. He smashed the computer cabinet off the desk, but it remained hanging in the air, suspended by a jumble of cables while the numbers on the screen raced forwards: 3 minutes, 30 seconds.

'No good, Geoffrey,' Ben said hoarsely. 'It's remote. If we've got to go, you've got to go, you lump of no-good shit!'

Abbott hurled Ben into a wall and knocked Janice off her feet as he thundered out of the house and headed madly towards the nearest protective shielding, yanking something from his pouch and hurling it desperately away. He was almost at the top of the ancient stones on the far side of the field when the air around him erupted into a vicious plasma of cracking thunder. For what seemed like an infinite moment his figure stood, arms outstretched, outlined in fire. Then it disintegrated into the darkness. Janice flinched, and Ben put his arm around her.

'It's over.'

Seconds later, another explosion shattered a nearby maple tree, sending a hail of branches over the driveway.

'Now it's over,' she said. Then her knees gave way, and he had to hold her up.

'I guess that was Major Leamington's bracelet,' Ben said. 'I wonder what happened to him.'

52

This is the story of how an arrogant and inept society took the lives of several innocent young people . . .

Ben stared at the computer screen for over an hour, unable to find the words to continue. Janice brought him a cup of tea, and he didn't notice. She read the screen and put the mug on the mat by his telephone. Eventually he deleted his sentence and after several minutes started again.

This is the story of how an arrogant and inept society caused the deaths of a young man called Wesley Freeman and other innocent people . . .

After another half an hour of blankness, he printed this and took the sheet of paper to Janice.

'Finished,' he said.

She smiled. 'That was quick.'

'Not really. Took a couple of hours, at least. Where're those matches?'

Janice opened one of the drawers in the dresser and took out the box.

Without another word they walked through the field to the willow tree by the river.

'Do the honours,' Ben said, holding out the paper.

'Are you sure about this?'

'It's symbolic. I've decided to team up with Norman Shelling on his TV documentary. With all the visual material I've got, it will be far more effective than a book. He's agreed to dedicate it to Wesley.'

'That's a lovely thing to do.'

Janice lit a match and held the flame to a corner of the sheet. Ben twisted and turned it carefully until only a tiny piece of white remained between his fingers. He flicked it after the blackened fragments of ash that were floating past the reeds where Wesley had been found.

'That kid from the estate agents – the one with all the pimples. What was his name?'

'Fletcher.'

'Right. Mr Fletcher. Let's give him a call. Brianne Mill is due for a set of new owners.'

Lindisfarm Organic Foods Limited

Fred Newson's company, Lindisfarm Organic Foods Limited, prospered as the market for organic food burgeoned, and he was able to acquire more land to keep pace with increasing demand. His disease-free produce was regularly judged to be more nutritious than any of his competitors'. Fred put this down to his special blend of good farming practice and the use of home-made fertilisers.

Fred had no trouble staffing his farms. There was a steady flow of new workers from Lindisholm and community mental hospitals, keen to work with the experienced people who had been with Fred in the days when he had managed Lindisholm Farm, eager to share the joys of working with nature, re-learning the old ways of farming.

The very old ways of farming.

Lindisholm International

Keith Melton's plans for franchising the Lindisholm Hospital concept internationally worked out well, despite the disaster of Open Day. The franchisees each had their reasons for such a development, but this was not Melton's concern. After the sixth franchise had been set up, he sold his shares in CareCorp and retired to an island he had bought in the Caribbean.

Roy Ormley persevered with CareCorp: lying, conniving, cheating and charming all and sundry. One of his ideas was to provide each new hospital with mementoes of the original in Wales. And what better than the more competent works of art that had so impressed Janice Kirby that day in the studio! The six pottery busts were sent to the franchise in the USA. They were given pride of place in the entrance foyer, and much admired.

Many years later, a cleaner knocked one off its plinth, and the fired clay shattered to reveal a human skull.

'Ingenious,' the director said, holding the earthly remains of Major Christopher Leamington in his hands. 'Why use wire for an armature when you can get the real thing? That's the kind of initiative I admire in the new breed of sculptor.'

In a spirit of artistic curiosity, he sent the skull to a friend who worked in an anthropological laboratory for a reconstruction of its owner, who turned out to be a gaunt man with a haunted expression.

'Ugly-looking brute,' the director said. 'I wonder who he was.'